What the Dead Know

LAURA LIPPMAN

ORION

First published in Great Britain in 2007
by Orion

This paperback edition published in 2019,
by Orion Fiction,
an imprint of The Orion Publishing Group Ltd
Carmelite House, 50 Victoria Embankment
London EC4Y 0DZ

An Hachette UK company

1 3 5 7 9 10 8 6 4 2

A CIP catalogue record for this book is
available from the British Library.

ISBN 978 1 4091 9023 3

Printed and bound in Great Britain by Clays Ltd,
Elcograf S.p.A.

MIX
Paper from
responsible sources
FSC® C104740

www.orionbooks.co.uk

For Sally Fellows and Doris Ann Norris

for Sally Fellows and Doris Ann Hart

*The living know that they will die, but the dead
    know nothing;*
*They have no more reward, and even the memory
    of them is lost.*
*Their love and their hate and their envy have
    already perished;*
*never again will they have any share in all that
    happens under the sun.*

—ECCLESIASTES 9:5–6

CHAPTER 1

Her stomach clutched at the sight of the water tower hovering above the still, bare trees, a spaceship come to earth. The water tower had been a key landmark in the old family game, although not *the* landmark. Once you spotted the white disk on its spindly legs, you knew it was time to prepare, like a runner crouched in blocks. *On your mark, get set, I see—*

It hadn't started as a game. Spotting the department store nestled in this bend of the Beltway had been a private contest with herself, a way to relieve the tedium of the two-day drive home from Florida. As far back as she could remember, they had made the trip every winter break, although no one in the family enjoyed this visit to Grandmother's house. Her Orlando apartment was cramped and smelly, her dogs mean, her meals inedible. Everyone was miserable, even their father, especially their father, although he pretended not to be and took great offense if anyone suggested that his mother was any of the things that she undeniably was—stingy, strange, unkind. Still, even he couldn't hide his relief as home drew nearer and he sang out each state line as they crossed. *Georgia,* he growled in a Ray Charles moan. They spent the night there, in a no-name motor court, and left before sunrise, quickly reaching South Carolina—"Nothing could be finah!"—followed by the long, slow teases of North Carolina and Virginia, where the only points of interest were, respectively, the lunch stop in Durham and the dancing cigarette packs on the billboards outside Richmond. Then finally Maryland, wonderful Maryland, home sweet home Maryland, which asked for only fifty miles or so, barely an hour back then. Today she had needed almost twice that much time to crawl up the parkway, but traffic was thinning now, up to normal speeds.

I see—

Hutzler's had been the city's grandest department store, and it marked the Christmas season by setting up an enormous fake chimney with a Santa poised on its ledge, caught in a perpetual straddle. Was he coming or going? She could never decide. She had taught herself to watch for that flash of red, the promise that home was near, the way certain birds told a sea captain that the shore was within reach. It had been a clandestine ritual, not unlike counting the broken stripes as they disappeared under the front wheels of the car, a practice that quelled the motion sickness she never quite outgrew. Even then, she was tight-lipped when it came to certain information about herself, clear about the distinction between eccentricities that might be interesting and compulsive habits that would mark her as odd as, say, her grandmother. Or, to be absolutely truthful, her father. But the phrase had popped out one day, joyful and unbidden, another secret dialogue with herself escaping into the world:

"I see Hutzler's."

Her father had gotten the significance instantly, unlike her mother and sister. Her father always seemed to understand the layers beneath what she said, which was comforting when she was really little, intimidating as she got older. The problem was that he insisted on turning her private homecoming salute into a game, a contest, and what had once been hers alone then had to be shared with the entire family. Her father was big on sharing, on taking what was private and making it communal. He believed in long, rambling family discussions, which he called "rap sessions" in the language of the day, and unlocked doors and casual seminudity, although their mother had broken him of that habit. If you tried to keep something for yourself—whether it was a bag of candy purchased with your own money or a feeling you didn't want to express—he accused you of hoarding. He sat you down, looked straight into your eyes, and told you that families didn't work that way. A family was a team, a unit, a country unto itself, the one part of her identity that would remain constant the rest of her life. "We lock our front door against strangers," he said, "but never against each other."

So he seized "I see Hutzler's" for the family good and encouraged everyone to vie for the right to say it first. Once the rest of the family decided to play, that last mile of Beltway had been unbearable in its suspense. The sisters craned their necks, leaning forward in the old lap seat belts, the ones worn only on long trips. That's how things were back then—seat belts for long trips only, no bicycle helmets ever, skateboards made from splintery planks of wood and old roller skates. Pinned by her seat belt, she felt her stomach flip and her pulse race, and for what? For the hollow honor of being the first to say out loud what she had always been the first to think. As with all her father's contests, there was no prize, no point. Since she could no longer be guaranteed victory, she did what she always did: She pretended not to care.

Yet here she was again, alone, guaranteed the win if she wanted it, hollow as that victory would be, and her stomach *still* flipped, unaware that the store was long gone, that everything around the once-familiar cloverleaf had changed. Changed and, yes, cheapened. The placid dowager that had been Hutzler's was now a tacky Value City. Opposite, on the south side of the highway, the Quality Inn had morphed into one of those storage places. It wasn't possible from this vantage point to see if Howard Johnson's, home of the family's weekly fish-fry suppers, remained at the intersection, but she somehow doubted it. Did Howard Johnson's exist anywhere anymore? Did she? Yes and no.

What happened next transpired in seconds. Everything does, if you think about it. She would say that later, under questioning. *The Ice Age happened in a matter of seconds; there were just a lot of them.* Oh, she could make people love her if absolutely necessary, and although the tactic was less essential to her survival now, the habit was hard to break. Her interrogators pretended exasperation, but she could tell she was having the desired effect on most of them.

By then her description of the accident was breathlessly vivid, a polished routine. She had glanced to the right, eastward, trying to recall all her childhood landmarks, forgetting the old admonition *Bridges may freeze first,* and felt a strange sensation, almost as if the steering wheel were slipping from her grasp, but the car was actually separating from the road, losing traction, although the sleet had not started and the pavement looked bone dry. It was oil, not ice, she would learn later, left from an earlier accident. How could one control for a coating of oil, invisible in the March twilight, for the inactions or incomplete actions of a crew of men she had never met, would never know? Somewhere in Baltimore, a man sat down to supper that night, unaware that he had destroyed someone else's life, and she envied him his ignorance.

She clutched the steering wheel and pounded on the pedals, but the car ignored her. The boxy sedan slid to the left, moving like the needle on a haywire tachometer. She bounced off the Jersey wall, spun around, slid to the other side of the highway. For a moment it seemed as if she were the only one driving, as if all the other cars and their drivers had frozen in deference and awe. The old Valiant—the name had seemed a good omen, a reminder of Prince Valiant and all that he stood for, back in the Sunday comics—moved swiftly and gracefully, a dancer among the stolid, earthbound commuters at the tail end of rush hour.

And then, just when she seemed to have the Valiant under control, when the tires once again connected to the pavement, she felt a soft thump to her right. She had sideswiped a white SUV, and although her car was so much smaller, the SUV seemed to reel from the touch, an elephant felled by a peashooter. She glimpsed a girl's face, or thought she did, a face with an expression not so much frightened as surprised by the realization that anything could collide with one's neat, well-ordered life at any time. The girl wore a ski jacket and large, cruelly unflattering glasses, made worse somehow by white fur earmuffs. Her mouth was round, a red gate of wonder. She was twelve, maybe eleven, and eleven was the same age when—and then the white SUV began its lazy flip-flops down the embankment.

I'm sorry, I'm sorry, I'm sorry, she thought. She knew she should slow down, stop, check on the SUV, but a chorus of honks and squealing brakes rose up behind her, a phalanx of sound that pushed her forward in spite of herself. *It wasn't my fault!* Everyone should know by now that SUVs were prone to tip. Her mild little nudge could never have caused that dramatic-looking accident. Besides, it had been such a long day and she was so close. Her exit was the next one, not even a mile ahead. She could still merge into the I-70 traffic and continue west to her destination.

But once on the long straightaway toward I-70, she found herself veering right instead of left, toward the sign that read LOCAL TRAFFIC ONLY, to that strange, unfinished road that her family had always called the highway to nowhere. How they had gloried in giving directions to their house. "Take the interstate east, to where it ends." "How can an interstate end?" And her father would triumphantly tell the tale of the protests, the citizens who had united across Baltimore to preserve the park and the wildlife and the then-modest rowhouses that ringed the harbor. It was one of her father's few successes in life, although he had been a minor player—just another signer of petitions, a marcher in demonstrations. He was never tapped to speak at the public rallies, much as he longed for that role.

The Valiant was making a terrible sound, the right rear wheel scraping against what must be a crushed fender. In her agitated state, it made perfect sense to park on the shoulder and continue on foot, although the sleet had now started and she became aware with each step that something was wrong. Her ribs hurt so that each breath was like a jab with a tiny knife, and it was hard to carry her purse as she had always been instructed—close to the body, not dangling from her wrist, a temptation for muggers and thieves. She hadn't been wearing her seat belt, and she had bounced around inside the Valiant, hitting the steering wheel and door. There was blood on her face, but she wasn't sure where it was coming from. Mouth? Forehead? She was warm, she was cold, she saw black stars. No, not stars. More like triangles twisting and turning, strung from the wires of an invisible mobile.

She had been walking no more than ten minutes when a patrol car stopped alongside her, lights flashing.

"That your Valiant back there?" the patrolman called out to her, lowering the window on the passenger side but not venturing from the car.

Was it? The question was more complicated than the young officer could know. Still, she nodded.

"You got any ID?"

"Sure," she said, digging into her purse but not finding her wallet. *Why, that—* She started to laugh, realizing how perfect that was. Of course she had no ID. She had no identity, not really. "Sorry. No. I—" She couldn't stop laughing. "It's gone."

He got out of the patrol car and attempted to take the purse to look for himself. Her scream shocked her even more than it did him. There was a fiery pain in her left forearm when he tried to slide the purse past her elbow. The patrolman spoke into his shoulder, calling for assistance. He pocketed her keys from her purse, walked back to her car, and poked around inside, then returned and stood with her in the sleeting rain that had finally started. He mumbled some familiar words to her but was otherwise silent.

"Is it bad?" she asked him.

"That's for a doctor to say when we get you to the ER."

"No, not me. Back there."

The distant whir of a helicopter answered her question. *I'm sorry, I'm sorry, I'm sorry.* But it wasn't her fault.

"It wasn't my fault. I couldn't control it—but still, I really didn't do anything—"

"I've read you your rights," he said. "The things you're saying—they count. Not that there's much doubt you left the scene of an accident."

"I was going to get help."

"This road dead-ends into a park-and-ride. If you really wanted to help them, you'd have pulled over back there or taken the Security Boulevard exit."

"There's the old Windsor Hills Pharmacy at Forest Park and Windsor Mill. I thought I could call from there."

She could tell that caught him off guard, her use of precise names, her familiarity with the area.

"I don't know of any pharmacy, although there's a gas station there, but— Don't you have a cell phone?"

"Not for my personal use, although I carry one at

8

work. I don't buy things until they work properly, until they're perfected. Cell phones lose their connections and people have to yell into them half the time, so you can't safeguard your privacy. When cells work as well as landlines, I'll buy one."

She heard her father's echo. All these years later, he was in her head, his pronouncements as definitive as ever. *Don't be the first to purchase any kind of technology. Keep your knives sharp. Eat tomatoes only when they're in season. Be kind to your sister. One day your mother and I will be gone, and you'll be all that each other has.*

The young patrol officer regarded her gravely, the kind of awed inspection that good children reserve for those who have misbehaved. It was ludicrous that he could be so skeptical of her. In this light, in these clothes, the rain flattening her short, spiky curls, she probably looked younger than she was. People were always placing her at a full decade below her real age, even on those rare occasions when she dressed up. Cutting her long hair last year had only made her look younger still. It was funny about her hair, how stubbornly blond it remained at an age when most women needed chemicals to achieve this light, variable hue. It was as if her hair resented its years of forced imprisonment under those home applications of Nice'n Easy Sassy Chestnut. Her hair could hold a grudge as well as she could.

"Bethany," she said. "I'm one of the Bethany girls."

"What?"

"You don't know?" she asked him. "You don't remember? But then I guess you're all of, what— twenty-four? Twenty-five?"

9

"I'll be twenty-six next week," he said.

She tried not to smile, but he was so much like a toddler claiming two and a half instead of two. At what age do we stop wishing to be older than we are, stop nudging the number up? Around thirty for most, she assumed, although it had happened to her far earlier. By eighteen she would have done anything to renounce adulthood and be given another chance at childhood.

"So you weren't even born when— And you're probably not from here either, so no, the name wouldn't mean anything to you."

"Registration in the car says it belongs to Penelope Jackson, from Asheville, North Carolina. That you? Car didn't come up stolen when I called the tag in."

She shook her head. Her story would be wasted on him. She'd wait for someone who could appreciate it, who would understand the full import of what she was trying to tell him. Already she was making the calculations that had long been second nature. Who was on her side, who would take care of her? Who was against her, who would betray her?

At St. Agnes Hospital, she continued to be selectively mum, answering only direct questions about what hurt where. Her injuries were relatively minor—a gash to the forehead that required four tiny stitches, which she was assured would leave no visible scar, something torn and broken in her left forearm. The arm could be stabilized and bandaged for now but would require surgery eventually, she was told. The young patrolman must have passed along the Bethany name, for the billing person pressed her on it, but she refused to speak of it again no matter how they poked and prodded. Under ordinary circumstances she would have been treated and released. But this was far from ordinary. The police put a uniformed patrolman outside her door and told her that she was not free to leave even if the hospital determined it was appropriate. "The law is very clear on this. You must tell us who you are," another cop told her, an older one, from traffic investigation. "If it weren't for your injuries, you'd be in jail tonight." Still she said nothing, although the thought of jail terrified her. To not be free to come and go as she liked, to be held anywhere—no, never again. The doctor entered the name "Jane Doe" on her chart, adding "Bethany?" in parentheses. Her fourth name, by her count, but maybe it was her fifth. It was easy to lose track.

She knew St. Agnes. Or, more correctly, had known it once. So many accidents, so many trips. A calf sliced open when a jar of fireflies was dropped, the shards ricocheting up from the sidewalk and nicking the roundest part. A flyswatter applied to an infected smallpox vaccination with nothing but good intentions. A knee opening like a flower after a fall in the underbrush, revealing the terrifying interior of bone and blood. A shin scraped on the rusty valve of an old tire, a huge inner tube from some tractor or truck, their father's makeshift version of a bouncy castle, obtained and erected in deference to their mother's Anglophilia. The trips to the emergency room had been family affairs, more father-enforced togetherness—terrifying for the injured party, tedious for those who had to tag along, but everyone got Mr. G's soft ice cream afterward, so it was worth it in the end.

This is not the homecoming I imagined, she thought, lying in the dark, allowing self-pity, her old friend, to come for her, envelop her.

11

And she *had* imagined returning, she realized now, although not today. Sometime, eventually, but on her own terms, not because of someone else's agenda. Three days ago the hard-won order of her life had jumped the track without warning, as out of her control as that pea-green Valiant. That car—it was as if there were a ghost in the machine all along, nudging her north, past the old landmarks, toward a moment not of her choosing. At the I-70 exit, when it would have been so easy to go west, toward her original destination, and possibly escape detection, the car had turned to the right and stopped on its own. Prince Valiant had brought her most of the way home, trying to trick her into doing what was right. That's why the name had popped out. That, or the head injury, or the events of the past three days, or her anxiety about the little girl in the SUV.

Floating on painkillers, she fantasized about the morning, what it would be like to say her name, her true name, for the first time in years. To answer a question that few people had to think about twice: *Who are you?*

Then she realized what the second question would be.

PART I
WEDNESDAY

CHAPTER 2

"That your phone?"

The sleep-creased woman staring at Kevin Infante was angry about something, not exactly a first for him. He also wasn't sure of her name, although he was reasonably sure it would come to him in a second or two. Again, not a first.

No, it was the combination—a strange woman *and* a baleful glare—that made this morning unique in what his sergeant liked to call the annals of Infante, which the boss invariably pronounced with a long *a* sound. If Infante didn't know a woman well enough to remember her name, what could he possibly have done to earn this martyred glare? He usually needed three or four months to inspire this kind of rage in a woman.

"That your phone?" the woman repeated, her voice as tight and dangerous as her expression.

"Yeah," he said, relieved to be starting with an easy question. "Absolutely."

It occurred to him that he should try to find the phone, perhaps even answer it, but the ringing had stopped. He waited for the landline to kick in behind the cell, then remembered he was not in his own bedroom. He fished around on the floor with his left arm, his right one still pinned beneath the woman, and found his trousers on the floor, the phone clipped to the belt. Even as he grabbed it, the phone vibrated in his hand and emitted a shrill chirp, another disgruntled scold.

"Just the office," he said, glancing at the number.

"An emergency?" the woman asked, and if he had been more on his game, he would have lied and said yes, absolutely, that's what it was, then gotten into his clothes and escaped.

Still sleep-fogged, he said, "There are no emergencies in my department."

"I thought you were a *cop*." He could hear the anger curdling at the edges of her words, the pent-up resentment.

"Detective."

"Same thing, right?"

"Pretty much."

"So don't cops have emergencies?"

"All the time." And this would count as one. "But in my line of work—" He stopped short of identifying himself as a murder police, fearful that she would find it too interesting and want to see him again, cultivate a relationship. There were a lot of cop groupies out there, a fact for which he was normally thankful. "The type of people I work with—they're very patient."

"You got, like, a desk job?"

"You could say that." He had a desk. He had a job.

Sometimes he did his job at his desk. "Debbie." He tried not to sound too proud of himself for pulling the name up. "You could say that, *Debbie*."

His eyes flicked around the room, searching for a clock but also taking in his surroundings. A bedroom, of course, and a reasonably nice one, with arty posters of flowers and what his ex-wife, the more recent one, always called a color scheme, which was supposed to be a good thing, but it never sounded right to Infante. A scheme was a plot, a plan to get away with something. But then a color scheme was part of a trap, too, if you thought about it, the one that began with a too-expensive ring, revolving credit at Shofer's, and a mortgage payment, then ended—twice in his experience so far—in a Baltimore County courtroom, with the woman taking all the stuff and leaving all the debt. The scheme here was pale yellow and green, not in the least objectionable, but it made him feel vaguely nauseous. As he sorted his clothes from hers, he began noticing other odd details about the room, things that didn't quite track. The built-in desk beneath the casement window, the boxy minifridge draped with a cloth, a small microwave on top of that, the pennant above the desk, extolling the Towson Tigers . . . *Fuck me,* he thought. *Fuck me.*

"So," he said. "What's your major?"

The girl—a real girl, a true girl, a probably-under-twenty-one girl, not that anything over sixteen was off the legal menu, but Infante had some standards—gave him an icy look and crawled over him, wrapping the yellow-and-green top sheet around her. With much conspicuous effort, she pulled a fluffy robe from a hook and arrayed it over herself, allowing the sheet to fall only after belting the robe. Still, he got a quick look and remembered what had brought him there. Lord knows it wasn't the face, although that had probably been more appealing when it wasn't puckered up this way. In the morning light, she was too all-over pale, this Debbie, one of those egg-faced blondes whose eyes disappeared without makeup. She grabbed a bucket from the floor of the closet, prompting a split second of panicky speculation. Was she going to hit him with it? Pour something on his head? But Debbie just huffed out of the room, on her way to the showers. Presumably to wash away any trace of her evening with Kevin Infante. How bad could it have been? He decided not to wait around and find out.

It was still early by college standards, and he was almost out of the dorm before he crossed another student's path, a plump, big-eyed girl who seemed unnerved by such an alien presence. Not just male but suited, older, so obviously not a student or even a teacher.

"Police," he said. "Baltimore County."

She didn't seem to find much comfort in this. "Has something happened?"

"No, just making a routine public-safety check. Don't forget, lock your doors and avoid unlighted areas in parking lots."

"Yes, Officer," she said solemnly.

The March morning was cold, the campus desolate. He found his car in an illegal spot not far from the dorm. He had thought it was an apartment house when he tried to drop her off last night. The evening was coming back to him. He had gone to Souris's, in need of a change from the usual place, Wagner's, where his coworkers went. There had been a gaggle of girls at the end of the bar, and although he'd told himself that he was just coming in for a quick drink, he soon felt compelled to cull one from the herd. He hadn't gotten the best one, but the one he *had* gotten had been pretty good. Eager to please, at any rate, blowing him in his car on Allegheny Avenue. He drove her back to this dowdy-looking midrise, quiet and hushed at 2:00 A.M. It had been his intention to watch her turn her key in the lock and then beat out a quick good-bye beep on the horn, but she had clearly expected more, so he'd followed her to her room and anted up. He was pretty sure he had made a good show of it before falling asleep. So what was up with the sour puss this morning?

A campus cop was getting ready to stroke his car, but Infante flashed his badge and the guy backed off, although he was clearly itching to argue. Probably the highlight of the poor mope's day, fighting over a ticket. He checked his cell phone—Nancy Porter, his former partner, whispering urgently into the phone, "Where are you?" Shit, he had missed roll call again. If he wanted to get to work in a reasonably timely fashion, he'd have to choose between a shower and breakfast, a real one that would settle his stomach. He decided he could handle being queasy for a few hours better than he could tolerate his own stink, so he drove to his apartment over in Northwest Baltimore. He could always claim that he had been chasing a lead on the . . . McGowan case, that was it. The inspiration came to him in the shower, and he stayed there longer than he should have, letting the hot water beat down on him, the night's odors rising up from his pores. He'd been looking for the girl's ex-boyfriend, not the most recent one, or even the one before, but three boyfriends ago. Come to think of it, that wasn't a bad idea. The girl's death, an old-fashioned stab-and-dump in Gunpowder Falls State Park, had a brutality to it that strangers seldom mustered. It hadn't been enough to cut her. The killer had also set her body alight, igniting a small brush fire that had brought fire trucks to the scene, when she otherwise might have languished undiscovered for days, weeks, months. Citizens were always surprised when cops couldn't find a body, but for all the endless development in the Baltimore metro area, there were still acres and acres of raw land. Every now and then a hunter stumbled on a pile of bones and it would turn out to be a vic from five, even ten years ago.

Early in his career, Infante had worked a case like that, one where murder was obvious but the body couldn't be found. The family had been rich and connected, with enough resources to drive the department crazy. When told that the things they wanted—searches, long-shot lab work—would have taken much of the department's budget for the year, they shrugged and said "So?" It was three years before the body showed up, not even ten yards off a state highway on the upper shore, discovered by a shy-bladder type who had walked into the weeds to take a piss. Blunt-force trauma, the medical examiner concluded, so it was a murder, all right. But there was nothing more to be gleaned from the body or the scene, and the husband, who had been the primary suspect since the start, was dead by then. The only lingering question in Infante's mind was if the fatal blow had been an accident, another Saturday-night fight in a house that had seen no shortage of such battles, or if there had been more intent to it. He'd spent a lot of time with the husband before cancer of the esophagus got him. The husband even came to believe that Infante came around out of friendship or kindness. He put on a good show of grief over his missing wife, and Infante decided that the guy saw himself as the victim. In his mind all he'd done was give her a push, a shove, no harder than any of the other pushes and shoves he'd meted out over the years, only this time she didn't get back up. So hubby picked her up, dumped her in the woods, and spent the rest of his days believing himself innocent. You'd think the wife's family would have been content that he died, fast and ugly at that, but it wasn't enough for them. For some people, it was never enough.

Infante stepped out of the shower. Theoretically, he was only thirty minutes late. But he was almost sick from hunger; and drive-through didn't do it for him. He went to the Bel-Loc Diner, where the waitresses fussed over him, made sure he got his steak-and-eggs exactly the way he liked them, the yolks just this side of runny. He pressed the tines of his fork into them, letting the juice flow over the steak, and wondered once again: *What the fuck did I do to piss off Debbie?*

"We got a babbling brook of a lunatic at St. Agnes Hospital, saying she knows about an old murder," his sergeant, Lenhardt, said to him. "Go."

"I'm on the McGowan case. In fact, I had to catch someone this morning, before he left for work. That's why I was late."

"I gotta send somebody to talk to her. Late boy is the lucky boy."

"I told you I was—"

"Yeah. I know what you *told* me. Still no reason to miss roll call, asshole."

Lenhardt had partnered with Infante last year, when the department had been shorthanded, and he seemed to be more of a hard-ass since he returned to his sergeant's duties full-time, as if Infante needed to be reminded who was in charge.

"What's the point? You said she's mental."

"Mental or making shit up to deflect attention from the fact that she left the scene of a bad accident."

"Do we even know what case she's promising to solve for us?"

"She was muttering something about Bethany last night."

"Bethany Beach? It's not even in the state, much less the county."

"The Bethany sisters, funny guy. An old missing-persons case."

"And you're betting she's a wack job."

"Yep."

"You're making me waste half my day—St. Agnes is about as far from here as you can get and still be in Baltimore County—to go talk to her?"

"Yep."

Infante turned to go, irritated and angry. Okay, he deserved to have his balls busted a little, but Lenhardt couldn't *know* that for sure, so it was unjust.

The sergeant called after him, "Hey, Kev?"

"Yeah?"

"You know that old expression, egg on your face? I

always thought of it as metaphorical, but you reminded me this morning that it can still be literal. You been out talking to people all morning, and no one mentioned that yellow smear on your face?"

Infante's hand flicked up, found the telltale bit of yolk at the corner of his mouth. "Breakfast meeting," he said. "I was working an informant that might know something about McGowan."

"You lie like that automatically?" The sergeant's voice was not unkind. "Or are you just trying to keep in practice until your next marriage?"

CHAPTER 3

The young doctor took a long time picking his pastry, pointing first to a cruller, then switching to a Danish, only to return to the cruller. Standing behind him, Kay Sullivan could feel his anticipatory delight, but also the guiltlessness of the decision. After all, he was no more than twenty-six or twenty-seven, lean as a greyhound, and running on the adrenaline of residency. He was years away from worrying about what he put into his mouth—assuming that ever happened. Some people didn't, especially men, and this one liked his food. The cruller was clearly the highlight of his morning, a reward at the end of a long night. His pleasure was so palpable that Kay felt almost as if she had chosen a pastry for herself, and was therefore less deprived when she settled for her usual black coffee with two packets of Splenda.

She took the coffee to a corner table and settled in with her emergency paperback, this one from her purse.

Kay stashed paperbacks in every nook and cranny of her life—purse, office, car, kitchen, bathroom. Five years ago, when the pain of the divorce was fresh and bright, the books had started as a way to distract herself from the fact that she had no life. But over time Kay came to realize that she preferred her books to other people's company. Reading was not a fallback position for her but an ideal state of being. At home she had to be hyperconscious not to use books to retreat from her own children. She would put her book aside, trying to watch whatever television program Grace and Seth had chosen, all the while casting longing glances at the volume so near to hand. Here at work, where she could have joined any number of colleagues for breaks and lunches, she almost always sat by herself, reading. Coworkers called her the *anti*social worker behind her back—or so they thought. For all Kay's seeming immersion in her books, she missed very little.

This morning, for example, she had picked up the details of the Jane Doe story within minutes of arriving and unlocking her office. The general consensus was that the woman was a faker, spouting nonsense out of desperation, but she did have a minor head injury, which could affect memory in various ways. There would be a psych examination, too, but Kay had transferred out of that department more than a year earlier, so it wasn't her concern. The woman's injuries were fresh, consistent with the accident, and she was not claiming homelessness, joblessness, or abuse by a partner—Kay's specialties. Of course, she also was refusing to say whether she had medical insurance, but that remained an administrative and billing problem for now. If she turned out to be uninsured, which Kay would put at even odds in this economy, it might fall to Kay to sort out the payment solution, try to figure out if they could bill her through a state or federal program.

But for now Jane Doe was someone else's problem, and Kay was safe in the world of Charlotte Brontë. *Jane Eyre,* her book club's selection this month. Kay didn't really much care for her book club, a neighborhood affair that she had joined when her marriage was on its last legs, but it provided a polite social cover for her constant reading. "Book club," she could say, holding up whatever paperback she was reading, "and I'm behind as always." The book club itself spent far more time on gossip and food than on the book at hand, but that was okay with Kay, too. She seldom had any desire to discuss what she read. Talking about the characters in a book she had enjoyed felt like gossiping about friends.

A gaggle of young doctors, so much younger than they knew, settled a table away. Kay was usually expert at tuning out ambient noise, but the lone female in the group had one of those sharp, clear voices that sliced the air.

"A murder!"

A week passed, and no news arrived of Mr. Rochester: ten days and still he did not come.

"Like that's news in Baltimore. There're, what, only five hundred a year?"

Fewer than three hundred in the city, Kay amended silently. And a tenth of that in the county. In Jane Eyre's world, the young governess was struggling with feelings she knew she should not have for her master. *I at once called my sensations to order; and it was*

*wonderful how I got over the temporary blunder—how
I cleared up the mistake of supposing Mr. Rochester's
movements a matter in which I had any cause to take
a vital interest.*

"My parents were terrified when they heard I was
going to be working here. If I was going to move to
Baltimore, why not Hopkins? Why not University? I
lied and told them that St. Agnes was in a very nice
suburban neighborhood."

Much smug laughter at this. St. Agnes was a good
hospital with a fat endowment, the city of Baltimore's
third-largest employer, but its good fortunes had not
helped the neighborhood around it. If anything, the
area had slipped a peg in recent years, from reliably
working class to seedy and marginal. These close-
in suburbs, which had boomed in the early years of
white flight, were finding out the hard way that urban
problems did not respect imaginary lines on a map.
Drugs, crime—they had barreled out of the inner city
and right over the city-county line. Those with the
means kept moving farther out and farther out. And
now downtown was booming, as yuppies and empty
nesters and equity-rich Washingtonians decided that
they wanted water views and decent restaurants, and
who cared if the schools were shit? Kay was grateful
that she had held on to the house in Hunting Ridge,
impractical and ruinous as it had seemed at the time
to stay in the city. Its value had more than tripled,
allowing her to tap the equity in hard times. And her
ex picked up the private-school tuition. He was good at
the big-ticket stuff, but he didn't have a clue about the
day-to-day costs of a child, what sneakers and peanut
butter and birthday gifts added up to over a year.

"I hear she's, what, like *forty*?" The cawing emphasis made it clear that forty was very, very old. "And she's saying this happened thirty years ago? So, what, she killed someone when she was ten and just didn't think to mention it until now?"

"I don't think she's saying she did it," a man's slower, deeper voice interjected. "Just that she knows of an unsolved crime. A famous one. Or so she says."

"What, like the Lindbergh baby?" It was not clear to Kay if the young woman was trying to be hyperbolic or if she thought that the Lindbergh kidnapping was in fact thirty years ago. Young doctors, bright as they were in their field, could be shockingly ignorant of other things, depending on how narrowly they had pursued their goals.

And then, with the suddenness of a migraine, Kay realized how insecure the young woman was. Her brittle speech functioned as a cover for someone who had no natural aptitude for the cool detachment required by her chosen profession. Oh, she was going to have a hard time, this one. She should pick a specialty such as pathology, where the patients were already dead, not because she was unfeeling but because she was *too* feeling. A bleeder, emotionally. Kay felt almost physically ill, exhausted and flu-achy. It was as if this strange young woman had crawled into her lap and asked for comfort. Not even *Jane Eyre* could shield her from this. She grabbed her coffee and left the cafeteria.

In her twenties and early thirties, Kay had believed that these sudden bursts of insight were limited to her own children. Their feelings washed over her and mingled with hers, as if there were no skin between them. She experienced their every joy, frustration, and sadness. But as Grace and Seth grew up, she found that she could sense others' feelings, too, on occasion. Usually these people were very young, because the very young had not yet learned how to shield their emotions. But, when conditions were right, adults got to her as well. This engulfing empathy was, perversely, a liability for a social worker, and she had learned to stay guarded in professional situations. It was in quiet moments, when someone caught her unawares, that it tripped her up.

She got back to her office in time to intercept Schumeier from psychiatry leaving a note on her door. He looked chagrined to be caught, and she wondered why he had risked coming to see her in person at all when he could have sent an e-mail. Schumeier was living proof that psychotherapy often attracted those most in need of it. He avoided face-to-face contact whenever possible, even voice-to-voice. E-mail had been a godsend for him.

"There's a woman who was brought in last night—" he began.

"The Jane Doe?"

"Yes." He wasn't surprised that Kay had heard about the woman, quite the opposite. He had probably sought Kay out because he knew there would be little explanation required and therefore less conversation involved. "She's refusing the psych exam. I mean, she spoke briefly to the doctor, but once the conversation became specific, she said she wouldn't talk to anyone without a lawyer present. Only she doesn't want to work with a public defender, and she says she doesn't know any attorneys."

Kay sighed. "Does she have money?"

"She says she does, but it's hard to know when she won't even give her name. She said she wouldn't do *anything* without a lawyer present."

"And you want me to . . . ?"

"Don't you have an . . . um, friend? That woman attorney who's in the newspapers all the time?"

"Gloria Bustamante? I know of her. We're not really friends, but we're both on the House of Ruth board." *And I'm not a lesbian,* Kay wanted to add, sure that this was the way Schumeier's mind worked. If Gloria Bustamante, sexually ambiguous attorney, was acquainted with Kay Sullivan, who had not dated anyone since her marriage ended, then it followed that Kay must be a lesbian, too. Kay sometimes thought she should get a little custom-made button: I'M NOT GAY, I JUST LIKE TO READ.

"Yes. That's it. Perhaps you could call her?"

"Before I do, I think I should check with the Jane Doe first. I don't want to summon Gloria out here unless she's going to talk to her. At the rates Gloria charges, the trip alone would be almost six hundred dollars."

Schumeier smiled. "You're curious, aren't you? You want to get a look at the hospital's mystery woman."

Kay ducked her head, searching her purse for one of the peppermints she'd grabbed the last time she splurged and took Grace and Seth to a restaurant. She had always disliked Schumeier's emphatic pronouncements about what others were thinking or feeling. It was another reason she had transferred out of his department. *You're a psychiatrist, not a psychic,* she wanted to say. Instead she muttered, "What room is she in?"

The young police officer posted outside room 3030 quizzed Kay endlessly, excited to have something to do at last, but finally let her go in. The room was dark, the blinds drawn against the winter-bright sky, and the woman appeared to have fallen asleep in an upright position, her head twisted awkwardly to the side, like a child in a car seat. Her hair was quite short, a dangerous style for anyone without exquisite bone structure. A fashion choice or the result of chemo?

"Hi," the woman said, her eyes opening suddenly. And Kay, who had counseled burn victims and accident victims, women whose faces had been all but vandalized by men, was more unnerved by this woman's relatively unmarred gaze than anything she had ever seen. There was an almost searing frailty to the woman in bed, and not just the usual shakiness of an accident victim. The woman *was* a bruise, her skin about as effective as an eggshell in keeping the pain of the world at bay. The fresh cut on her forehead was nothing compared to the wounded eyes.

"I'm Kay Sullivan, one of the social workers on staff here."

"Why do I need a social worker?"

"You don't, but Dr. Schumeier thought I might be able to help you get an attorney."

"No public defenders. I need someone good, someone who can concentrate on *me*."

"It's true, they do carry heavy caseloads, but they're still—"

"It's not that I don't admire them, their commitment. It's just—I need someone independent. Someone not reliant on the government in any fashion. Public defenders get paid by the government in the end. In the end—my father always said—they never forget where their bread is buttered. Government workers. He was one. Once. And he disliked them intensely."

Kay couldn't be sure of the woman's age. The young doctor had said forty, but she could have been five years younger or older. Too old to be speaking of her father in such reverent tones, at any rate, as if he were an oracle. Most people outgrew that by eighteen. "Yes . . ." Kay began, trying to find a footing in the conversation.

"It was an accident. I panicked. I mean, if you knew the things going through my head, how I hadn't seen that stretch of highway for— How's the little girl? I saw a little girl. I'll kill myself if . . . Well, I don't even want to say it out loud. I'm poison. Just by existing, I bring pain and death. It's his curse. I can't escape it, no matter what I do."

Kay suddenly recalled the state fair up at Timonium, the freak-show tent, how at age thirteen she had worked up the nerve to go in, only to find just slightly odd people—fat, tattooed, skinny, big—sitting placidly. Schumeier had her pegged, after all: There was a bit of voyeurism in her mission here, a desire to look, nothing more. But this woman was talking to her, drawing her in, babbling as if Kay knew, or should know, everything about her. Kay had worked with many clients like this, people who spoke as if they were celebrities, with their every moment of existence documented in tabloids and television shows.

But at least the woman in the bed seemed to *see* Kay, which was more than some self-involved clients managed. "Are you from here?"

"Yes, all my life. I grew up in Northwest Baltimore."

32

"And you're what? Forty-five?"

Ah, that hurt. Kay was used to, even liked, the version of herself she glimpsed in mirrors and windows, but now she was forced to consider what a stranger saw—the short, squat body, the shoulder-length gray hair that aged her more than anything else. She was in good shape by every internal measure, but it was hard to convey one's blood-pressure, bone-density, and cholesterol numbers via wardrobe or casual conversation. "Thirty-nine, actually."

"I'm going to say a name."

"Your name?"

"Don't think that way, not yet. I'm going to say a name—"

"Yes?"

"It's a name you'll know. Or maybe not. It depends on how I say it, how I tell it. There's a girl, and she's dead, and that won't surprise anyone. They've believed she was dead, all these years. But there's another girl, and she's not dead, and that's the harder part to explain."

"Are you—"

"The Bethany girls. Easter weekend, 1975."

"The Bethany . . . oh. Oh." And just like that it came back to Kay. Two sisters, who went to . . . what, a movie? The mall? She saw their likenesses—the older one with smooth ponytails fastened behind the ears, the younger one in pigtails—remembered the panic that had gripped the city, with children herded into assemblies and shown cautionary yet elliptical films. *Girls Beware* and *Boys Beware*. It had been years before Kay had understood the euphemistic warnings therein: *After accompanying the strange boys to the beach party, Sally was found wandering down the highway, barefoot and confused. . . . Jimmy's parents told him that it wasn't his fault that Greg had befriended him and taken him fishing but made it clear to him that such friendships with older men were not natural. . . . She got in the stranger's car—and was never seen again.*

There were rumors, too—sightings of the girls as far away as Georgia, bogus ransom demands, fears of cults and counterculturists. After all, Patty Hearst had been taken just a year before. Kidnapping was big in the seventies. There was a businessman's wife redeemed for a hundred thousand dollars, which had seemed like a fortune, a rich girl buried in a box with a breathing tube, the Getty heir with the severed ear. But the Bethanys were not wealthy, not in Kay's memory, and the longer the story went without an official ending, the less memorable it had become. The last time that Kay thought about the Bethany sisters had probably been the last time she went to the movies at Security Square, at least a decade ago. That was it—Security Square Mall, relatively new at the time, something of a ghost town now.

"Are you . . . ?"

"Get me a lawyer, Kay. A good one."

CHAPTER 4

Infante took the as-the-crow-flies route to the hospital, traveling straight through the city instead of taking the Beltway around it. Damn, downtown Baltimore was getting shiny. Who'd have thought it? He almost regretted not buying a place in town ten years ago, not that he'd still have it anyway. Besides, he had been raised in the suburbs—Massapequa, out on Long Island—and he had a soft spot for the jumbled secondary highways and modest apartment complexes where he lived up in Parkville. IHOPs, Applebee's, Target, Toys "R" Us, gas stations, craft stores—to him this was what home looked like. Not that he had any intention of going back there, where it was now almost impossible to live on a police officer's salary. He kept his allegiance to the Yankees and played the part of the brash Noo Yawkah for his colleagues' amusement. But in his head, he knew that this town, this job, was right for him. He was good at what he did, with one of the better clearance rates in the department. "Baltimore punk is my second language," he liked to say. Lenhardt was on him to take the sergeant's exam, but then—people always thought you should do what they did. *Be a firefighter,* his dad said, *on the island.* His first wife had cajoled, *C'mon, watch* Law & Order *with me.* She wanted her favorite show to be his favorite show, her favorite meal to be his. She even tried to convert him to Rolling Rock over Bud, to Bushmills over Jameson. It was as if she were working backward, trying to create a logical match from one that had been all heat and desire from the jump. In that way she reminded Infante of himself in high school. He decided where he wanted to go to college—Nassau Community College, no major brain bust, that, it was all they could afford—then gave the guidance counselor the info that would make her computer spit out that school. That way his only option became a choice, instead of something that was forced on him.

He breezed through the city, making the hospital in less than forty minutes. But it wasn't good enough. Gloria Bustamante—the biggest ballbuster of any defense attorney he knew, male or female, straight or gay—was in the hospital corridor.

Fuck me.

"You look absolutely crestfallen," the alcoholic old lizard said. "You know, I don't think I've ever had cause to use that word in a sentence before, but now I see it—crestfallen. Like a blue jay whose little tuft is drooping in the front."

She pulled at her own forelock, a stray piece of red-brown hair that showed an inch of gray at the root.

Bustamante was her usual wreck of a self—lipstick in and out of the natural line of mouth, suit missing a button. Her shoes, expensive ones once upon a time, were scuffed and banged up on the toes, as if she'd been kicking something very hard over and over again. Probably a detective's shin.

"She hire you?"

"I think we have an arrangement, yes."

"It's yes or no, Gloria. Are you her lawyer?"

"For now. I'm taking her at her word that she can pay my fee." Her eyes flicked over him. "You're here for homicide, right? Not traffic investigation?"

"I could give a fuck what she did with her car."

"If she talks to you about the murder, can we make the traffic thing go away? No one was really at fault, she panicked—"

"Shit, Gloria. Who do you think you are, Monty fuckin' Hall, trading me the accident for what's behind the curtain? Any deal requires a prosecutor's approval. You know that."

"Well, then maybe I won't make her available to you this morning. She's exhausted, she has a head injury. I'm not sure she should speak to anyone until a doctor can determine if the injury has affected her memory."

"They checked her out last night."

"She was treated for her injuries. And she's just passed a psych exam. But I'd like to bring an expert in, someone from neurosurgery. She might not even remember the collision. She might not be aware that she left the scene of the accident."

"Save the bullshit for a summation, Gloria, and put the goods on the table. I have to determine that this case is in our jurisdiction."

"Oh, it's very much in your jurisdiction, Detective." Gloria made it sound kind of dirty, her style when talking to men. When Infante first got to know her, he thought the innuendos were a way of her fronting, trying to hide her sexual orientation. But Lenhardt insisted it was a highly developed sense of irony, the kind of mindfuck that a professional mindfucker like Gloria used just to stay in practice.

"So can I talk to her?"

"About the old case, not about the accident."

"Shit, Gloria, I'm a murder police. I could give a crap about some fender bender on the Beltway. Unless— Wait, did she do it on purpose? Was she trying to kill the people in the other car? Man, maybe this is my lucky day and I can get two clearances, just like that." He snapped his fingers.

Gloria flicked her eyes over him, bored. "Leave the humor to your sergeant, Kevin. He's the funny one. You're the pretty boy."

The woman in the hospital bed had her eyes closed tight, a kid playing possum. The light in the room showed up the fine hairs on her arm and the side of her face, blond peach fuzz, nothing intense. And there was a hollowed-out look beneath the eyes, a long-lived exhaustion. The eyes flickered open for only a moment, then closed again.

"I'm so tired," she murmured. "Do we have to do this now, Gloria?"

"He won't stay long, sweetie." *Sweetie?* "He just needs the first part."

The first part? Then what was the second?

"But that's the hardest part to talk about. Can't *you* just tell him and let me be?"

He needed to assert himself, stop waiting for the introduction that Gloria didn't seem intent on making.

"I'm Kevin Infante, a detective with Baltimore County homicide."

"Infante? As in Italian for baby?" Eyes still closed. He needed her to open them, he realized. Until this moment Infante had never considered how vital open eyes were to what he did. Sure, he had thought about eye contact, studied the way that various people used it, knew what it meant when someone couldn't meet his gaze. But he'd never had a subject sit there—lie there in this case—with eyes closed tight.

"Sure," he said, as if he'd never heard that before, as if two ex-wives hadn't thrown that back at him time and again.

Her eyes opened then. They were a particularly vivid blue, kind of wasted on a blonde. A blue-eyed brunette, that was his ideal, the light and the dark, an Irish girl with eyes put in with a dirty finger.

"You don't look like a baby," she said. Her voice, unlike Gloria's, carried no whiff of flirtation. She wasn't playing it that way. "It's funny, for a moment I had this vision of the cartoon character, the giant one who wore the diaper and the little cap."

"Baby Huey," he said.

"Yes. Was he a duck? Or a chicken? Or was he a *baby*-baby?"

"A chicken, I think." Maybe they should get the neurosurgeon in to see her. "You told someone you knew about an old murder here in Baltimore County. That's what I need to talk to you about."

"It began in Baltimore County. It ended— actually, I'm not sure where it ended. I'm not sure it ever ended."

"You're saying someone started killing somebody in Baltimore County and finished it elsewhere?"

"I'm not sure—in the end . . . well, not the end but the part where bad things happened. By then I didn't know where we were."

"Why don't you just tell me your story and let me figure it out?"

She turned to Gloria. "Do people—I mean, are we known? Still?"

"If they were here, they remember," the old lizard said in a much-gentler-than-usual voice. Was she hot for her? Was that why she was willing to risk taking a case that might not pay? It was hard enough to figure out other men's taste in women sometimes, much less a woman's, and Gloria wasn't sentimental that way in Infante's experience with her. "Maybe not the name, but the moment they hear the circumstances. But Detective Infante's not from here."

"Then what's the point of speaking to him?" She closed her eyes and settled back on the pillow. Gloria actually gave an embarrassed what-can-I-do shrug. Infante had never seen her so gentle with a client, so solicitous. Gloria took good care of the people she represented, but she insisted on being the boss. Now she was all deferential, motioning him to follow her out into the hall. He shook his head and stood his ground.

"*You* tell me," he said to Gloria.

"In March 1975 two sisters left their family's house to go to Security Square Mall. Sunny and Heather

Bethany. They were never seen again. And they weren't not seen again in the sense that police had a hunch what happened but couldn't prove anything. Not like the Powers case."

Powers was shorthand for a decade-old homicide, one in which a young woman had vanished, but no one doubted that her estranged husband was at the heart of that disappearance. They just couldn't prove it. The conventional wisdom was that the guy had hired someone and lucked out, finding the tightest-lipped, most loyal hit man ever, a guy who never had a reason to trade the information. A guy who never got locked up or bragged drunkenly to a girlfriend, *Yeah, I did that.*

"So she knows what happened?"

"I can *hear* you," the woman in the bed said. "I'm right here."

"Look, you're free to participate in the conversation if you like," Infante said. Was it possible to roll one's eyes when they were closed? Her expression shifted subtly, as if she were a peeved teenager who just wanted Mom and Dad to leave her alone, but she didn't say anything else.

"There were some seeming leads in the early days. An attempt to collect ransom. Some, I think, what we would call persons-of-interest today. But nothing panned out. Virtually no evidence—"

"Sunny was short for Sunshine," said the woman in the bed. "She hated it." She started to cry but didn't seem to notice she was crying, just lay in the bed letting the tears flow down her face. Infante was still trying to work out the math. Thirty years ago, two sisters. How young? Gloria hadn't said. Young, obviously, young enough so that running away was ruled out and homicide assumed. Two. Who grabs two? That struck him as wildly ambitious and prone to failure. Wouldn't taking two sisters suggest something personal, a grudge against the family?

"Arthur Goode kidnapped more than one boy," Gloria said, as if reading his thoughts. "But that was before your time, too. He kidnapped a newspaper-delivery boy here in Baltimore and made him watch while . . . At any rate, he released the delivery boy unharmed. Goode was later executed in Florida, for similar crimes there."

"I remember that," said the woman in the bed. "Because it was like us, but not like us. Because we were sisters. And because—"

Here she broke down. She brought her knees to her chest, hugged them with her good arm, the one not bandaged and wrapped, and cried the way someone might heave after food poisoning. The tears and sobs kept coming, unstoppable. Infante began to worry that she might dehydrate herself.

"This is Heather Bethany," Gloria said. "Or was, many years ago. Apparently it's been a long time since she's used her real name."

"Where has she has been? What happened to her sister?"

"Killed," moaned the keening woman. "Murdered. Her neck snapped right in front of me."

"And who did this? Where did it happen?" Infante had been standing all this time, but now he pulled up a chair, realizing he would be there for hours, that he would need to set up the tape recorder, take an official statement. He wondered if the case was really the sensation that Gloria said it was. But even if she was exaggerating its fame, it was the kind of story that would mutate into a clusterfuck when the news got out. They would have to proceed slowly, be delicate in their handling of it. "Where have you been, and why has it taken so long for you to come forward?"

Bracing herself on her right arm, Heather returned herself to a sitting position, then wiped her eyes and nose with the back of her hand, a child's gesture.

"I'm sorry, but I can't tell you. I just can't. I wish I had never said anything in the first place."

Infante shot Gloria a what-the-fuck look. Again she shrugged helplessly.

"She doesn't want to be Heather Bethany," Gloria said. "She wants to go back to the life she's made for herself and put this behind her. Her sister's dead. She says her parents are dead, too, and that jibes with my memory. There is no Heather Bethany, for better or worse."

"Whatever she calls herself, wherever she's been, she is by her own account the witness to the murder of a— How old was your sister?"

"Fifteen. And I was just about to turn twelve."

"The murder of a fifteen-year-old girl. She doesn't get to drop a bomb like that and waltz out of here."

"There's no one to arrest," the woman in the bed said. "He's long gone. Everyone's long gone. There's no point to any of this. I hit my head, I said something that I never meant to say. Let's just forget about it, okay?"

Infante motioned Gloria to follow him into the hall.

"Who is that?"

43

"Heather Bethany."

"No, I mean, what name is she going by now? Where does she live? What has she been up to? The cop who brought her in said the car was registered to Penelope Jackson. Is that her?"

"Even if I *do* have that information—and I'm not saying I do—I'm not authorized to give it to you."

"Fuck authorized. The law is really clear on this, Gloria, all the way up to the Supreme fucking Court. She was driving a car, she was in an accident. She has to provide ID. If she doesn't want to do that, she can go straight from here to jail."

For a moment Gloria dropped all her arch mannerisms—the cocked eyebrow, the half smirk. Strangely, it made her even less attractive. "I know, I know. But bear with me. This woman has been through hell, and she wants to hand you the clearance of a lifetime, if you can be a little patient. Why not indulge her for a day or two? The way I see it, she's genuinely terrified of revealing her current identity. She needs to trust *you* before she can tell you everything."

"Why? What's the big deal? Unless she's wanted for some other crime?"

"She swears up and down that she's not, that her only concern—and this is a direct quote—is becoming 'wacko of the week' on cable news. Once she's revealed as Heather Bethany, her life as she knows it is over. She wants to find a way to give you the case without giving up herself."

"I don't know, Gloria. This isn't my call. Something like this has to go up the chain of command, and they still might send me back to lock her up."

"Lock her up and she won't give you the Bethany

case. She'll say it was a delusion born of the accident. Look, you should be delirious with her terms. She doesn't want any publicity, and your department hates being in the media. *I'm* the loser here, the one who won't get any bump, and may not even get paid."

At this, she reverted to form, batting her eyelashes and puffing out her lips in a monstrous pout. Shit, if anyone resembled Baby Huey, it was Gloria, with that fish mouth and beak of a nose. *Beak*—that was it, he had the image in his mind now. Not a beak, but a bill. Baby Huey was definitely a duck, and lord fuck a duck, as the old saying went.

CHAPTER 5

A radio was playing somewhere. Or perhaps it was a television in a nearby room. Her room was dead silent, and the light was finally fading, which she found restful. She thought about work. Had she been missed yet? She had called in sick yesterday, but today she hadn't known what to do. It was a long-distance call, but she didn't have a calling card handy and she wasn't sure what would happen if she went through the hospital switchboard and she couldn't get to the pay phone in the hall without going past the patrolman outside her door. Did calling cards mask one's movements anyway? She couldn't take the chance. She had to protect the only thing she had, this sixteen-year existence built on someone's death, just as everything in her life had been made possible by someone's death. It was her *real* life, for better or worse, the longest life she had inhabited to date. For sixteen years she'd managed to have this thing that others would call a normal life, and she wasn't about to give it up.

It wasn't much of a life, to be sure. She had no real friends, only friendly colleagues and clerks who knew her well enough to smile. She didn't even have a pet. But she had an apartment, small and spare and neat. She had a car, her precious Camry, a purchase she had rationalized because of the commute to work, an hour on a good day. Lately she'd been listening to books on tapes, fat womanly novels as she thought of them. Maeve Binchy, Gail Godwin, Marian Keyes. Pat Conroy—not a woman, obviously, but the same kind of storyteller, unafraid of big emotions and big stories. *Shit*, she had three tapes due back at the library Saturday. For sixteen years she had never been late for anything—a payment, a library book, an appointment. She hadn't dared to be. What happened if you turned in tapes late? Did the fines accrue? Did they report you somewhere?

It was ironic, given her work on Y2K compliance, but she had long lived in fear of centralization, a day when the machines would learn to speak to one another, compare notes. Even as she was paid to prevent it, she had been secretly rooting for a systemic breakdown that would wipe all the tapes clean, destroy every bit of institutional memory. The pieces were out there, somewhere, waiting for someone to put them together. *This woman—she has the name of a child who died in Florida in 1963. How odd—because this woman, who resembles her, had the name of a child who died in Nebraska in 1962. Yet this woman was a child who died in Kansas in 1964. And this one? She was from Ohio, born in 1962 as well.*

47

At least it would be easy to remember who she was now: Heather Bethany, born April 3, 1963. Resident of Algonquin Lane 1966–78. Ace student at Dickey Hill Elementary. Where had the family lived before? An apartment in Randallstown, but she wouldn't be expected to remember anything about that time. That was the tricky part. Not knowing what she should know but remembering what she *wouldn't* know.

What else? School #201. Dickey Hill. Predictable jokes about the name. A newer building at the time. Jungle gym, chin-up bars in three heights, a slide that became hot to the touch on June days, hopscotch and foursquare grids painted in bright yellow. There had been a merry-go-round, not the kind with horses but one of those rickety metal ones. No, wait, that hadn't been at the school but somewhere nearby, someplace vaguely forbidden. In the Wakefield apartments that surrounded the school? In her mind she remembered the dirt track first, because she pushed more often than she rode. Head down, like a horse in harness, she had lined up behind the boys, linking her left arm into the metal bar and beginning to run, making the riders scream with delight. She saw the toe of her—she needed a second to remember the shoes. Not athletic shoes, which is why she got in trouble. She was wearing her school shoes, brown, always brown, because brown was practical. But even practical brown couldn't stand up to the orange dust of that playground, especially after the April rains. She had come home with dirt caked onto the toes, much to her mother's exasperation.

What else could she tell them? There were eight sixth-grade teachers that year. Heather had the nice one, Mrs. Koger. They took the Iowa Basic Skills

Test, and she was in the ninety-ninth percentile in everything. They did science projects that fall. She had netted crawfish from Gwynns Falls and put together an elaborate aquarium, but all four had died. Her father theorized that clean water was a shock to their systems after the murky, polluted stream and her exploration of that thesis had earned her an A anyway. Thirty years later she was beginning to have a clue how the crawfish had felt. You knew what you knew, you wanted what you wanted, even if it was literally scum.

But, of course, this was not what they would demand of her. They didn't want the story of Heather Bethany *before* 1975. They wanted to know about the subsequent thirty years, and small details would not satisfy. She could not placate them with anecdotes about, say, her boxy little tape recorder. It was the first purchase she was allowed to make, a reward for six months of living by their rules, for proving her trustworthiness. They were okay with the tape recorder but appalled by the handful of tapes she bought as well. The Who, Jethro Tull, even some of the earlier punk bands. She would lie on the bumpy chenille bedspread, still in her school uniform, and listen to the New York Dolls and, later, the Clash. "Turn it down," she was ordered. "Get your shoes off the bedspread." She would obey, but everyone was still appalled. Perhaps they knew that she, like Holly in the Lou Reed song, was plotting to get on the bus and go take a walk on the wild side.

The irony was that *they* put her on the bus, sent her away as if she were the criminal. They meant to be kind. Well, he did. Her? *She* was glad to see her leave. Irene had always resented her presence in the household—not because of the pretense required in the external world but because of the reality of what happened within the house. *She* was the one who carped about the shoes on the bedspread and insisted that the music be turned down to a whisper. *She* was the one who offered neither solace nor salve for the bruises, wouldn't even help concoct a reasonable cover story for those badges of occasional resistance—the cut lip, the black eye, the hobbled walk. *You got yourself into this,* Irene's placid manner seemed to suggest. *You brought this on yourself and destroyed my family in the bargain.* In her head she shouted back, *I'm a little girl! I'm just a little girl!* But she knew better than to raise her voice to Irene.

The music drowned it all out. Even when it was turned down to whispery volumes, the music made everything go away—the assaults, physical and spiritual, the exhaustion brought on by the double life that was really a triple life, the sadness in his face every morning. *Make it stop,* she pleaded with him silently from across the round breakfast table, so homey and warm, so everything she had thought she wanted. *Please make it stop.* His eyes replied, *I can't.* But they both knew that was a lie. He had started it, and he was the only person who could find an end to it. Eventually, he proved that he had the power all along to save her, but it was too late. By the time he let her go, she was more broken than Humpty Dumpty, more shattered than the heads of Irene's precious china dolls, which she had smashed with a poker one brilliant fall afternoon. Composure finally lost, Irene had flown at her, screaming, and even he had pretended not to understand why she would do such a thing.

"They wouldn't stop looking at me," she said.

The real problem, of course, was that no one looked at her, no one saw. Every day she walked out into the world with nothing more than a name and a hair color to disguise her—and no one ever noticed. She came to the breakfast table, aching in parts of herself that she barely knew, and the only thing anyone said was, "Do you want jelly on your toast?" Or, "It's a cold morning, so I made hot chocolate." *See me,* Roger Daltrey sang on her little red tape recorder. *See me.* Irene called up the stairs, *Turn that noise down.* She yelled back, *It's opera. I'm listening to an* opera. *Don't sass me. You have chores.*

Chores. Yes, she had a lot of *chores,* and they didn't end at nightfall. Sometimes she made a list, called Who-I-Hate-the-Most, and Irene was never lower than three, and sometimes she made it as high as two.

Number one, however, was hers and hers alone.

PART II
THE MAN WITH THE BLUE GUITAR (1975)

CHAPTER 6

"Take your sister," their father said, in both girls' hearing, so Sunny couldn't lie about it later. Otherwise, Heather knew, her older sister would have nodded and pretended agreement, then left her at home anyhow. Sunny was sneaky that way. Or tried to be, but Heather was forever catching her in her schemes.

"Why?" Sunny protested automatically. She must have known that the argument was lost before it began. It was pointless to argue with their father, although, unlike their mother, he didn't mind when they talked back. He was happy to have long discussions in which he debated their points. He even helped them shape their side of things, build their cases like lawyers, which he was always reminding them that they could be. They could be anything they wanted, their father told them frequently. Yet in an argument with him, they could never be right. It was not unlike playing checkers with him, when he

would guide his opponent's hand with small shakes and nods of his head, letting the girls avert disastrous moves that might result in double- or even triple-jumps. Still, he somehow claimed victory in the final play, even when he was down to just one king.

"Heather's only eleven," he said in what the sisters thought of as his reasoning voice. "She can't stay home alone. Your mother's already left for work, and I have to be at the shop by ten."

Head lowered over her plate, Heather watched them through her lashes, still as a cat studying a squirrel. She was torn. Normally she pushed for greater privileges whenever possible. She wasn't a *baby*. She would be twelve next week. She should be allowed to stay at home alone on a Saturday afternoon. Since her mother had started working last fall, Heather was alone for at least an hour every afternoon, and the only rules were that she mustn't touch the stove or have friends over. Heather liked that hour. She got to watch what she wanted on television—*The Big Valley,* usually—and eat as many graham crackers as she wanted.

That bit of freedom, however, had been forced on her parents. They had wanted Heather to wait in the Dickey Hill Elementary School library after school until Sunny could collect her, the same plan they had used when Heather was in fifth grade and fourth grade before that. But Dickey Hill got out at three and Sunny didn't get home from junior high until past four now that her bus ride was so long. The principal at Dickey Hill had told Heather's parents in no uncertain terms—that was her mother's recounting of the story, and the phrase had stuck with Heather, *in no uncertain terms*—that her librarian was not a baby-sitter. So Heather's parents, always eager not to be seen as people who expected special treatment, had decided that Heather could be in the house by herself. And if she could be by herself for an hour every day, Monday through Friday, then why couldn't she be alone for three hours on a Saturday? Five was greater than three. Plus, if she won the right to stay home today, maybe she would never have to spend another deadly dull Saturday in her father's store, much less her mother's real-estate office.

But that long-term possibility paled alongside the prospect of a Saturday at Security Square Mall, a place of great novelty to Heather. Over the past year, Sunny had fought for and won the right to be dropped off there on Saturday afternoons, once a month, to meet friends for matinees. Sunny also got to baby-sit, earning seventy-five cents an hour. Heather hoped to start doing that, too, once she was twelve, which was just next week. Sunny complained that she spent years trying to gain her privileges, only to see Heather awarded them at a younger age. So what? That was the price of progress. Heather couldn't remember where she had heard that phrase, but she had adopted it for her own. You couldn't argue with progress. Unless it was something like the highway through the park, and then you could. But that was because there were deer and other wildlife. That was the *environment,* which was more important than progress.

"You can go to the mall today if you take your sister," their father repeated, "or you can stay home with her. Those are your choices."

"If I have to stay at home with Heather, shouldn't I be paid for baby-sitting?" Sunny asked.

"Family members don't charge one another for doing things for the family," their father said. "That's why your allowance isn't chore-based. You get spending money because your mother and I recognize that you need some discretionary income, even if we don't always approve of the things you buy. The family is an entity, joined in a common good. So no, you don't get money for taking care of your sister. But I will provide bus fare for both of you if you want to go to the mall."

"Big whoop," Sunny muttered, chopping up her pancakes but not really eating them.

"What did you say?" her father asked, his tone dangerous.

"Nothing. I'll take Heather to the mall."

Heather was elated. Bus fare. That was an extra thirty-five cents to spend as she wanted. Not that thirty-five cents could buy that much, but it was thirty-five cents of her own she didn't have to spend and could therefore save. Heather was good at saving money. Hoarding, her father called it, and he was being critical, but Heather didn't care. She had thirty-nine dollars in a metal box bound with a complicated system of elastic bands, so she could tell if anyone had tried to get inside it. But she wouldn't take her money to the mall today, because then she couldn't be tempted to spend it. No, she would compare prices and study sales, then return with her birthday money when she had made a careful decision about what she wanted. She wouldn't waste her money on an impulse as Sunny often did. Last fall Sunny had bought a poor-boy knit sweater, off-white, with a red placket. The red trim had bled on the first washing, creating twin tracks on the sweater's back. But it was the kind of sale that said no returns, and Sunny would have been out eleven dollars if their mother hadn't gone to the store and berated the salesperson, embarrassing Sunny so much that she wouldn't even say thank you.

Their father put the dishes on the drain board and left the kitchen, whistling. He had been fun this morning, much more fun than usual, making pancakes with Bisquick and even throwing in chocolate chips, real ones, not the carob ones he normally used in baking. He had let Heather pick the radio station, too, and although Sunny made fun of her choice, Heather knew it was the same station that Sunny used to listen to in her room, late at night. Heather knew lots of things about Sunny and what went on in her room. She considered it her business to spy on her older sister, and it was another reason she liked her hour alone on weekdays. That's how she had come to find the bus schedule in Sunny's desk drawer yesterday, the Saturday times for the Number 15 carefully highlighted.

Heather had been looking for her sister's diary, a miniature book of Moroccan leather with a real lock. But anyone could figure out how to jiggle it open without the key. She had found Sunny's diary only once, more than six months before, and it had been sadly boring. Reading her sister's diary, she had almost felt sorry for her. Heather's life was much more interesting. Maybe that was how it was: People with interesting lives didn't have time to write about them in diaries. But then Sunny had tricked her, drawing Heather into a conversation about one of the entries, only to point out that Heather couldn't know of the incident on the bus unless she'd read Sunny's diary. Heather had gotten into quite a bit of trouble for that, although she didn't understand why. If the family was supposed to share everything, then why was Sunny allowed to lock up her thoughts?

"Heather just admires her big sister so," their mother had told Sunny. "She wants to be like you, do everything you do. That's how little sisters grow up."

Wrong, Heather wanted to say. Sunny was the last person to whom she would look for guidance. Almost in high school, Sunny didn't even have a boyfriend, while Heather sort of did. Jamie Altman sat next to her on field trips and paired up with her whenever the teacher made them go boy-girl. He also had given her a Whitman sampler on Valentine's Day. It was the small one, only four chocolates, and none of them with nuts, but Heather was the only girl in all of sixth grade to receive chocolates from a boy other than her father, so it made quite the stir. Heather didn't need Sunny to show her how to do anything.

She picked up the Accent section and read her horoscope. In just five days, there would be a horoscope especially for her. Well, for her and the other people born on April 3. She couldn't wait to see what it said. And next week there would be a party, bowling at Westview Lanes and a bakery cake—devil's food with white icing and blue roses. Maybe she should buy something new to wear. No, not yet. But she would take her new purse to the mall, an early birthday gift from her father's store. It was actually multiple purses that buttoned to the same wooden handles, so you could match it to your outfit. She had chosen denim with red rickrack, a madras plaid, and one with a print of large orange flowers. Her father hadn't planned to stock the purses, but her mother had noticed how Heather

60

studied the samples and pressed him to include it in the orders he made back in February. They were by far the most successful new item in his store this spring, but that just seemed to make her father grumpier.

"Faddish," he said. "You won't want to carry it a year from now."

Of course, Heather thought. Next year there would be another purse or top that was the thing to have, and her father should be glad for that. Even at eleven she had figured out that you couldn't run a successful store if people didn't keep buying things, year in and year out.

Sunny, frustrated almost to the point of tears, watched silently as her father left the kitchen. He had been so odd this morning—making pancakes, letting Heather listen to WCBM, singing along and even commenting on the songs.

"I like that one," he said of each song. "The girl—"

"Minnie Riperton," Heather said.

"Her voice sounds like birdsong, don't you think?" He attempted to imitate the cascading notes, and Heather laughed at how poorly he did it, but Sunny simply felt uncomfortable. A father wasn't supposed to know songs like "Lovin' You," much less sing along with them. Besides, her father was the biggest liar. He didn't like any of these songs. The very fact that a song was Top 40—the very fact of popularity in anything, whether it was music or movies or television or fashion—disqualified it from serious consideration in her father's life. On his headphones, in his study, he played jazz, Bob Dylan, and the Grateful Dead, which seemed as formless and pointless as jazz to Sunny. Listening to the radio with her father and sister made Sunny feel queer, as if they were reading her diary in front of her, as if they knew what she was thinking late at night when she went to bed with her transistor radio plugged into one ear. Her tastes were changing, but she still found certain love songs irresistible: "You Are So Beautiful." "Poetry Man." "My Eyes Adored You." Twitching in her seat, cutting her pancakes into ever-smaller pieces, she had yearned to jump up and turn the radio off.

Then Ringo came on with the "No No Song" and her father did it for her, saying, "There's only so much a man can take. When I think—"

"What, Daddy?" Heather asked, playing up to him.

"Nothing. What do my girls have planned today?"

And that's when Heather said, "Sunny's going to the mall." She spoke with a lisping baby quality, a voice she had long outgrown, a voice she never really had to begin with. When Heather petitioned for a new freedom for herself—permission to ride her bike to the shopping district in Woodlawn, for example—she spoke in her regular voice. But when she was trying to show up Sunny, Heather used this little-girl tone. Even so, their mother was onto her. Sunny had heard her mother tell someone on the phone that Heather was eleven going on forty. Sunny had waited to hear what *her* relative age was, but it hadn't come up.

Sunny added her dish to the stack her father had left on the drain board. She tried to come up with a rationalization not to do them now, but she knew that was unfair to her mother, who would be left with a pile of sticky dishes at the end of a long workday. It never even occurred to her father to wash them, Sunny knew, although he was liberated, compared to other fathers. The kids in the neighborhood called him the "hippie," because of the shop, his hair, and his VW bus, which was a simple robin's-egg blue, not anything remotely psychedelic. But although their father cooked—when he felt like it—and said he "supported" his wife's decision to work as a real-estate agent, there were certain household chores he never attempted.

If he had to wash the dishes every day, Sunny thought, scraping the leftover pancakes into the trash, *he wouldn't have been so dead set against putting in a dishwasher.* She had shown him the ads for the portable models, explaining how they could roll it from the sink to the covered back porch when it wasn't in use, but her father had said the machines were wasteful, using too much water and energy. Meanwhile he was always upgrading his stereo. But his study was a place of contemplation, he reminded Sunny when she complained, the place where he conducted the sunrise and sunset rituals known as the Agnihotra, part of the Fivefold Path, which wasn't a religion but something better, according to Sunny's father.

"Have you been spying on me?" Sunny asked her sister, who was humming to herself and winding a lock of hair around her finger, lost in some secret joy. Their mother often said that their names should be switched, that Heather was always happy and bright, while Sunny was prickly as a thistle. "How did you know I planned to take the bus to the mall?"

"You left the schedule out on your desk, with the departure times underlined."

"What were you doing in my room? You know you're not supposed to go in there."

"Looking for my hairbrush. You're always taking it."

"I am not."

"Anyway"—Heather gave a blithe shrug—"I saw the schedule and I guessed."

"When we get there, I go my way and you go yours. Don't be hanging around me. Okay?"

"Like I want to follow you around. The only thing you do is go to the Singer store and flip through the pattern books, when you all but flunked out of home ec at Rock Glen last year."

"The machines there are all torn up, from so many kids using them. The needles are always breaking." This was the excuse her mother had offered for Sunny's poor grade in home ec, and she had been happy to take it. She just wished there had been excuses for her other not-great grades. Dreaminess was the kindest reason that her parents could muster. *Does not work to ability,* her homeroom teacher had written. "The shift dress I made at home, with Mom's help, was perfectly good," Sunny reminded her sister.

Heather gave her a knowing look. Technically, the dress had been well made, and Sunny had executed even the tricky parts—the darts in the bodice, the cutting of the fabric so the pattern was consistent—with finesse. But Heather seemed to have been born knowing things that escaped Sunny. Heather would never have chosen the heavy, almost muslinlike material, with its motif of ears of corn in vertical rows. In hindsight the teasing that Sunny had suffered was so predictable. *Corny, cornpone, corn-fed.* But she had felt so pretty getting ready that morning, her hair pulled into side ponytails and tied with green ribbons, so they played off the shiny gold ears encased in green stalks. Even their mother thought she looked nice. But the moment she stepped onto the bus—even before the shouts of "Cornball!" and "Corn-fed!"—Sunny knew that the dress was yet another mistake on her part. It didn't help that the darts, while properly executed, made the bodice pull tightly across the breasts that she wasn't quite ready to have.

"Anyway, once we get there, you're not to tag along after me. Dad said he'd pick us up at five-thirty, outside. I'll meet you at Karmelkorn at twenty after."

"And you'll buy me one?"

"What? Sure. Karmelkorn or Baskin-Robbins, if you like. Whatever you want. In fact, I'll give you five dollars if you'll promise to leave me alone."

"Five whole dollars?" Heather loved money, money and things, but she hated to part with money in order to have things. Their parents worried about this streak in her, Sunny knew. They tried to pass it off as a joke, calling her the little magpie, saying her eye was drawn to anything shiny and new, which she then took home to her nest. But this wasn't Bethany behavior, and Sunny knew that her parents worried about Heather. "She has an eye too soon made glad," their father said gloomily, paraphrasing some poem about a duchess.

"Yes, so you won't have to dip into your savings at all." *And,* Sunny thought, *so you won't open your metal card box and see I've had to borrow money from you, so the five dollars I'm giving you is actually yours.* Heather wasn't the only person who sneaked into other people's rooms and poked at things that she wasn't supposed to touch. Sunny had even figured out the pattern of the rubber bands that Heather used on the box.

Served her right, for being a spy.

65

CHAPTER 7

There was a vending machine in the motel room, actually *in* it, not down the hall or tucked away in a breezeway. Miriam lingered in front of the machine, testing the knobs, scooping her fingers in the change bin the way a child might. The wrappers on the candy bars looked a little faded. Given that it cost seventy-five cents to purchase a Zagnut or a Clark bar that could be had for thirty-five cents in the machine back in the lobby, cheaper still at the grocery store across the street, it had probably been a while since anyone had tried to justify the novelty of an in-room candy bar purchase. Still, how Sunny and Heather would have gloried in this machine, so many forbidden marvels crammed into one silvery box—sugary candy sold at exorbitant prices, yours for a quick yank on a handle. If they had ever stayed in such a motel—unlikely enough in itself, given Dave's preference for motor courts and campsites, "real" places, as he called them, which also had the virtue of being cheap places—the girls would have pleaded for coins to feed the machine as Dave grumped and harrumphed about the wastefulness of it. Miriam would have caved, and he would have remonstrated with her for not presenting a united front, then been cold and distant for the rest of the evening.

What else would happen on this fantasy trip to a motel not even five miles from where they lived? They would have watched television as they did at home—each girl picking one program—then turned it off and read until bedtime. If the room had a radio, Dave might have tuned it to a jazz station, or Mr. Harley's Saturday-night show of standards. She imagined them seeking refuge here during a storm, one not unlike Hurricane Agnes three years before, when the rising creek waters a few blocks away had briefly trapped them on Algonquin Lane. The lights had gone out, but it had seemed like an adventure at the time, reading by flashlight and listening to the news reports on Dave's battery-powered radio. Miriam had almost been disappointed when the water had receded and the electricity returned.

A key turned in the lock, and Miriam started. But it was Jeff, of course, returning with the filled ice bucket.

"Gallo," he said, and she thought for a moment that it was some sort of play on "hello," then realized he was introducing the wine he had brought.

"It will take some time to chill," he added.

"Sure," she said, although Miriam knew a trick to speed the process. One put the bottle in a bucket of ice and then rotated it clockwise one hundred times, exactly, and voilà—cold wine. It was when Miriam discovered herself rolling the neck of a bottle between her anxious palms at two o'clock in the afternoon that she decided she should get a job. Yes, they had needed the money—rather desperately, in fact—but that had been less urgent to her than the prospect of becoming a pickled, desultory housewife, boozy breath washing over her children as they ate their after-school snacks and recounted their days.

Jeff stepped closer to her, taking her chin in his hand. His hand was still cold from carrying the bucket, but she didn't flinch or pull back. Their teeth bumped painfully as the kiss began, and they had to adjust their mouths, as if they'd never kissed before. Funny, they had managed to make love so gracefully in a variety of tight and inconvenient locations—a closet at the office, a restaurant bathroom, the backseat of his little sports car—and now that they had space and, relative to what they were used to, time, they couldn't be clumsier.

She tried to shut down her mind, give in to her usual urgency for Jeff, and it started to work. This was, what, their seventh time, and it still amazed her how much *fun* it was. Sex with Dave had always been a little somber, as if he needed to prove his feminist credentials by making the act joyless for both of them, plying her with his endless earnest questions. Socratic sex, as Miriam thought of it. *How does this feel? What if I do this? Or if I vary it this way?* If she had tried to explain this to her girlfriends—if, in fact, she had female friends, which Miriam did not—she knew this would sound grumpy and ungrateful. She would not be able to convey her sense that Dave, in pretending to care for nothing but her pleasure, was actually intent on making sure she didn't enjoy herself. He had always seemed to pity her, just a bit, and regard himself as a gift he had conferred on her, the dark, sheltered girl from the north.

Jeff flipped her over, planted her feet on the floor, and placed her hands on the still-made bed, locking his fingers over hers and slipping into her from behind. This wasn't new to Miriam—Dave was also a dutiful student of the *Kama Sutra*—but Jeff's silence and directness made everything feel novel. Physiologically, according to Dave—yes, Dave was forever explaining her own anatomy to her—she shouldn't even be able to come in this position, yet with Jeff it happened frequently. Not yet, though, not just now. With an entire afternoon to spend in a motel room, they were taking it slowly. Or trying to.

Miriam had not been thinking of an affair when she entered the work world, or even an office flirtation. She was certain of that much. Sex wasn't important to Miriam, or so she had reasoned when she decided to marry Dave. Her sexual experience was somewhat limited, as the mores of her time had dictated. Not just the mores but the stakes—birth control was far from perfect and hard for a single girl to get. Still, Miriam was not a virgin when she met Dave. Jesus no, she was twenty-two and had once been engaged for six months, to her college sweetheart, with whom she had wonderful sex. "Mind-blowing," as they said now, but Miriam's mind had blown only when her fiancé decamped suddenly and without satisfactory explanation, fulfilling her mother's dire prophecies about cows and free milk.

A nervous breakdown, they called it, and Miriam

thought the term quite perfect. It was as if her nervous system had ceased to function. She was spastic and off-kilter, with all the basic bodily functions—sleeping, eating, shitting—unpredictable. One week she might sleep no more than four hours, while eating nothing at all. The next she would rise from her bed only to gorge herself on odd foods, a pregnant woman's cravings—batches of raw brownie mix, coddled eggs with ice cream, carrots and molasses. She had dropped out of school and moved back home to Ottawa, where her parents saw her problems as a direct consequence of her dalliance not with the college boyfriend, whom they had quite liked, but with the United States itself. They had not approved of Miriam's insistence on attending college in the States. Perhaps they suspected that it was the first step in a plan to leave Canada forever and, by extension, them.

Jeff pushed Miriam's entire body onto the bed. He had not said a single word since "It takes some time to chill," had barely even grunted. Now he flipped her again, as easily as if he were turning a pancake, and buried his face between her legs. Miriam was self-conscious about this act, something else she blamed on Dave. "You're Jewish, right?" Dave had asked the first time he tried that. "I mean, I know you're not observant, but that's your heritage, isn't it?" Stunned, she had been able only to nod. "Well, the mikvah has its utility. There's a lot about your religion that I don't like, but a careful cleansing after menstruation doesn't hurt anyone."

Dave had odd pockets of anti-Semitism, although he always insisted that his biases were about class, not religion, a reaction to the rich neighborhood where he had been the only poor kid. Miriam hadn't resorted to milk baths, but she had become, briefly, the world's great consumer of sprays and douches. Then she read an article that said the whole industry was bullshit, another manufactured solution for a problem that didn't exist. Still, she'd never gotten over the idea that she perpetually tasted of blood, rusty and metallic. If so, Jeff clearly didn't care. Jeff, who just happened to represent everything Dave hated—a rich Pikesville Jew with a country-club membership, an ostentatious house, and three indulged, bratty children. Miriam wasn't stereotyping. She'd met the children at the office, and they were hideous. But she had not chosen Jeff because he so neatly encapsulated everything that Dave loathed. She had chosen him, to the extent that such a decision could ever be called a choice, because he was there and he wanted her, and she was so pleased to be wanted that she couldn't imagine how to say no.

It was dangerous, meeting today. Their spouses weren't stupid. Well, hers wasn't. Tomorrow, when Dave read the Sunday paper, he might notice the dearth of open house notices, given that it was Easter, and wonder why Miriam had been needed at the real-estate office on a weekend when there was nothing to do. The whole affair was dangerous, because neither Miriam nor Jeff wanted to leave their marriages or disrupt their lives. Well, Jeff probably didn't. Miriam was no longer sure what she wanted, what she was doing.

Jeff was getting impatient with her. She was usually so fast, almost too fast, but today she could not still her thoughts. And Jeff, while generally polite, would abandon her eventually and pursue his own pleasure if she didn't get going. She focused on that one part of herself, syncing her movements to his mouth, aligning things better, and soon she felt it. Her orgasms with Jeff were like the trick of a soprano shattering glass; it was the resonating frequency, not the pitch, that broke her. She was useless afterward, barely able to move, but Jeff was accustomed to that. He arranged her rag-doll limbs beneath him and pushed into her rather violently until he also was done.

Now what? Usually they just pulled their clothes on, not that they had ever gotten them totally off before, and returned to work, or home, or wherever. Jeff fetched the bottle of wine from the plastic ice bucket. "No corkscrew," he said, amused by his own mistake. Casually, as if it were the most natural thing in the world, he broke the bottle's neck on the rim of the bathroom sink and then filled the water glasses, picking out a few glass fragments that were caught when the wine flowed over the bottle's broken neck.

"I like screwing you in a bed," Jeff said.

"Our first time was in a bed," Miriam said.

"That didn't count."

Why not? she wondered, yet didn't ask. Their first time had been in a client's house, and the violation of the space with which they'd been entrusted had seemed more shocking than the actual fact of adultery. When Jeff asked her to go over to see the new listing, she had known that they were going to have sex, but she pretended naïveté. *The woman always sets the pace,* her mother had told Miriam in her euphemistic way when probing for the reason behind Miriam's breakdown. Miriam liked to pretend that Jeff had controlled everything, as easily as he manipulated her body in bed. Jeff made Miriam feel wispy, featherlight, almost as if she were in her girlhood body again. She had not gained weight as she aged, but she had thickened a little, a fact that she had been able to ignore until she noticed her own daughters' bodies, so impossibly narrow and slim-hipped. Both looked as if they could be snapped in half at the waist.

"What now?" she asked.

"Now, as in here, this specific moment? Or now as in tomorrow and next week and the month after?"

She wasn't sure. "Both."

"Now, here, today, we'll have sex again. Maybe twice, if we're lucky. Tomorrow, while you're in church, acknowledging Jesus's alleged resurrection—"

"I don't go to church."

"I thought—"

"He didn't ask me to convert. He just told me he didn't want the girls raised in any organized religion or exposed to anything but the more nonsecular traditions. Christmas trees, Easter baskets."

She had broken an unwritten rule, mentioning her children, and the conversation stalled awkwardly. Miriam didn't know how to raise the topic she really wanted to discuss. *How do we end this? If we're doing this just because the sex is fun, will it stop being fun in a convenient and mutual way? Will I yearn for you while you move on to someone else? Or vice versa? How did affairs end?*

Theirs was ending that very moment, Miriam would realize later, in ways both banal and cataclysmic. Maybe it had always been this way. A mushroom cloud formed over Hiroshima, and some of those

73

who ran through the streets, stunned and burned, had been routed from beds not their own, from places they shouldn't be. Tsunamis washed over illicit lovers, adulterers were put on the train to Auschwitz, just not for that particular reason.

This was her legacy, this was her before, the moment she would return to again and again. When Miriam tried to remember the last time she was happy, all she could summon up was a warmish glass of Gallo wine with slivers of glass in it and a dusty Fifth Avenue candy bar that was, in fact, quite stale.

CHAPTER 8

The bus shelter on Forest Park Avenue was a more-than-familiar place to Sunny, part of her school-day routine going back almost three years, but she found herself studying it that afternoon as if seeing it for the first time. Although its purpose was basic—keep bus riders from the damp, if not the cold—someone had cared enough to add a few nonessential flourishes so it might be mistaken for attractive. The roof was off-green, a shade their mother had wanted to use for the trim on their house, but their father had said it was too dark, and their father, as the artistic one, always won such arguments. The pale beige bricks had a rough texture, while the slatted bench inside the structure was the same shade as the roof.

Boys in the neighborhood, indifferent to the bus shelter's efforts, had scrawled rude graffiti on the walls in chalk and paint. Someone had come behind them and tried to remove the worst of it, but a few stubborn

75

curses and character assassinations remained. Heather inspected these solemnly.

"Do they ever—" she began.

"No," Sunny said swiftly. "They leave me alone."

"Oh." Heather's tone sounded almost as if she felt sorry for Sunny.

"They don't like me because of the fight. The kids on the bus."

"But they don't live here," Heather said. "The graffiti is done by people who live here, right?"

"I'm the only one who goes to Rock Glen. Everyone else is older or younger, by a lot. That was the problem, remember? 'We had right, but they had might.' Majority rules."

Bored with this family story in which she had played no part, Heather sat on the bench, opened her purse, and examined its contents, humming to herself. The bus was not due for another fifteen minutes, but Sunny hadn't wanted to risk missing it.

The battle over the school bus route had been Sunny's first brush with gross unfairness, a lesson in how money can triumph over principle. Most of the students on Sunny's bus lived far up Forest Park Avenue, all the way on the other side of Garrison Boulevard. But under the city's open-enrollment plan, they could choose to attend school wherever they liked, and they had bypassed the all-black school nearest them and picked Rock Glen on the city's southwest side, which was still mostly white. A private bus service, paid for by all the parents, was set up. Sunny's stop, the little shelter on Forest Park Avenue, was the last stop every morning and the first one every afternoon. For two years this seemed a logical plan to everyone involved.

And then it didn't.

Last summer the parents at the far end of the route began to grumble that their children would have a much shorter trip if the bus didn't have to stop on the lower part of Forest Park Avenue for Sunny. Or, as they called her, "Just the one." As in, "Just the one student." Or, "Why should just the one student inconvenience so many?" They threatened to find another bus service, leaving the company with "just the one," which would never cover the cost of the route. Sunny's parents were appalled, but there was nothing they could do. If they wanted to continue using the bus service—essential, given that they both worked—they had to agree to a compromise: The route would be reversed in the afternoon. So every afternoon Sunny watched her own block fly past as the bus headed to the beginning of its route and dropped students off in reverse order, backtracking to Forest Park Avenue. Given that their families had won, the other students should have been gracious, but Sunny discovered it didn't work that way. They disliked her more than ever because her parents had all but called their parents racists. "N.L.," one of the larger boys hissed at her. "You and your parents are N.L.ers." She had no idea what it meant, but it sounded terrifying.

The mass-transit system, unlike Mercer Transportation, could not be bullied. If it took twenty-five minutes to get to Security Square, with stops, then it took twenty-five minutes to get home again. The MTA was *egalitarian,* a word that she picked up from her father and particularly liked because it reminded her of *The Three Musketeers* with Michael York. When Sunny started Western High School next year, the plan was for her to take the MTA, using the free coupons distributed to students in monthly packs. To prepare for this, her parents had started allowing her to take practice runs—trips downtown, to Howard Street and the big department stores. That's how she had come to reason that she could take the bus to Security Square and not tell anyone. Sunny was practically blasé about taking the bus places.

But Heather, who had never taken a public bus anywhere, bounced with excitement on the wooden bench, one hand clutching her fare, the other wrapped around the handle of her new purse. Sunny also had a purse from her father's store, a macramé one, but they didn't get such things for free despite what the other kids assumed. If the item wasn't a gift, like Heather's purse, then they were expected to pay the wholesale price, because their father said his "margins" wouldn't allow for freebies. Margins always made Sunny think of her typing class, which she was failing, although not because of margins. Her problem was that she performed horribly at the timed trials, making so many mistakes that she ended up with a negative word-per-minute score. When she wasn't being timed, she typed very well.

Sunny wondered why her parents had insisted that she take the typing elective in junior high, if they thought she was going to have to type for a living. Ever since sixth grade, when most of her friends were placed in the "enriched" track at Rock Glen, while she was merely "high regular," she couldn't help worrying that her future had been derailed while she wasn't paying attention, that she'd lost options she never knew she had. When she was little, Grandpoppa and

Grandmama had given her a nurse's kit, while Heather had gotten a doctor's kit. At the time the nurse's kit was the better thing to have, because it had a pretty girl on its plastic cover and the doctor's kit had a boy. How Sunny had lorded that over Heather. "You're a *boy*." But maybe it would have been better to be the doctor? Or at least to have people tell you that you *could be* the doctor? Their father said they could be anything they wanted to be, but Sunny wasn't convinced that he really believed this.

Heather, of course, was going to be enriched when she entered Rock Glen next year, not that the placements had been announced yet. Heather would be enriched and then, most likely, in the A course at Western, which meant that she would skip the last year of junior high and enter high school in ninth grade instead of tenth. It wasn't that Heather was smarter than Sunny. Their mother said that IQ tests showed that both sisters were smart, near genius. But Heather was good at school, the way someone else might be good at track or baseball. She understood the rules, whereas Sunny seemed to trip herself up by trying too hard to be creative and different. And while those were the very values that her parents professed to cherish above straight A's and rote memorization, their expectations for Sunny had clearly flagged when she didn't make enriched. Was that why she was so angry with them all the time? Her mother laughed and called it a phase, while her father encouraged her to argue—"But rationally," a directive that only made her more irrational. Lately she had taken to challenging his politics, the thing he held most dear, but her father had remained maddeningly calm, treating her like a little girl, like Heather.

"If you want to support Gerald Ford in next year's election, then by all means do it," he told her just a few weeks ago. "All I ask is that you have reasoned positions, that you research his positions on the issues."

Sunny wasn't going to support *anyone* in the election. Politics was stupid. It embarrassed her to think of her impassioned speeches for McGovern back in 1972, part of her sixth-grade teacher's current-events debates on Friday. Only six kids in a class of twenty-seven had voted for McGovern when their mock Election Day came—one fewer than had voted for him in the initial poll when school started. "Sunny talked me out of it," Lyle Malone, a smugly handsome boy, said when asked if he wanted to explain his change of mind. "I figured anyone she liked that much couldn't be much good."

Yet if Heather had spoken for McGovern, then everyone in her class would have followed her. Heather had that effect on people. People liked to look at her, make her laugh, win her approval. Even now the MTA driver, a type that usually screamed at anyone who dawdled at the open door, seem charmed by the excited girl with the denim purse held tightly to her chest. "Drop your fare here, sweetie," the bus driver said, and Sunny wanted to yell, *She's not that sweet!* Instead she climbed the steps, looking at her shoes, wedgies purchased just two weeks ago. The weather really wasn't right for them, but she had been dying to wear them, and today was the day.

CHAPTER 9

Woodlawn Avenue was busier than usual the Saturday before Easter, with steady streams of people in and out of the barbershop and the bakery. The impending resurrection of Jesus apparently required fresh Parker House rolls and trimmed, exposed necks, at least for those Baltimore throwbacks who still believed in haircuts. There also was a spring festival at the elementary school, an old-fashioned fair with cotton candy and goldfish free to anyone who could land a Ping-Pong ball in the narrow neck of a fishbowl. *This is a city where change is slow to catch on,* thought Dave, an eternal outsider in his own hometown. He had traveled all over the world, determined to live somewhere else, anywhere else, yet somehow ended up back here. In opening his shop, he had rationalized that he might bring the world to Baltimore, but Baltimore wasn't having it. For all the people on the sidewalks, not a single one had stopped to inspect his window displays, much less come inside.

Now that it was almost 3:00 P.M., according to the "Time for a Haircut" clock over the barbershop across the street, Dave had run out of ways to occupy himself. If he hadn't agreed to pick up Sunny and Heather at the mall, he might have packed it in and closed up early. But what if a customer arrived in that final posted hour, a customer of taste and means, determined to buy lots of things, and he lost that person's business forever? Miriam worried ceaselessly over this scenario. "It just takes once," she would say. "One time, one person pulling on the door when it should be open, and you've lost not just that customer but whatever word of mouth he or she might have generated."

If only things really were that simple, if all that success required was showing up early, leaving late, and working hard every minute in between. Miriam didn't have enough experience in the professional realm to realize how touchingly naïve her views were. She still believed that the early bird caught the worm, slow and steady won the race, all those clichés. Then again, if she hadn't held those beliefs, she might not have agreed so readily to his plan to open the store, given that it meant leaving his state job, a job that was all but guaranteed for life. Lately he had begun to wonder if Miriam figured that she would benefit either way. The store would make them rich or provide her with something to hold over Dave's head the rest of their lives. She had given him his chance, and he had blown it. Now every disagreement between them was rooted in that

unspoken context: *I believed in you / You blew it.*
Had she hoped all along that he would fail?

No, Miriam was not that Machiavellian, he was sure of that much. Miriam was the most honest person Dave had ever known, quick to give credit where credit was due. She always admitted that she had never seen the potential in the house on Algonquin Lane, a rambling, run-down farmhouse that had been the victim of repeated architectural insults—a cupola, a so-called Florida room. Dave had restored the house to its original bones, creating a simple, organic structure that seemed of a piece with its large, untamed yard. People who came to their house were always exclaiming over Dave's eye, pointing out objects he had collected in his travels and demanding to know how much they had cost, then announcing they would pay five, ten, twenty times as much if he would only open a store.

Dave had taken those words at face value. He still did. Those compliments could not possibly have been social niceties because Dave had never inspired that kind of effusive tact. Quite the opposite—he had always been a magnet for blunt, unpleasant truths, aggression disguised as candor.

On their very first date, Miriam had said to him, "Look, I hate to tell you this. . . ."

He was familiar with such beginnings, but his heart still sagged a little. He had thought this trim young woman, with her Canadian manners and vowels, would be different. She was working as a clerk-typist in the state Department of Budget and Revenue, where Dave was an analyst, and it had taken him three months just to ask her out.

"Yes?"

"It's about your breath."

Reflexively, he had clapped his hand to his mouth, Adam shielding his nakedness after a bite of the apple. But Miriam patted the hand that remained on the table.

"No-no-no—my father is a dentist. It's really quite simple." It was. With the introduction of dental floss and Stimudents and, eventually, gum surgery, Miriam rescued Dave from a life in which people had always reared back, ever so slightly, when talking to him. It was only when this behavior ended that Dave understood what it meant when people pulled their chins in and lowered their noses. *He stank. They were trying not to inhale.* He couldn't help wondering if those first twenty-five years, the fetid years, as he thought of them—had damaged him irreparably. When you spend a quarter of a century seeing people recoil from you, can you ever expect to be embraced and accepted?

His daughters had offered his only chance at a clean slate. After all, even Miriam had known bad-breath Dave, however briefly. The girls' hero worship of him had been so pronounced that Dave had been foolish enough to believe that they would never tire of him. But now Sunny seemed to regard him a corporeal embarrassment, the walking embodiment of a fart or a belch. Heather, precocious as ever, was already imitating big sister's coolness at times. But although his daughters now tried to keep him at arm's length, they could not keep him from knowing them. He felt as if he lived inside their skulls, saw the world through their eyes, experienced all their triumphs and disappointments. "You don't understand," Sunny snarled at him with increasing frequency. The real problem was that he did.

Take this newfound obsession with the mall. Sunny thought Dave hated shopping centers because of their emphasis on cheap, mass-produced consumer pleasures, the diametric aesthetic to the one-of-a-kind handicrafts sold in his store. But what he really disliked was the mall's effect on Sunny. It called to her as surely as the sirens had serenaded Ulysses. He knew what she did there. It wasn't that much different from what he had done in his own teenage years in Pikesville, walking up and down the business district along Reisterstown Road, hoping that someone, anyone, would pay attention to him. He had been very much the odd boy out, the son of a single mother when everyone else had parents, a nominal Protestant in a neighborhood of well-to-do Jewish families. His mother had worked as a waitress at the old Pimlico Restaurant, so their household's fortunes were tied to the generosity of his classmates' fathers, men who sat in judgment of Dave's mother at meal's end, taking her tip up twenty-five cents or down fifty, and every penny had mattered. Oh, no one had taunted him openly for being poor. He wasn't worth the bother of ridicule, which seemed worse in a way.

And now Sunny was stuck in the same life. He could almost smell the yearning on her. And while desperation was sad enough for a teenage boy, it was downright dangerous for a girl. He was terrified for Sunny. When Miriam tried to minimize his fears, he wanted to say, *I know.* I know. *You can't begin to understand what goes through a man's mind at the sight of a girl in a tight sweater, just how base and primary those urges are.* But if he told Miriam this, she might ask what went through his mind, every day, when he saw the girls from Woodlawn High School stroll past, heading to the bakery or High's Dairy Store or Robin's Nest Pizza.

Not that he wanted anything to do with teenagers, far from it. Sometimes he wanted to *be* a teenager, or at least a man in his twenties. He wanted the freedom to wander in this new world, where the girls' hair swung long and free and their braless breasts bounced in slinky print shirts. The freedom to wander and gawk, but nothing more. When he was still working for the state, he'd seen plenty of colleagues succumb to this desire. Even in the cultural backwater of the accounting division, men suddenly sprouted sideburns and bought sharp new clothes. About ten months later—really, Dave could have put together a chart, predicting that the appearance of sideburns on a man presaged the end of his marriage by exactly ten months—the guy would move out of the house and into one of those new apartment complexes, explaining earnestly that his kids couldn't be happy if he wasn't happy. *Uga-duh*, as Sunny might have snorted. Dave, having grown up in a fatherless household, would never subject his daughters to that.

The hour hand on the "Time for a Haircut" clock crawled toward 4:00 P.M. Almost six hours into his day, and not a single customer had come into the shop. Was it possible that the site was cursed? A few weeks back, Dave had chatted up one of the counterwomen at Bauhof's Bakery as she dropped cookies into a waxed-paper bag. The bakery still used the old-fashioned counterbalances, the ones that were being phased out by electronic scales that could measure weight to one-hundredth of a pound. Dave preferred the inexact elegance of the old scales, enjoyed watching them slowly align as each cookie dropped.

"Let's see," said the counterwoman, Elsie, who had to stand on tiptoe to reach the scale. "For years and years, it was a hardware store, Fortunato's. Then, in 1968, the old man got upset by the riots and sold, moved to Florida."

"There weren't any riots in Woodlawn. The trouble was miles away."

"No, but it aggravated him all the same. So Benny sold to some woman who sold children's clothes, but they were too dear."

"Dear?"

"Pricey. Who's gonna spend twenty dollars on a sweater that a baby's gonna wear all of a month? So she sold out to this restaurant, but it just didn't take. The young couple just didn't know which end was up, couldn't get a western omelet on the table in under forty-five minutes. And then there was a bookstore, but what with Gordon's up to Westview and Waldenbooks at Security, who's gonna come to Woodlawn to buy a book? And then there was the tux rental—"

"The Darts," Dave said, remembering the round-shouldered man with a measuring tape about his neck, the shy woman who peered out from a great curtain of long, prematurely gray hair. "I took over their lease."

"Nice couple, sensible types, but people go to where they've always gone when they want formalwear. Tuxes is traditional. Like funeral homes. You go to the place where your dad went, and he went to the place that his dad went, and so on. You want to *open* a new place, you got to *go* to a new neighborhood, where people don't have loyalties."

"So four different businesses in less than seven years."

"Yep. It's one of those black holes. Every block has one, the one store that never works." She brought her hand up to her mouth, the waxed grabbing paper still in her hand. "I'm sorry, Mr. Bethany. I'm sure you'll make a go of it with your little, um . . ."

"Tchotchkes?"

"What?"

"Nothing." In a German bakery that sold "Jewish" rye bread, without irony or apology, it was probably too much to expect Yiddish to be understood, much less the self-lacerating mockery in Dave's use of the word. Tchotchkes indeed. The items in his store were beautiful, unique. Yet even the families he knew through the Fivefold Path, like-minded people when it came to spiritual matters, had been slow to embrace his material goods. If he had been in New York, or San Francisco, or even Chicago, the store would be a hit. But he was in Baltimore, which he'd never intended. Then again, it was here that he'd met Miriam, had his family. How could he wish that away?

The wind chime over the front door keened softly. A middle-aged woman, and Dave wrote her off instantly, assuming she must be in need of directions. Then he realized she was probably only a few years removed from him, no more than forty-five or so. Her clothes— a fussy pink knit suit and boxy handbag—had thrown him off.

"I thought you might have unusual items for Easter baskets," she said, stumbling a little over the words, as if worried that this *unusual* store required an *unusual* etiquette. "Something that could be used as a keepsake?"

Fuck. Miriam had suggested that he stock more seasonal items and he had ignored her. He had done Christmas, of course. But Easter had seemed far-fetched. "I'm afraid not."

"Nothing?" The woman's distress seemed disproportionate. "It doesn't have to be for Easter, just Easter-themed. An egg, a chick, a rabbit. Anything."

"Rabbits," he repeated. "You know, I think we have some wooden rabbits from Mexico. But they're a little large for an Easter basket."

He went to the shelves that held Latin American art and gently pulled down one of the rabbit carvings, passing it to the woman as if it were an infant that needed to be cradled. She held it in front of her with straight, stiff arms. The rabbit was simple and primitive, a sculpture created with a few swift, sure cuts of a knife, far too nice to be a consolation prize in some child's Easter basket. It wasn't a toy. It was art.

"Seventeen dollars?" the woman asked, looking at the handwritten price tag on its base. "And so plain."

"Yes, but the simplicity . . ." Dave didn't even bother to finish his own sentence. He had clearly lost the sale. But he thought of Miriam, her poignant faith in him, and made one last attempt. "You know, I might have some wooden darning eggs in the back room. I found them at a West Virginia craft fair, and they're painted in bright primary colors—red, blue."

"Really?" She seemed oddly excited by this prospect. "Would you get them for me?"

"Well . . ." The request was a delicate one, for it would mean leaving her alone in the shop. This was the consequence of not being able to afford a part-time helper. Sometimes Dave invited customers into

89

the back room, made it seem like he was conferring special honor on them, rather than insult them by suggesting he was worried about theft. But he couldn't imagine this woman pocketing anything, or trying to get into his cash register, an old-fashioned one that would ring clamorously if opened. "Wait here, I'll see if I can find them."

It took longer to find the eggs than it should have. In his head, Miriam's voice nagged him—gently, but a nag was a nag—reminding him about the need for inventory and procedures and systems. But the point of the shop had been to escape such things, to set himself free from the rigors of numbers. He still remembered his disappointment when Miriam had failed to understand the significance of the store's name.

"The Man with the Blue Guitar—won't people think it's a music store?"

"You don't get it?"

"Well, I can see it's kind of . . . zany, the way things are now. The Velvet Mushroom, that kind of thing. Still, it might confuse people."

"It's from Wallace Stevens. The poet who was also an insurance agent."

"Oh, the 'Emperor of Ice-Cream' guy. Sure."

"Stevens was like me—an artist trapped inside a businessman. He sold insurance, but he was a poet. I was a fiscal analyst, but that didn't fulfill me. Can't you see?"

"Wasn't Stevens the vice president of an insurance agency? And didn't he keep working, even as he wrote poems?"

"Well, yes, it's not an exact parallel. But it's the same emotionally."

Miriam hadn't said anything to that.

The eggs located, he carried them out to counter. The store was empty again. Immediately he checked the register, but his meager supply of cash was there, and a quick survey of the more precious items— well, semiprecious, by definition, jewelry made from opals and amethysts—indicated they had been left undisturbed in the glass case. It was only then that he noticed the envelope on top of the counter, addressed to Dave Bethany. Had the mailman come and gone while he was in the back? But this was unstamped, with no designation other than his name.

He opened it and found a note, the handwriting wavy with emotion, not unlike the voice of the woman in the pink suit.

Dear Mr. Bethany:
You should know that your wife is having an affair with her boss, Jeff Baumgarten. Why don't you put a stop to this? There are children involved. Besides, Mr. Baumgarten is very happily married and will never leave his wife. This is why mothers do not belong in offices.

The letter was unsigned, but Dave had no doubt that it was written by Mrs. Baumgarten, which meant that her Easter mission had been an elaborate bit of fakery. Dave didn't know much about Miriam's boss, but he knew he was Jewish, prominently Jewish, probably just a few years ahead of Dave at Pikesville High School. Perhaps Mrs. Baumgarten had planned to drop this letter on the counter without being seen but had been undone by the empty shop. Or she had written it as a fallback, in case she couldn't summon the nerve to confront him directly. How odd, that last line, as if she needed a larger social issue to buttress her position as the wronged party. In the split second it took Dave's mind to find the word *cuckold* and apply it to himself, he felt a twinge of pity for this proper middle-class woman with her anonymous note. Not too long ago, the local news had been full of stories about the governor's wife, who had to learn from her husband's press secretary that she was being divorced. She had holed herself up in the governor's mansion and refused to come out, sure that her husband would return to his senses. She had been a woman not unlike this one—Northwest Baltimore, Jewish, plump and well dressed, an integral part of her husband's success. Affairs were a man's perquisite, something that wives either tolerated or didn't. The women in affairs were young and toothsome and unencumbered—secretaries and stewardesses, Goldie Hawn in *Cactus Flower*. Miriam couldn't have an affair. She was a mother, a good one. Poor Mrs. Baumgarten. Her husband was clearly cheating on her, but she had lashed out blindly, settling on Miriam because she was a handy target.

He dialed Miriam's office number, and let it ring, but the receptionist didn't pick up. Ah well, Miriam was probably still out at an open house, and the receptionist had left for the day. He would ask her about it tonight, something he should do more often anyway. Ask Miriam about her work. Because surely it was her work that had given her so much confidence recently. It was the commissions that accounted for the glow in her face, the bounce in her step, the tears in the bathroom late at night.

The tears in the bathroom . . . but no, that was Sunny, poor sensitive Sunny, for whom ninth grade had been a torture of ostracism, all because he and Miriam had tried to fight the other parents over the bus route. At least that's what he'd told himself when, sitting in his study late at night, he had heard those muffled sobs in the bathroom at the head of the stairs, the one that the whole family shared. He'd sat in his study, pretending to listen to music, pretending he was respecting the privacy of the crying female just a stair climb away.

Dave tore the letter in pieces, grabbed his keys, and locked up, heading down the street to Monaghan's Tavern, another Woodlawn establishment doing a booming business on the Saturday before Easter.

CHAPTER 10

"You were supposed to stay away from me," Sunny hissed at Heather after the usher dragged them both out of the movie theater and said they were banned for the day. "You *promised.*"

"I got worried when you didn't come back from the bathroom. I just wanted to make sure you were all right."

It wasn't a lie, not exactly. Certainly Heather had *wondered* why Sunny had left fifteen minutes into *Escape to Witch Mountain* and not returned. And she'd been worried that Sunny was trying to dump her, so she had gone outside, looked in the bathroom, then sneaked into the other side, where the R-rated *Chinatown* was playing. Sunny must have been pulling this trick for a while, Heather figured, buying a ticket for the PG movie on one side of the theater, then using a bathroom visit to gain entrance to the R-rated one while no one was looking.

She took a seat two rows back from Sunny, the same maneuver she'd used in *Escape to Witch Mountain*. ("It's a free country," she announced airily when Sunny had glared at her.) This time she'd gone undetected until the moment the little man had inserted his knife in the other man's nose. Then she had gasped, quite audibly, and Sunny had turned at the sound of her voice.

Heather had assumed that Sunny would ignore her, rather than draw attention to both of them. But Sunny came back to where she was sitting and, in urgent whispers, told her that she had to leave immediately. Heather shook her head, pointing out that she was observing the rules that Sunny had set down. She wasn't with her. She just happened to be at the same movie theater. Like she said, it was a free country. An old woman called the usher, and they were both thrown out when they couldn't produce the proper ticket stubs. Heather, being Heather, had lied and said she'd lost hers, but slow-thinking Sunny had produced the ticket for Theater One, where *Escape* was playing. A shame, because busty as she was, Sunny might have passed for seventeen. If their ages were reversed, if Heather were the older one, she would have been able to get them out of it—lying smoothly to the usher about her lost ticket, claiming to be seventeen and arguing that a sister counted as the adult supervision required for an R movie. What was the good of an older sister if she didn't act like one? Here was Sunny, on the verge of tears because of a stupid movie. Heather thought it was crazy, spending precious mall time to sit in the dark, when there were so many things to see and smell and taste.

"It was boring anyway," Heather said. "Although it was scary when that guy got his nose cut."

"You don't know *anything*," Sunny said. "That movie was directed by the man with the knife. Mr. Roman Polanski, whose wife was killed by Charles Manson. He's a genius."

"Let's go to Hoschild's. Or the Pants Corral. I want to look at the Sta-Prest slacks."

"Slacks don't wrinkle that much," Sunny said, still snuffling a bit. "That's stupid."

"It's what all the girls are wearing now that we're allowed to wear pants to school."

"You shouldn't want a thing just because everyone else has it. You don't want to run with the herd." That was their father's voice coming through Sunny's mouth, and Heather knew that Sunny herself didn't believe a word of it.

"Okay, let's go to Harmony Hut, then, or the bookstore." On her last visit to the mall, Heather had sneaked a look at what seemed to be a dirty book, although she couldn't be sure. There were lots of promising descriptions of the heroine's breasts pressing against the thin fabric of her dress, usually a good sign that something dirty was about to happen. She was trying to work up her nerve to read the book with the zipper on the cover—not a real zipper, like the Rolling Stones album cover that Sunny owned, but one that nevertheless revealed a portion of a woman's naked body. She needed to find a bigger book to put in front of it, so she could read it without drawing attention to herself. The staff at Waldenbooks didn't care how long you stood there reading a book without buying it, as long as you didn't try to sit down on the carpet. Then they chased you out.

"I don't want to do anything with you," Sunny said. "I don't care where you go. Just do your own thing and come back here at five-twenty."

"And you'll buy me Karmelkorn."

"I gave you five dollars. Buy your own Karmelkorn."

"You said five dollars *and* Karmelkorn."

"Fine, fine, what does it matter? Come back here at five-twenty and you'll get your precious Karmelkorn. But not if I see you hanging around me again. That was the deal, remember?"

"Why are you so mad at me?"

"I just don't want to hang out with a *baby*. Is that so hard to understand?"

She headed toward the Sears end of the mall, the corridor with Harmony Hut and Singer Fashions. Heather thought about following her, Karmelkorn notwithstanding. Sunny had no right to call her a baby. Sunny was the babyish one, crying so easily over the smallest things. Heather wasn't a baby.

Once Heather had loved being the baby, had reveled in it. And when their mom had gotten pregnant, back when Heather was almost four, and they had started talking about "the baby," it had bothered her. "I'm the baby," she said hysterically, pushing a finger into the middle of her chest. "Heather's the baby." As if there could be only one baby in their family, in all the world.

That was when they moved to Algonquin Lane, to the house where everyone could have her own bedroom. Even then Heather could recognize a bribe when she saw one—*you can have a bedroom, but you*

97

won't be the baby. The house was huge compared to their apartment, big enough so that four children could have their own bedrooms. That made Heather feel better somehow. Even the new baby wouldn't always be the baby. And Heather would get second dibs on whatever room she wanted. She thought she should get first dibs, given that she was losing baby status, but her parents explained that because Sunny was older, she would be in her room a shorter amount of time before going to college, so she should have first choice. If Heather really wanted the room that Sunny chose, then it could be hers for three years, most of high school. Even at four going on five, something in Heather rebelled at that logic, but she didn't have the words to make an argument, and her parents were never impressed by tantrums. Her mother said exactly that when she tried: "I'm not impressed, Heather." Her father said, "I don't respond to that kind of behavior." But he didn't respond to any behavior that Heather could see. Look at Sunny. She played by their rules, marshaled her arguments and presented them in orderly fashion, and she almost never got what she wanted. Heather was much sneakier, and she usually got her way. She even got to stay the baby, although that wasn't because of anything she did. As it turned out, the baby just hadn't been strong enough to live outside their mother's stomach.

When the baby died, their father made a point of telling Heather and Sunny exactly what a miscarriage was. To do that he had to explain how the baby had gotten inside their mother in the first place. Much to their dismay, he used all the proper words—penis, vagina, uterus.

"Why would Mommy let you do that?" Sunny had demanded to know.

"Because that's how babies are made. Besides, it feels good. When you're a grown-up," her father had added. "When you're a grown-up, it feels good to do that, even if it doesn't make a baby. It's a very sacred thing, the way you show love."

"But . . . but—pee comes out of there. You might have peed inside her."

"Urine, Sunny. And the penis knows not to do that when it's inside a woman."

"How?"

Their father started to explain how the penis grew when it wanted to make a baby, how it had this different kind of liquid inside filled with seed called sperm, until Sunny put her hands over her ears and said, "Eew, I don't want to know. It could still get confused. It could still pee in there."

"How big does it get?" Heather wanted to know. Her father had held out his hands, like a man showing the size of a fish he'd caught, but she didn't believe him.

Given that she knew everything about baby making before she entered kindergarten, Heather was surprised when she got to Dickey Hill Elementary and discovered that sex education was not taught until the sixth grade and it was considered a big deal, requiring permission slips from all the parents. Still, she didn't brag about her knowledge or draw attention to it. That was another thing that Sunny never understood, that it was good to keep things back, not volunteer everything at once. No one liked a show-off.

In fourth grade, however, Heather's friend Beth's

mother got pregnant, and Beth's parents told her that God had put the baby there. Like her father, Heather could not bear to let misinformation stand. She convened a quick class beneath the jungle gym on the playground, recounting everything she knew about baby making. Beth's parents complained, and Heather's parents were called to school, but her father was not only unapologetic, he was proud of Heather. "I can't be held accountable for those who prefer to lie to their children," he said, right in front of Heather. "And I won't ask my daughter to say she was wrong for speaking the truth about something natural."

Natural was good. It was her father's highest form of praise. Natural fabrics, natural foods, natural hair. After he opened the shop, he had grown his hair into a large, woolly Afro, much to Sunny's embarrassment. He even combed it with a Black Power pick, one whose handle ended in a clenched fist. He would, in fact, not approve of the Sta-prest pants, which definitely had something unnatural in them to keep them unwrinkled. Yet Heather was sure she could persuade him or her mother to let her have a pair, if she used her birthday money.

She walked toward the Pants Corral. Mr. Pincharelli, Sunny's music teacher, was playing the organ at Jordan Kitt's. Sunny once had a crush on him, Heather knew from reading her diary. But the last time they'd come to the mall together, Sunny had hurried by the organ store, as if embarrassed by him. Today he was standing up, playing "Easter Parade" with a lot of energy, and a small crowd had gathered around. Mr. Pincharelli's face was shiny with sweat, and there were pit stains along the underarm seams of his short-sleeved dress shirt. Heather couldn't imagine having a crush on him. If he were her music teacher, she never would have stopped making fun of him. Yet the crowd seemed genuine in its admiration and enjoyment, and Heather found herself caught up in the mood and she perched on the edge of a nearby fountain. She was puzzling over one of the phrases—*you'll find that you're in a photo so pure?*—when someone grabbed her elbow.

"Hey, you were supposed to—" The voice was angry, not loud, but sharp enough to be heard above the music, so those standing nearby turned and looked. The man dropped her arm quickly, mumbled, "Never mind," and disappeared back into the throngs of shoppers. Heather watched him go. She was glad she wasn't the girl that he was looking for. That girl was definitely in trouble.

"Easter Parade" gave way to "Superstar," a Carpenters song, not the one about Jesus. Just last week Sunny had given Heather all her Carpenters albums, proclaiming them lame. Music was the one area where Sunny's taste might be worth imitating, and if she thought the Carpenters lame, then Heather wasn't sure she wanted any part of them either. *Five dollars*—that was enough to buy an album and still have some left over. Maybe she would go down to Harmony Hut after all, buy something by . . . Jethro Tull. He seemed pretty cool. And if Sunny happened to be at the record store, too—well, it was a free country.

PART III
THURSDAY

CHAPTER 11

"The thing is," Infante said to Lenhardt, "she doesn't *look* like a Penelope."

The sergeant bit. "What does a Penelope look like?"

"I dunno. Blond hair. Pink helmet."

"*What?*" Drawing it out to two syllables.

"That old cartoon? The one where there was a car race every Saturday and they sucked you into believing that the outcome was somehow unknown? Anyway, Penelope Pit Stop was the name of the pretty one. They hardly ever let her win."

"It's Greek, though, right? I mean, not to take anything away from Hanna-Barbera, but I think there's some famous story about Penelope, something to do with knitting and a dog."

"What, like Betsy fuckin' Ross?"

"Slightly before that. Like a few thousand years, asshole."

Just twenty-four hours ago, when Infante was on the

shit list, this conversation would have been completely different—same words, perhaps, but a much less friendly tone. Yesterday Lenhardt would have been up for the same bullshit conversation, but the insults, the digs at Infante's intelligence, would have been serious, barbed rebukes. Today, however, Infante was a good boy. Two hours of overtime last night, at his desk bright and early, despite having stopped at the impound lot on his way in, and now at his computer, where he had pulled up Penelope Jackson's North Carolina driver's-license info and quickly arranged to get a copy of her photo faxed by the state police there.

Lenhardt squinted at the likeness, fuzzy from being enlarged on a photocopier. "So is it her?"

"It *could* be. Theoretically. The age, thirty-eight, isn't that far off the mark, although our girl's claiming older, which you don't get much. Hair and eye color are consistent. Hair's long in the photograph, cropped short in real life. The one in the hospital is definitely thinner than this."

"Women cut their hair all the time," Lenhardt said, his voice a little wistful, as if this fact made him sad. "And some even manage to drop a few pounds around the time they turn forty, or so I'm told." Mrs. Lenhardt was a knockout, but a bit on the plump side.

"Still, I don't think it's the same face. This one here's got a look to it. Kind of surly and cunning. The Jane Doe at St. Agnes, she's softer. I mean, I don't doubt she's lying to me—"

"Of course." Lying was assumed in their line of work.

"But I'm not sure what she's lying *about,* or to what purpose. If she isn't Heather Bethany—if she's Penelope Jackson or someone else still—then how does she know to bring up this thirty-year-old case when she's arrested? And how does she have the good fortune to fit the description, more or less?"

Infante pulled up another file on the computer, this one from a national database on missing children. He hadn't known how to do this, but a quick call to his old partner, Nancy Porter, had pointed the way. Here were the two girls, Heather and Sunny, as they had been at eleven and fourteen, their last school pictures. Below the actual photos were an artist's interpretations of how those girls might look today.

"She look like that?" Lenhardt asked, tapping the photo of Heather with his index finger—and leaving a little smear on Infante's screen, right in the middle of the girl's nose.

"Kinda. Maybe. Yes and no."

"You been to a reunion, college or high school?"

"Naw. That stuff doesn't do anything for me. And it's all the way back on Long Island, where I got no people now."

"I went to my thirty-year high school reunion a few years back. People age all different ways. Some, yeah, they looked like themselves, just a little older. Some just *go*, male and female. Like, you know, they got tired of trying. There were cheerleaders who weighed three hundred pounds, former football stars who managed the trick of going bald and developing dandruff. I mean, they bear no resemblance to the people they used to be."

"I bet you liked that—going into the reunion with a pretty wife fifteen years younger than you."

Lenhardt raised his eyebrows in mock surprise, as if it had never occurred to him that his wife was hot, when Infante knew the guy lived for the covetous glances thrown his way.

"But there's a third type, female division only," he said. "New and improved, better than they ever were. Sometimes with plastic surgery, but not always. They work out. They dye their hair. They've totally reinvented themselves, and they know it. That's why they show up, so you'll know it, too. The only way you could tell their age at all was by looking at their elbows."

"Who looks at a woman's elbows, you sick fuck?"

"I'm just saying it's the one place that a woman can't hide her age. My wife told me. She lemons hers sometimes. Cuts a lemon in half, hollows it out, fills it with olive oil and kosher salt and sits at her vanity, arms up like a little bunny." Lenhardt demonstrated the pose. "I tell you, Kevin, it's like going to bed with a fucking tossed salad."

Infante laughed. Yesterday he wouldn't have dreamed of admitting to himself how anxious it made him feel, being on the boss's bad side. He had preferred to rage instead at the unfairness of it all. But today he was redeemed, a good detective with a damned interesting case, and he couldn't deny the relief. If this woman was Heather Bethany, she was going to give them a sweet clearance. If she wasn't—well, she almost certainly knew something about something.

"Here's what struck me," he said, flipping to the notes he had taken at the impound lot. "We have this car registered in North Carolina two years ago. Penelope Jackson is no longer at that address, and her landlord, when I tracked him down, said she wasn't the kind of solid citizen who left a forwarding address. Said she followed whatever man she got her hooks into, picked up bartending and waitressing jobs. So she moved out almost ten months ago but didn't update her registration or license."

"Such *wickedness*," Lenhardt said with a whistle. "How long did you live in Maryland before you got around to registering your car?"

"You can't believe how they screw out-of-state people on title transfers," Infante said. "But then—you're one of those Baltimorons who thinks you've seen the world because you moved twenty miles out of the city. Anyway, the car's backseat is trashed—burger wrappers, some of 'em pretty fresh, cigarette butts, although the gal in the hospital isn't a smoker. You'd smell it on her if she were, and she'd be jumpy from nicotine withdrawal. It's a car that looks as if it's traveled a ways. But no suitcase. A purse, but no wallet on her when she's picked up and no cash. It's just garbage and the registration. How do you travel more than three hundred, four hundred miles without a credit card or a wad of cash?"

Lenhardt reached around Infante, pressing a few computer keys, toggling back and forth between Penelope Jackson of Asheville, North Carolina, and Heather Bethany of yesterday and today. "I wish we had one of those computers that movie cops had," he said.

"Yeah—then all we'd have to do is input Penelope Jackson and her last-known address and her whole life would be open to us. I can't wait until they get around to inventing those computers. Those and jetpacks."

"Nothing in NCIC?"

"Nothing in NCIC. No military record. And no report that this is a stolen vehicle."

"You know," Lenhardt said, reading through the

information on the missing children site, "there's a lot of detail here. Enough for a true-crime junkie to bone up, as it were."

"Yeah, I thought of that. But there's some stuff that's *not* here. Their exact address, for example, on Algonquin Lane. And the patrol who pulled her over? He said she was babbling about an old pharmacy at Windsor Mill and Forest Park. There's no such thing now. But I called the reference room at the Pratt, and there was a Windsor Hills Pharmacy there, around the time the girls disappeared."

"Kevin called the lie-berry? Man, you are bucking for employee of the month. So what about the case file? That's where you're going to find the level of detail that will make it impossible for some Internet surfer to fake you out."

Infante just gave his boss a look, the kind of look that conveys a world of meaning, a look available only to long-married couples or coworkers who've shared many years in the same bureaucracy.

"Do *not* fucking tell me—"

"I called for it yesterday afternoon, soon as I got back from the hospital. It's not here."

"Gone? Gone-gone? What the fuck?"

"There's a note where the file should be, left by the former primary—a guy who's since made sergeant and been posted to Hunt Valley. He was pretty sheepish when I tracked him down. Admitted he took it out for his predecessor on the case and just plain forgot about it."

"Sheepish? He should have been shitting himself. Bad enough to let the file leave the building, but to send it off with a former police and forget about it?" Lenhardt shook his head at the excess of idiocy involved. "So who has it?"

Infante glanced down at the name. "Chester V. Willoughby IV. Know him?"

"Know of him. He retired before I started out here, but he showed up at some of the homicide reunions. You could say he was . . . uh, atypical."

"Atypical?"

"Well, for one thing he's a fucking fourth. You might meet a junior police, but you ever know a fourth? And he came from money, didn't even have to work. When did the file go out?"

"Two years ago."

"Let's just hope he hasn't died since then. It wouldn't be the first time that some obsessed old coot took a file home and we all but had to go to probate to get it back."

"Man, I hope I'm not never like that."

Lenhardt had reached for the in-house directory and began thumbing through it, then punching in numbers, starting the hunt for the old cop's home address. "Hello—yeah, I'll hold." He rolled his eyes. "On fuckin' hold with my own department. And who are you kidding, Infante?"

"What?"

"There are supposed to be cases that eat at you. If there aren't, you're just lucky. Or stupid. This guy caught the reddest of red balls, two angelic-looking girls, vanishing at a mall on a Saturday afternoon with hundreds of people around. I wouldn't wipe my ass with a police who didn't carry that with him for the rest of his life." Then, back into the phone. "Yeah? Yeah. Chester Willoughby. You got an address on him?" Lenhardt was clearly put on hold again, and he mimed an up-and-down pumping motion with his left hand until the person came back on the line. "Great. Thanks."

He hung up, laughing.

"What's so funny?"

"In the time that took, you coulda walked over there. He's in Edenwald, behind the Towson Town Center mall, not even a mile from here."

"Edenwald?"

"Retirement community, one of the pricey ones where you pay extra money so you can die in your own bed. Like I said, he comes from money."

"Do you think that rich cops work more OT or less?"

"They probably work more, but don't put in for it. Hey, maybe you ought to pretend you're rich sometimes, see what it's like to work an hour out of love."

"Not even for your baby blues."

"What if I kiss you first?"

"I'd rather take it up the ass and get the cash."

"Well, that makes you a faggot *and* a whore."

Whistling, Infante grabbed his keys and headed out, feeling about as content as he ever did.

CHAPTER 12

"Buenos días, Señora Toles."

Miriam fished her keys out of her battered leather bag—"distressed" is what she would say if she were trying to sell it to someone—and unlocked the door to the gallery. She loved the way "Toles" sounded in Spanish—Toe-lez, instead of the flat, ugly syllable it was meant to be, "Tolls," a word that denoted fees and payments. No matter how long she lived in Mexico, it never got old, this aural transformation of her maiden name.

"Buenos días, Javier."

"Hace frío, Señora Toles." Javier rubbed his bare arms, which were goose-pimply. Such a March day would have been considered a godsend back in Baltimore, not to mention Canada, but it was frigid by San Miguel de Allende's standards.

"Perhaps it will snow," she said in Spanish, and Javier laughed. He was simple-minded and laughed at almost anything, but Miriam still appreciated his ready laughter. Once, *before,* her sense of humor had been a key part of her personality. It was rare now that she made anyone laugh, which puzzled her, because Miriam felt she remained capable of wit. In her head she amused herself constantly. Granted, it was a cruel wit, but her sensibility had always been on the cynical side, even when the cynicism was unearned.

Javier had attached himself to the gallery and Miriam shortly after she began working there. A teenager at the time, he hosed down the sidewalk in front of the shop, cleaned its windows without being asked, and told the *turistas* in a confidential whisper that it was *el mejor,* the very best of all San Miguel de Allende's shops. The owner, Joe Fleming, considered him a mixed blessing. "With that walleye and that cleft palate, he probably scares away as many customers as he brings us," he complained to Miriam. But she liked the young man, whose affection for her seemed rooted in something much deeper than the tips she slipped him.

"*¿Ha visto nieve?*" *Have you seen snow, Señora Toles?*

Miriam thought of her childhood in Canada, the endless winters that made her feel as if her family had been exiled from some more desirable climate. She had never gotten a satisfactory answer as to why her parents chose to leave England for Canada. Her mind skipped ahead to the blizzard of 1966 in Baltimore, a freak meteorological legend. It had fallen on Sunny's sixth birthday, and they'd taken six little girls from her class to see *The Sound of Music* in a downtown theater. It had been sunny and cloudless when they entered. Two-plus hours later, the Nazis vanquished and the world safe once again for family singing troupes, the party emerged to find a city in near-whiteout conditions. How she and Dave had struggled through the streets of Baltimore, delivering each daughter to her parents—literally delivering them, carrying them so their party shoes would not be ruined, handing them to mothers and fathers standing worriedly in their doorways. They laughed about it later, but it had been terrifying at the time, the old station wagon slithering over the roads, the girls shrieking in the back. Yet Sunny and Heather later remembered it as a grand adventure. That was the miracle wrought by a happy ending. You were free to relive a terrifying story as if it were merely exciting.

"No," she told Javier. "I've never seen snow."

She told such small lies all the time. It was easier. Mexico required less lying than the places she'd lived before, because it was a place full of people trying to leave various things and people behind. She assumed all the ex-pats lied as much as she did.

Miriam had come to San Miguel de Allende for a weekend in 1989 and essentially never left. She had intended to choose a less Americanized Mexican city in which to settle—and, not incidentally, a cheaper one, where she might have been able to live on her savings and investments alone, not work at all. But within two days of alighting from the train, she couldn't imagine living anywhere else. She had returned to Cuernavaca to collect the rest of her things, then arranged to sell her possessions in storage back in the States. When she bought her little house, her *casita,* she started with only a bed and her clothes. Today she didn't have much more. That was something else, like hearing the Spanish-soft version of her name, that never got old—waking up in a bare, uncluttered space of whitewashed walls and fluttering, sheer white curtains. The furniture, what there was of it, was pine. The Saltillo floors had been left bare. The only colors in Miriam's apartment were in her dishes and housewares, vivid blues and greens, purchased on discount from the gallery. If she decided to move again, it would take her no more than a day or two to dispose of her things. She had no intention of moving again, but she liked having the option.

The house on Algonquin Lane had been full of stuff, bursting with it. Miriam hadn't minded at first. For one thing, so much of what they carried then had belonged to the girls. Children didn't travel light, not even in those pre-car-seat days. They had toys and hats and mittens and dolls and stuffed animals and those hideous plastic trolls and, in Heather's case, a blanket known as "Bud," whose intermittent disappearances kept the household in a frenzy. Sunny, not to be outdone, had an imaginary friend, a dog named Fitz. Strangely, Fitz was as capable of getting lost as Bud. In fact, Fitz got lost whenever Bud got lost, and then some, and Fitz proved much harder to find. Sunny would stomp up and down the stairs of the house, reporting grimly on his non-whereabouts. "Not in the basement." "Not in the bathroom." "Not in your bed." "Not under the sink." For an imaginary dog, Fitz required a lot of care. Sunny began putting food down for him, refusing to understand that this was an invitation for roaches and rodents. She left the back door open, so Fitz could go outside. On rainy days Miriam came to believe that she could smell a wet dog.

The house on Algonquin Lane had baggage of its own, as it turned out. Purchased at auction, Miriam's first taste of her talent for real estate, it had come "as is." Miriam and Dave had understood that this meant the systems weren't guaranteed, that it was a bit of a *Let's Make a Deal* gamble. What they hadn't realized was that the house wouldn't be cleaned in any way. The longtime residence of an elderly woman, it had the feel of a life interrupted, as if aliens had swept in and kidnapped the people there. A cup and saucer sat on the table, a spoon at the ready for a pot of tea that was never made. A book lay on the stairs, as if to remind someone to carry it up. The old furniture was draped with antimacassars, a few askew, waiting for a gentle hand to set them straight. It reminded Miriam of a nineteenth-century version of the automated house in that Bradbury story "There Will Come Soft Rains." The family was gone, but the house lived on.

Initially, the things left behind had seemed a bonus, a windfall. Some of the furniture was usable, and the dishes were actually valuable—Lowestoft china, too good for everyday use, nicer even than Miriam's dinner-party china. In the backyard the girls found the remains of tea sets hidden in odd places—in the gnarled roots of the old oaks, beneath the lilac bushes, where they had rusted just a little. But these discovered treasures quickly became oppressive. They had to move as many things *out* as they did in. Why had so much stuff been left behind? They had been in the house for two months when a helpful neighbor volunteered that the former owner had been murdered in the kitchen by her own nephew, her only heir.

"That's why it went to auction," said the neighbor, Tillie Bingham. "She was dead and he was in prison, so he couldn't inherit."

She lowered her voice, although the girls were out of earshot and uninterested in this over-the-fence conversation. "Drugs."

Spooked, Miriam had tried to persuade Dave to put the house back on the market, even if it meant taking a loss. They could be downtown homesteaders, she told him, knowing what would appeal to him, settling in one of the grand old town houses of Bolton Hill. This was before the era of the dollar house, before the great revival of downtown, but Miriam's instincts about real estate were always sound. If Dave had heeded her advice, they would have had a far more valuable house in the end, for the values in their little corner of Northwest Baltimore remained flat for years.

And, of course, the girls would be alive.

That was the secret game that Miriam could never stop playing with herself, unhelpful as she knew it to be. Go back into history, change one thing. Not the day itself. That was too obvious, too easy. Their doom was sealed before that day dawned, when Sunny decided to spend the afternoon at the mall and Heather lobbied for permission to join her. But if she could go a little further back, then destiny could be thwarted. If they had put the house on Algonquin Lane up for sale as Miriam had urged, if they had never purchased it at all, then the chain of events could be disrupted. She wondered who owned it now, if the current residents knew of its talent for death. One murder in a house was bad enough, but if a buyer knew the full story of Algonquin Lane . . . No, not even Miriam could sell that house, and Miriam, in her heyday, could sell almost anything.

Hindsight was twenty-twenty, as the cliché would have it, but not always. After the girls had disappeared, Dave had proved to be even more myopic about their past than he had been about their present. Their problem, their curse, he insisted to neutral third parties, was that they were *happy*. Life was perfect, and therefore they had to fall. To hear Dave tell it, Algonquin Lane was a veritable Eden, and some unknown force had slithered through their lives and pinned its crimes on them.

The media had bought it, too. People were less cynical then, resources fewer. Today the shock of two missing sisters would have dominated national news channels, an armchair detective story for those lucky parents who knew where their children were. Back then, the girls' disappearance had been a local story, generating only a passing mention in a *Time* magazine piece on missing children. More national attention might have helped achieve what Miriam was always careful to think of as a resolution, but she supposed they'd been better off without the intrusion. Nowadays it would probably take a day for an amateur blogger to uncover the nature of Miriam's alibi, not to mention the debts that were weighing the family down. Thirty years ago the police could keep such secrets, while Equitable Trust had quietly paid off their first and second mortgages. (Children missing and presumed dead? Then you deserve a free house.)

Yet Dave's version—spin, as it might be called

now—had proved to be good for his business, not to mention her own career. Especially in that first year, Miriam could tell when it was her name, more than anything else, that had been the chief factor in attracting a new client. Midway through her spiel, while laying out what she could do for a motivated seller, how the firm could help with financing for pre-qualified buyers, she would catch one of the clients, usually the wife, inspecting her gravely. *How do you go on?* was the unspoken question. *How do you not?* was Miriam's unstated answer. *What are my choices?*

She sometimes wished Dave could see her now, working in a store not unlike the one he had run. He would appreciate the irony—Miriam, who had so loathed The Man with the Blue Guitar, selling the very same Oaxacan pottery that Dave had tried to persuade middle-class Baltimore to buy long before it was ready for such wares. But she'd needed a job and, although she had little use for the gallery owner's taste, she liked him immediately. Joe Fleming was a jolly, flamboyantly gay man—when he was talking to customers. But Miriam had known from the moment she met him that it was an act, a cover for something dark and sad. Faux Joe, she called it now. "Here come some customers," she would call out to him. "Time to put on our faces, the ones we keep in the jars by the door." "I'll be right there, Miss Rigby," Joe replied, exaggerating his Texas drawl. And although Miriam didn't share Joe's taste, she was superb at selling the things he stocked. Her secret was that she really didn't give a shit. With her good posture and her marvelous figure still intact, her dark hair shot through with wiry strands of silver, she had a reserved, cool manner that whipped shoppers into a frenzy of buying, as if this might win her approval, prove their taste equal to hers.

It was quiet in the shop this morning. The snowbirds had started migrating north; the frenzy generated by Easter was still a week away. Miriam had first arrived in San Miguel de Allende in Easter Week 1989, completely by accident. *Before,* Easter had been a secular holiday to her, more about the baskets that she assembled so painstakingly, the elaborate egg hunts that Dave staged in the yard. Neither one of them had grown up in observant homes; Miriam was "Jewish" and Dave was "Lutheran" in the same way that she was German and he was a Scot. And while many had counseled a return to religion as a way of coping with her grief, Miriam had even less use for it after the girls disappeared. "Faith explains nothing," she told her parents. "It simply asks you to wait for an explanation that may or may not come after you die."

But the faith to which Miriam had been exposed was polite, demure. Even the Fivefold Path, as practiced by Dave, was restrained and low-key. In Mexico there was still something savage and outlaw about religion. She wondered if that was a consequence of the years that it had been prohibited, when Catholicism had been driven underground in the 1930s, but that theory wouldn't come to her until she'd been there several years and immersed herself in books such as Alan Riding's *Distant Neighbors* and Graham Greene's *The Lawless Roads*. On the day she arrived in San Miguel, she knew only that the crowd had the panting intensity of people waiting for a rock concert, and she joined them out of base curiosity.

At last the processional came into view, a startlingly lifelike mannequin of Jesus in a glass coffin, held aloft by women dressed in black and purple. Miriam had been repulsed by Jesus under glass, but liked the fact that it was women who carried him. That was Good Friday. By Easter Sunday, she had decided she wanted to live in San Miguel.

Anniversaries. There was a date, of course, a specific one—March 29, and it would be logical to mourn her daughters on that day. But it was the moving target of the Saturday that fell between Good Friday and Easter Sunday that got to Miriam. It was the day, more than the date, that mattered. It had been foolish to pretend that she was working that day. Even Dave, naïve as he was, should have been able to figure out that a real-estate saleswoman, even Baumgarten's hard-driving number one saleswoman, didn't have to go into work on Saturday when there were no open houses on Sunday. If only Dave hadn't ignored all the evidence of a philandering wife, if only he had called her on what she was doing a week or two earlier. But he had probably been scared that she would leave him. To this day, she didn't know if she would have, not if the children had lived.

Joe arrived late, the owner's prerogative. "Texans," he said, gesturing over his shoulder at the window, where a group of tourists were studying the displays skeptically. He hissed the word the way a cowboy might have said "Injuns" in an old-fashioned movie. "Cover me."

"You're a Texan," Miriam reminded him.

"That's why I can't deal with them. You take them. I'll be in the back."

Miriam watched Joe disappear between the bright curtains that separated the gallery from a workshop in the back. With his red face and huge belly blooming beneath his oxford-cloth shirt, he looked unhealthy, but then he always had. When she met him in 1990, she assumed he had HIV, but his midsection had only grown more and more rotund, while his legs remained stick-thin and wobbly. Faux Joe the Folk Art Ho. They had enjoyed their own don't-ask-don't-tell policy from the beginning, maintaining their superficial bonhomie for fifteen years. *Ask me no questions and I'll tell you no lies. Tell me no secrets and I'll do you the same favor.* Once, after a long, drunken dinner party when Joe had been spurned by a young man he'd courted for months, he seemed on the verge of confiding in Miriam, spilling all his secrets. Miriam, sensing his need, had headed off the confession by jumping ahead to the benediction he clearly needed.

"We're such good friends we don't need to go into specifics, Joe," she'd said, patting his hand. "I know. I *know*. Something bad happened, something you seldom speak of. And you know what? You're right to keep it inside. Everyone says just the opposite, but they're wrong. It's better not to speak of some things. Whatever you've done, whatever happened, you don't need to justify it to me or anyone. You don't need to justify it even to yourself. Keep it locked up."

And the next morning, when they met at the gallery, she could tell that Joe was glad for her advice. They were best friends who told each other nothing of significance, and that's the way it needed to be.

"Is this real silver?" one of the Texans asked, barging through the door and grabbing a bracelet from the window display. "I hear that there are a lot of fakes down here."

"It's easy enough to tell," Miriam said, flipping it to show the woman the stamp that certified it as silver. But she didn't hand the bracelet back to the woman, her own private technique. She held it as if suddenly reluctant to surrender the object, as if she had just realized she wanted it for herself. A simple trick, but it made the right kind of customer wild to own the thing in hand.

The Texans turned out to be good for a lot of jewelry, which was typical. One of the women, however, had better-than-average taste, and she gravitated toward an antique *retablo* of the Virgen de Guadalupe. Miriam, seeing her interest, moved in for the kill, telling the story of the beloved figure, how a cape full of rose petals burned itself into the cloak that a peasant brought to the cardinal.

"Oh, it's darling," the woman trilled. "Just darling. How much?"

"You sure can sling the shit," Joe said, coming out as the quartet left, accompanied by Javier's effusive good wishes.

"Thanks," Miriam said, sniffing at the burst of breeze that entered the shop in the Texans' wake. "Do you . . . is there a strange smell in here this morning?"

"Just the usual mustiness that we get in this chilly weather. Why, what do you think you smell?"

"I don't know. Something like . . . wet dog."

Not in the bedroom, Sunny would report. *Not in the basement. Not under the lilac bush. Not on the porch.* There are, of course, an infinite number of places where one is *not,* yet only one place where one actually is. Miriam liked to think that Fitz, at least, had found his way to the girls, and stayed with them all these years, a loyal guardian.

As for Bud, Heather's hapless blanket, reduced to a small square—it was here in Mexico with Miriam, a faded scrap of blue cloth, preserved in a frame that she kept on her nightstand. No one ever asked her about it. If they had, she would have lied.

CHAPTER 13

Infante's momentum, so strong all day, faltered at the driveway to Edenwald. Nursing homes—and whatever they called these places, retirement communities or assisted living, they were still nursing homes—were creepy to him. Instead of making a right into Edenwald's parking lot, he found himself going left into the mall, toward TGI Friday's. It was going on 1:00 P.M., and he was hungry. He had a right to be hungry at 1:00 P.M. He hadn't been in a Friday's for a few years, but the staff still wore those striped referee tops, which he had never quite gotten. A ref—timekeeper, custodian of the rules—didn't convey fun to him.

The menu was also full of mixed messages, pushing plates of cheesy things and fried things, then including the breakdown of net carbs and trans fats in other items. His old partner had analyzed every bite this way, depending on which diet she was trying. By calorie, by carb, by fat, and, always, by virtue. "I'm being good,"

Nancy would say. "I'm being bad." It was the only thing he didn't miss about pairing with her, the endless dissection of what she put in her mouth. Infante had once told Nancy that she didn't know what bad was if she thought it was something found in a doughnut.

Thinking of which—he smiled at the waitress, not his, but one at a nearby table. It was a defensive smile, an in-case-I-know-you smile because she looked a little familiar, with that high-on-the-head ponytail. She flashed him an automatic grin but didn't make eye contact. So she wasn't someone he knew. Or—this had never occurred to him before—maybe *she* had forgotten him.

He paid his bill and decided to leave his car where it was, cutting across Fairmount Avenue to Edenwald. What was it about the air in these places? Whether super-posh, like this one, or just a step up from a county hospital, they all smelled and felt the same: overheated and cold at the same time, stuffy, room deodorizers and aerosols battling the medicinal air. Death's waiting room. And the more they fought it, like this place with all its brightly colored flyers around the lobby—museum trip, opera trip, New York trip— the more obvious it seemed. Infante's father had spent his last years in a nursing home on Long Island, a no-frills place that all but announced "You're here to die, please hurry up." There was something to be said for the honesty of its approach. But if you could afford a place like this, of course you'd ante up for it. At least it cut down on a family's guilt.

He stopped at the front desk, where he could tell that the women were checking him out, wondering if he was going to be a regular. He inspected them back but didn't see anything of note.

"Mr. Willoughby is home," the receptionist said.

Of course, Infante thought. *Where else would he be? What else did he have to do?*

"Call me chet," said the man in the brown cardigan, which looked expensive, maybe cashmere. Infante had been gearing up to meet someone feeble and ancient, so this trim, well-dressed man was a bit of a shock. Willoughby was probably this side of seventy, not much older than Lenhardt and considerably healthier-looking. Hell, in some ways he looked healthier than Infante.

"Thanks for seeing me with no notice."

"You got lucky," he said. "I usually play golf over at Elkridge on Thursday afternoons, but this last gasp of winter forced us to cancel. Do I detect some New York in your voice?"

"Some. They beat most of it out of me in the twelve years I've lived here. Ten more years and I'll be saying 'warter' and 'zinc.' "

"Of course the so-called Bawlmer accent is a working-class accent. It hews very close to Cockney. There are families who go back four hundred years in Baltimore, and I can assure you they don't speak that way."

On the surface it was an asshole thing to say, a clever way of saying *My family is old and rich,* just in case the casual mention of Elkridge Country Club hadn't done the trick. Infante wondered if the guy had been like that as a detective, trying to have it both ways. A cop, but a cop who never let his coworkers forget that he didn't have to be one.

If so, he must have been hated.

Willoughby settled into an armchair, his regular seat judging by the sweat line where his close-trimmed hair ended. Infante perched on the sofa, clearly a woman's purchase—rose-colored and uncomfortable as hell. Yet Infante had known the moment he crossed the threshold that it had been some time since a woman lived there. The apartment was neat and well kept, but there was a palpable absence. Of sound, of smells. And then there were the little things, like that grease line on the easy chair. He knew the feeling from his own place. You could always tell whether a woman was a regular on the premises.

"According to the records, you've got the Bethany case file. I was hoping I could pick it up."

"I have the . . ." Willoughby seemed confused. Infante hoped he wasn't edging into senility. He looked great, but maybe that's why he had moved into Edenwald so young. But the brown eyes quickly turned shrewd. "Has there been a development?"

Infante had anticipated this question and prepared for it. "Probably not. But we've got a woman in St. Agnes."

"Claiming to know something?"

"Yeah."

"Claiming to *be* someone?"

Infante's instinct was to lie. The fewer people in the loop, the better. How could he trust that this guy wouldn't spread the news all over Edenwald, using it as a chance to relive his own glory days? Then again Willoughby had been the original primary. No matter how good the file was, he might have valuable insights.

"This doesn't leave the room—"

"Of course." Promised quickly, with a brisk nod.

"She says she's the younger one."

"Heather."

"Right."

"And does she say where she's been, what she's been up to, what happened to her sister?"

"She's not saying much of anything anymore. She asked for a lawyer, and now they're both stonewalling us. The thing is, when she started slinging this shit yesterday, she thought she was in a lot of trouble. She was in an accident on the Beltway—serious injuries, but probably no-fault—and fled the scene. She was found walking on the shoulder of I-70, where it dead-ends into the park-and-ride."

"That's not even a mile from the Bethany house." Willoughby's voice was a murmur, almost as if he were speaking to himself. "Is she crazy?"

"Not *officially*. Not in a way that gets picked up on a preliminary psych exam. But, in my unofficial opinion, she's a fuckin' nut job. She says she has a new identity, a new life that she wants to protect. She says she'll give us the case, but not her current identity. I can't help thinking there's a lot more to it. But if I'm going to trip her up, I need to know the case forward and backward."

"I do have the file," Willoughby said, his manner slightly sheepish—but just slightly. "About a year ago—"

"File's been out for two years."

"Two years? Jesus, time changes when you're not going to the job. I'd need a second to tell you that this was Thursday and if I didn't play golf regularly—anyway, there was an obituary in the paper, and it got me thinking about something, and I asked for a chance to review it. I shouldn't have held on to it—I know better—but Evelyn, my wife, took a bad turn about the same time and . . . Well, it wasn't long before I had another obituary to worry about. I forgot that I had it, but I'm sure it's in my den."

He rose, and Infante was already calculating the dynamic of what was about to happen. Willoughby was going to insist on carrying the box, and robust and healthy as the older man looked, Infante should figure out a way to do it for him without insulting him. He had seen this with his own father, when he was still in the house in Massapequa, his insistence on trying to grab his son's suitcase out of the trunk of the car. He followed the man to the den. But, sure enough, Willoughby hoisted the box in his arms before Infante could figure a way around it, grunting and grimacing a bit before he placed it on the Oriental rug in the living room.

"The obituary's on top," he said. "I'm sure of that."

Infante opened the lid of the cardboard box and saw a clipping from the *Beacon-Light*: "Roy Pincharelli, 58, longtime teacher." As it often happened with obits, the photo was from a much earlier time, perhaps even twenty years earlier. *The strange vanity of the dead,* Infante thought. The guy had dark eyes and hair, a dense cloud in the black-and-white photo, and he held himself as if he thought himself quite the dreamboat. On first glance he was okay. But study the photo for more than a second and the flaws revealed themselves—the weak chin, the slightly hooked nose.

"Complications from pneumonia," Willoughby recited from memory. "That's often a code for AIDS."

"So he was gay? How does that track with the disappearance of the Bethany sisters?"

"As the article says, he was a longtime band teacher in the city and county school systems. In 1975 he was teaching at Rock Glen Junior High, where Sunny was one of his students. On weekends he had a part-time gig—selling organs at Jordan Kitt's Music Store. In Security Square Mall."

"Man, teachers and cops and their part-time jobs. We do the heavy lifting for society, and we still need OT gigs. Nothing ever changes, does it?"

Willoughby's look was blank, uncomprehending, and Infante recalled that the man was rich, that he had never known what it was like trying to make ends meet on a police's salary. *How nice for you.*

"Did you talk to him at the time?"

"Of course. And, in fact, he said he noticed Heather early that afternoon. She was in the crowd, watching him play Easter songs."

"You said he taught Sunny. How did he know Heather?"

"The family had attended school concerts and the like. The Bethanys were very big on family solidarity. Well, Dave Bethany was big on it, to be precise. Anyway, Pincharelli said he saw Heather in the crowd that day. A man, maybe in his twenties, grabbed her arm, began to yell at her, then just as quickly walked away."

"And he notices all this while he's banging on his organ?"

Willoughby smiled and nodded. "Exactly. A mall on a Saturday is a busy, antic place. Why would you notice that one encounter? Unless—"

"Unless you were already fixated on the girl. But he was gay."

"That's my inference." It killed Infante the way this guy talked, using two-dollar words without even a hint of irony or self-mockery. He must have been a good police beneath the bullshit, or the others would have torn him down in no time.

"So why does a gay guy care about two girls?"

"First of all, the crime wasn't necessarily sexual in nature. That's an obvious conclusion, but it's not the only one. We had a case in Baltimore County, a few years before the Bethany girls, where a man flipped and killed a young girl because something in her manner reminded him of his mother, whom he loathed. That said, I've often wondered if Heather saw something that day, something that she didn't realize she saw, but which terrified the teacher. If he was gay, he most certainly was closeted at the time and probably feared losing his job if discovered."

"So how do both girls end up missing?"

Willoughby sighed. "It always comes back to that. Why two? How do you even get *two*? But if it was the teacher and he grabbed Heather first and stashed her somewhere—the back of his van, for example— and then found Sunny, he would have had a huge advantage. He was her teacher, someone she knew and trusted. If he told her to come with him, she would have done it automatically."

"Did you ever break him down, get him to change his story?"

"No. He was consistent, albeit in the way that liars are consistent. Maybe he was getting a blow job in the mall bathroom that afternoon from some teenage

133

boy and feared that getting out. At any rate, he never changed his story, and now he's dead."

"I'm assuming you checked out the parents?"

"Parents, neighbors, friends. You'll find it all in there. And there were extortion calls, too, claims from people who said they had the girls. Nothing ever checked out. It was almost enough to make you believe in the supernatural or alien abductions."

"Given that you read the obituaries so closely—"

"You will, too, one day." Willoughby had a way of smiling, a kind of double-edged superiority. Irritating as hell. "Sooner than you think."

"I guess you know whether the parents are alive? I didn't get any hits on them."

"Dave passed away the year I retired, 1989. Miriam moved to Texas, then Mexico. She sent me Christmas cards for a while. . . ."

He got up and went to a highly polished piece of furniture that Infante thought of as a ladies' desk, because it was small and impractical, with dozens of little drawers and a tiny, slanted writing surface that couldn't even hold a computer. The old cop may have needed reminding that he had the Bethany file, but he knew exactly where that Christmas card was. *Jesus,* Infante thought, *I don't care what Lenhardt says. I hope I never have a case like this.*

Then he remembered that he did, that he was sitting with a cardboard legacy at his feet. He saw himself thirty years in the future, passing the box along to another detective, telling the story of the Jane Doe and how she'd hoaxed them for a couple of days, then turned out to be a fake. Once you got inside something like the Bethany case, did you ever really get out?

134

"The envelope's long gone, so if there was a return address, I couldn't tell you what it was. But I remember the town—San Miguel de Allende. See? She mentions it here."

Infante inspected the card, a lacy green cutout of a dove overlaid on a heavy piece of vellum. Inside, FELIZ NAVIDAD had been printed in red ink, and a few lines had been scrawled beneath it. *Hope this finds you well. San Miguel de Allende seems to be my home now, for better or worse.*

"When was this?"

"At least five years ago."

Infante jumped on the date. "The twenty-fifth year of their disappearance."

"In Miriam's case that was probably subconscious. She was very intent on pushing the memories down, trying to move on. Dave was the exact opposite. Every day he lived was a conscious tribute to those girls."

"And that's when she moved, after he died?"

"When— Oh, no. My mistake. Speaking from what my wife called 'deep context,' as if everything known to me is known to you. Even more unforgivable, when one has been hoarding the context. Miriam and Dave separated a little more than a year after the girls disappeared, and she went back to using her maiden name, Toles. It wasn't a happy marriage, even before. I liked Dave. In fact, I considered him a friend. But he didn't appreciate what he had in Miriam."

Infante fingered the card, studying the older man's face. *But you did, didn't you?* It wasn't just the sense of a job undone that had led Willoughby to file this card in a place he remembered so readily. Infante wondered what the mother looked like, if she was a sunny little blonde like the daughters. A certain kind of police—a guy like this Willoughby—he'd be a sucker for a good-looking woman in distress.

"I'm assuming the medical records are in here?"

"Such as they are."

"What's that mean?"

"Dave had some, um, interesting ideas about doctors. Less was more, in his opinion. No tonsillectomies for his daughters, and as I understand it, he was ahead of his time on that. But also no X-rays, because he believed that even small doses of radiation were dangerous."

"You mean—" *Fuck me*.

"Right. The dental records include exactly one set of X-rays, taken when Sunny was nine and Heather was six. And that's it."

No adult dental records, no blood information on record, not even type. Infante didn't have the tools he would have expected to have in 1975, much less 2005.

"Any advice?" he asked, putting the lid back on the box.

"If your Jane Doe's story doesn't fall apart in the face of the information in the file, then find Miriam and bring her back. I'd put everything on her maternal instincts."

Yeah, and you'd probably like to get a look at your old crush, you being a widower and all.

"Anything else?"

Willoughby shook his head. "No, I have to— If you knew what I felt, just looking at that box. It isn't healthy. It's all I can do to let you walk out of here with it, not to beg to come along to the hospital with you and interrogate the woman. I know so much about these girls, about their lives, especially that last day. In some ways, I'm surer of the facts of their lives than I am of my own. Maybe I know them too well. Wouldn't it be something if a pair of fresh eyes saw something that had been staring me in the face all those years ago?"

"Look, I'll keep you in the loop. If you like. Up or down, I'll call you, tell you how it turns out."

"Okay," he said in a tone that suggested he wasn't at all sure that was okay, and Infante felt as if he were pressing a drink on a guy who swore he needed to quit but could never quite manage it. He probably should leave the guy be, if possible. He thought he would have been more intrigued, having the old case resurface. But Willoughby looked out the window, studying the sky, seemingly more interested in the weather than the long-gone Bethany girls.

CHAPTER 14

"Heather . . ."

"Yes, Kay?"

Heather's face filled with light at the sound of her name. Just hearing it was a homecoming, a reunion. Why had it been denied to her for so long? Where could she have been, what could have happened to her that she didn't, couldn't, reclaim her identity years ago?

"I hate to do this, but there's so much that has to be straightened out. A discharge plan, insurance—"

"I do have insurance. I *do*. The hospital will be paid. But I just can't tell you yet the account, the ID number."

"Sure, I understand." Kay paused, thinking about what she'd said, something she said every day, a phrase others used all the time. It was automatic. It was also seldom true. "Actually, I *don't* understand, Heather." That little beam of resurrection again. "Whatever happened, you're clearly the victim here.

Are you frightened? Are you trying to hide from someone? Perhaps you'd like to speak to someone on the psychiatric staff, someone with experience in post-traumatic stress disorder."

"I talked to someone." Heather made a face. "Strange little man."

Kay couldn't disagree with that assessment of Schumeier. "He administered a basic psych exam. But if you'd like to explore other . . . issues, I could arrange that."

Heather's smile was mirthless, mocking. "You speak sometimes as if you ran the hospital, as if the doctors did what you told them to do."

"No, not exactly, it's just that I've been here so long, almost twenty years, and worked in so many departments . . ." Kay was stammering as if she'd been caught in a lie, or at least in the very act of self-aggrandizement that Heather was suggesting. The initial psych report had indicated that Heather was sane by clinical definition, but not particularly empathetic or interested in people. Yet she noticed things, Kay was beginning to realize, picked up subtle details quickly. *Strange little man.* That was Schumeier in a nutshell. *You speak sometimes as if you ran the hospital.* She noticed things and used them against people.

Gloria Bustamante sailed in, the usual physical wreck, but her eyes bright and focused.

"What are we talking about?" she asked, settling in the room's only chair. Her voice was brisk and not a little acidic.

"Discharge," Kay said.

"Kay," Heather said.

"An interesting topic," Gloria said. "Discharge,

I mean. Not Kay. Although Kay is *fascinating* in her own right." Was her smile faintly lascivious? Had she misunderstood Kay's solicitation of this favor? Did anyone really know what Gloria's sexual orientation was, or were the rumors about her as groundless as the things said about Kay behind her back?

"I hit my head," Heather said. Petulant now, her pouting-child act. "I fractured a bone in my forearm. Why can't I stay in the hospital?"

Gloria shook her head. "Sweetie, you could have your head amputated and they'd be trying to get you out of this costly little bed, which they bill at the same rate as a suite at the Ritz-Carlton. And given that you won't tell us your insurance carrier, the hospital is all the more desperate to get rid of you, lest they be stuck with the bill."

"Indigent patients mean higher board costs for all," Kay said, registering her own priggish tone. "It really is a waste of a bed. Under normal circumstances a patient such as Heather might have been kept overnight for observation, because of the head injury. But there's no medical reason for her to remain here, and the issue needs to be resolved."

"Everyone's clock is ticking," Gloria said. "The hospital's, mine. The only person *not* worried about billing right now is Detective Kevin Infante. He told me this morning that if Heather declines to go before a grand jury, she could be held on the hit-and-run. The best I can do is push for home detention."

Heather jerked up in bed, wincing in pain as she did so. "Where—not jail, not police custody. I'd die. I'd absolutely die."

"Not to worry," Gloria assured her. "I pointed out

to the police that it would be disastrous, publicity-wise, to lock up the missing Bethany sister."

"But I don't want *any* publicity, so how can you use this as leverage?"

"I know that. You know that." A sideways glance at Kay. "And now *she* knows that, for better or worse. I'm going to trust you not to run and tattle, Kay. I came here as a favor to you, so you owe me that much."

"I would never—"

Gloria plowed on, indifferent to what Kay had to say. It would be interesting to know what a psych exam on Gloria Bustamante might reveal.

"The boy is not that badly injured, as it turns out. It looked awful, apparently, and they were worried about a spinal injury, but he's been moved from Shock Trauma to ICU already."

"The boy?" Heather asked, brow furrowed.

"In the SUV that tipped over after you sideswiped it."

"But I saw a girl—I was so sure that I saw a girl, a girl in rabbit-fur earmuffs. . . ."

"There was no girl in the car," Gloria said. "It was a little boy who was taken to Shock Trauma."

Heather sat up straighter in bed. "And I didn't sideswipe anyone. The driver of the SUV hit me, and he overreacted. It's *not* my fault."

"That's an easier case to make," Gloria said dryly, "when you don't flee the scene and leave your damaged car on the roadside. But we're going to chalk that up to the head injury, try the Halle Berry defense."

"Who?" Kay asked, and the other two women regarded her as if she were genuinely freakish.

Gloria perched on a corner of Heather's bed. "The more pressing problem is that the police continue to insist that you're required to provide the name and address under which your driver's license was issued. Without those, you can be jailed in connection with the accident. So far, I've managed to persuade them that your potential as a material witness trumps your role as a defendant in a highway collision that was really no one's fault. But they're getting restless. We need to throw them a few facts to satiate them. How long has it been since you were Heather, Heather?"

She closed her eyes. Her skin was so fair and the lids so thin that it appeared as if she were wearing blue-pink eye shadow, lightly applied.

"Heather disappeared thirty years ago. The last time I changed names—it's been sixteen years. My longest stretch yet. I've been this me longer than I've been any other me."

"Penelope Jackson?" Kay asked, knowing of the name the patrol cop had used when Heather was admitted Tuesday night.

"No," Heather said sharply, eyes flying open. "I am *not* Penelope Jackson. I don't even know Penelope Jackson."

"Then how—"

Gloria held up a hand to stave off Kay's questions, and it was impossible not to notice how ragged her manicure was, how dull her diamond rings were. A piece of jewelry must be very dirty indeed if Kay's eyes registered it as dull.

"Kay, I trust you, I do. And I need your help. But you have to respect boundaries. There are some things that must remain, for now, between Heather and me. *If*— always if, understand that I am speaking speculatively for now—Heather obtained her current identity illegally, then I'm going to argue she's entitled to protect that information under the Fifth Amendment—no self-incrimination. She's trying to protect her life and I'm trying to protect her rights."

"Fine. But it's harder to help if I don't have sufficient information."

Gloria smiled, not buying it. "I don't need a second chair, Kay. I need someone who can guarantee housing for Heather while this is being straightened out. Housing and, perhaps, public assistance, short term."

Kay did not bother to ask why Gloria couldn't lend her client money or take her into her home. Such things would have been anathema to the attorney, who had already violated her own standards by taking a case without a big fat retainer up front.

"Gloria, you are so out of the loop. There hasn't been financial assistance for single adults in Maryland since . . . shit, the early 1990s. And to qualify for anything, you need papers. Birth certificate, Social Security."

"What about a victims' assistance network? Isn't there some advocacy group we could plug Heather into?"

"They specialize in emotional support, not financial."

"This is what the police are counting on," Gloria said. "Heather Bethany has no money, nowhere to go—except jail. In order to prevent that, she has to reveal where she's been living, what she's been doing. But Heather doesn't want to do that."

Heather shook her head. "At this point the life I've made for myself is all I have."

"You have to see," Kay said, "how impossible that will be."

"Why?" A child's question, asked in a child's tone.

Gloria answered. "The Bethany case is the kind of thing that attracts a lot of attention."

"But I've already told you that I don't want to be *that* girl."

Foolishly, Kay couldn't help thinking of the old television show, Marlo Thomas with her enormous eyes and shiny bangs, a small-town girl breezing through the big city. Now there was a name she knew.

"You don't want to be who you are?" Gloria asked.

"I don't want to go back to the life I managed to make for myself and have everyone treat me like some freak, the girl of the moment—the runaway bride, the Central Park jogger, whoever. Look, it took a lot for me to get to a place of even seminormalcy. I was taken from my parents when I was a kid. I saw . . . things. I didn't finish college, I drifted through a lot of jobs before I found one that suits me, allows me to have the kind of life that everyone takes for granted."

"Heather, not to be crass, but there will be financial opportunities for you, if you choose to pursue them. Your story is a commodity." Gloria's smile was wry. "At least I assume it is. I've taken it on faith that you are who you say you are."

"I am. Ask me anything about my family. Dave Bethany, son of Felicia Bethany, abandoned by her husband early in the marriage. She worked as a waitress at the old Pimlico Restaurant, and she preferred to be called 'Bop-Bop' instead of anything grandmotherly. She retired to Florida, to the Orlando area. We visited her every year, but we never went to Disney World because my father didn't approve of it. My dad was born in 1934 and died, I think, in 1989. At least, that's when his phone was cut off." She rushed on, as if fearful of letting anyone else speak or ask questions. "Of course I kept tabs. My mother, Miriam, must have died, too, because there's no trace of her. Maybe that has something to do with her being Canadian. At any rate, there's no record of her, not anywhere I checked, so I assumed she was dead."

"Your mother was Canadian?" Kay echoed back stupidly, even as Gloria said, "But your mother is alive, Heather. At least that's what the detective thinks. She was living in Mexico five years ago, and they're trying to track her now."

"My mother's . . . alive?" The collision of emotions in Heather's face was strangely beautiful, like one of those thunder bursts in the middle of a sunny summer day, the kind that made old women nod and say: *The devil must be beating his wife.* Kay had never seen grief and joy in such extremes, trying to coexist in the same place. The joy she could understand. Here was Heather Bethany, thinking herself an orphan, with nothing to claim but a name and tabloid tale. Yet her mother was alive. She was not alone.

But there was anger, too, the skepticism of someone who trusted no one.

"Are you sure?" Heather demanded. "You say she was in Mexico five years ago, but are you sure she's alive now?"

"The original detective seemed to think so, but it's true, they haven't found her yet."

"And if they do find her . . ."

"They'll probably bring her here." Gloria made a point of capturing Heather's eyes in hers, holding the look. It was a snake charmer's gaze, if one could imagine a mildly exasperated snake charmer in a rumpled knit suit. "Once she's here, Heather, they'll want to do DNA tests. You understand, you get where this is going?"

"I'm not lying." Her voice was dull and listless, as if to suggest that lying was simply too much effort. "When will she get here?"

"It all depends on when they find her and what they tell her when they do." Gloria turned to Kay. "Can't the hospital keep Heather until, say, her mother arrives? I'm sure she'll be happy to put her up."

"It's impossible, Gloria. She has to leave today. The administration is very clear on that."

"You're playing into the police's hands, giving them the leverage they want to rush this thing through, force Heather on to their timetable. If she's discharged without a plan, they're going to put her in jail—"

Heather moaned, an unearthly, inhuman sound.

"What about House of Ruth? Can't she go there?"

"It's a battered-women's shelter, and you know as well as I do that it's full up."

"I *was* abused," Heather said. "Doesn't that count for something?"

"You're talking about thirty years ago, right?" Kay felt that rush of unbecoming prurience, the desire to know exactly what had happened to this woman. "I hardly think—"

"Okay, okay, okay, okay, *okay*." Even as her words seemed to promise agreement, Heather swung her head vehemently side to side, so her blond curls, short as they were, bounced and shook. "I'll tell you. I'll tell you, and you'll know why I can't go to jail, why I can't trust these people not to hurt me."

"Not in front of Kay," Gloria commanded, but

Heather was wound up now, impossible to stop. *She doesn't know I'm here,* Kay thought. *Or she knows but doesn't care.* Was it trust or indifference, a vote of confidence or a reminder that Kay was of no significance to her?

"It was a policeman, okay? A policeman came to me and said something had happened to my sister and I needed to come quick. And I went, and that was how he got both of us. First her, then me. He locked us in the back of the van and took us."

"A man pretending to be a cop," Gloria clarified.

"Not *pretending*. A real police officer, from right here in Baltimore, from the county, with a badge and everything. Although he wasn't wearing a uniform—but policemen didn't always wear uniforms. Michael Douglas and Karl Malden—*The Streets of San Francisco*—they didn't wear uniforms. He was a policeman, and he said everything would be all right, and I believed him. That's the only real mistake I ever made, believing that man, and it ruined my life."

With that final word, *life,* some long-held emotion was released and Heather began crying with such raw force that Gloria reared back from her, unsure of what to do. What could Kay do, what would any feeling person do, but reach around Gloria and try to comfort Heather, remembering to be especially gentle, given the temporary splint on the left forearm, the general all-over soreness left by a car accident.

"We'll work something out," she said. "We'll find a place for you. I know someone—a family in my neighborhood, away for spring break. At the very least, you can stay there for a few days."

"No police," Heather choked out. "No jail."

"Of course not," Kay said, catching Gloria's eyes to see if she approved of Kay's solution. But Gloria was smiling, smug and triumphant.

"Now this," the attorney said, her tongue darting over her lower lip, as close to a literal smacking as Kay had ever seen, "*this* gives us leverage."

CHAPTER 15

One more night. One more night. Everyone had said she couldn't stay in the hospital beyond today, but she'd gotten one more night out of them, which just proved what she had always believed: Everybody lied, all the time. *One more night.* There had been a hideous pop song with that title, years ago, a spurned lover begging for a final bout of lovemaking. It was a frequent motif in pop music, come to think of it. *Touch me in the morning. I can't make you love me if you don't.* She had never understood this. When she was younger, still trying to date—and, big surprise, failing miserably time and time again—the men usually ended up leaving her a few months in, almost as if they could smell the rottenness coming off her, as if they had found her secret sell-by date and realized how ruined she was. At any rate, when a man broke off with her, the last thing she wanted from him was one more night. Sometimes she threw things, and sometimes she cried. Sometimes she laughed, relieved. But she never resorted to begging for one more night, a touch in the morning, a pity fuck however you sliced or diced it. You took your pride where you could find it.

She eased herself out of the bed, everything aching, her body already sensing that the left arm was not to be counted on, not for a while, that the right arm had to pick up the slack. Amazing how quickly the body adjusted, much faster than the mind. Her mind was far from reliable these days. *Did I see a boy and think he was a girl, or was there never a face at the window at all?* She went to the window, pulled aside the curtain, and studied the landscape—the parking lot, the smudge of city skyline in the distance, the clogged lanes of I-95 at rush hour. *Come to the window, sweet is the night-air!* A line of poetry stuck in her head, a legacy of the nuns, who believed you could memorize your way to intelligence. The highway was near, not even a mile away. Could she get there, put out her thumb and hitch a ride home? No, she'd be a fugitive twice over then. She had to tough this out. But how?

It wasn't the lies that worried her. She could keep track of the lies. It was the bits of truths that put her at risk. A good liar survives by using as little truth as possible, because the truth trips you up far more often. Back when she'd been in the habit of changing names, she had learned to create each new identity fresh, to carry nothing forward. But the threat of jail this afternoon, just like the possibility of arrest that first night, had freaked her out. She had to say *something*. It had seemed pretty inspired, telling them about the cop, throwing Karl Malden into the mix. Odd, tangential details like that made everything else sound authentic.

But they weren't going to settle for Karl Malden. They were clamoring for a real name, and she was going to have to give them something, someone.

"I'm sorry," she whispered to the night sky.

She wasn't sure who worried her more, the dead or the living, who posed the most risk. But at least you could bluff the living. You couldn't put anything over on the dead.

PART IV
PRAJAPATAYE SVAHA.
PRAJAPATAYE IDAM
NA MAMA. (1976)

Agnihotra mantras are to be uttered in
their original form in Sanskrit. They are not to
be translated into any other language. . . .

Agnihotra mantras are to be
uttered in rhythmically balanced tone
so the sound vibrates throughout the entire household.
The tone should not be too loud or too weak
nor should it be done in a hurry. . . .
The feeling of total surrender is developed through
the utterance of these mantras.

—Adapted from instructions on how to perform
the Agnihotra, the sunrise/sunset ritual
central to the practice of the Fivefold Path

CHAPTER 16

Sunset fast approaching, Dave grabbed the ghee from the refrigerator and headed into the study, leaving Chet at the kitchen table with Miriam and their mugs of tea. They weren't even trying to speak, just sipping herbal tea and staring off into space. Everyone was exhausted and hoarse after the full day of interviews, although Dave had done most of the talking. Miriam deferred to Dave, and the detective seldom spoke at all. Sometimes Dave found Willoughby's silence comforting. Men of action should be laconic. Other times he suspected that these still waters didn't run particularly deep. But Chet was familiar to them now, like a dignified stray they had adopted after years of saying they didn't want the bother of a dog.

In his study he sat cross-legged on his rug, not a proper prayer rug—other than the copper pot for the offering, the Agnihotra did not require ritual objects, which was a large part of its charm—but a dhurrie he'd found in an Indian market years ago, when he was traveling after college. His mother had still lived in Baltimore then, and he'd shipped his treasures to her apartment, despite her complaints and suspicions. "What's in these boxes?" she had berated him upon his homecoming. "*Drugs?* If the police come to my door, I am not lying for you."

He put a dung cake in the pot, adding a piece of ghee-soaked camphor, followed by the rest of the dung and the rice grains, checking his watch to see if the exact moment of sunset had arrived.

"Agnaye Svaha," he said, offering the first part of the ghee-smeared rice grains. "Agnaye Idam Na Mama."

People often assumed that the Fivefold Path was another souvenir from his travels, but Dave was married to Miriam and working for the state when he first heard about it, at a party in Northwest Baltimore. The Fivefold Path turned out to be the nexus for most of the people at the party, held at a beautiful Victorian in Old Sudbrook. Dave had not known such houses existed when he was growing up in Pikesville, much less such people, yet Herb and Estelle Turner lived less than two miles from his mother's former apartment. The Turners were at once warm and reserved, and Dave assumed that their grave dignity derived from the Fivefold Path. It would be some time before he knew about their troubles with their daughter, or Estelle's fragile health. And although Miriam had always been skeptical of the couple, claiming they'd been fishing for converts that night, they only brought up the Fivefold Path when Dave asked about the house's sweet, smoky smell, so unexpected on a warm spring night. He had suspected, hoped for, grass, which he and Miriam were anxious to try. But the fragrance was from the sunrise/sunset ritual of the Agnihotra, and it was almost as if it had baked its way into the bones of the house. As Estelle Turner explained the smell, and its connection to the Fivefold Path, Dave saw it as a way to *be* the Turners—gracious, poised, living in a beautiful yet unostentatious house.

For her part, Miriam said the Agnihotra made the house smell like shit, literally. Once they moved to Algonquin Lane, she had been adamant that Dave confine the practice to his study, with the doors closed. Even then she had despaired at the greasy residue the ghee left on the walls, a filmy sheen that resisted any and all cleaning methods. Now, Dave suspected, he could set up the 'Hotra on the dining room table and Miriam wouldn't make a peep. She never reproached him anymore. He almost missed it. Almost.

Still your mind, he urged himself. *Focus on your mantra.* There was no point to the practice if he couldn't lose himself in it.

"Prajapataye Svaha," he said, making the second offering. "Prajapataye Idam Na Mama."

Now he must meditate until the fire was out.

The reporters had come in threes—three newspapers, three television stations, three radio stations, three wire services. In each group there had been one reporter who pushed for an exclusive, a private chat with Dave and Miriam, but those young comers professed to understand when Chet told them that the Bethanys preferred to tell the story only so many times, once to each medium. The reporters were uniformly polite and kind, wiping their feet on the welcome mat, expressing admiration for the remodeled farmhouse, not that any work had been done in the past year. Their voices were gentle, their questions circumspect. One young woman, from Channel 13, teared up prettily while looking at the girls' photos. These were not the school photos, the head shots against the sky-blue background. The television types explained to Dave and Miriam that these photos had been shown so many times that they had "lost their impact," and it would be helpful to use new ones. They chose candid snapshots that Dave kept in his study, souvenirs of a trip to the Enchanted Forest on Route 40. Heather was sitting on a toadstool, cross-legged, while Sunny stood with arms akimbo, trying to pretend she wasn't having a good time. But it had been a wonderful day, as Dave remembered it, with Sunny's adolescent moodiness barely in evidence, everyone tender and sweet with each other.

The newspaper reporters, the last to troop through that day, had no qualms about using the school photos that had been circulating since the girls disappeared. Yet they insisted on a new photo of Dave and Miriam, sitting with the framed school photos on the coffee table in front of them. How Dave dreaded seeing that tableau in tomorrow's newspaper—the awkward lie of his arm across Miriam's shoulders, the distance between their bodies, their faces turned away from each other.

"I know that there was one ransom demand, in the first week," said the reporter for the *Beacon,* the morning newspaper. "And it turned out to be a hoax. Have there been any similar dead ends over the past year?"

"I don't know—" Dave looked to Miriam, but she would not speak unless pressed directly.

"I wouldn't expect you to tell me anything that could hurt the investigation."

"There were other calls. Not ransom demands. More like . . . taunts. Obscene phone calls, although not in the traditional sense." He stroked his chin, where he was growing a beard, or trying to, and glanced at Chet, who was frowning. "You know, maybe you shouldn't put that in? The police determined it was just some sick kid. He didn't know us, or the girls. It didn't mean anything."

"Of course," the *Beacon* reporter said, nodding in robust sympathy. Forty or so, he had been a war correspondent in Vietnam and spent time in the *Beacon*'s foreign bureaus—London, Tokyo, São Paulo. He had arrived first and managed to convey this information about himself in the flurry of introductions at the beginning. His credentials were supposed to be a comfort, Dave supposed, an assurance that the assignment had been given to an accomplished professional. But Dave couldn't help feeling that the man was trying to console himself, too. Two missing girls were not on a par with wars and foreign policy. He looked liked a drinker, his nose sprouting with broken blood vessels, his cheeks an unhealthy red.

"The one ransom demand—the one down at War Memorial Plaza—did they ever figure out who called that in?" This was the *Light* reporter, tiny and feisty. With her short pixie cut and miniskirt, she looked to be barely out of college. A jogger, Dave thought, eyeing the hard calves pressed into the lower rung of her straight-backed chair. He had started running after the first of the year, although it wasn't the result of a New Year's resolution. Like someone summoned by unseen voices, he had gotten up one day, put on sneakers and headed to Leakin Park, circling the tennis courts and the miniature train track. He had run to Crimea, the summer mansion built by the family that founded the B&O Railroad, passing the old church that his girls had believed was haunted. He was up to five miles a day now, but he had liked jogging better in the beginning, when it was hard and he had to focus on every rasping breath. Now that he reached the so-called runner's high within minutes, his mind was free to roam again, and it always ended up in the same place.

"No . . . I . . . no— Look, there's nothing new. I'm sorry. It's been a year, and there's nothing new. I'm sorry. We're talking to you because we're hopeful that your articles might prompt someone's memory, might reach that one person who knows something. . . . I'm sorry."

Miriam shot him a look that only a spouse could interpret: *Stop apologizing.* His eyes replied, *I'll stop when you start.*

The reporters didn't seem to notice. Did they know? Had Chet told them—off the record, of course—all the family's secrets, then persuaded them that they were irrelevant to the girls' disappearance? Dave almost wished now that the whole story had come out. On his best days, he knew it wasn't Miriam's fault. Wherever Miriam had been that day—at an open house, here on Algonquin Lane, in a motel, in a motel, *in a fucking motel*—she couldn't have saved the girls. Besides, he'd been in a bar for much of the afternoon, although he had managed to pull himself together and arrive at the mall to fetch the girls, no more than five minutes late. His chest still hurt, thinking about how he had felt that afternoon. *Anger,* assuming that the girls were late, inconsiderate. *Panic,* but a safe, this-will-soon-pass-and-I-can-be-angry-again panic. When forty-five minutes had passed, he checked with the mall security, and he still remembered with great affection the overweight security guard who had walked the corridors with him, his voice a rumbling bass of benign possibilities. "Maybe they took the bus home. Maybe they decided to take one of those shopper surveys, back in the offices. Maybe they got a ride home with a friend's mother or father and thought they could get home in time to call you at your work."

Dave had seized on the security guard's words as if they were a promise, racing home in his VW bus, certain that the girls would be there, finding only Miriam. It had been so strange, seeing her, wanting to confront her, yet having to put aside the suddenly minor fact of her infidelity. Miriam had been marvelously calm, calling the police, agreeing that Dave should go back to the mall and continue searching while she stayed at the house in case they showed up. At 7:00 P.M., they still assumed the girls would show up. It was hard to describe how slowly that expectation, that hope—what had once seemed their *right*—had slipped away. Yet emotion was not linear, and the absence of a definitive answer still made Dave's imagination jump and lurch, concocting far-fetched endings. This was the stuff of soap operas, so why shouldn't it have a soap-opera ending? Simultaneous amnesia, an eccentric Greek billionaire whisking Dave's children away, unharmed, to live in a Bavarian castle. Why not?

Whatever Miriam's sins, Dave had been the one to

give permission for the mall trip, and although Miriam had assured him again and again that he had not erred, he still blamed . . . *her*. He'd been distracted, anxious. At the time he'd thought he was worried about the business, but he saw in hindsight that he'd known that something was wrong in their marriage, that his subconscious was picking up signals it didn't know how to translate. If he'd been more *present* that day, if he'd been focused on his daughters, he might have realized they were too young to be given that much freedom. Miriam had set him up.

He felt no guilt over Jeff Baumgarten or his wife, who had been subjected to repeated police interviews after Miriam volunteered the truth. After all, Thelma Baumgarten had been in Dave's store at 3:00 P.M., and the store wasn't more than three miles from the mall. The motel was even closer, as it turned out. But Dave hated Mrs. Baumgarten more than he hated Jeff. Jeff had fucked his wife, but Mrs. Baumgarten . . . Well, Mrs. Baumgarten, with her stupid little note, had tried to project all this on Dave. Fat little hausfrau. If she'd kept her husband happy, maybe he would have left Miriam alone.

"Were there any strong suspects along the way?" Dave looked at Chet, longing for permission, for encouragement, to tell everything about the Baumgartens. Chet shook his head, ever so slightly. *It would only muddy the waters,* he'd told Dave whenever he lobbied to make everything—*everything*—public on the grounds that every bit of truth mattered, that it was not only a virtue in and of itself, but essential to learning what had happened to his daughters. The more the public knew, the better equipped people were to help them. Maybe Mrs. Baumgarten had hired someone. Maybe Jeff Baumgarten had arranged for the children to be kidnapped to force Miriam to continue their illicit affair. Maybe something had gone wrong with his plan. Candor was liberating, Dave argued, and it would be rewarded. They should put everything out there and let the chips fall where they may.

Maybe that was why Chet had decided he should be here for the interviews. Dave couldn't see any other reason. Very little had been held back in the early weeks of the investigation—the discovery of Heather's purse, the calls that placed the girls in various states (South Carolina, West Virginia, Virginia, Vermont) and various states (alive and laughing, swimming and playing, eating hamburgers, bound and gagged). Funny, but those delusional types were worse than the pranksters in their own way. They thought their fantasies were helpful, but all they brought was pain.

"Do you—can you—" The *Star* reporter, an absolute throwback, with a hat on the back of his head and a narrow tie, groped for words in a way that Dave knew could end up in only one place. "Do you continue to hope that your daughters will be found alive?"

"Of course. Hope is essential." *Mutual amnesia, a castle in Bavaria, a gentle eccentric who wanted two golden-haired daughters, but would never, ever harm them.*

"No," Miriam said.

In the corner of the room, Chet tensed, as if he thought he might have to intercede. Had the detective finally detected something? Could he know that it was Dave's instinct, at that very moment, to slap his wife? It wouldn't be the first time that he had fought down

163

that impulse in the past year. The reporters seemed shocked, too, as if Miriam had broken some unwritten protocol of the mourning parent.

"You'll have to excuse my wife," Dave said. "She's very emotional, and this is such a difficult time—"

"I'm not a child who didn't get my nap today," Miriam said. "And I'm no more emotional today than I was yesterday or I'll be tomorrow. I would love to be wrong about this. But if I don't accept the *probability* of their deaths at this point, how do I live? How do I go on?"

The reporters did not take notes during this outburst, Dave noticed. Their instinct, like everyone else's, always, was to protect Miriam, to assume that her inappropriate comments had come out of grief. Reporters were supposed to be cynical, and maybe they were, when they were covering stories of Watergate-like intrigue and conspiracy. But in Dave's experience they were among the most naïve and optimistic people he had ever met.

"I'm sorry," he said, and even he didn't know why he was apologizing this time.

After a beat, Miriam nodded as well, rounding her shoulders in a way that invited Dave to put his arm around her. "It's hard," she said. "Remaining open to hope, yet needing to grieve. Whatever I do or say, I feel as if I'm betraying my daughters. We just want to *know*."

"Is there a moment in the day when you're not thinking about this?" asked the *Light* reporter.

The question caught Dave off guard, in part because it was new. *How do you go on, how do you not think about this?* Those he knew. But was he ever *not* thinking about the girls? Rationally, there must be such moments, but he couldn't identify them now that he was trying. When he made preparations for dinner, he still reviewed the girls' likes and dislikes. *Meat loaf again?* Stopped at a red light in afternoon traffic, he would relive the conversations they once had about the nearby Social Security Administration and why it had so many employees who clogged the streets every day at 4:00 P.M. *They'll give us money when we're old? Cool!* If he started thinking about how much he hated Jeff Baumgarten, how he wanted to wait outside his Pikesville home and run over him with the VW bus when he came out to pick up the morning newspaper from the circular driveway—even that was really about the girls, wasn't it? When he opened the mailbox and found his copy of *New York* magazine, he would see the Ronrico rum ad on the back and be reminded of how fascinated Heather was by its campy re-creations, while Sunny had giggled over the weekly word contests. Every object in the world—the collapsed lean-to that the girls had built in the backyard, the glittering green of a Genesee ale can in the gutter, Miriam's ratty blue bathrobe—brought him back to his daughters. Conventional wisdom held that he could not continue at this level of intensity forever, that all pain fades, but he *wanted* to keep it going. The dull fury he felt was like a lamp lighted in the window, waiting for the girls to find their way home.

Even now his mind would not stop racing, which defeated the purpose of the Agnihotra. He had tried, delicately, to bring this up with the others who followed the Fivefold Path. Estelle Turner was long dead, of course, and Herb had wandered out to Northern

California after she was gone, saying he had to cut all ties in order to go on. Dave had called him about the girls, but Herb had seemed vaguely resentful to be reminded of his prior life in Baltimore and had turned the conversation inside out so it ended up being about *him*, his various disillusionments and losses. "I just can't find the *way*, buddy," he said repeatedly. But then everything had been an abstraction to Herb—except for Estelle. Even the death of Herb's own daughter had been shrugged off as some kind of spiritual test, part of his goddamn *journey*.

There were still others in Baltimore who followed the Fivefold Path and they had been exceptionally kind to Dave over the last twelve months, providing what Miriam dryly called a never-ending supply of soybean casseroles. Yet even these friends seemed upset when he tried to suggest that their mutual belief system might not be large enough to get him through this. What did it mean if he could not clear his mind for the daily meditation? Should he abandon it until he could find the necessary concentration, or should he continue to try, every sunrise and sunset, to empty his head and embrace the now? Here he was, coming to the end of the sunset ritual, and he remembered none of it, had failed to find any peace or contentment. Instead he was beginning to see the Agnihotra as Miriam had always seen it—a shitty smell, a greasy smoke that coated the walls of the study.

The fire was out. He bagged the ashes, which he used as fertilizer, and drifted back to the kitchen, pouring a glass of wine for himself and a shot of whiskey for Chet. As an afterthought, he gave Miriam a glass of wine, too.

"Really, Chet—has there been any progress? Can you look back at the past year and say we've learned anything?" He thought it was generous, using "we." Privately, Dave thought the cops, while kind and earnest, had been nothing short of inept.

"We've eliminated a lot of scenarios. The Rock Glen chorus teacher. Um . . . others." Even in private, Chet wouldn't rub Miriam's nose in the Baumgarten mess. It killed Dave how the cops had all but congratulated Miriam for being so forthcoming about the affair, how they had nodded approvingly that Sunday evening as she volunteered everything. Truthful Miriam, candid Miriam, putting aside the usual instinct of self-protection and preservation to do whatever it took to find her daughters. But if Miriam hadn't had a talent for deceit to begin with—if she hadn't been involved in the stupid affair—then she wouldn't have had anything to hide. Dave sure didn't.

Yet it was Dave who had lied at first, skipping over the part about Mrs. Baumgarten's visit, stammering inexpertly about why he'd chosen to close the shop early and go drink beer at the tavern down the block. He'd been nervous and halting in those early interviews with police, his eyes darting around the room. Had that been the problem? Had the police been so focused on Dave's odd behavior that they assumed he was the culprit? They denied it now, but Dave was sure he was a suspect.

"Did you chant?" Chet knew Dave's routines well by now.

"Yeah," Dave said. "Another day, another sunset. And in three hundred sixty-five more sunsets, will we be here again, telling the story again, hoping again that someone will come forward? Or do the anniversaries begin to space out after the first year? Five years, ten years, then twenty, then fifty?"

"Three hundred sixty-six," Miriam said.

"What?"

"This was a leap year: 1976. So there was an extra day. It's been three hundred sixty-six years since the girls disappeared. I mean days, three hundred sixty-six days."

"Well, bully for you, Miriam, having it down to the day. I guess you loved them more than me, after all. Except today is the twenty-seventh, not the twenty-ninth. The reporters needed time to ready their stories and reports for the Monday papers, the actual anniversary. So it's really day three hundred sixty-four."

"Dave—" This was Chet's real role in their lives, more peacemaker than policeman. But Dave already felt contrite. A year ago—well, 364 days—he had thought losing his wife would be the great tragedy of his life. Hunched over the bar at Monaghan's, he had experienced the cuckold's usual emotions—anger, vengeance, self-pity, fear. He'd played with the idea of divorcing Miriam, confident that he was one father who could retain custody of his children, considering the circumstances. Instead he lost his children and kept his wife.

Given a choice—but he hadn't been given a choice. Who really was, when it came to anything that mattered? But if he had been asked to choose, he would have sacrificed Miriam in a heartbeat if it meant getting Sunny and Heather back, and it was understood that she would do the same to him. Their marriage was a brittle memorial to their lost daughters, truly the very least they could do.

He said good night to Chet and took his drink to the back porch, studying the tire swing that hung from the one truly sturdy tree in the yard, the pile of sticks and timber near the fence line. When the girls were little, they'd been fond of building forts in the backyard, lean-tos of limbs and branches, with "carpets" made from moss that they transplanted from other parts of the yard, and stores of onion grass and dandelions for their food supply. The girls had outgrown such things years ago, but their last fort had stood until this past winter, when it collapsed from the weight and moisture of the snow. Dave felt as if he lived in a house of broken sticks, as if he were, in fact, impaled on the sharp ends, the moss long dead, the supply of wild onions depleted.

CHAPTER 17

Alone at last—alone again, *naturally,* as the song would have it, a song that Sunny had listened to over and over again when she was eleven, eventually driving them all crazy—Miriam walked over to the sink and poured her glass of wine down the drain. She didn't have much of a taste for alcohol anymore, not that Dave noticed such things. In order for Dave to observe how little Miriam drank these days, he would have to see how much more he drank, and that particular brand of self-knowledge didn't interest him.

The sink was directly beneath a large window that overlooked the backyard, the only change that Miriam had sought during the house's renovation. *A woman has to have a window over the sink,* she argued when she saw Dave's original plans, in which the sink was to face a backsplash of Mexican tile. This was her mother's dictate, and Miriam had inculcated this principle in her own daughters. She remembered

Heather, arranging her Creative Playthings dollhouse. A modular affair, this open-air rectangle of blue wood was quite different from the furbelowed Victorian that Heather would have picked out for herself. It even had Danish modern furniture, made from sturdy hardwoods. "The sink has to go in front of the woman," the rubbery mama doll told the rubbery daddy doll when Heather set it up the first time, and Miriam hadn't corrected Heather's mangling of her edict. The dolls had been the only flimsy things in that set, crumbling and drying as rubber inevitably does, the paint on their faces melting away. But the house and the furniture were still in Heather's closet, waiting for . . . what? For whom?

Overall the girls' rooms remained as they had been, although Miriam had finally broken down and washed the linens, making the beds that had been left tumbled and tossed, in Heather's case, smooth and barely wrinkled in Sunny's case. Each girl had used her own sleeping style to argue against bed making. "I'm just going to mess it up again," Heather said. "You can barely tell I've been in it," Sunny said. They had reached a compromise: Beds would be made, Monday through Friday, then left alone on the weekend. For weeks Miriam had taken great comfort in looking at those unmade beds, proof that their daughters intended to sleep in them again, that the week would return, and her daughters with it.

In the immediate aftermath— But no, "aftermath" was the wrong word, for it suggested a tangible event, something definitive. Where was the "math" in their situation, what was the "after"? In the first forty-eight hours, when nothing was known and everything was possible, Miriam felt as if she had been plunged into a cold, rushing stream, and her only instinct was to survive the shock of it all. She ate nothing, she seldom slept, and she stoked her body on caffeine because she needed to be ready, alert. The one thing she assumed, in the early going, was that an answer would be forthcoming. With the ringing of the telephone, a knock on the door, all would be revealed.

How grandiose that expectation turned out to be.

Detective Willoughby—he was not yet Chet to her, just the detective, the police officer—Detective Willoughby thought she was so brave and selfless to admit, before the weekend was over, exactly where she'd been that afternoon. "The natural instinct is to lie," he told her. "About the smallest things. You'd be amazed how naturally and automatically people lie to police."

"If it helps find my daughters, then who cares? And if it doesn't . . . who cares?"

This was the Sunday after the girls had disappeared. The first twenty-four hours, the first forty-eight hours—everyone seemed to have a rule of thumb about the crucial window of opportunity. And everyone seemed to be wrong. There were no rules, Miriam found out. They didn't have to wait, for example, to report the girls missing. The police had taken them seriously from the very first call, sending officers to the house and then to the mall, where they walked through the thinning Saturday-evening crowds with Miriam and Dave. Other people had been helpful, too. The usher at the cinema remembered the girls—and remembered that they had bought tickets for *Escape to Witch Mountain,* then tried to sneak into *Chinatown.* Miriam had a strange surge of pride in Sunny, hearing that. Docile, goody-goody Sunny, sneaking into an R-rated movie—and such a good one at that. Miriam didn't know she had it in her. When she saw her again, she wouldn't be angry, not in the least. In fact, she would sit down with Sunny and the movie listings, ask her if there were other R movies she wanted to see. Coppola, Fellini, Herzog—she and Sunny would become art house aficionados together.

What other promises did she make that Saturday evening? She would find her way back to some sort of spiritual life. Not Dave's Fivefold Path, but maybe Judaism or, in a pinch, the Unitarian Church. And she wouldn't *hock* Dave anymore about the path, wouldn't tease him about the fact that he had adopted a spiritual practice because he envied the material goods of the people who introduced him to it. Much as she was grateful to the Turners, she didn't share Dave's gaga admiration of them. Their generosity to the Bethanys had been rooted in selfishness, contradictory as that might sound.

Other promises. She would be a better mother, making good meals, relying less on Chinese takeout and Marino's pizza. The girls' laundry would be done with meticulous care. Perhaps it was time to redecorate Sunny's room, to mark the rite of passage into high school next year? And wasn't Heather going to outgrow the elaborate *Where the Wild Things Are* border in her room, beautiful as it was? Miriam had made that by buying two copies of the book, breaking the binding, then shellacking the pages to the wall, so the entire story was told. They could go, the three of them, to the flea market at Westview Drive-In and the

Purple Heart, find old furniture and paint it bright, mod colors. Good linens couldn't be faked, so she would have to shop the so-called white sales at the department stores, come next January—

All of this was going through Miriam's head that evening when the sight of the blue denim bag, which looked like a stain in the dim light of the parking lot, brought her back from the future with an abrupt, sickening thump. She gave a little cry and fell to her knees in the parking lot, but the young officer had restrained her.

"Don't touch it, ma'am. We should—Please, ma'am. There's a way to do this."

Little girls lose things. Purses and keys and hair ribbons and schoolbooks and jackets and sweaters and hats and mittens. To lose things is the nature of childhood. Being separated from this purse would be reason enough for Heather—stubborn, materialistic Heather—to refuse to go home, tracing and retracing her steps again and again and again and again. "Have you ever stopped to think," Miriam had asked her just a few weeks before, "why when you find something you lost, it's always in the last place you look?" How Heather had rejoiced in that bit of verbal tomfoolery, once she got it. Literal-minded Sunny had simply said, "Of course it is."

On her knees in the parking lot, Miriam yearned to grab the purse as if it were her daughter, but the young officer continued to hold her back. There was a mark on it—a footprint, a tire track. How Heather would anguish over that. The purse had come with two other sheaths, but this denim one was Heather's favorite. They would replace it, no recriminations about her carelessness. And tomorrow they would have an Easter-egg hunt, although the girls had claimed they were too old this year. That is, Sunny had said she was too old, not to bother, and Heather had swiftly agreed. A special hunt, with chocolates but also amazing treasures. Miriam could get the candy eggs from High's, but where would she find treasures at this time of night? The mall was open for another twenty minutes or so. Or she could go to the Blue Guitar and help herself to Dave's wares, and who cared how red the ink ran? She would pick out jewelry and toys and ceramic vases, which could be used for the daffodils and crocuses just beginning to poke their heads into the world.

Life was never as *sharp* again as it was at that moment. With each day as the possibility of an answer receded a little more, Miriam's senses dulled. The girls would not be found unharmed. The girls would not be found alive. The girls would not be found . . . intact, the all-purpose euphemism that Miriam used to denote everything from sexual assault to actual dismemberment. But it was a long time before it occurred to anyone that the girls might not be found.

And Miriam had been waiting for the girls to be found, she realized, not just because she was desperate to know what had happened but because she'd been planning to leave Dave once this was settled. The tragedy of their daughters—the blame of it, the weight of it—was marital property as surely as the house and the furniture and the store. She needed to know the whole story so that it could be divided between them, fifty-fifty, fair and square. But what if the ending never came? Did she have to stay with Dave? Even if she were to blame for her daughters' deaths—and Miriam, in her darkest moments, could not believe that any god, in any belief system, would kill two children to punish a philandering mother, and if there were such a god, she wanted no part of him or her or it—did she have to serve a life sentence in this marriage? It had been deadening enough before, leavened only by their joy in the girls. How long did she have to stay? How much did she owe Dave?

She studied her reflection in the window above the sink. *A woman must have a window over her sink,* her mother had said. *Washing dishes is so boring there must be a view.* To her knowledge it was the only demand her mother had ever uttered. Certainly, she had never questioned that it was the woman who would wash the dishes and make the meals and clean the house, much less seek a place for herself outside the house. Women of Miriam's generation were beginning to ask for so much, but her mother, miserable as she was living in Ottawa, had asked for nothing but a window, and Miriam had followed suit. Here, during daylight hours, she could see the large, overgrown-verging-on-wild yard. The wildness was a carefully cultivated illusion. Miriam had tended to her yard as she had reared her children, allowing it to follow its instincts, respecting what was there—honeysuckle, mint, jack-in-the-pulpit—and not trying to force things that were never meant to be, such as roses or hydrangeas. The things she added had been compatible, unobtrusive, perennials capable of thriving in the shade.

But once the sun went down, all the window provided was one's own face. The woman that Miriam saw looked exhausted, yet still attractive. She would have no problem finding a new man. In fact, men seemed more drawn to her than ever in the past year. Chet clearly had a crush on her, and not only because she was a damsel in distress. The knowledge of Miriam's affair, the secret that he had continued to safeguard, excited him. She was a bad woman. And Willoughby, despite being a detective, didn't seem to have a lot of firsthand experience with bad women.

Other men, not privy to what Willoughby knew, were attracted to Miriam by the palpable sense of doom and damage, the exhausted eyes that clearly said, *I'm out of the game.* It was frightening, really, how many men responded to damage in a woman. Yes, she could easily find another man. But she didn't want another man. What she wanted was an excuse to leave, a definitive reason to go upstairs, pack a bag and drive away, without being seen as the cold, unnatural woman who had abandoned her husband when he needed her most. The husband who had forgiven her, so generously, so unstintingly. Then again, how magnanimous was a gesture if one were constantly aware of its magnanimity?

She would give it six more months. That would take them to October. But October had been so hard on Dave last fall—the beautiful weather, Halloween, with neighborhood children in their costumes. November, December? But the holidays were more painful still. January brought Sunny's birthday, and then it would be March again, the second anniversary, with Heather's birthday the following week. There would never be a right time to leave, Miriam thought. There would just be a time. Soon.

She imagined herself on the highway, heading

to . . . Texas. She knew a girl from her college days who had settled in Austin and raved about its free-and-easy lifestyle. Miriam saw herself in her car, driving west, then south through Virginia, through the long Shenandoah Valley, past the destinations they had visited with the girls—Luray Caverns, Skyline Drive, Monticello—deeper and deeper, all the way to Abingdon and into Tennessee. She experienced a chill. Ah, right. Abingdon was the locale of another alleged sighting. A well-intentioned one, but those clueless busybodies bothered Miriam more than the out-and-out hoaxes did.

Of all the things that she had cause to resent, Miriam most despised how her private tragedy had become a public one, something that others claimed to be affected by. Look at these reporters today, pretending they had a clue how she felt. The deluded witnesses were just another variation, people seeking ownership, as if the "Bethany girls" were a public resource or treasure, too great for one family to own, like the Hope Diamond down in the Smithsonian. Of course, that gem was said to be cursed.

The Hope Diamond made her think of that huge diamond that Richard Burton gave Elizabeth Taylor. Miriam remembered watching the once-glorious couple on *Here's Lucy,* with Sunny and Heather. Lucille Ball always made Miriam slightly anxious; a beautiful woman should not have to be so silly to get attention. Beauty was its own excuse for being—just look at Elizabeth Taylor if you doubted that fact. But the girls loved Lucy as if she were a cherished aunt, and the comedienne had raised them in a sense, amusing them many an afternoon, on the fuzzy feed from one of the Washington stations. Even the girls recognized that the current nighttime series couldn't begin to touch the magic of the original, but they watched out of loyalty. In the show Miriam remembered, Ball tried on Taylor's ring and couldn't get it off. High jinks ensued, with lots of popping eyes and wide mouths.

People tried on Miriam's pain in that way, modeled it for her, almost as if they expected her to be flattered by their interest. But they never had any trouble shedding it when the time came. They plucked it off and handed it back to her, continuing with their blessedly uneventful lives.

CHAPTER 18

It had taken a lot of begging and promising and negotiating, but she finally got permission to attend a party. She had argued—well, not argued, a voice raised in anger was considered unacceptable—she had said that it would appear odd, forever saying no to the invitations at school. She was supposed to be a kid like any other, and kids went to parties. Uncle and Auntie, as she had been instructed to call them in public, were keen not to seem odd to others. That made sense to her, given all the secrets they were keeping and all the lies they were telling, but she couldn't understand how they managed to hide their oddness from themselves. How could they not know how weird they were, how out of step in every way? Outside the house it was 1976, the year of the Bicentennial, in the middle of a decade that had proved that anything could happen, even in a small town such as this. A war had ended, a president had been toppled, because people had demanded change. Spoke for it, marched for it, died for it in some cases. She was not thinking of the soldiers in Vietnam. She never thought about them. She was thinking about Kent State, an event she wished she'd paid more attention to when it happened, but she'd been so much younger then. It wasn't the kind of thing that a little girl could understand, much less care about.

She cared about it now, though. In the library she had found a copy of *Time* magazine with the photo of the girl crouching by the boy. The girl was a runaway, dislocated, not where she was supposed to be, and she had wandered into history. The photograph became a kind of promise: She could run away. She could find history. And if she found history, if she could do something large and important enough, then maybe she could be forgiven.

But, for now, she was happy to be in a basement party room in a house in town, waiting to see if anyone would call her number for Five Minutes in Heaven. The game had started contentiously, not because some girls didn't want to play—everyone had been eager to play—but because there was much disagreement on how long couples should stay in the closet. Some said two, citing no less an authority than *Are You There God? It's Me, Margaret,* while others said it should be seven, because that sounded right: *Seven* Minutes in *Heaven.* "We'll split the difference," decreed the hostess, Kathy. A popular girl but a nice one, she wielded her power with grace. If Kathy said it was okay to play Five Minutes in Heaven, then it was definitely okay.

That was something else that Uncle and Auntie didn't know about the world right outside their door:

Sex was everywhere, even here, even among the very young, especially among the very young. Doctor, Spin the Bottle, now Five Minutes (or Two or Seven) in Heaven. Sex came first, well before drinking and drugs, although drugs were largely disdained here. Too hippie-ish. Her classmates were groping their way into adolescence, literally and figuratively.

She was the only one having full-out intercourse in a feather bed, however. She was pretty sure of that, not that she dared to compare notes. If she told anyone about life at home, they would take her away, and that might actually be worse.

It was hard to think about kissing in daylight, on a Saturday afternoon. Sex was a nighttime activity, grim and silent, in a house where everyone pretended not to hear the squeak of the springs, the way the bedstead swayed, pressing against the wall with a muted thump, like waves lapping a pier. Waves against a pier . . . She was in Annapolis, at the clam festival. She was eight. She wore orange-and-pink culottes. She didn't like clams, but she liked the festival. Everyone was happy, back when she was eight.

By day she was a distant cousin, arrived from Ohio, saddled with a name she truly hated, Ruth. So plain, so stark that name. Ruth. If she had to have a new one, why not Cordelia or Geraldine, one of the names that Anne of Green Gables had chosen for herself? But Uncle explained that the choices were limited, and Ruth was the best he could do. Ruth was a real girl, once upon a time, a girl who lived to be only three or four, then burned up in a fire with her whole family in a place called Bexley. Ruth had a different birthday than she did, so they put her in the wrong grade, which she had expected to be boring and repetitive. But her new school, Shrine of the Little Flower, was actually harder than her old one. She wasn't sure if that was because of the nuns or the fact that the class was small, maybe both. With so much schoolwork, she didn't have time to learn all the things she should know about her new self, and she worried that someone was going to ask her questions about Ohio that she couldn't answer—the capital, the state flower, the state bird. But no one ever did. Her new classmates had grown up together and had little experience dealing with strangers. And they'd been instructed explicitly not to talk to Ruth about the horrible things that had happened to her family back in Ohio.

One girl, someone who would have been called a spastic back home, although that term didn't appear to be in use here, asked her about the cigars.

"Cigars?"

"From the burns?"

"Oh. Scars." She needed to think for only a second. Lying was becoming second nature to her. "They're where you can't see them."

She regretted this, because it got back to the boys from Little Flower and they had been gossiping about who might be the first to see Ruth's secret scars. Even today, when Five Minutes in Heaven was proposed, she saw Jeffrey point to her and punch Bill in the arm, saying in a hoarse stage whisper, "Maybe you'll get to see Ruth's scars." She knew that Jeffrey liked her, that his teasing was a form of flirtation, but she was too tired to care. If the girls at Little Flower didn't know what to do with a new girl, the boys did, or thought they did. They liked her, mysterious, forbidden Ruth, with her tragic history that no one was supposed to mention. She worried that they could smell all the sex on her, despite the long showers she took morning and night, earning her harsh lectures about the limits of well water and the cost of natural gas.

"Forty-seven!" Bill called out. That was her number. The other kids whooped, as they did each time. She walked to the closet with as much dignity as possible, knowing that Bill was capering after her, making faces at his buddies behind her back. Again, this was what all the confident boys did, she reminded herself.

The closet was really a pantry, where Kathy's mom put up her summer canning. Tomatoes and peppers and peaches stared down at them. They made her think of the jars in a horror movie, of the brains floating in brine in *Young Frankenstein*. Abbie. Abbie Normal! That would be a good fake name. Auntie put up food, too, and made wonderful jams and preserves. Apple, peach, plum, cherries— No, don't think about the cherry tree. There was a large cooler on the floor, and they sat on it, hip to hip, shy and awkward.

"What do you want to do?" Bill asked.

"What do you want to do?" she countered.

He shrugged, as if the situation bored him, as if he'd seen it all and done it all.

"Do you want to kiss me?" she ventured.

"Yeah, I guess."

His breath tasted of cake and potato chips, which was kind of pleasant. He parted his lips but didn't try to put his tongue in her mouth. And he kept his hands to his sides, almost as if he were afraid to touch her.

"Nice," she said, being polite but also meaning it.

"Do you want to do it again?"

"Sure." They had five minutes.

This time he stuck the tiniest tip of his tongue between her lips and let it hang there, barely breathing, as if he expected her to object or push him away. Instead she had to concentrate on not widening her mouth reflexively and drawing his tongue in the rest of the way. She was well trained by now, expert in the techniques it took to speed through the nightly transaction. What would Ruth, the real Ruth, do, if she hadn't burned up in a fire when she was four years old? What would Ruth know, how would she act? The tip of Bill's tongue rested on her lower lip, like a fleck of food or a strand of hair she wanted to brush away. But she let it stay.

"What else do you want to do?" Bill asked, pulling back to breathe.

He didn't know, she realized. He had no idea of all the things that could be done, even in five minutes. For one moment she considered showing him, but she knew that would be disastrous. When their five minutes finally ended with the others pounding on the closet door, screaming at them to put back on the clothes that weren't even disheveled, Bill was still as ignorant as she wished she were. Then Kathy's mother called downstairs that it was time to go home, and she didn't have to call anyone's number.

"How was the party?" Uncle asked.

"Boring," she said, telling the truth, but a truth she knew that would make him happy. If the party were boring, maybe she wouldn't want to go to another one. He worried about her when she was out in public, without someone in the family watching her. He didn't quite trust her when she was out of the house. Besides, she liked to make him happy. In his own strange way, he was on her side, and no one else in the house really was, not even the dogs, who were rough and nasty, good only for muddying coats and tearing her tights.

"I thought I'd go outside," she said.

"Cold as it is?"

"Just around the property. Not far."

She walked to the orchard, to the cherry tree. This time of year, it was hard to say if one really saw buds or if it was just wishful thinking, a trick of the March dusk, creating gray-green shadows that looked like the promise of new life.

"I kissed a boy today," she told the tree, the twilight, the ground. No one was impressed, but the normalcy of it made her feel that maybe she could be normal again, that she could retrace her steps and get things right. One day.

She was Ruth, from Bexley, Ohio. Her whole family burned up in a fire when she was three or four. She had jumped out the second-floor window, breaking her ankle. That's why she was a grade behind where she should be, because of all the time in the hospital. No, she had not been left back. She just didn't get to do any schoolwork that year. And school was different in Ohio. That's why she didn't know some things she should know.

Yes, she had scars, but they weren't where you could see them, even when she wore a bathing suit.

PART V
FRIDAY

CHAPTER 19

"I can't," she said. "I just can't."

Odd, the things that stuck with you from school. Infante hadn't been much of a student, but he'd liked history for a while there. In Jane Doe's hospital room Friday morning—and he was insisting on thinking of her as Jane Doe, now more than ever—Infante was reminded of something he once heard about Louis XIV. Or maybe XVI. The point was, he remembered how certain kings made their servants watch them dress, and that was supposed to establish their power. Dress and bathe and God knows what else. As a fourteen-year-old in Massapequa, he hadn't bought it. Who looked less powerful than a naked man, or a guy taking a dump? But watching Jane D. do her thing this morning, the history lesson came back to him.

Which isn't to say she was disrobing for him—anything but. She was still in her hospital gown, her bony shoulders draped with a bright shawl. Yet she was ordering around Gloria and the hospital social worker, what's-her-name, in this very queenly fashion, acting as if he weren't in the room at all. If he didn't know the first thing about her—and, again, he was sticking by that notion—he would have diagnosed her a rich bitch, or a daddy's girl at the very least, someone used to getting her way. With men *and* women. These two were jumping, vying for the right to do things for her.

"My clothes—" she began, eyeing the outfit she had been wearing when she was admitted, and even Kevin could see why she wouldn't want to put them on again. They were sweat-type things, a loose top and yoga pants, the Under Armor brand that was so hot locally, and they were giving off a stale smell—not the hard-core acrid odor of a workout but that slept-in, lived-in-too-long kind of smell. He wondered how many miles she had driven in them before the accident. *All the way from Asheville? Then how did you buy gas, with no billfold or cash?* Could she have flung her wallet out of the car? Gloria kept trying to portray the events after the accident as pure panic, the faulty decisions made by adrenaline. But you could counter that it was all calculated, that she had fled the scene to give herself time to come up with a story.

A story that had been enlarged to include a cop-perpetrator when this woman learned that the state's attorney thought she should be grand juried or locked up. And sure enough, the state's attorney had blinked, agreed to let her stay out of jail as long as Gloria would vouch for her remaining in Baltimore. Infante had to admit, a person would have to be really ballsy to flee Gloria. She'd hunt the woman down for her fee alone.

"There's a Salvation Army over on Patapsco Avenue," said the social worker. Kay, that was it. "Really, they have some very nice things."

"Patapsco Avenue," Lady X said in a musing, remembering tone, a little arch to Infante's ears. "I think there was a discount seafood place up there, once upon a time. It's where my family bought crabs."

He jumped on that. "You came all the way over here to buy seafood, living in Northwest Baltimore?"

"My dad was big on bargains. Bargains and . . . idiosyncrasy. You know, why drive ten minutes for steamed crabs if you could go clear across the city, save a buck a dozen, *and* have a story to tell? Come to think of it, wasn't there a place around here that served deep-fried green-pepper rings dipped in powdered sugar?"

Kay shook her head. "I've heard people speak of them, but I've lived in Baltimore my whole life and never seen such a thing on any menu."

"Just because you don't see something doesn't mean it doesn't exist." She was queenly again, lifting her chin. "I sat in plain sight for years and no one ever saw me."

Good, she was finally in the neighborhood of where this conversation should have been going all along. "Your appearance wasn't altered at all?"

"Nice'n Easy took my hair two shades darker. I asked to be a redhead like Anne of Green Gables, but what *I* wanted was seldom of interest." She met his gaze. "I'm guessing you weren't much of an L. M. Montgomery fan."

"Who was he?" he asked obediently, knowing he was being set up, letting the trio of women laugh at him. He could afford such laughter—use it to his advantage, even. Let her think he was an idiot. Wouldn't it be great if Gloria went on the clothes-shopping mission with Kay? But he was never going to get that lucky. "Seriously—"

"I started to grow," she said, as if anticipating where he was going. "And although everyone knew that I'd have to grow if I was still alive, I think that was part of the reason no one ever recognized me. That, and being just the one."

"Yeah, your sister. What happened to her? That would be a good place to start."

"No," she said. "It wouldn't be."

"Gloria said you had lots to say. About a cop, in fact. I was summoned here this morning on the understanding that you were ready to tell me everything."

"I can do the generalities. I'm still not sure I should deal in specifics, yet. I don't feel that you're on my side."

"You're saying you're a victim, a hostage held against her will, and you're implying that your sister was killed. Why wouldn't I be on your side?"

"See, there it is: *You're saying*. Not that I am but that I claim to be. Your skepticism makes it very hard for me to trust you. That, and the likelihood that you'll do everything you can to discredit a story that doesn't reflect well on one of your department's own."

She had hit a nerve there, but he wasn't going to give her the satisfaction of seeing how much it bugged him, how it had set off all sorts of alarms in the department. "It's a way of talking, that's all. Don't read so much into it."

She ran her right hand, the one that wasn't bandaged, through her hair, and held his gaze. Their game of

192

visual chicken dragged on until she blinked, fluttering her eyelids as if exhausted. Yet he had the sense that she was simply allowing him the illusion of winning, that she could have gone much longer. Piece o' work, this one, a real piece o' work.

"I knew a girl—" she began, behind closed eyes.

"Heather Bethany? Penelope Jackson?"

"This was high school. While I was still with *him*."

"Where—"

"Later. In good time." Eyes open now, but trained on the wall to her left. "I knew a girl, and she was popular. A cheerleader, a good student. Sweet, though. The kind of girl that adults admired. She dated, a lot. Older boys, college boys. In—where this was—there was a lake, and kids went there on date nights to drink and make out. Her parents didn't want her to be in cars late at night, driving on those roads with inexperienced boys. So they made her a deal. If she would bring her dates home, to their house, they would respect her privacy. She and her date would have the rec room to themselves. There would be no curfew. Beer could be consumed, within reason. After all, they could have crossed the state line, where the drinking age was eighteen at the time. In the rec room, they could drink beer and watch television and know that—short of her screaming 'Fire!' or 'Rape!'—no parent would enter the room. Her parents would stay in their bedroom, two floors away, and respect her privacy. What do you think happened?"

"I don't know." *Christ, I don't care*. But he had to pretend that he did. This one drank up attention like water.

"She did everything. *Everything*. She perfected the

193

art of the blow job. She lost her virginity. Her parents thought they had figured it out so neatly, that they could give her freedom and she would be too inhibited to use it. They thought she wouldn't really take them at their word, that she would worry about them crossing the threshold. So here was this girl, this sweet, popular girl, all but starring in pornos in her parents' rec room, and it didn't change her reputation one whit."

"Is this a story about you?"

"No. It's a story about perceptions, about what you get to be in public and what you are in private. Right now I'm a private person. Anonymous, unknown, ordinary. But when I start to tell you what happened to me, you're going to think I'm dirty. Nasty. You won't be able to help yourself. The cheerleader in the basement can give out all the blow jobs she likes. But the little girl who doesn't try to escape from her captor and abuser, who gets raped every night, she's harder to understand. She must have liked it, if she didn't run away. Right? And that's without the guy being a cop on top of everything else."

"I'm a police," he said. "I don't blame victims."

"But you categorize them, right? You feel differently about, say, a woman beaten to death by her husband than you do about a drug dealer killed by a rival. That's just human nature. And you're human—right?" Kevin glanced over at Gloria. In his experience, she kept her clients on a tight leash, interrupting and directing interviews. But she was letting this one run the show. In fact, she seemed a little mesmerized by her. "I want to help you, but I want to preserve what little normalcy I have. I don't want to be the freak of the week on all those news channels. I don't want police officers poking around in my present life, talking to neighbors and coworkers and bosses."

"And friends? Family?"

"I don't have those."

"But you know we're trying to find your mother, Miriam, down in Mexico."

"Are you sure she's alive? Because—" She stopped herself.

"Because what? Because you think she's dead? Because you *counted* on her being dead?"

"Why don't you ever use my name when you speak to me?"

"What?"

"Gloria does. Kay does. But you never call me anything. You used my mother's name just then, but you've never used mine. Don't you believe me?"

She listened well, better than most. You had to really listen to pick up on the omissions in another person's conversation, and she was right—there was no way he was going to call her Heather. He didn't believe her, plain and simple, had her pegged as a liar from the first time he met her. "Look, it's not about belief or trust or sympathy. I like to work from established facts. Things that can be verified, and you haven't really given me any of those. Why were you so sure your mother was dead?"

"Around the time I turned eighteen—"

"What year was that?"

"April third, 1981. Please, Detective. I know my own birthday. No small miracle, given how many different birthdays I've had in my life."

"Heather Bethany's birthday is on the Internet. It

was in the news stories. Everyone knows that Heather Bethany was just days away from her twelfth birthday when she disappeared."

She didn't bother to answer things she didn't want to answer, more evidence of her shrewdness. "Anyway, around the time I turned eighteen, I was on my own. Cut loose, put on a bus, given lovely parting gifts, and sayonara."

"He freed you, just like that? Kept you for six years and then waved bye-bye, with no fear of where you would go or what you would tell people?"

"He told me every day that my parents didn't want me, that no one was looking for me, that I had no family to return to, that my parents had broken up and moved away. Eventually I came to believe that."

"Still, what happens when you're eighteen? Why does he let you go?"

She shrugged. "He'd lost interest. I was less . . . malleable as time went on. Still under his thumb, but beginning to nip at that thumb, make my own demands. It was time for me to support myself. I got on a bus—"

"Where?"

"Not yet. I won't tell you where I started. But I got off in Chicago. It was so cold for April. I never knew April could be so cold. And there was a ticker-tape parade downtown, for the shuttle astronauts who had just returned. I remember wandering out of the bus station, into the Loop, and finding myself in the aftermath of this huge celebration. But I had missed the good part. All that was left was the trash."

"That's a nice story, I guess. Is it true or is it just a metaphor?"

"You're *smart*." Admiring and insulting at the same time.

"Why wouldn't I be? Because I'm a cop?"

"Because you're handsome." To his own irritation he blushed, although it was far from the first time a woman had praised his looks. "It cuts both ways, you know. Men think pretty girls are dumb, but women think the same thing about a certain kind of man. One of the worst things you can do, as a woman, is have a boyfriend prettier than yourself. You could never be my boyfriend, Detective Infante."

Through all of this, Gloria Bustamante had been still as a stone gooney-eyed gargoyle, but now she cleared her throat noisily, filling the awkward silence. Maybe she was even more freaked out by this conversation than Infante was.

"Heather does have something she's willing to give you," Gloria said. "A factoid, something you can check out and it will go a long way to establishing the authenticity of all her claims."

"Why can't she just give a statement?" he asked. "Dates, times, places. The name of the man who kidnapped her and killed her sister. She lived with him for six years. Presumably she knows his goddamn name."

The woman in the hospital bed—he was running out of ways to think of her—jumped in, eyes gleaming. "Did you know that 'factoid' actually means false? Originally. Its meaning has . . . migrated, if you will, so the dictionary now accepts 'small fact' as one of its definitions. I was kind of disappointed in that. I think language should hold the line, not allow its own corruption."

"I'm not here to talk about language."

"Okay, here's what you want. Up Interstate 83, just over the Pennsylvania line, the first exit, up around Shrewsbury. It wasn't very developed then, and street names may have changed. But there was a farm on something called Old Town Road, which ran from Glen Rock to Shrewsbury, all the way to York. The farm used a P.O. box to get its mail, but there was a mailbox at the foot of the drive, and the number was 13350. The driveway is a mile long, almost exactly. The house was stone, the door was painted bright red. There was a barn. Not far from the barn was an orchard. You'll find my sister's grave there, beneath a cherry tree."

"How many cherry trees are there?"

"Several, and there were other kinds of trees mixed in as well. Apple and pear, a few dogwoods for color. Over time, when I wasn't being observed, I managed to scratch a random pattern into the bark. Not her initials. That would have been noticed. Just a little ring of X's."

"We're talking thirty years ago. The tree could be gone. The house could be gone. Earth *moves*."

"But property records remain. And if you research the address I've given you, then I'm confident that you'll find a name you'll be able to cross-reference with the personnel files of the Baltimore County Police Department."

"Why not just tell me the fuckin' name of the man who did this to you?"

"I want you to believe me. I want you to see the farm, see his name on the records, then match it with your own files. I want you to have my sister's bones.

Then when you find him—if you find him, he could be dead for all I know—you'll know that much is true."

"Why not go there with us and show me? Wouldn't that be simpler, and faster?" *Or is simple and fast the one thing you don't want, girlie? What are you stalling for? What's your angle?*

"That," she said, "is the one thing I will never do. Not even after almost twenty-five years. I never want to see that place again."

He believed that much—but only that much. The fear in her face was real, the shudder in her shoulders visible even beneath the shawl. She could not stomach the thought of this journey. Wherever she'd been headed Tuesday night, it wasn't Pennsylvania.

But that still didn't mean that she was Heather Bethany.

CHAPTER 20

Heather wrinkled up her nose the moment she crossed the threshold into the Forrest house.

"I'm allergic to cats," she told Kay, speaking as if Kay were a dim-witted real-estate agent. "This won't work."

"But I thought you understood—I told you my son, Seth, was earning extra money by looking after the family's plants and pets."

"I guess I heard only the plant part. I'm sorry, but—" She turned her head and sneezed, a dainty, dry sneeze. A catlike sneeze, in fact. "In just minutes I'll be all red and puffy. I couldn't possibly stay here."

Her cheeks did seem to be reddening, her eyes watering. Kay followed Heather back outside, onto the fieldstone porch on the front of the house. A black woman was walking down the street with her daughter, and although the girl was astride a bike with training wheels, she was outrageously well dressed in a pale yellow pinafore and matching shoes. The mother wore a complementary shade of celery green. She turned to study the two women on the porch, clearly suspicious of them. A neighbor, Cynthia something. Mrs. Forrest had said she was a one-woman neighborhood watch, that she wouldn't have worried about the house at all during their vacation if it weren't for the plants and the cat, Felix. Kay waved, hoping the gesture would reassure the woman, but she did not wave back or even smile, just narrowed her eyes and nodded curtly as if in warning. *I see you. I'll remember you if anything happens.*

"Well, now I'm stumped," Kay said. "You can't stay here, but I can't take you back to the hospital either. And without those options—"

"Not jail," Heather said, her voice raspy and hoarse, but maybe it was still the effect of the cat. "Kay, you have to see why a woman who's accusing a police officer wouldn't feel safe there. It's hard enough having a cop posted wherever I stay. And not a shelter," she added, as if in anticipation of Kay's next question. "I just couldn't do a shelter. Too many rules. I'm not great with rules, with other people telling me what to do."

"That's true of emergency shelters, where beds are given out daily on a first-come, first-served basis. But there are mid-range placements, too. Not many, but if I made some calls—"

"It just wouldn't work for me. I'm used to being alone."

"You've never lived with anyone? I mean, not since . . ."

"Since I left the farm? Oh, I've moved in with a

boyfriend a time or two. But it's not for me." She smiled with one half of her mouth. "I have intimacy issues. Go figure."

"You've been to counseling, then?"

"No." Fierce, insulted. "What makes you think that?"

"I just assumed. . . . I mean, by the phrases you used. And because of what you've been through? It would seem . . ."

Heather sat on the porch, and although Kay could feel the cold and damp through the soles of her shoes, it seemed only right to join her there, to be on her level, instead of looming over her.

"What would I tell a shrink? And what would a shrink tell me back? My life was taken from me when I was barely a teenager. My sister was killed in front of me. The fact is, I think I've done pretty well. Up until seventy-two hours ago, my life was fine."

"And by fine you mean . . ."

"I had a job. Nothing impressive or fascinating, but I did it well and I paid my bills. On weekends, when the weather was good, I biked. If the weather was bad, I picked a recipe out of a book, something challenging, and tried to replicate it. I had as many failures as successes, but that's part of the learning process. I rented movies. I read books. I was— You wouldn't call it happy. I gave up on happy a long time ago."

"Content?" Kay thought about how sorry she had felt for herself after the divorce, how easily she had tossed around words such as *unhappy* and *sad* and *depressed*.

"That's closer to it. *Not* unhappy. That's what I aspired to."

"That's so sad."

"I'm alive. That's more than my sister got."

"What about your parents, though? Did you ever think about what they must be feeling?"

Heather tapped two fingers against pursed lips. Kay had noticed the gesture before. It was almost as if the answer were right there, inside her mouth, ready to jump out, but she first wanted to think through all the consequences.

"Can we have secrets?"

"Legally? I have no standing—"

"Not legally. I know that you could be forced to tell what you know in a courtroom. But I don't expect to see the inside of a courtroom. Gloria says I won't even have to talk to a grand jury. As people, human beings, can we have secrets?"

"You mean, can you trust me?"

"I wouldn't go that far." Heather instantly registered that her words were hurtful, unkind. "Kay, I don't *trust* anyone. How could I? But really, in my own fucked-up way, don't you think I'm a success story? The fact that I get up every day and I breathe and I feed myself and I go to work and I do my job and I come home and watch crap television, then get up the next day and do it all over again, and I never hurt anyone"— here, her lip started to tremble—"never hurt anyone on purpose."

"The child in the accident is going to be fine. No brain injury, no spinal-cord damage."

"No *brain* damage," Heather repeated bitterly. "*Just* a broken leg. Oh, boy!"

"For which the father is equally at fault, if not more so. Consider his pain."

"To be truthful, that's hard for me. Other people's

pain. When I'm at work and I hear people talking about what they think is painful or difficult, it's like I want to explode, want something horrible and slimy to burst from my innards, like in a science-fiction film. Other people's notions of pain are pretty lame. This father, okay, he can beat himself up all he likes about what happened. But he was reacting to my error—"

"An error caused by road conditions that weren't your fault," Kay reminded her.

"Yeah, but . . . do you think the person in the previous accident, much less the half-assed county worker who didn't hose down the highway properly—do you think they've even made the connection? No, and they never will. Blame falls where it falls, fair or not."

They had wandered away from whatever Heather had been on the verge of confiding. Kay wondered if she could guide her back there. Her interest was not prurient, she was sure of that this time. She felt as if she might be the closest thing Heather had to a disinterested ally. The police, Gloria—this woman was almost secondary to their agendas. Kay didn't care who she was now, she didn't care about solving the mystery of her disappearance.

"We can have secrets," she said, remembering the original phrase. "You can tell me things, and I won't repeat them, not unless they involve harming yourself or someone else."

Another ragged half grin. "Everyone has a loophole."

"It's called ethics."

"Okay, here's my secret: Once I was on my own, I tried to keep track of my parents, over the years. My dad was easy to find, because he was at the old house.

I was told he wasn't, but he was. But my mom—I couldn't find my mom. That is, I found her, then I lost her again about sixteen years ago. I assumed she was dead, but I didn't look that hard, didn't do everything I knew how to do. It was a weird kind of relief, thinking she was dead, because I had come to believe what they told me, that she didn't care, that she wouldn't want to see me."

"How could you believe that?"

A shrug, so like a teenager's, like Kay's own daughter, Grace.

"As for my dad," she said, not even bothering to answer Kay's question. "As for my dad, a day came when . . . well, I don't want to get too specific. A day came when I knew he wasn't at the same address anymore, and I couldn't imagine him moving. This would have been in 1990 or so. He would have been in his fifties then. That freaked me out, because it had to be, you know, a heart thing or cancer. So I've been walking around, assuming I wouldn't live much past fifty. Now they say my mother's alive, but I just can't believe it. She's been dead to me for so long. And I've been dead to her, most likely. The fact is, much as I want to see her, I'm kind of dreading it, too. Because she's not going to be the person I've been remembering all this time, and I'm not going to be the person she's been remembering."

"Did you ever—I'm sorry, this may be inappropriate."

"Feel free."

"Did you ever look at those drawings on the Internet? The ones that attempted to guess what you would look like as you aged?"

This time her smile was genuine, not ironic. "Pretty

spooky, huh? How close they came. It can't work that way for everyone. I mean, some people get *fat*. Oh—sorry."

If it hadn't been for the apology, Kay would not have connected that remark to herself. She'd noticed this childlike tactlessness in Heather before.

"Look," Heather said, her gaffe already behind her, "I'm sure you don't make much money, but couldn't you put me up in a motel, some old chain? The Quality Inn on Route 40 may not still be there, but something like that. You could put it on a credit card, and assuming we get all this sorted out before long, I'll be able to pay you back. Hey, maybe my *mom* will pay you back."

The thought seemed to amuse her.

"I'm sorry, Heather," Kay said, "but my kids and I live pretty close to the bone. And it's just not right. I'm a social worker. There are lines that I can't cross."

"But you're not *my* social worker, not really. All you did was find Gloria for me. Time will tell how that works out."

"You don't like Gloria?"

"It's not about *liking*. I'm just not sure her self-interest aligns with mine. And forced to choose, who do you think she'll pick?"

"Her client's. Gloria is odd, I grant you, and she loves publicity for herself. But she'll do things your way. As long as you're not lying to her."

Again the tapping motion, two fingers against her lips. It reminded Kay of the way young children once played Indian, making war whoops with their hands by beating a similar tattoo on the mouth. She wondered if children still did that, or if heightened sensitivity had meant the end of such games. Certain cultural icons did disappear. Alley Oop, for example, cavemen dragging their women around by the hair, and who could really feel nostalgia for that? Did Andy Capp and Flo still go at it in the comics? She hadn't glanced at the comics page in years.

"C'mon, Kay. There's got to be a solution."

"Perhaps if I took Felix to our house?"

"No, this place is *suffused* with cat hair and dander. But what if you and the kids came here and I took your house?"

The very reasonableness with which Heather made this proposal floored Kay. She did not see it as an imposition, much less as odd. Kay was careful about throwing around clinical terms, but there was a shading of narcissism in Heather. Then again, perhaps that had been essential to her survival.

"No, Seth and Grace would not be agreeable to that. Like most kids, they're creatures of routine. But—" She knew she was walking a fine line. Hell, she was crossing a thick one, agreeing to a breach that could get her in a lot of trouble at work. Still, she plunged ahead. "We have a small room, over our garage. Not heated, and not air-conditioned, but that shouldn't be an issue this time of year, not with a space heater. It was set up as an office, but there's a couch, a small bath with a shower. Perhaps you could stay there, at least until your mother arrives."

It wouldn't be more than a day or two, Kay reasoned. And she *wasn't* Heather's caseworker, not officially. This would be nothing more than a favor to Gloria. Besides, she couldn't allow the police to lock Heather up. Jail would be devastating for a woman who'd spent much of her youth imprisoned.

"Do you think she's rich?" Heather asked.

"*What?*"

"My mother. We never were, quite the opposite. But he said she's living in Mexico—that seems kind of rich. Maybe I'm an heiress. I always wondered what happened to my dad's business and the house, after he died. Sometimes I'd read those legal listings. You know, unclaimed bank accounts and safe-deposit boxes? But I never found one in my name. I guess he couldn't put me in his will, with everyone thinking I was dead and all. I don't know what happened to our college funds, not that there was that much in them."

Kay felt the dampness of the stone seeping into her skirt, yet her palms were strangely hot and sweaty.

"And now she's coming back, you say. I'm going to call Gloria, see what she thinks about all this. Maybe I should go in voluntarily tomorrow, give them the whole story after all. By then, they'll be ready to believe me, I bet."

CHAPTER 21

Babies floated across the computer screen. No, not babies plural—just one baby, *the* baby, the only baby that mattered in the new millennium. *Move over, Jesus,* Kevin thought, *Andrew Porter Jr. has come to town.* And his now computer-savvy mother had fed endless images of him into the computer, so when it went into rest mode, the little Andy slide show began. Andy as a tiny infant, cradled by his impossibly huge father. Andy eating, Andy with a picture book, Andy squinting at a Christmas tree. His father's genes were stamped all over the boy's face and bulky body, but Kevin liked to think he saw Nancy Porter's sweet skepticism in that squint. *You're saying there's this guy, and he brings me presents? What's in it for him? And what the hell does the tree have to do with any of it?*

"Pennsylvania records are fucked," Nancy said, moving her cursor so Andy disappeared and her computer opened on an archived Web page. "Or else

I don't get how they work. In Maryland all I need is the address and the county, and I can research a property going back years. I haven't been able to find an equivalent page in Pennsylvania, though. The only hit I got on the address you gave me showed it was owned by an LLC, which sold the property a few years back."

"An LLC?"

"Limited liability corporation, somebody's small business. Mercer Inc. Could have been anything, from a produce stand to a cleaning service. But there's no Mercer in our personnel records, so it must be the previous owner we want."

Fair and pleasantly plump before motherhood, Nancy liked to say she was frankly fat now, but the issue of her weight didn't seem to bother her as much. When she returned to work, she'd asked for the transfer to cold cases, a request that Infante had secretly disdained. It seemed dreary stuff to him, poring over old files and looking for lucky breaks—the witness who was finally ready to tell the truth after all these years, the spouse who was tired of keeping secrets. He could see why a new mom would want a job that guaranteed regular hours, but he wasn't sure he considered it real police work. Nancy, however, had a knack for computers and an unerring sense for finding information without ever leaving her desk. The Goddess of Small Things, as Lenhardt had once dubbed her, she now tracked down the tiniest bits of data the way she'd once been able to spot a bullet casing at a hundred paces. She wasn't used to being stymied, but the old Keystone State's record-keeping had thrown her for a loop.

"Probably a wild-goose chase," Infante said as Nancy

clicked to the map, showing him the location. "But I'll go up there, see what gives, canvass neighbors."

"Thirty years ago. Twenty-four, if she left in 1981 the way she claimed. Does anyone live in the same place that long, anymore?"

"We just need one. Preferably one nosy old busybody with a razor-sharp memory and a photo album."

Kevin headed north, marveling at the steady stream of southbound traffic at midday. Lenhardt lived out this way, and he complained constantly about the drain of commuting. He spoke of it as a kind of war, a battle waged daily. *So why do it?* Infante asked when he tired of the bitching. He got the usual answers: kids, schools, problems that an unencumbered guy didn't know from.

He almost had, though. There'd been a scare, with his first wife. Or so they'd framed the incident in hindsight, when it became apparent that she wasn't pregnant. A scare, a danger averted. He hadn't really felt that way at the time, although he had cause to think of it that way later, when the marriage broke up. He'd been a little hopeful, actually, trying on the role of daddy in his head and feeling it fit pretty well. It was Tabitha who had been worried, fretting over her new job at the mortgage broker's office, wondering what this would do to her plans to do real-estate closings. So they called it a scare, and she became more vigilant about protection. Then she just stopped having sex with him, and he started cheating on her. Which came first had been the chicken-or-the-egg debate at the center of their divorce. The thing that galled Infante was that even when Tabby conceded he was telling the truth, that he hadn't fucked around until she stopped fucking, she refused to grant him cause and effect.

"You have to fight for a marriage!" she screamed at him. "You should have talked to me directly, or asked for counseling, or thought about what might make me feel . . . like a woman again." He'd never been sure about the last part, but he thought it had something to do with foot rubbing, maybe bubble baths and impromptu gifts. "I'm fighting for it now," he had screamed back. "I'm talking to you. I'm sitting here in counseling, which isn't covered under health insurance, by the way."

But it was over, her decision. Everywhere he went, it was the same story with divorce: The women were the ones who really wanted it. True, there were assholes, guys who cared for no one's feelings, who dumped their wives for new models. Yet in Infante's experience, these out-and-out jerks were few and far between. Most of the divorced guys he knew were people like himself, guys who made mistakes but had every intention of staying married. Lenhardt, whose second marriage had made him a bit sanctimonious in the family-happiness department, liked to say that a request for counseling was the first sign that your wife was ready to leave you. "Relationships are chess for women," he said. "They can see the whole board, plan way ahead. They're the queens, after all. We're the kings, limited to one square in any direction, on defense for the whole fucking game."

Infante and his second wife, Patty, hadn't even bothered with counseling. They had gone straight to the mattresses, hiring lawyers they couldn't afford, going into debt over bragging rights to their paltry possessions. Again he had been grateful there were no kids. No student of the Bible—no student of anything— Patty would have carved a kid up even before Solomon offered. Only instead of making a top-to-toe cut, she would have done it at the waist and given Infante the lower half, the one that shit and pissed. And the thing was, he'd *known*. He had stood there in the church— because Patty, while married twice before, was big on celebrating herself—and realized it was a huge mistake. Watching her come down the aisle had been like seeing a truck bear down on him.

The sex had been great, though.

Interstate 83 went to shit the second he crossed into Pennsylvania and the speed limit dropped ten miles. Still, he could see why some Baltimore workers chose to live up here, a good forty miles out, and not just because the taxes were lower. It was pretty in that rolling-fields, amber-waves-of-grain kind of way. He took the first exit and, using the instructions that Nancy had printed out from the Internet, followed a winding road west, then turned northeast. A McDonald's, a Kmart, a Wal-Mart—the area was pretty built up. His tires seemed to hum with worry. What were the odds that forty acres had gone undisturbed in the midst of all this development?

Exactly nil. Although he was clearly in the 13350 block, he drove a few miles past Glen Rock Estates before he doubled back, in hopes that he was wrong. No, the address was now a development, one promising an "exclusive community of executive-style homes on generous lots." In this case "generous" appeared to be defined as between one and two acres, and these "exclusive" homes were two or three years old, judging by the spindly trees and slightly raw landscaping. As for executives—the cars in the driveways spoke more to middle-management types, Subarus and Camrys and Jeep Cherokees. In a truly rich development, there would be a Lexus or two, maybe a Mercedes. Rich people didn't have to move this far out to have family rooms and two-car garages.

As for orchards? Long gone. Assuming they had ever been there.

"Isn't that convenient?" he said aloud to himself, using the intonation from the old *Saturday Night Live* bit. She had been pretty persuasive in her panic about returning here, but now he wondered if she simply didn't want to go to the trouble of acting out her dismay all over again. He wrote down the name of the company that had developed the property. He would check with local police to see if there'd been any bones discovered during the excavation, get Nancy to cross-check it on a Nexis search. Baltimore County and York County might lie next to each other, but it was all too plausible that bones found here wouldn't be matched to any Maryland case, much less a thirty-year-old one involving two missing girls. Again, it wasn't like there was a national database, Bones-R-Us, where you typed in some info and all the missing-persons cases popped up, yours for the asking.

He dialed Nancy's cell.

"Anything?" she asked. "Because I've got—"

"The property's been developed. But I had an idea. Could you check York County for—I don't know how you would phrase it—something like 'York

County' and 'bones,' plug in the street name. If there was a grave, it should have been disturbed when they prepared the lots, right?"

"Oh, you mean a Boolean search."

"Boo-yah what?"

"Never mind. I know what you want. Now, here's what *I* got, sitting comfy at my desk."

Infante thought it would be ungallant to mention what else Nancy was getting, sitting comfy at her desk. Her ass was a lot wider these days. "Yeah?"

"I managed to find the property records. The deed was transferred to Mercer Inc. in 1978, but the previous resident was Stan Dunham. And Dunham was in fact a county police, a sergeant in robbery. Retired in 1974."

A former cop at the time of the girls' disappearance, then, but that distinction wouldn't have been meaningful to a child. Still, it would be slightly easier for the department to stomach. Slightly.

"Is he still alive?"

"In a manner of speaking. His pension checks go to an address out in Carroll County, around Sykesville. It's an assisted-living community. Based on what the people out there told me, he's more assisted than living."

"What's that mean?"

"He was diagnosed with Alzheimer's three years ago. He barely knows who he is, day in and day out. No living relatives, according to the hospital, no one to contact when he goes, but he's got a power of attorney on record."

"Name?"

"Raymond Hertzbach. And he's up in York,

so you might as well try him out before you head back. Sorry."

"Hey, I *like* getting out of the office. I didn't become a police so I could sit at a desk all day."

"Neither did I. But things change."

She sounded just a little bit smug, which wasn't Nancy's way at all. Maybe she had picked up the unvoiced observation about what her work habits were doing to her butt. Fair enough, then.

The highway actually got worse around York, and Kevin was glad that he wasn't subjecting his personal vehicle to the ruts and potholes of Pennsylvania. The lawyer, Hertzbach, appeared very much the big fish in a small pond, the kind of attorney who had a billboard on the interstate and a converted Victorian for his office. Puffy and shiny, he wore a pink shirt and a flowery pink tie, which went nicely with his pink face.

"Stan Dunham came to me about the time he sold the property."

"When was that?"

"Five years ago, I think."

The new owner must have flipped the property fast, probably gotten even more money for it.

"It was a windfall for him, but he had the foresight to realize that he needed to be prepared for the long term. His wife had died—I was under the impression that he wouldn't have sold the land while she was alive—and he told me that he had no children, no heirs. He purchased several insurance products that I recommended—long-term care, a couple of annuities.

Those were handled through someone else here in town, Donald Leonard, friend of mine through Rotary."

And you got a nice kickback, Infante thought.

"Did Dunham ask for any advice on criminal matters?"

Hertzbach found this amusing. "If he did, you know I couldn't comment on it. Confidentiality."

"But it's my understanding that he's now not competent—"

"Yes, he's deteriorated badly."

"And if he dies, there's no one to notify? No next of kin, no friends?"

"Not to my knowledge. But a woman did call me recently, curious about his finances."

Infante's brain almost sang like a teakettle at that detail—a woman, interested in money. "Did she give you a name?"

"I'm sure she did, but I'd have to get my secretary to go over the log, pinpoint the date and the name. She was . . . rather coarse. She wanted to know who was named in his will, if anyone, and how much money he had. Of course, I couldn't have told her that. I asked her what her relationship was to Mr. Dunham, and she hung up on me. I wondered if it was someone from the nursing home itself, who might have tried to inveigle her way into his good graces, back when he was still alert. Given the timing."

"The timing?"

"Mr. Dunham was moved to hospice care in February, which means the facility doesn't expect him to live more than six months."

"He's dying from the dementia? Is that possible?"

"Lung cancer, and he quit smoking when he

217

was forty. I have to say, he's one of the more spectacularly unlucky men I've ever met. Sells his land for a tidy sum, then his health fails him. There's a lesson in that."

"What would that be, exactly?"

Kevin wasn't trying to be a smart-ass, but Hertzbach appeared to be struck dumb by the question. "Why, to . . . I don't know, take advantage of every day," he said at last. "Live life to the fullest."

Thanks for the insight, pal.

He left the office, bumping and bouncing back to the Maryland line, wondering at the coincidence of that telephone call from a woman who, according to the secretary's logs, had identified herself as the oh-so-creative Jane Jones. That call had come in on March 1, not even three weeks earlier. A strange woman, asking questions about an old cop's money. Did she know he was dying? How? Had she been thinking of bringing a civil action against the man? She had to know there was no statute of limitations for her sister's murder.

But also no money in a criminal case.

Again he was struck by how convenient it all was—the old farm, gone, and who knows what had happened to the alleged gravesite? The old man, as good as gone.

As he crossed into Maryland, he fumbled for his cell phone and dialed Willoughby, to ask him if he had ever heard of Dunham, although Lenhardt had been out in the country less than a decade. No answer. He decided to hit Nancy again, see what she had learned.

"Infante," she said. He was still getting used

to the fact that phone calls no longer involved any mystery, that his name popped up on Nancy's screen, identifying him instantly.

"The lawyer had some interesting nuggets, but Dunham's pretty much a dead end at this point. Are you now the leading expert on all things Bethany?"

"Getting there. Managed to find the mom—her old real-estate firm, in Austin, knew how to get in touch with her. No answer and no machine, but Lenhardt's going to keep trying her. Here's the big find, though—"

"We should keep her away, until we know for sure."

"Yeah, but, Infante—"

"I mean, she's going to *want* to believe, so we have to control for that. And we don't want to waste her time if we can discredit her."

"Infante—"

"At the very least, she has to understand that this is not guaranteed, that—"

"Infante, shut up and listen for a second. I took a flier, plugged Penelope Jackson's name into the Nexis newspaper database on a hunch. You didn't do that, right?"

Shit. He hated it when Nancy one-upped him this way. "I did the criminal searches, things like that. And Google, but there were hundreds of hits. The name's too common. Besides, why would I care if she made news some other way?"

"She popped up in an article in some Georgia newspaper"—a pause as Nancy clicked away, looking for what she had stored—"the *Brunswick Times*. Christmas of last year. A man was killed in a fire Christmas Eve, ruled an accident by investigators. His girlfriend, home at the time, was named Penelope Jackson."

"Could be a coincidence."

"Could be," Nancy agreed, her smugness apparent even over the unstable cell phone line. "But the man who was killed? His name was *Tony* Dunham."

"Guy's lawyer said he had no heirs, even five years ago."

"And cops down there were told—by the girlfriend—that there was no next of kin to notify, that Tony's parents were dead. Yet the age works—he was fifty-three when he died, and his Social Security number begins with twenty-one, which indicates it was issued in Maryland. The Dunhams probably lived in Maryland before they moved to Pennsylvania."

"But thirty years ago, he was twenty-three. He might not even have been living at home then." And now dead, dead in an accident. Why did everything dead-end with this case, this woman? That family she sideswiped was lucky to be in as good shape as they were, given her track record. "Hell, he could have been drafted for all we know. You check military records?"

"Not yet," she admitted, and that gave him a small buzz of satisfaction, petty as it was. *I thought of a record you didn't.*

"Where's Brunswick anyway? How do you get there?"

"Sergeant has you booked on a Southwest flight into Jacksonville, leaving at seven. Brunswick is about an hour north. Penelope Jackson worked at a restaurant, Mullet Bay, in some nearby resort called St. Simons Island, but she quit about a month ago.

She might still be in the area, though, but no longer at the same address."

Or she might be in Baltimore, playing some creepy con on them all.

CHAPTER 22

"You sure you'll be fine?"

"Sure," she said, thinking, *Go, go, please go.* "I could even take care of Seth, if he doesn't want to go."

"Great," the boy began, even as Kay said, "No, no, I wouldn't dream of imposing on you like that."

Wouldn't risk it, you mean. But that's okay, Kay. I wouldn't leave a child with me, either. I only offered so you wouldn't find me suspect.

"It is okay if I stay in your house, though, watch television?"

She could tell that Kay didn't want to offer her that much hospitality. Kay didn't trust her, and she was right not to trust her, although she couldn't know that. There was a brief inward struggle, but Kay's sense of fairness ultimately won out. Oh, she loved Kay, who could always be trusted to do the kind thing, the right thing. It would be nice, to be like Kay, but kindness and fairness were luxuries she couldn't afford.

"Of course. And help yourself to anything—"

"After that wonderful dinner?" She patted her stomach. "I couldn't possibly eat another bite."

"Only someone who had been in the hospital for two days could consider Wung Fu's wonderful."

"My family went there for Chinese food. Oh, I know it's not the same place or family. But I remembered it when we drove over there."

A skeptical look from Kay. Was she laying it on too thick, trying too hard? But it was true, this part was true. Perhaps she had gotten to the point where her lies were more believable than her truths. Was that the consequence of living a lie for so long?

"Duck sauce," she said, conscious not to speak too brightly, too rapidly. "I thought it came from a duck the way that milk comes from a cow. I used to think that if we got to the park over in Woodlawn, the one near the Gwynns Falls, early enough in the morning, I would see Chinese people milking the ducks. I imagined them in those straw hats—oh, Lord, we called them coolie hats, I'm afraid. God, we were racists then."

"Why?" asked Seth. She liked him, him and Grace, too, almost in spite of herself. She despised most children, resented them in fact. But there was a sweetness about Kay's kids, a kindness inherited or learned from their mother. They were solicitous of Kay, too, perhaps a by-product of the divorce.

"We didn't know better. And thirty years from now you'll probably be saying the same thing to someone else young, who can't believe the things *you* said and did and wore and thought."

She could tell from Seth's expression that he wasn't persuaded, but he was too polite to contradict her.

His generation was going to get it right, be perfect in every way, unlock every mystery. After all, they had iPods. It seemed to make them think that anything was possible, that they would be able to control life the way they controlled and managed their music, flipping around on a little track wheel. Right, sweetie. It was just one big playlist waiting to be designed, the brave new world of Tivo. What you wanted, when you wanted, all the time.

"We shouldn't be more than an hour," Kay said.

"Don't worry about me." *Or, as Uncle used to say, "Don't go away mad, just go."*

Left alone in the house, she turned on the television in the den and forced herself to sit through some amazingly stupid program for ten minutes. Kids always forgot something, she figured, but after you'd been in the car for ten minutes, the item would have to be critical for a parent to turn back. When the program went into its second commercial break, she turned on the family computer. *No passwords, no passwords, no passwords,* she prayed, and of course there weren't. The poky little Dell was wide open. She would leave tracks, that was unavoidable, but who would think to hunt for them here? Working quickly, she scanned her e-mail via the Web, looking for anything urgent. She then e-mailed her supervisor, explaining that there'd been an accident and a family emergency—true enough, she was her own family—and she'd left town suddenly. She sent it, then immediately quit her e-mail program in case her supervisor was online and fired back a fast reply. Then, although she knew it was risky, she began to type "Heather Bethany" into the Google search engine.

H-e— Two letters in, Google offered her own search back to her. Why, that nosy little Kay. She had been doing quite a bit of extracurricular homework over the past few days. It made her feel better somehow, knowing that Kay wasn't quite so noble and helpful, that she was capable of base curiosity. She scanned the history, curious to see where Kay's searches had taken her, but it was all the obvious places, the basic ones. Kay had gone into the *Beacon-Light* archives but balked at paying the fees. No matter; she had those stories practically memorized. There was the missing-children site, with those eerie aged photographs, the basic facts. And a really creepy blog maintained by some man in Ohio, purporting to have solved the Bethany case. O-kay.

How she wished that Kay, as a social worker, had access to some secret government files, where confidential details were stored. But of course no such place existed, and if it had, she would have found it on her own and hacked her way into it. She had exhausted the available computer resources ages ago.

Reluctantly, she disconnected from the Internet and turned the screen back off. She missed her computer. Until this moment she had never pondered her relationship with it, never acknowledged to herself how many hours a day she spent staring into screens. But this bit of self-knowledge, now that she had it, didn't feel pathetic. Quite the opposite. She liked computers, their logic and tidiness. In the past few years, she had snorted with laughter at all the concern over the Internet, how it could be used to gain access to underage girls and boys, how it increased the reach of child pornography, as if the world had been so safe before computers came along. If her missteps had started with an IM conversation, her parents would have had a chance of catching it. Instead she had been out in the world, talking to somebody one-on-one, and that's where the trouble all began, with a simple conversation, the most innocent conversation that anyone could imagine.

Do you like this song?

What?

Do you like this song?

Yes. She didn't, really. It wasn't at all the kind of song she liked, but the conversation—the conversation was something else, something she hoped would never end. *Yes, I do.*

CHAPTER 23

And, finally, the phone rang.

That's how Miriam would remember the moment. She started creating the memory even as it was happening to her, revising the present in the present. Later she would tell herself that she sensed the momentousness of the call in the dull, flat ring itself, which came as she was setting the table for a supper. But it was really a few seconds later, after a man cleared his throat and began to speak in those strange Baltimore vowel sounds, odd and jarring and yet familiar to her ear after all these years, that she knew.

They had found them.

They had found bodies, and it might be them.

Another lunatic had started babbling in jail, desperate for a deal, or just attention.

They had found them.

Bodies found, them be might it.

Lunatic in jail babbling long shot but hear him out have to.

Them found had they.

Sunny. Heather. Dave dead, poor dead Dave, not here for the end of the story. Or was he lucky Dave, spared from hearing a truth that he could never quite admit to himself?

They had found them.

"Miriam Bethany?" It was the "Bethany" that gave it away. There was only one context in which she remained Miriam Bethany.

"Yes?"

"My name is Harold Lenhardt, and I'm a sergeant with the Baltimore County Police Department."

Found them, found them, found them.

"A few days ago, a woman was in a car accident, and when police came to the scene, she said—"

Lunatic, lunatic, another fucking lunatic. Another crazy, indifferent to the pain and hurt she was causing.

"That she's your daughter. The younger one, Heather. She says she's your daughter."

And Miriam's mind exploded.

PHONEMATES (1983)

CHAPTER 24

The telephone rang at 6:30 A.M. and Dave grabbed the receiver without thinking. He knew better. Just last week, in anticipation of this annual call, he had purchased a PhoneMate answering machine at Wilson's, the catalog store on Security Boulevard. They supposedly had lower prices, although Dave could never tell for sure, because he didn't have the patience to comparison-shop. Still, as a fellow retailer, albeit on a much smaller scale, he was interested in how the store reduced overhead by keeping salespeople to a minimum and not stocking inventory on the floor. Shoppers jotted down the codes of the items they wanted, stood in one line to pick them up, another to purchase. Perhaps the trick was that such an onerous system simply made people *believe* they were getting a deal. All the waiting in line—it had to pay off somehow, right? The Soviets lined up for toilet paper, Americans queued for PhoneMates and WaterPiks and fourteen-karat-gold necklaces.

Answering machines were new, a technology that had caught fire in the wake of the AT&T breakup, and now suddenly everyone was getting them—recording silly messages, performing skits, even singing in some cases. It turned out that the United States was a desperately lonely place, where everyone had been worrying that a single missed phone call might change one's destiny. The old Dave, the *before* Dave, would have gone as long as possible before succumbing to a gadget such as this, if ever. But there was always the chance that someone might call once and never call again. And then there were the calls you didn't want to take, and the machine allowed you to listen to those, decide for yourself if you wanted to talk to the real person. Dave hadn't worked out the etiquette of that yet—once you revealed to someone that you had eavesdropped on the incoming message, how could you ever fail to take that person's call again? Or did you just pretend that you weren't there? Maybe it would be better *never* to answer. It had taken him almost three hours to come up with his outgoing message. *"This is Dave Bethany, and I'm not at home now—"* Not necessarily true, and he didn't like to lie, even to strangers, much less encourage burglars. *"You have reached the Bethany household—"* But there was no Bethany household, just a single Bethany in an increasingly neglected house, where nothing was broken, but nothing really worked as it should. *"This is Dave. Leave your message at the beep."* Unoriginal, but it got the job done.

The PhoneMate was set to ring four times before it answered, and Dave, groggy from the dreamless sleep that he now considered a blessing, reached out blindly and grabbed the receiver. At the split second he lifted it to his ear, he remembered the date, the very reason he'd made a point of purchasing the PhoneMate. Too late.

"I know where they are," said a man's voice, raspy and thin.

"Fuck you," Dave said, slamming down the phone, but not before he registered the sound of a fist, furiously working.

These calls had started four years earlier and were always the same, at least in the way they were worded. The voice sounded different from year to year, and Dave had figured out that the annual caller suffered from allergies, which affected the timbre. Did the obscene caller sound hoarse this year? Spring must be precocious, pollen already in the air. The guy was his personal groundhog. His *PhoneMate*.

Dutifully, Dave recorded the date, time, and content of the call on the pad he kept by the telephone. Detective Willoughby said he should report everything, even hang-up calls, but although Dave kept a record, he had never confided in Willoughby about this particular rite of spring. "Let us decide what's important," Willoughby had told him many times over the last eight years, but Dave couldn't live that way. He needed to make distinctions, if only for his own sanity. Hope was an impossible emotion to live with, he was finding out, a demanding and abusive companion. Emily Dickinson had called it the thing with feathers, but her hope was small and dainty, a friendly presence perched inside the rib cage. The hope that Dave Bethany knew also had feathers, but it was more of a griffin, with glinting eyes and sharp talons. *Claws,* he corrected himself. The griffin had the head of an eagle but the body of a lion. Dave Bethany's version of hope sat on his chest, working its claws in and out, piercing the meaty surface of his heart.

He didn't need to leave bed for at least another hour, but it was useless to try to return to sleep. He got up, shuffled out to grab the newspaper, and started boiling water for his coffee. Dave had always insisted on using a Chemex for coffee, no matter how Miriam wheedled for an electric maker, which had become all the rage when Joe DiMaggio started pitching them. Now the food-obsessed, a decadent class in Dave's opinion, were returning to the old ways of making coffee, although they ground their beans in little domed machines that whirred with pompous ceremony, oversize dildos for the gourmet fetishist. *See,* he said to his invisible breakfast partner as he poured the steaming water over the grounds. *I told you everything comes around again.*

He had never broken the habit of speaking to Miriam over breakfast. In fact, he enjoyed it more since she'd left, for there were no contradictions, no teasing or doubt. He held forth, and Miriam silently agreed with everything he said. He couldn't imagine a more satisfactory arrangement.

He scanned the *Beacon*'s local section. No mention of the date's significance, but that was to be expected. There'd been a story at one year, again at two years, but nothing after that. It had puzzled him, when year five came and went without any acknowledgment. When would his daughters matter again? At ten years, at twenty? At their silver anniversary, or their gold?

"The media's done what it can," Willoughby had

said just last month as they watched crews digging holes on an old farm out toward Finksburg.

"Still, if only from a historical standpoint, the fact that it happened . . ." The countryside was beautiful here. Why had he never come to Finksburg before, seen how beautiful it was despite its bum name? But the highway had been extended to this part of the county only recently. Before the road construction, it would have been impossible to live here and work in town.

"At this point it's going to come down to an arrest," Willoughby had said as the day wore on and more holes were dug, and the detective gave up on the enterprise in progress. "Someone who knows something and will want to use it as a bartering chip. Or perhaps the guy himself. I wouldn't be surprised if he's already in custody for another crime. There are lots of unsolved cases that have gotten all the publicity in the world—Etan Patz, Adam Walsh."

"They came *after*," Dave said, as if this were an issue of primogeniture. "And Adam Walsh's parents at least have a body."

"They have a head," Willoughby said, his pedantic nature coming to the fore. "They never found the body."

"You know what? I'd kill for a head at this point."

The call about that Finksburg farm had been so promising. For one thing, it had come from a woman, and while women in general were no more sane than men, they did not have the kind of craziness that sought release in taunting the family of two presumed murder victims. Besides, this was a neighbor, a woman who had provided her full name. A man named Lyman Tanner had moved to the area in the spring of 1975, just before the girls disappeared. She recalled him washing his car very early on Easter Sunday, the day after the girls disappeared, which struck her as odd, because rain was in the forecast.

She had been asked, Willoughby reported back to Dave, why she would remember such a detail eight years later.

"Simple," said the woman, Yvonne Yepletsky. "I'm Orthodox—Romanian Orthodox, but I go to the Greek Orthodox church downtown, like most of the Romanian Orthodox. On our calendar Easter falls on a different day, and my mother used to say it always rains on *their* Easter. And sure enough it usually does."

Still, the oddness of that car wash did not come back to her until a few months ago, when Lyman Tanner died and left his farm to some distant relatives. Yvonne Yepletsky remembered then that her neighbor had worked at Social Security, so close to the mall, and that he had seemed unusually interested in her own daughters, young teenagers when he first moved in next door. He hadn't even minded the old graveyard bordering his property, which had deterred so many other buyers.

"And he made a big to-do about putting in crops, rented a tractor and all to till up the field, but then he never done nothing with it," Mrs. Yepletsky said.

The Baltimore County Police Department hired a bulldozer.

The crew was on its twelfth hole when another neighbor helpfully informed them that Mrs. Yepletsky was disgruntled because her husband wanted to buy the land and Tanner's heirs wouldn't sell. The Yepletskys weren't liars, not quite. They had come to believe the stories they told about Tanner. A man whose heirs wouldn't sell to you for a good price—why, he must be odd. *He had washed his car when rain was in the forecast. Wasn't that about the time those girls had disappeared? He musta done it.* Hope, which had moved to Dave's shoulder for all of a week, settled back on his chest, kneading its claws in and out.

Given that his breakfast consisted solely of black coffee, Dave required only twenty minutes to finish it and the paper, rinse out his cup, and head upstairs to get dressed. It was barely 7:00 A.M. Three hundred and sixty-four days of the year, he kept his daughters' bedroom doors closed, but he always opened them on this day, allowed himself a little tour. He felt not unlike Bluebeard in reverse. If a woman were to join him in this house—unimaginable to him, but theoretically possible—he would forbid her to enter these rooms. She would, of course, defy him and sneak in behind his back. But instead of discovering the corpses of his previous wives, she would find preserved time capsules of two girls' lives, April 1975.

In Heather's pink-and-white room, Max of *Where the Wild Things Are* circled the world, found the island of the wild things, yet still made it home in time for supper. A few teen idols had crept onto the walls beneath Max, toothy boys all, indistinguishable to Dave's eyes. Next door, Sunny's room was very much a teenager's room, with only one trace of childhood left: a wall hanging, her sixth-grade marine-biology project, for which she had laboriously constructed an underwater scene in cross-stitch. She'd gotten an A for that project, but only after the teacher had interrogated

Miriam at length, not trusting that Sunny had done this on her own. How angry Dave had been that someone would doubt his daughter's talent, her word.

One might expect that the rooms, shut up and untouched, would get dirty and musty, yet Dave found them startlingly fresh and alive. It was reasonable, sitting on the beds in these rooms—and this morning he tried out the beds in both, bold as Goldilocks—to imagine that their owners would return by nightfall. Even the police, who had briefly considered the possibility that the girls were runaways, had conceded that these rooms showed that the occupants expected to return. True, it was odd that Heather had taken all her money to the mall, but perhaps that had been the source of the trouble. There were people who might hurt a child for forty dollars, and the money was not in her purse when it was found.

Of course, the moment the police ruled out the fact that the girls had left on their own, it was Dave's turn to be the suspect. To this day Willoughby had never acknowledged, much less apologized for, the unfairness and awkwardness of that inquiry, or the vital hours that had been lost in this misdirection. Dave subsequently learned that family members were always suspect in such cases, but the specifics of his life—the crumbling marriage, the failing shop, the college trust funds started by Miriam's parents—had made the accusation specifically heinous. "You think I killed my children for money?" he asked, all but lunging at Willoughby. The detective hadn't taken it personally. "I'm not thinking anything just yet," he said with a shrug. "There are questions, and I'm getting answers. That's all."

To this day Dave wasn't sure what was worse: being suspected of a financial motive in his daughters' deaths or being accused of killing them to get back at his philandering spouse. Miriam had acted as if she were so noble, spilling her secret to the cops so quickly, but her secret had also provided the perfect alibi for her *and* her lover. "What if they did it?" Dave asked the police. "What if they did it and framed me, so they could run off together?" But not even he believed that scenario.

He didn't mind so much that Miriam had left him, but he lost all respect for her when she left Baltimore as well. She had abandoned the vigil. She was not strong enough to live with the kneading, needling hope and the impossible possibilities it whispered in his ear. "They're dead, Dave," Miriam said the last time they spoke, over two years ago. "The only thing we have to look forward to is the official discovery of what we know is true. The only thing to cling to is that it's less horrific than we've dared to imagine. That someone took them and shot them, or killed them in a way that involved no suffering. That they weren't sexually assaulted, that—"

"Shut up, shut up, shut up, SHUT UP!" Those were almost the last words he ever spoke to Miriam. But neither one of them wanted that. He apologized and she apologized, and *those* were their last words. Miriam, who had always loved new things, had gotten an answering machine last year. He called sometimes and listened to her outgoing message, but he never left one. He wondered if Miriam listened in on her messages, if she would pick up if she heard his voice on the machine. Probably not.

239

Under Maryland law he could have petitioned as early as 1981 to have the girls presumed legally dead, a judicial finding that would have freed the money in their college accounts. But he had no interest in their money, less interest still in having a court codify his worst fears. He let the money languish. That would show everyone.

Perhaps a kindly family stole them, the hope-griffin whispered in his ear. *A kindly family in the Peace Corps, who whisked them off to Africa. Or they met up with a band of free spirits, younger versions of Kesey and his gang, and hit the road together, doing exactly what you might have done, if you didn't have children.*

Why don't they call, then?

Because they hate you.

Why?

Because kids hate their parents. You hated yours. When was the last time you called your mother? Long distance doesn't cost that much.

Still, are those my only choices? Alive but so filled with hatred for me that they refuse to call? Or full of love for me but dead?

No, those aren't the only choices. There's also the possibility that they're chained in some sicko's basement where—

Shut up, shut up, shut up, SHUT UP.

Finally it was time to head to the Blue Guitar. The store wouldn't open for another three hours, but there was plenty to do before then. Of all the ironies in his life, this one was the most painful. The store had thrived in the wake of the publicity about his daughters. Initially, people had come to gawk at the grieving father, only to find the efficient and empathetic Miss Wanda from the bakery. She had volunteered her time, insisting that Dave would not only want to return to work eventually but that he would *need* to return to work. The gawkers turned into shoppers, and word of mouth for the store was so strong that his business grew beyond his modest dreams. He had actually expanded, adding a line of clothing and small housewares—drawer pulls, decorative wall plates. And the things he imported from Mexico were very hot just now. The carved rabbit that Mrs. Baumgarten had disdained, the one she couldn't imagine paying thirty dollars for? A San Francisco museum that was opening a folk-art wing had offered to pay Dave a thousand dollars for it, recognizing it for the valuable piece it was—an early, less self-conscious piece by one of the Oaxacan masters. He had loaned it to the inaugural exhibit instead.

He stopped on the front porch, drinking in the light. With the trees still relatively bare and the world on standard time for a few more weeks, the mornings had a bittersweet clarity. Most people welcomed daylight savings, but Dave had always thought it a poor trade-off, losing these mornings so you could have extra light at the end of the day. Morning was the last time he'd been happy. Sort of. He'd been *trying* to be happy that morning, focusing on the girls because he knew that Miriam was up to something—he just wasn't ready to confront what it was. He'd been trying to distract himself, playing the superattentive dad, and Heather had bought it, believed in it. Sunny—Sunny hadn't been fooled. She'd known he wasn't really present, that he was lost in his own thoughts. If only he'd stayed there, if he hadn't snapped to and insisted that Sunny take Heather with her. If only— But what was he arguing for? One dead daughter instead of two? That was *Sophie's Choice,* not that Dave could bear to read the book, although Styron's *The Confessions of Nat Turner* had been a great favorite of his. Styron needed the Holocaust to explain the worst thing that could happen to a parent. The thing was—it still wasn't big enough. Six million dead meant nothing when you had lost your own child.

He got into the old VW van, another relic he couldn't let go of, another piece of his Miss Havisham existence. Hope hopped into the passenger seat, the old vinyl shredding and cracking beneath its always-working claws. The griffin turned its bile-colored eyes on Dave, and reminded him to fasten his seat belt.

Who cares if I live or die?

No one, Hope admitted. *But when you die, who will remember them? Miriam? Willoughby? Their old classmates, some of whom have graduated college by now? You're all they have, Dave. Without you, they truly are gone.*

CHAPTER 25

Miriam had a secret love—butter pecan yogurt from I Can't Believe It's Yogurt. She could, in fact, believe it was yogurt. She further believed that it wasn't quite the health food that others seemed to think, and that its calories counted as much as any other calories. Miriam wasn't deceived by any of the promises made by I Can't Believe It's Yogurt, real or implied. But she liked it, and she was sorely tempted to take a small detour right now and buy some. The day was warm, summer-hot by her standards if not by Texas ones, hot enough to make an afternoon at Barton Springs seem eminently reasonable. Miriam thought about taking the afternoon off and doing just that, or going all the way out to the lake, but she had two appointments with prospective sellers in the Clarksville section.

Still, it worried her that she'd considered, even for a moment, driving over to the public swimming area. She had really settled in here. If she didn't watch it, she'd soon be joining the local chorus of "But you should have lived here when—" The endless lament about how hip, how happy, how affordable Austin used to be. Then there was the invocation of the places that used to exist—the Armadillo, the Liberty Lunch. Look at Guadalupe Street, the Drag, where she couldn't find a parking spot today. She'd have to forgo the yogurt and continue on to her appointment.

A shiver ran through her, and she worked backward through her thoughts to find what was making her feel anxious. Parking—Austin—Barton Springs—*lake*. There had been a murder at the lake last fall, two girls, found on a lot where an expensive new house was under construction. Two girls—not sisters, but the mere configuration demanded her attention—and no possible motive that anyone could discern. Miriam, more expert than others in reading between the lines of news accounts, understood that the police really did have no information, but her friends had inferred all sorts of strange conspiracies from the barest of facts. Trained by television, they kept expecting it to turn into a *story,* something explicable and—although her earnest Austin friends would never use this word— *satisfying.* To them, obsessed with the way Austin was changing—mutating, the old-timers said; growing and progressing, according to the newcomers who had staked their fortunes on this booming city—the murders must somehow be rooted in the phenomenon of growth. The girls were locals, biker chicks of a sort, from families who had lived in the area before it was desirable. According to news reports, they had long used this cove off Lake Travis for partying with their friends and saw no reason to stop simply because a house was going up. It seemed to Miriam that the girls were most likely killed by their own surly acquaintances, but police had interviewed the lot's owner and the various workmen from the site.

In focusing on the clash between old and new, progress and status quo, Miriam's Austin friends didn't realize that they were really arguing for their own connection to the crime, that they were trying to take an isolated horror and make it—loathsome word—relatable. Which was, of course, the one thing it could never be, not in liberal Austin. Austin was so sweetly, reliably liberal that Miriam was beginning to wonder just how liberal she really was.

Take the death penalty, which had resumed in Texas the year before. There was much discussion among her coworkers and neighbors about how shameful this was, how unbecomingly eager Texas was to put men to death now that Utah had led the way, although only one man had been executed so far. Miriam never joined in these discussions, because she was afraid that she would find herself arguing heatedly for it, which could lead to the trump card of personal experience, something she never wanted to lay on the table. Since her arrival in Texas seven years earlier, she had been allowed the luxury of not being the martyred mother, poor sad Miriam Bethany. She was, in fact, no longer Miriam Bethany. She was Miriam Toles. Even if someone were to know of the Bethany girls, if the names were to come up in the endless speculating about the double murders at Lake Travis, no one would make the connection. She had even glossed over the Baltimore part of her past. *Bad marriage, didn't work out, no children, thank God, originally from Ottawa, much prefer the climate here.* That was what people knew about her.

There had been moments—wine-soaked or pot-infused camaraderie, usually late at night—when Miriam flirted with the idea of confiding in someone. Never a man, because although she found it remarkably easy to meet and bed men, she did not want a boyfriend of any stripe, and that kind of revelation might inspire a man to take her seriously. But she had made female friends, including one, Rose, who hinted at her own secrets. An anthropology student at thirty-seven—Austin was filled with people who seemed determined to spend their lives as students—she had stayed late after a party, taking Miriam up on her offer to get into the backyard hot tub. As they worked through a bottle of wine, she began to speak of a remote village in Belize where she'd lived for several years. "It was surreal," she said. "After living there I'm not so sure that magical realism is a literary style. I just think those guys are writing the truth." Rape was alluded to, vaguely, but all the personal pronouns seemed to drop from Rose's speech, and it was impossible to know if she was the victim or a bystander who had failed to act. She and Miriam danced around the flames of their respective pasts, each casting beautiful shadows that allowed the other to draw whatever conclusions she wished. But they hadn't gotten so personal again, much to Miriam's relief, and possibly to Rose's. In fact, they had barely seen each other at all.

At the next stoplight, Miriam flipped open her Filofax in the passenger seat and glanced at the address for the first appointment. A man on the street stared at her, and she had an awareness of herself as a self-made woman, although not in the usual sense of the phrase. True, she had done well financially, starting with very little here. The camel-colored Filofax, the Joan Vass knits and shoes, the air-conditioned Saab—these details allowed her to broadcast her success in an Austin-appropriate way. But Miriam was more interested in the creation of this different person, Miriam Toles, who was allowed to move through her days without tragedy tugging visibly at everything she did. It was hard enough to be Miriam Bethany on the inside. Miriam Toles was the candy-coated shell, the thin layer that kept all the messy stuff inside, just barely.

"They do melt," Heather had complained, showing her mother a palm smeared with orange, yellow, red, and green. "How can they lie like that?"

"All commercials lie," said Sunny, a sage at eleven. "Remember when we ordered the one hundred dolls from the back of the Millie the Model comic, and they were so teensy?" She held her fingers apart to show how small the dolls were, how large the lie.

Her car still idling at the light, Miriam's eyes fell on the date: March 29. The day. That day. It was the first time she had ever managed to ease into it without an overweening awareness, the first time that she had not gone to sleep dreading the so-called anniversary, the first time she had not awakened bathed in the sweat of vicious nightmares. It helped that Austin springs were so different, that it was verging on hot by late March. It helped that Easter had come and gone, early again. Easter was usually the sign that she'd passed into what she thought of as the safe season. If they were alive—oh Lord, if they were alive, Sunny would be twenty-three, Heather verging on twenty.

But they weren't alive. If she was sure of anything, it was that fact.

A honk, then another and another, and Miriam lurched forward almost blindly. She was trying to think of reasons that Sunny and Heather would be glad they weren't here. The Reagan presidency? But she doubted that either girl would have sacrificed her life to avoid that. Music was actually better, to Miriam's middle-aged ears, and she liked the clothes as well, the merger between comfort and fashion, at least in some of the lines. They would have liked Austin, too, even if the locals thought it had been ruined, ruined, ruined. They could have gone to college here cheaply, hung out at the clubs, eaten burgers at Mad Dog & Beans, tasted migas at Las Mañanitas, slurped frozen margaritas at Jorge's, shopped at Whole Foods, which managed the trick of being simultaneously organic (millet in bulk) and decadent (five different kinds of brie). Sunny and Heather, grown, would have shared her sense of humor, Miriam decided now, joined in her awareness of how absurd Austin was at moments, how precious. They could have lived here.

And died here. People died here, too. They got murdered at construction sites. They were killed in boozy car accidents on the twisty farm-to-market roads in the Hill Country. They drowned in the Memorial Day weekend flood of 1981, when water had risen so fast and furiously, turning streets into treacherous rivers.

Miriam secretly believed—or secretly rationalized—

that it was her daughters' destiny to be murdered, that if she could go back in time and change the circumstances of that day, all she would do was postpone and reconfigure the tragedy. Her daughters had been marked at birth, imprinted with a fate Miriam could not control. That was the one oddity about being an adoptive parent, the sense that there were biological factors she could never control. At the time she had thought it was healthy, that she had given in to a reality that biological parents—never "natural," although even in well-intentioned Austin one still heard that tactless expression—that biological parents found it harder to accept. She could not control everything when it came to her children.

Of course, she had the advantage of knowing part of Sunny and Heather's family, their maternal grandparents, Estelle and Herb Turner. How guilty Miriam had felt about her unkind first impression of them when she learned their whole story—the beautiful daughter, Sally, who had run away at age seventeen to marry a man of whom her parents didn't approve, then refused their help until it was much too late. This would have been 1959, when elopement was still presented as a comic adventure—the ladder at the window, the young couple always caught, only to win the parents' blessing in the end. This was when married couples on television slept in twin beds and sex was so hidden that young people must have felt as if they were going to explode with the feelings and sensations that no one ever discussed. Miriam knew. Miriam remembered. She wasn't that much older than Sally Turner.

She had pieced the rest together on her own—the

loutish, brutish beau of a different social class, the Turners' objections, which Sally had written off as snobbery but had really been a parent's unerring instinct. Having run away and married her bad boy, Sally must have been proud, too proud to call her parents and ask for help as the marriage became increasingly violent. Sunny had just turned three, and Heather was an infant when their father shot their mother, then killed himself. The Turners discovered almost simultaneously that their daughter was dead and that they had two grandchildren who needed someone to care for them.

Unfortunately, they had learned a month earlier that Estelle had liver cancer.

It had been Dave's idea to volunteer to adopt the children, and while Miriam had doubts about his motives—she thought Dave was more interested in the bond it would establish with Estelle than the girls themselves—she had been eager to do it. Only twenty-five, she had already miscarried three times. Here were two beautiful girls, ready for them, girls that would not require a drawn-out adoption process. The Turners, as the girls' guardians—the girls' only family, as far as anyone knew, a fact that would be verified years later, when Detective Willoughby tried to ascertain if their dead father had any relatives—could assign guardianship to the Bethanys. It had been simple. And, cruel as it may sound, Miriam was relieved when Estelle finally died and Herb drifted away, as they all had known he would. The girls reminded him too much of his lost wife and daughter. Grateful as Miriam was for his decampment, she despised him for it, too. What kind of man wouldn't want to be part of his granddaughters' lives? Even now that she knew the whole story, she still couldn't get past her initial dislike of the Turners, Herb's uxorious regard for Estelle, his inability to love or care about anyone else. It was likely that Sally had run away because there was no room for her in that beautiful Sudbrook home, filled as it was with Herb's excessive love for Estelle.

The girls never learned the entire story. They knew they were adopted, of course, although Heather had always refused to believe it, even as Sunny pretended to greater memories than she could possibly have. ("We had a house in Nevada," she would announce to Heather. "A house with a fence. And a pony!") But even let's-be-honest, let-it-all-hang-out Dave could not bear to tell the girls the complete truth— the young runaways, their biological father's deadly rage, the loss of two lives because Sally could not bear to pick up the phone and ask her parents for help to get away from the husband they had disapproved of from the start. Miriam had been of the opinion that the girls should never be told everything, while Dave thought it would mark their passage into adulthood, at age eighteen or so.

But she had been even more uncomfortable with the gentle fantasy Dave created for the girls in the interim.

"Tell me about my other mommy," Sunny or Heather would say at bedtime.

"Well, she was beautiful—"

"Do I look like her?"

"Yes, exactly." They did. Miriam had seen the photos in the Turners' home. Sally had the same flyaway blond hair, the small-boned frame. "She was beautiful and she married a man and went away to live. But there was an accident—"

"A car accident?"

"Something like that."

"What was it?"

"Yes, a car accident. They died in a car accident."

"Were we there?"

"No." But they had been. That part worried Miriam. The girls had been found in the house, Heather in a crib, Sunny in a playpen. They were in a different room, but what had they seen, what had they heard? What if Sunny remembered something that was more real than Nevada and a house and a pony?

"Where were we?"

"At home with a baby-sitter."

"What was her name?"

And Dave would keep going, making up details until it was simply the most colossal lie that Miriam had ever heard. "We'll tell them the truth when they're eighteen," he said.

To think that the truth could be assigned an age, as if it were beer or the right to vote. Oh, what busy but inexpert beavers Dave and Miriam had been, slapping together makeshift dams against all their secrets, trying to stem the trickle of a mere creek when an earthquake lay in wait for them. In the end all their lies had been released into the world, only to go unnoticed, because who would take note of such puny things in a postapocalyptic world, when so much debris was lying around? On the day that Estelle and Herb Turner came to them seeking their help, Miriam had thought she was providing a fresh start for two innocents. But in the end it was the girls who gave her the chance to reinvent herself. And when they were gone, she had lost that part of herself as well.

Fuck it, she thought, making an erratic and illegal left turn, *I will go to Barton Springs*. But she turned back to her original route a block later. The Austin real-estate market was beginning to slow. She couldn't risk losing a single client.

CHAPTER 26

"You think faster than the cash register," said Randy, the Swiss Colony manager.

"Excuse me?"

"The new cash register calculates change, does all the thinking for you. But you don't let it, I can tell. You're a step ahead, Sylvia."

"Syl," she said, pulling at the sleeves of the Swiss Miss outfit they were forced to wear, complete with dirndl and puffy sleeves. The girls all hated the low-cut necklines, which exposed their breasts as they leaned over to fetch cheese and sausage from the cases. In winter they wore turtlenecks beneath their dresses, though now, with April almost here, it was hard to justify the turtlenecks. "It's Syl, not Sylvia."

"But you can't wrap for shit," he said. "I've never seen anyone get more lost in a roll of plastic wrap. And you don't suggestive-sell. If they buy the summer sausage, you gotta push the mustard.

If they want the small gift basket, you gotta suggest a larger one."

We don't get commissions, she wanted to say, but she knew it was the wrong thing. She pulled up the right sleeve and the left one slid down, pulled up the left and the right slid down. Fine, let Randy look at her shoulder.

"Don't you need this job, Sylvia?"

"Syl," she said. "It's short for Priscilla, not Sylvia." She was trying to make the new name her own. She was Priscilla Browne now, twenty-two according to the documents she carried—a birth certificate, a Social Security card, and a state ID card, but no driver's license.

"You're kinda spoiled, aren't you?"

"Excuse me?"

"You didn't have a lot of work experience. You said you weren't allowed to work in high school, and here you are . . . what?"—he glanced at the sheet in front of him—"in Fairfax Community College? A daddy's girl, huh?"

"What?"

"He gave you a nice allowance, you didn't have to work. Spoiled you."

"I guess so." Oh, yes, he definitely *spoiled* me.

"Well, things are slow now. Been slow since Christmas, you want to know. So I have to thin things out. . . ."

He looked at her expectantly, one of the moments that she dreaded. Since forced out on her own, she had been thrust into this situation again and again, trying to converse in what she thought of as the dialect of "normal." The words were more or less the same as the language she knew, but she had trouble following the meanings. When someone left a sentence open-ended, expecting her to fill it in, she was afraid her response would be so off the charts that she would be automatically suspect. Right now, for example, she wanted to provide ". . . and introduce a line of low-calorie foods." But that clearly wasn't what Randy meant by thinning things out. He meant— Oh, shit, she was getting fired. Again.

"You're not a people person," he said. "You're bright, but you shouldn't be in sales."

"I didn't know I *was* in sales," she said, her eyes brimming.

"You're a salesgirl," he said. "That's the job title. Salesgirl."

"I could do better . . . with the selling and the wrapping. I could—" She looked up at Randy through her wet lashes and abandoned the plea. He wasn't someone she could sway. Her instincts on this were unerring. "Is this effective as of today? Or do I have to work the rest of my scheduled hours?"

"That's your call," he said. "You want your last four hours on the clock, they're yours. You don't work 'em, you don't get paid."

She considered, for all of a second, stripping out of the costume and marching off in her underwear. She'd seen an actress do that in a movie once, and it had been very effective. But there was no one here to cheer her liberation. The mall was empty at this time of day, which was part of the problem. Even a conscientious, gung-ho salesgirl couldn't sell cheese to people who weren't there. Someone on the staff had to be let go, and she was the right one—the last hired, the least competent, the most sulky. She didn't suggestive-sell. If anything, she tried to talk people out of purchases, especially the stinkier cheeses, because she could barely wrap them without wanting to throw up.

This was the second job she had lost in the last eight months, and for the same reasons. Not a people person. Not a self-starter. Showed no initiative. She wanted to argue that minimum-wage jobs such as this shouldn't require initiative. She knew how to live inside an hour, how to weather the slow passing of time. She could endure boredom better than anyone she knew. Wasn't that enough? Apparently not.

She had figured out during the job interview last November, when they were taking people on for the Christmas rush, that Randy would not be kindly inclined toward her. She didn't engage his protective juices. He was gay, but that wasn't the reason. She didn't use sex if she could avoid it. No, there were some people who responded to her and some who didn't, and she had long ago ceased trying to figure out why. It mattered only that she identify those she could manipulate, if needed. In his own way, Uncle had wanted to take care of her, while Auntie had loathed her. People seemed to make up their minds about her in the first minute they met her, and there was no changing them.

"You know what?" she said to Randy. "I don't want to work today if I'm fired. I'll come in for my final paycheck on Friday, and you can have the dress then."

"You won't get paid," he said.

"Right, you said that." She turned her back on him and fluffed out the full red skirt.

"Dry-cleaned," he called after her. "Those dresses should be dry-cleaned."

She walked out into the mall, a sad, run-down place that had lost much of its business to Tysons Corner, the newer and shinier mall to the west. But this one was convenient to the Metro, which was why she had chosen to work there. She didn't have a car. In fact, she didn't know how to drive. It was one thing that Uncle wouldn't teach her. And by the time they both agreed that leaving was the only recourse open to her, there wasn't time to learn. Even when she was working steady, she couldn't imagine parting with the money to go to driving school. She'd just have to continue to live in places with public transportation or find someone who would teach her. She thought about the kind of relationship that would be required if someone was going to teach her to drive and grimaced. It wasn't that she never felt any natural impulse for sex. She had liked looking at Mel Gibson, in that movie called *The Road Warrior*. In fact, she thought that was a world she could negotiate pretty well, if she had to, a place with one commodity and everyone for himself. Or herself. The problem was that sex had been something she used to keep herself safe, a defensive posture. *Okay, okay, I'll do it, don't hurt me again.* It was a currency to her now, and she didn't know how to change it back. If Randy had been straight, for example, she'd probably be on her knees in front of him right now, although that was a last-ditch thing for her. The better play was to promise it and seldom deliver. That had worked on her boss in Chicago, at the pizza restaurant. Until his wife came in that day.

When Uncle gave her five thousand dollars and a

new name, she thought she would end up in a city. Cities allowed for more anonymity, yet the crush of people and buildings would make her feel safe. She'd chosen San Francisco—Oakland, really—but it had been a poor fit for her. Gradually, almost without realizing it, she headed back east by fits and starts. Phoenix, Albuquerque, Wichita, Chicago again. Finally she ended up in northern Virginia, in Arlington, which had the density and energy of a city, but the added bonus of transience, with people coming and going often enough that no one forced friendship on you. She lived in Crystal City, a name she found hilarious. It sounded so fake, a location in a science-fiction film. Baltimore was not even fifty miles away, Glen Rock another thirty, but the Potomac River seemed as wide and nonnavigable to her as an ocean, a continent, a galaxy. She even avoided the District proper.

She sat on a bench in the desolate mall, bunching her voluminous skirt around her hips, then flattening it out, only to see it spring back to life. Mall—now, that was a language she spoke. There was a comforting sameness to them, wherever one went. Some were glossy and high-end, pulsing with energy, while others, like this one, were a little sad, shot through with a sense of abandonment. But certain things were universal—the overly sweet cookie and cinnamon smells that hung in the air, the scent of new clothes, the perfume counters at the department stores.

She wandered down to the video arcade, a place she had spent her breaks. She played the kiddie games—Ms. Pac-Man and Frogger—and she was getting very good at them, good enough so that she could finance an hour with nothing more than a dollar or two. She was beginning to see patterns in the games, how finite the possibilities were. At this time of day, a few hours before school would let out, she was virtually alone in the arcade, and she was sure she looked odd, a young woman in a Swiss Miss outfit yanking on the joystick so some yellow blob could gobble up dots. She got far enough into Ms. Pac-Man today to see the meeting and the chase, but she used up her last life before the baby Pac arrived in its carriage. She seldom made it to Baby Pac on this machine. It was programmed a hair fast, and it cheated you on the invincibility portion of the game, where every millisecond counted.

She used her last quarter to buy the *Washington Star,* and she read the want ads on the Metro, sneaking her hand into her purse to eat a few contraband M&M's. Eating and drinking were strictly prohibited on the Metro, and she liked circumventing stupid rules. She reasoned it kept her in practice for when she really needed to cheat at something. She wished she could outthink the fare system as well, which charged different prices according to the routes traveled and required a ticket to exit. Jumping a turnstile would never be her style, but there had to be a way around the fares, which weren't exactly cheap.

She had not planned to be this way. Sneaky, that is. Arguably, she didn't need to be this way anymore. She had a new name and therefore a new life. "A blank slate," Uncle had promised her. "A chance to start over, with no one bothering you. You can be whatever you want to be. And I'll always be here for you if you really, really need me." She couldn't imagine needing him. She hoped never to see him again. She brought her hands up to her face but dropped them quickly. They smelled of plastic and cheese. She hadn't even worked her shift, and still she smelled of plastic and cheese.

Back home in her studio apartment, she took the dress down to the basement laundry room. Despite what Randy said, it didn't have to be dry-cleaned. He was full of shit. But she left it in on high for an hour, forgetting how strong these apartment machines were, and it had shrunk several sizes—it would fit a twelve-year-old maybe, or a midget. Randy would probably use that as an excuse not to cut her final check, then make some poor girl wear it anyway, so the male customers could get a little thrill while buying their stupid cheese. Fuck him. She threw the dress in the trash can and went upstairs to do her homework. She owed a paper in her statistics class, but the professor was an old man whose hands shook violently when she spoke to him. He'd cut her some slack.

PART VII
SATURDAY

CHAPTER 27

Brunswick, Georgia, smelled. At first Infante tried to chalk it up to his own imagination, his reflexive dislike for the deep-fried South-with-a-capital-S. Baltimore had been enough of a culture shock when he moved there in his early twenties, although he had gotten used to it, even come to prefer it. A police could live on his salary and overtime in Baltimore, unlike Long Island. Maybe money went further still down here, but he couldn't see making *that* transition. There was no getting around it, Brunswick flat-out stank.

The waitress at the Waffle House must have seen the way his nose was puckered when he came in from outside.

"Pehpermeal," she said in a low tone, as if offering the password to a secret club.

"Pepper mill?" He was really having a hard time understanding the people down here, despite how slowly they spoke.

"Peh. Per. Meal," she repeated. "That's what you smell. Don't worry, you'll get used to it fast."

"I'm not going to have time to get used to anything here." He gave her his best smile. He loved women who brought him food. Even when they were plain and unattractive, like this dumpy, pockmarked girl, he loved them.

It had been almost ten when he got into Brunswick the night before, too dark and too late to visit the neighborhood where Penelope Jackson and her boyfriend had lived. But he'd cruised the block this morning, on his way to this meeting with the local fire inspector. Reynolds Street, at least the particular block where Tony Dunham had lived and died, looked kind of scrappy. It was on its way either up or down. Then again, much of Brunswick looked that way to Kevin, as if it were sliding into despair or picking itself back up after a long slump. *Not for me,* he thought, regarding the town from the bubble of the Chevy Charisma that Alamo Rent-a-Car had provided. But when he got closer to the water and felt the soft, sweet breeze and remembered how spring had yet to get started up in Baltimore, he began to get the point. There was a gentleness to the weather here, and the people, too. He respected it—in the weather.

"Oh, it was assuredly an accident," said the inspector from the local fire department, a man named Wayne Tolliver, who met Infante for a cup of coffee at the end of his breakfast, just as Infante had timed it. He didn't like to conduct business while eating, and he was glad that he had given himself wholeheartedly to this particular meal, a satisfying spread of eggs, sausage, and grits. "She was in the front room, watching television, and he was in the bedroom, smoking and drinking. He fell asleep, knocked the ashtray on a little rug next to the bed, and the place"— he threw his hands open, as if tossing an invisible wad of confetti—"went up."

"What did she do?"

"The smoke alarms weren't working." Tolliver made a face. He was a round-faced man, pink-cheeked and kind-looking, probably not as old as his freckled bald head made him look. "People think we're overly concerned, telling them to change batteries when they change their clocks every six months, but it's better'n *never*. Anyway, it was Christmas Eve, cold for these parts, and she had a space heater going where she was. The TV was in an old Florida room, didn't have any central heating. By the time she noticed the smoke, it was too late. She told us she went to the door but felt it first, like you're supposed to, and saw it was hot to the touch. She said she banged on it, screamed his name, then called 911. Windows were nailed shut—a violation on the landlord's part, to be sure, but the fellow probably never had a fighting chance, drunk as he was. My guess is that he was dead from smoke inhalation, or on his way there, before she even realized what was going on."

"And that was that."

Tolliver picked up the judgment in Infante's voice. "No accelerants. Only one point of origin, the rug. We looked at her. We looked at her real close. Here's the thing that sold me—she didn't take nary a thing out of that room. It went up with all her clothes, whatever jewelry she owned, and it's not like he had any money to leave her. Quite the opposite. He had an annuity that stopped with his death, so she lost whatever income he provided."

"An annuity?" The lawyer up in York had said that Stan Dunham purchased one after selling the farm, so that fit. But he also said the man didn't have any living relatives.

"A policy that paid him a monthly sum, for up to ten years. You know when ballplayers get those big salaries? They're underwritten by annuities. Bigger ones than this, of course. It wasn't a lot—judging by their lifestyle, it was just enough to get the two of them fucked up, regular. They were partyers, those two. You think they'd have grown out of that behavior, at their ages—he was in his fifties—but some people never do."

There was a whiff of sorrow in that statement, as if Tolliver had some personal experience on this front, a loved one who had never grown up and caused him some heartache. But Infante wasn't here to talk about Tolliver.

"What else did you learn about the two of them?"

"It was a . . . familiar address to our brothers in blue. Noise complaints. Suspected domestic violence, but those calls came from the neighbors, not from her, and they said they were never sure who was getting the worst of it. She was a hellcat, one of those hillbilly gals out of the hollows of North Carolina."

Everything was relative. If this guy was calling someone a hillbilly, she must have been really low-rent—rope belt, Daisy Dukes, the full Elly May Clampett.

"How long had she lived at the Reynolds Street address?"

"Not sure. She didn't appear on any of the official documents—the lease, the utility bills. That was all in his name. He'd been there five years or so. He drove trucks, but not regular for any one company. The way the neighbors tell it, he met her on the road and brought her back. He wasn't much, but he always managed to have a woman around. She was the third one, the neighbors."

"Did you do a tox screen on him?"

Another insulted look. "Yes. And it was consistent with being dead drunk, with an Ambien behind it, and nothing more. Guy was like a lot of truckers—he relied on pills to stay awake, to make his days, and then he needed help to calm down when he was home. He had just come back from a job the day before."

"Still . . ."

"Look, I get where you're trying to go with this. But I know fires. Allow me that much? An upended ashtray on a cheap cotton rug. If she'da set that fire, do you know how calculating she'd have to be, how calm? Oh, it's easy enough to throw a lit cigarette on the rug, but she's got to be sure he won't wake up, right? She has to stand there, watch the fire get under way, wait until it's the inferno that she's going to call in. If it doesn't catch, she can't throw another one down, because we'll pick up on that. Right? She's got to hope the neighbors don't see anything—"

"It was Christmas Eve. How many were home?"

Tolliver steamed past that. "I've met the woman. She didn't have the wiles to pull that off. Firefighters had to hold her back from going into the house."

But she had the presence of mind not to go into the bedroom when the door was hot to the touch.

Again Tolliver picked up on what Infante didn't say. "People can be real calm and composed in an

269

emergency. Self-protection kicks in. She saved herself, but when she realized he was in there, that he was really gone, she went crazy. I've listened to the 911 call. She was scared." *Skeered.* And people made fun of Infante's alleged New York accent, which was actually pretty mild, a shadow of the real thing.

"Where is she now?"

"I don't know. House is condemned, so she's not living there. Could be in town, could have left. She can do what she pleases. She's free, white, and twenty-one."

If Infante had ever heard that phrase in his life, it would have been in a movie or a television show, and not a recent one. Said in today's workplace, this was the kind of careless sentiment that resulted in meetings with human-resources facilitators. Yet Tolliver didn't seem to realize that the comment was off in any way. And, to be fair, Infante's own father and uncles had let loose with far worse, much more consciously.

Leaving the Waffle House, he wondered what had brought Tony Dunham south, why he'd ended up making his home here. The weather could be reason enough. And as a long-haul trucker, it wasn't like the guy was burning with ambition. Born in the early 1950s, Dunham would have been just old enough that college was still optional. Even a high school dropout could make a living back in the sixties, if he got in with a good union. Nancy's record check indicated that Tony Dunham wasn't a veteran, but it wasn't clear if he'd been living at home during the years that the alleged Heather Bethany claimed to live there. She hadn't mentioned anyone else in the house. Then again, she hadn't provided much beyond the address and Stan Dunham's name. Had she wanted them to find the link to Tony or not? And where did Penelope Jackson fit into this?

Photos didn't lie: The woman in Baltimore wasn't Penelope, not the Penelope in the driver's-license photo. But who was she? What if Penelope was Heather Bethany and this woman had stolen her life story along with her car? Then where was Penelope? He could only hope that folks on Reynolds Street might recognize his mystery woman, be able to explain her relationship to these people.

Southern hospitality was notably lacking when Infante returned to Reynolds Street and began asking questions about Penelope Jackson and Tony Dunham. Granted, the first man he encountered may have wanted to be helpful, but he spoke more Spanish than English, and the mere sight of Infante's official ID shut him down. Still, he nodded at the photocopy of Penelope Jackson's North Carolina driver's license, saying, "*Sí, sí,* is Miss Penelope," then shrugged at the photo of the other woman, showing no sign of recognition. The neighbor to the east, a heavyset black woman who seemed to have five or six children, sighed as if to suggest that she had seen so much that she didn't have time to see anything else. "I minded my business and they minded theirs," she said when asked if she knew where Penelope Jackson might be.

On the other side of the charred blue house, an older man was pulling a bamboo rake over the yellow-green lawn, loosening winter debris. Cold and curt at first, he became friendlier when he realized he was dealing with someone official.

"I hate to say it, but I'd rather have the place a burnt-out shell than have those two back," said the man, Aaron Parrish. "Unkind of me—and I wouldn't have wished such a tragedy on them. But they were awful people. Oh, the fights and the yelling. Plus—" He lowered his voice as if about to speak of something truly shameful. "Plus, he parked his pickup on the front lawn. I complained to the landlord, but he said they kept up on their rent, unlike the Mexicans. But I find the Mexicans to be better neighbors, once you explain a few things about America to them."

"Fights, yelling—between the two of them?"

"Frequently."

"Did you call the cops?"

A nervous look around, as if someone might be listening. "Anonymously. A few times. My wife even tried to talk to Penelope about it, but she said it was none of our business, only she didn't say it quite so *nicely*."

"This her?"

Parrish peered at the driver's-license photo, enlarged and printed out by Nancy. "Appears so. Although she was prettier in person. Petite, but with a lovely figure, like a little doll."

"This woman look familiar?" He had a photo of quote–Heather Bethany–unquote, taken with a digital camera during their second interview.

"No, never seen her. My, they look a little bit alike, don't they?"

Did they? Infante looked at the two photos, but he saw only the most superficial resemblance—

hair, eyes, maybe build. Much as he disliked and disbelieved Heather Bethany, he saw a frailty there that Penelope Jackson didn't have. Jackson looked like one tough customer.

"Did she tell you anything about herself? Penelope Jackson, I mean. Where she was from? Where Tony was from? How they met?"

"She wasn't one who was inclined to chat. I know she worked over on St. Simons, at a place called Mullet Bay. Tony did work on the island, too, sometimes, when he couldn't find long-haul work. He picked up jobs with a landscaping service. But of course they couldn't live there."

"Why not?"

Aaron Parrish laughed at Infante's naïveté. "Prices, son. Almost none of the folks who work on the island can afford to live there. This house"—he waved at the charred remains of the three-bedroom rancher with blue siding—"that would be a quarter of a million, as is, if you could just pick it up and airlift it five miles east. St. Simons is for millionaires, Sea Island dearer still."

Infante thanked Mr. Parrish and let himself into the unlocked house, which still held the smell of the fire. He didn't see why the structure had to be condemned; the damage had been largely contained to the bedroom. The landlord probably stood to make more money on the insurance claim that way.

The door to the bedroom was swollen and stuck, but he managed to open it by throwing his full weight behind his shoulder. Tolliver had said that Tony Dunham had been dead before he burned, killed by smoke inhalation, but it was hard to forget that

273

his flesh had sizzled and popped like barbecue for a time. That smell remained, too. Infante stood in the doorway, trying to imagine it. You would have to have some big balls to try killing someone this way—tossing the ashtray on the rug, waiting for the fire to engage. As Tolliver said, you couldn't throw a second cigarette down if it didn't get going. And if the guy woke up, you'd better be able to persuade him that it was an accident and you just walked in, a nervy chance to take if he was already smacking you regular. You also needed the discipline not to reach for a single cherished possession, to let it all go. You had to stand there until you were almost choking from the smoke, then close the door, wash your face to clear it of the watery tears caused by the fire, then go back and wait until you were sure that no one could save the man on the other side.

The woman up in Baltimore, whatever her name was—she could do that, he was sure of it. But he also was convinced that she wasn't Penelope Jackson. It was the only real fact he had. *I don't know Penelope Jackson,* she had said. But wouldn't a true stranger have modified the name? *I don't know a Penelope Jackson, I don't know any Penelope Jackson.* Then how the fuck did you come to have her car? She had managed to avoid answering that question by offering them the solution to an infamous crime, then setting up a police officer as the perp. She had thrown a lot of things at them—to what end? What didn't she want them to see?

He left the house, left Reynolds Street. It was a sad house, even before the fire. A house where two un- happy people had coexisted with frustration and disappointment. A house of quarrels and insults. He could tell because he had lived in such a house, twice. Well—once, his second marriage. His first marriage had been okay, until it wasn't. Tabby had been a sweet girl. If he met her now . . . But he could never meet her again, not the Tabby he had first glimpsed in the Wharf Rat twelve years ago. She was lost to him, replaced by a woman who knew Kevin Infante as a cheat and a runaround. He ran into Tabby sometimes—Baltimore was small that way—and she was always polite, civil, as was he. Friendly, even, laughing about their marriage as if it were nothing more than an accident-plagued road trip, a merry misadventure. A decade out, they could be generous to their younger selves.

Yet there was a film in her eyes that would never quite disappear, a sheen of disappointment. He would give anything to see Tabby one more time as she had regarded him that first night in the Wharf Rat, when he was still someone she could admire and respect.

One of the pamphlets from the Best Western lobby said there was some sort of fort over on St. Simons Island, and he decided to kill time there until Mullet Bay, the restaurant-bar where Penelope Jackson had worked, began prepping for the dinner rush. He was used to historical disappointments—he had seen the Alamo when he was just ten years old—but there was no structure at all where Fort Frederica once stood. He was staring at a sea of weeds known as the Bloody Marsh when his cell rang.

"Hey, Nancy."

"Hey, Infante." He knew that tone. He was more

attuned to Nancy's tones than he had been to either wife's. She was going to drop some bad news on him.

"Out with it, Nancy."

"Our gal has decided she wants to talk. Today."

"I'm back tonight. Can't it wait?"

"I thought so, but Lenhardt says we gotta humor her. He's going to send me in there with her. I think he's worried about media, once her mom gets here. No one expected her to get out of Mexico so fast, with so little notice, and . . . well, we can't control the mom as easily. We've got no charge hanging over her head. She can talk to whoever she wants to."

Free, white, and twenty-one, as Tolliver might say.

"Yeah, it could be a clusterfuck." It was amazing that they had flown beneath the radar as long as they had, their only bit of luck. "Fuck, though. When does the mom get in?"

"Ten P.M., right behind you. That's another thing . . ."

"Aw, c'mon. I've got to pick her up? Did I get demoted in the last twenty-four hours?"

"Sarge thought it would be nice if someone met her, and we don't know how long this thing will go. Nice and . . . well, prudent. We want to keep her in our sights, you know?"

"Yeah."

Infante snapped his phone shut in disgust and returned to staring at the marsh. The battle hadn't apparently been all that bloody. British troops had repelled a Spanish invasion during something called the War of Jenkins' Ear. What a small-stakes name for a war, but then he was fighting his own meaningless battle, wasn't he, wandering around Georgia while his former partner vaulted into the lead position, conducted an interview that should have been his. *The War of Infante's Left Testicle*. It was worse, in a way, knowing that Nancy hadn't backstabbed him or maneuvered this. She had never been the scheming type. He wondered if maybe-Heather knew he had gone to Georgia and that's why she was suddenly keen to tell all.

Fuck, he hated Brunswick.

CHAPTER 28

"The thing is, we could really use your help."

Willoughby heard the words, made sense of them, yet couldn't quite process his way to an answer. He was too taken with the speaker, enthralled and delighted by her mere presence. *An old-fashioned girl.* Willoughby knew he was being sexist, but he couldn't help thinking of the young detective that way. She was so curvy, a nineteenth-century body type here in the early days of the twenty-first, with such pretty red cheeks and slippery blond hair falling out of a careless topknot. There had been women in the department when he was there. By the late 1980s, some had even made homicide. But they sure hadn't looked like this one.

"I was up until almost four A.M.," the detective, Nancy, was saying earnestly, "going over what's filtered out about the case and what was kept in the file. But it's so much to take in at once, I thought you could help me focus on the key details."

She pushed two printouts toward him. Not just typed but color-coded, red and blue. Red for what was known publicly, blue for what had been kept back. It seemed a little girly to him, but maybe all police did such things now that they had computers. Certainly he would never have dared using a system like this in his day, given how his coworkers were always on the alert for any sign of weakness or softness in him. Effeteness was the precise word, but if he had ever uttered it aloud, his colleagues would have seized upon it as evidence that he was, in fact, effete.

"Four A.M.?" he murmured. "And here it is only noon. You must be exhausted."

"I have a six-month-old son. Exhausted is my natural state. Actually, I got four straight hours, so I feel relatively well rested."

Willoughby pretended to study the papers in front of him, but he didn't want to focus, didn't want to surrender to those red and blue sirens. There was a whirlpool beneath this placid assortment of old facts. He had no desire to get sucked into this again, to think about all the ways he had failed. Not that anyone had ever rebuked him or suggested he was at fault in any way. His superiors, much as they had wanted a resolution in the Bethany matter—and that was the word they had come to use over time, *matter*—understood that it was bad luck, one of those rare cases that could have come straight from *The Twilight Zone*. Not even Dave, in the end, had faulted him. And by the time Willoughby left the department, he had in many ways carved out the image he'd wanted. One of the guys. Tough. Dogged. Never soft, much less effete.

Yet it had long gnawed at him that he'd never made

significant inroads into learning what happened to the Bethany girls. And now here was this young woman—gosh, she was pretty, and a new mother, too, imagine that—telling him that a police had been accused, one of their own. One of *his* own, practically a contemporary. He didn't remember Stan Dunham, and this Nancy girl said he had retired from the theft division in 1974, but still: This would be so embarrassing. He knew how it would look, if the Jane Doe girl—the woman—was telling the truth. *Right under their own noses, all these years.* There might be suggestions of a cover-up, a conspiracy. People loved conspiracies.

"This," he said, pointing his finger at a line in blue ink, a line that had been capitalized and highlighted. "You got it. This is what you want. Only a very few people could talk about this in any detail—me, Miriam, Dave, the young cop who was with us that night, whoever had access to the evidence room."

"That's not a small number of people. Plus, the accused is a police, someone who might have had sources inside the department."

"You're thinking she's not who she says she is, but that Stan still might be involved."

"Everything's in play right now. Information, it's—" She paused, gathering her thoughts. "It's alive, in its own way. It grows, it changes. Since I started working cold cases and spending more and more time with case files and computers, I think about information differently. It's like a Lego set, you know? There are different ways to put it together, but some pieces will never join, no matter how you pound on them."

The tea on the table between them had grown cold, but he took a sip anyway. He had insisted on making the tea, injecting a lot of ceremony into two mugs and two bags of Lipton, and she had indulged him in his wish, probably thinking he was lonely and wanted to draw out the visit. He wasn't lonely, far from it, and he didn't want her to stay one minute longer than necessary. His eyes slid toward his wife's old desk and he heard a bird's mournful coo somewhere in the eaves of Edenwald. *Too late. Too late.*

"The thing about *this*," Willoughby said, "is that the person who took the girls doesn't necessarily know about it and almost certainly doesn't remember it. It wouldn't have mattered to him. But a girl—a girl would remember it. You would, wouldn't you? At that age?"

"Well, I was more of a tomboy, as you might guess, but yeah, I would remember."

"So work your way to that. Get her good and drunk on her own words. That's all you need to do. But you know that, right? You say you were in homicide, before your maternity leave." He found himself blushing, as if it were impolite to remind this woman that she had bodily functions, that she had reproduced. "You know your way around an interrogation. In fact, I bet you're darn good at it."

It was her turn to drink cold tea, to stall a little. When he was younger, he might not have been drawn to her. In his twenties he had liked the women of his class, as his own snobbish mother might have said, the thin-to-the-point-of-brittle women, Katharine Hepburn types, with those pelvis-forward walks and hips that could cut you. Evelyn had been such a woman, elegant at every angle. But softness had its virtues, and this Nancy Porter had such a doll-like face, with those red cheeks and pale blue eyes. Peasant stock, his mother would have said, but his family tree could have used some sturdier genes.

"We thought—*they* thought—Sergeant Lenhardt, who supervises Infante, and the commissioner himself—we thought you should be present."

"Watching, you mean?"

"Maybe even . . . talking."

"Is that legal?"

"Sometimes retired police still work for the department. Sort of a noncommissioned, consultancy gig. We could make that happen."

"Dear—"

"*Nancy.*"

"I wasn't being a sexist—I lost your name for a second and was trying to cover up. That's how it works, don't you see? I'm in my sixties. I forget things. I'm not as sharp as I was. I don't remember every detail. Right now you know this case better than I do. I have nothing to contribute."

"Just your presence might make her think twice about trying to fake us out. With Infante in Georgia and the mother due to arrive tonight—"

"Miriam is coming? You found Miriam?"

"In Mexico, just as you said. She kept a bank account in Texas, and we got the contact info from them. Lenhardt found her last night, but we never thought she'd get here so fast. He tried to talk her out of coming at all. She'll have to travel all day, but once she's here, I don't see how we can keep her away. It wasn't our idea to sit down today, but my boss says it may be an opportunity, after all."

"You mean, if she's a fake, she may fool Miriam and

begin gleaning information from her, almost without her knowing." He shook his head. "She won't fool Miriam. No one could fool Miriam about anything."

"We're not too worried about that. If it comes to it, we'll always have epithelial cells. But if we could eliminate her definitively, trip her up on the facts, that wouldn't be a bad thing."

"Epi . . . ?"

"DNA. I'm just being fancy using a scientific term, and not even accurately."

"DNA. Of course. The policeman's new best friend." He took another sip of cold tea. So Miriam hadn't told them, and they hadn't asked. She assumed and they assumed, and why wouldn't they? Things had gone unsaid, inferences had been made. His fault, he supposed, and he had considered undoing it so many times over the years. But he had owed Dave that much.

He pushed the papers away with enough force that some skidded off the slick surface of his mahogany coffee table. A table that, he noticed now, in the presence of this vibrant young woman, was dusty and overwaxed.

"You can't imagine being through with something like this, can you? You think the juices can always be engaged. The old cliché is that warhorses react when they smell smoke. But does that mean the horse wants to go to war or that he wants to avoid it? I've always thought it might be the latter. I did some good work as a detective. When I retired, I made peace with the fact that this one case would remain open, that some things cannot be known. I even—don't laugh—thought about supernatural explanations. Alien abductions. Why not?"

"But if there are answers to be had . . ."

"In my gut I feel that this is going to prove to be a hoax, an ugly waste of everyone's time and energy. I grieve for Miriam, flying back here, being forced to contemplate the one thing she seldom allowed herself to believe. Dave was the one who clung to hope, and it killed him. It was Miriam who could accept reality, who found a way to survive and get on with her life, diminished as it was."

"Your gut—that's what we need. In the room with me, making eye contact with her. The commissioner says he'll talk to you further about this, if it will make a difference."

Willoughby walked to the window. It was overcast and cool, even by March's temperamental standards. Still, he could play golf if he wanted to. Golf, the game one never perfects, the game that reminds you every time how human you are, how flawed. He had always said he would never play, never be drawn into the country-club life that was practically his birthright, but in the empty days of retirement he had fallen into it, and now he was stuck. He'd been forty-five when he retired. Who retires at forty-five?

A failure.

He hadn't meant to be a career police. The plan, long ago, had been to go into police work for a mere five years or so, then switch to the state's attorney's office, run for attorney general as the candidate who knew the law at every level, maybe even take a run at governor one day. As a young man, fresh out of UVA law school, he had plotted his future with that kind of confidence—five-year plans, ten-year plans, twenty-year plans. Then he became a murder police at age thirty and decided to stay a little longer, maybe work a famous case or two to boost his profile. Within that first year, he caught the Bethany case. He stayed another five years, then another ten.

It wasn't only because of the Bethany case, not exactly. But justice seemed less and less important to him. The courtroom wasn't a place for answers. It was the world of epilogues, a stage setting where the players assembled the exact same facts, fitting them together—how had this young woman put it? Yes, like Legos. *Here's my version, here's his version. Which appeals to you the most?* Legos. There were an infinite number of ways to put them together. He thought of the downtown library at Christmastime, where the windows were filled with magnificent Lego constructions made by local architectural firms. He thought about how carelessly he had assumed he would walk his own children, then grandchildren, past those windows. But his wife couldn't have children, as it turned out. "You can adopt," Dave had told him, and Willoughby had said unthinkingly, "But you never know what you're going to get."

Dave, to his credit, had said only, "No one ever does, Chet." The debt to Dave weighed on him still, and it was not paid, it would never be paid. His one effort to repay it had resulted in this debacle—Miriam on a plane, the detectives assuming that science was on their side, that when all else failed they would get a subpoena and prove she was a liar, via her blood or her teeth—or her mother's DNA. Yes, it would be better for everyone if this woman's story could be debunked before Miriam arrived tonight.

"I'll accompany you," he said at last. "I won't go

in, but I'll watch and listen, and you can consult me as you need to. But I'll need some lunch, and then you better get some caffeine into me. This is going to be a long afternoon, and I'm used to enjoying a nice postprandial nap."

He knew he was giving her something to ridicule, with that postprandial bit. She would probably repeat that around the department later. "He couldn't say 'after lunch' like a normal person—he had to say 'postprandial.' " But that had always been part of his police persona. He had deliberately allowed other police to take the piss out of him every now and then, to give them reasons to mock his grandiosity, his manners.

Their hostility to him, their suspicion of his motives in being a police, had always puzzled him. The best detectives loved what they did and were proud of it. They, too, could make more money doing other things, but they had chosen police work. Chet was simply doing the same thing, and his love was purer still. Yet they never got that. In the end they just couldn't trust the guy who didn't need the paycheck. This red-cheeked girl was no different. Right now she required his help, or thought she did. But when it was all over, she'd mock him behind his back. So be it. He would do this for Dave—and Miriam.

He wondered how she had aged, how much gray was in her dark hair, if Mexico had weathered that lovely olive skin.

CHAPTER 29

The blankness of her passport reminded Miriam how immobile she had been for the last sixteen years, barely moving out of San Miguel, much less traveling beyond Mexico's borders. She hadn't, in fact, flown since long before 9/11, but she wasn't sure she would have noted the changes if she had not been primed to look for them. Customs in Dallas–Fort Worth had probably never been a particularly pleasant experience in the most hopeful of times. She wasn't surprised at how rudely she was treated, or how they peered at her, then the photo on the passport, which was due to expire in a year. She had become a U.S. citizen in 1963 because it simplified everything. Contrary to what people thought, citizenship wasn't conferred automatically upon marriage. If it hadn't been for the girls, she might never have changed her citizenship. Even in 1963 she had a sense that she wasn't meant to be an "American," as residents of the United States so blithely called themselves, as if no other country in the hemisphere existed. But she took on that identity for her family's sake.

"What's the nature of your visit in the United States?" the immigration agent asked in a rapid monotone. She was black, forty-something, and so bored by her job that it seemed an enormous effort for her to rest her considerable bulk on the high, padded stool afforded her in the little booth.

"Uh . . ." It was only a split second of hesitation, but it seemed to be the excitement the immigration official had been longing for, the off-kilter answer that her ears were trained to pick up. Suddenly the woman's spine was straight, her eyes sharp.

"What's the nature of your visit?" she repeated, her voice now inflected. *Vi-sit.*

"Why, I—" Miriam remembered just in time that she was not required to tell the story of her life, standing here in immigration. She did not have to tell this woman that her children had been missing and presumed murdered for thirty years, much less that now, against all hope, one of them might be alive. She did not have to tell her about the affair with Baumgarten, the divorce, the move to Texas, the move to Mexico, Dave's death. She did not have to explain why she became a U.S. citizen, or why she had reverted to her maiden name after the divorce, or even why she had chosen to settle in San Miguel de Allende. Her life belonged to her still, at least for now. That could change, in the next twenty-four hours, and she could become public property once again.

All she had to say was, "Personal. A family matter. A relative was in a car accident."

"I'm sorry," the woman said. "That's awful."

"It's not serious," Miriam assured her, gathering her bags and moving on to the domestic terminal, where she had a numbing four hours to kill before the flight to Baltimore.

"It's not serious," the sergeant had told her the evening before, when she had recovered from the shock. Like someone thrown into deep, cold water, Miriam had been disoriented and stunned, her instincts overwhelmed. It had taken several moments for her to center herself, to do the natural thing and head for the surface, to break through to the place where she could breathe again. "The car accident, I mean," the man clarified. "Obviously, the claims she's making are very serious."

"I'll have to fly all day, but I could be back there by tomorrow night if I leave first thing," she said. She was weeping, but it was the kind of crying that didn't impede her voice, her thoughts. Her mind was flipping through her contacts in San Miguel, people who could and would do her favors. There was one particularly good hotel where the management was used to catering to rich types, with their sudden whims. They could probably book her ticket. Money was no object.

"It really would be better if you waited . . . We're not sure, in fact—"

"No, no, I could never wait." Then she got it. "You think she might be a liar?"

"We think she's damn odd, but she knows some things that only someone with intimate knowledge of the case could have, and we are developing some new leads, but it's all very tentative."

"So even if she's not my daughter, she almost certainly knows something about her. And what of Sunny? What has she said about her sister?"

A pause, the kind of grave pause that told her the man on the other end of the phone was a parent. "She was killed soon after they were taken. According to this woman."

In sixteen-plus years of living in Mexico, Miriam had never once suffered a stomach ailment. But at that moment she felt the sharp, stabbing gut pain that was the hallmark of *turista*. Of all the things she had allowed herself to imagine for thirty years—the discovery of a grave, an arrest, the end of the story and yes, in some secret chamber of her heart, the impossible possibility of reunion—this had never occurred to her. One, but not the other? She felt as if her body might break down under the strain of trying to harbor such polarized feelings. Heather, alive, and the promise of answers after so many years. Sunny, dead, and the horror of answers after so many years. She glanced at her expression in the tin-framed mirror over the primitive pine buffet, expecting to see it bifurcated, the mask of comedy and tragedy combined in one face. But she looked as she usually did.

"I'll be there. As soon as humanly possible."

"That's your choice, of course. But you might want to let us check out a few of these leads. I've got a detective in Georgia, working on something. I'd hate for you to come all this way—"

"Look, there are only two possibilities. One is that this is my daughter, in which case I cannot get there soon enough. The other is that this is someone who knows something about my daughter and is exploiting the knowledge for whatever reason. If that's so, I want to confront her. Besides, I'll know. The moment I see her, I'll know."

"Still, a day won't change much, and if we should discredit her . . ." He didn't want her to come, for whatever reason, not yet, which only strengthened Miriam's resolve to be there as soon as possible. Dave was dead, she was in charge. She would behave as he would, if he were still around. She owed him that much.

Now, not even twenty-four hours later, wheeling her luggage past the hideous shops in the airport, Miriam was rethinking her certitude. What if she *didn't* know? What if her desire to see her daughter alive tainted her maternal instinct? What if maternal instinct was bullshit? There had always been those eager to disavow Miriam's motherhood, people who unthinkingly and unfeelingly demoted her because she had no biological claim on the children she was raising. What if they were right and Miriam was missing some key sense? Did the very fact that she had bonded so thoroughly with children who were not her biological kin prove how suggestive she was by nature? She remembered a cat they had owned, a superb calico mouser. Spayed, the cat had never thrown a litter. But one day she had discovered a little stuffed seal of Heather's, a repulsive thing made of actual seal fur, a gift from Dave's clueless mother. If the seal hadn't come from his mother, Dave never would have allowed Heather to keep it; he had made Miriam get rid of her beaver coat, a remnant of her Canadian life, passed down from her grandmother, and far more defensible. But all sorts of exceptions were made for Florence Bethany. The cat, Eleanor, discovered the seal and adopted it, dragging it around by the neck as she might have carried her own kitten, endlessly washing it, hissing at anyone who tried to take it from her. Eventually, of course, she ruined it, her wet, rough tongue removing all the hair until it was something truly hideous, a fetal bit of canvas.

What if Miriam's instincts were on a par with the calico mouser's? Having learned to love another woman's children as her own, was she capable of claiming any child, if she wanted to believe badly enough? Was she going to grab a stuffed seal by the neck and pretend it was her kitten?

In the year before she disappeared, Sunny had asked more and more questions about her "real" mother. She had been a typical adolescent at the time, so moody and temperamental that the family called her Stormy, and she kept tiptoeing up to the edge of the story, then retreating. She wanted to know. She wasn't ready to know. "Was it a one-car accident?" she asked. "What caused it? Who was driving?" The sweet, polite stories they had told for so long were now lies, plain and simple, and neither Miriam nor Dave knew how to navigate that change. Lying was the greatest sin in a teenager's eyes, the only excuse needed to reject all parental rules and strictures. If they had armed Sunny with the evidence of their deceit and hypocrisy, she would have been impossible. But, eventually, she would have to know, if only because there was an object lesson in her mother's mistakes, a reminder of how fatal it can be not to confide in a parent, to be proud in the wake of a mistake. If Sally Turner had been able to go to her parents in her time of need, then Sunny and Heather might never have come to be the

Bethany girls. And as much as Miriam hated that idea, she knew that it would have been for the best. Not because of biology but because if the girls' mother had lived, they might have lived, too.

The police had looked long and hard into the father's family, but his few remaining relatives seemed to neither know nor care what had happened to that violent young man's offspring. He was an orphan, and the aunt who raised him had disapproved of Sally as much as Estelle and Herb had disapproved of him. Leonard, or Leo. Something like that. It was impossible to single out any indignity in the aftermath of the girls' disappearance, but Miriam had disliked the keen interest in the girls' parentage even more than the probing into her licentiousness. And Dave, who usually wanted every avenue explored, even the most crackpot theories, had been driven insane by that line of inquiry. "They are *our* daughters," he said to Chet repeatedly. "This has nothing to do with the Turners, or that idiot who did nothing more than a stray dog might have done. You're wasting your time." He was almost hysterical on the subject.

Once, years earlier, someone—a friend until this incident, which revealed that the person was not a friend and had never been one—had asked Miriam if the children could be Dave's, biologically, if he had impregnated the Turners' daughter during some long, clandestine affair and they had all conspired to concoct this elaborate story when she died, from whatever cause. Miriam had gotten used to the fact that no one would ever see a likeness between her and the girls, but she found it strange that this woman thought she could see Dave in them. Yes, his hair was light, but bushy and curly. Yes, his skin was fair, but his eyes were brown, his frame completely different. Yet, time and time again, people had said, *Oh, the girls favor their father,* which created a moment beyond awkward, for Miriam did not want to be put in the position of disavowing the girls in their hearing, but nor could she bear for the misinformation to stand. *They are like me,* she wanted to say. *They are so like me.* They are my daughters, and I have shaped them. They will be better versions of me, strong and more self-aware, capable of getting what they want without feeling selfish or greedy, the way women of my generation did.

Four hours. Four hours to kill in an airport and then almost three hours for the flight itself, and she had already been traveling for almost eight hours—up at 6:00 A.M. for the car, arranged by Joe, that took her to the local airport, then a long delay in Mexico City. There were good books in the airport bookstore, but she could not imagine focusing on any of them, and the magazines seemed too trivial, too outside her existence. She didn't even know who most of the actresses were, living as she did without a satellite dish. In face and figure, they looked shockingly alike to Miriam, as indistinguishable from one another as Madame Alexander dolls. The headlines screamed of personal matters—engagements, divorces, births. *Give Chet credit,* she thought. He had kept so much from local media. How docile reporters had been, how circumspect. Now the whole story would come out— the adoption, her affair, their money woes. Everything.

It still might, Miriam realized. *It still might.* Today's world would never allow this reunion, if it proved to be that, remain private. It was almost enough to make her hope that the woman in Baltimore *was* a liar. But she couldn't sustain the wish. She would give up everything—the truth about herself, ugly and unpleasant as it was, the truth about Dave and how she had treated him—she would trade it all, without a second thought, to see one of her daughters again.

She scooped up an armful of tabloids, deciding to think of them as homework, the future text of her life.

CHAPTER 30

"Do you think this will finish it?" Heather asked, staring out the car window. She had been humming under her breath since they got in the car, a hum that had risen to a high-pitched drone when Kay took the entrance to the Beltway. It wasn't clear to Kay if she was aware of what she was doing.

"Finish it?"

"Will it be over, once I tell them everything?"

Kay was never glib, even about the smallest matters, and this question struck her as particularly grave. *Will it be over?* Gloria hadn't bothered to provide that information when she called and asked Kay—told her, really, issuing orders as if Kay worked for her, as if she were the one who'd been doing all the favors and Kay was in *her* debt—to bring Heather to the Public Safety Building by 4:00 P.M. And now they were running late because Heather had fussed so over her clothes. She'd been as petulant as Grace dressing for school, and almost as impossible to satisfy. Ultimately, she settled on a pale blue button-down and a stretchy tweed skirt, which worked, in spite of itself, with her clunky black shoes, the only items of her own wardrobe that she was still willing to wear. All this bother seemed funny to Kay, because Heather didn't give off the vibe of someone who thought about her appearance. A shame, really, because she was such a striking woman, blessed with things that only nature could bestow—high cheekbones, the kind of willowy frame that age never thickened, good skin.

"Nothing's changed with the boy, if that's what you mean. His condition's improving steadily. Gloria seems confident there won't be serious charges in connection with the collision."

"I wasn't really thinking about him."

"Oh." It bothered Kay, how seldom Heather thought of anyone but herself. But that would be the logical consequence of what had happened—assuming that Kay's theories were right. Working from the scant details that Heather had meted out so far, Kay had decided that Stan Dunham had taken both girls but killed Sunny because, at fifteen, she was too old to interest him. He had kept Heather until she, too, ceased to be of use to a pedophile, then retained her for a few extra years until Heather was sufficiently traumatized to keep his secrets. How? Kay didn't want to think about that. Clearly, he had turned her into his accomplice somehow, made her feel as if she were a criminal, too. Or simply left her so racked with fear that she would never consider telling anyone what had happened. Kay was not troubled, as the detectives seemed to be, by the fact that Heather had not tried to get away or tell anyone what was happening to her during those six or so years. Perhaps he told her that her parents were dead, or even that they'd arranged for him to take the girls. Children were so suggestible, so malleable. Even Heather's continuing reluctance to tell the full story was logical to Kay. Her new identity, whatever it was, had been central to her survival. Why should she entrust anyone with it—particularly men and women who had worked in the same department as her abductor?

"Do you think they know anything new?" Heather asked.

"New?"

"Maybe they found my sister's body. I told them where it was."

"Even if they did—and I think that might have made the news, since it would be hard to excavate an old grave without drawing attention to it—it would take weeks to identify her remains."

"Really? Wouldn't this be a high-priority case, something they could rush through?" She seemed a little insulted not to be given the treatment she thought was her due.

"Only on television." Through her work with the House of Ruth, the same channels in which she'd become acquainted with Gloria, Kay had gotten to know a forensic anthropologist from College Park, who was a rueful guide to the pedestrian restraints, mainly budgetary, that kept her from producing the miracles the public expected. "There are some things they can tell right away—"

"Like what?"

Kay realized she wasn't sure. "Well, certain . . . um,

damage to the body. Blunt-force trauma or gunshot. But also the gender, I think, the approximate age."

"How do they do that?"

"I don't know exactly. But, obviously, skeletons change in puberty. However, if your old dentist is still around, he'll be able to ID your sister pretty quickly. I understand that dentists are very good at recognizing their own work."

"John Martielli, D.D.S.," Heather said, her voice almost dreamy. "His office was upstairs, above the drugstore. There were *Highlights* magazines, of course. Goofus and Gallant. If we didn't have cavities—and we *never* had cavities—we were allowed to go around the corner and buy whatever we liked from the bakery, no matter how much white sugar it had in it."

"You've never had a cavity?" Kay thought of her own poor, tortured mouth. Just this year she'd undergone the tedium of having every silver filling replaced, and now there were crowns aging out, the result of cracked teeth that Kay considered the legacy of her divorce. She had ground her teeth until two sheared off, the bits coming up with the granola bar she was eating at the time. The crowns had led to an infection and a root canal, and the dentist thought she might need additional surgery still. She knew that her dental woes weren't her fault, but the problems in her mouth made her feel vaguely unclean, unhygienic.

"No. Even when I didn't go to the dentist for years—because I didn't have health insurance in my twenties—my teeth were perfect. Now I go every six months." She bared her teeth, showing them off. Good teeth, great bone structure, a naturally slender frame, lovely skin—if Kay hadn't known Heather's story, she would have hated her a little.

"Could we stop?" Heather asked, holding her stomach as if she had a cramp.

"We're running late as it is, but if you're carsick or need something to eat—"

"I thought we could go to the mall."

"The mall?"

"Security Square?" Kay glanced at Heather. It was hard to make eye contact while driving, especially when one was trying to merge onto the Beltway, but she had learned from dealing with Grace that eye contact was overrated. She got more information out of her daughter when they were staring straight ahead, through the same windshield. The mall was one exit past where Heather had been picked up Tuesday night. "Is that where you were trying to go, all along?"

"Not consciously. But maybe I was. At any rate, I need to go there now, before I do this. Please, Kay? It's not the worst thing in the world, being late."

"I'm not as worried about the detectives as I am about Gloria. She doesn't value anyone's time but her own."

"I'll call her on your cell, explain we're running behind." Without waiting for Kay's agreement, Heather grabbed the phone from the cup holder between the seats and used its received-calls log to find Gloria's number and call her back. She manipulated the phone with ease, as comfortable with gadgetry as Seth or Grace. "Gloria? It's Heather. We're just getting on the road. Kay's ex-husband was late picking up the kids, and we couldn't very well leave them there, could we?" She didn't give Gloria time to reply. "See you in a few."

What a brilliant excuse, Kay thought. *She pinned*

*it on someone that no one knows, that no one would
think to question.*

It took a split second, but the larger implications
of this observation seemed to vibrate beneath her
tires as she merged onto the long, sweeping exit to
Security Boulevard.

"I thought things got smaller as you aged," Heather
said. "This seems larger. Did they expand it?"

They were standing in a corridor where, according
to Heather, the movie theater, all two screens, had
once been. For a Saturday the mall was severely
underpopulated, and while it had some of the usual
offerings—Old Navy, a chain music store, a Sears, and
a Hecht's—the other stores were unknown to Kay, and
there was a general sense of abandonment. In one
corner a former department store—Hoschild's, Heather
insisted—had been deconstructed, its walls torn away
so that only its escalators remained. These now took
shoppers to an Asian food court. There must be a big
Asian population in the area, for the name Seoul Plaza
had been affixed to the facade of the mall's south end.
Kay found the Seoul Plaza part vaguely hopeful, a sign
of how things changed and adapted. It was exciting,
on one level, that this section of Baltimore County
needed such a specialty store. But she wasn't much of
a fan of malls in particular, and this one was so forlorn,
so seedy and forgotten.

She wondered what it looked like to Heather.

"You could smell the Karmelkorn even here,"
Heather was saying now. "It filled this central area.
That's where we were supposed to meet that day."

301

Heather began to walk, head down, as if there were clues to follow. Upon reaching the mall's atrium, she turned right. "The organ store was up here, near the bookstore. The sewing supplies—Singer, not Jo-Ann—were the other way, along with Harmony Hut. We were supposed to meet our father at the health food store, the GNC, at five-thirty. He bought brewer's yeast there, and sesame candy. It was pretty here then. Full of people, festive."

It was as if Heather were prepping, reviewing information for a test. But if she was Heather Bethany, why would she worry about having the right answers? And if she wasn't, she must see that the mall was so changed that no one could check her memories of it, contradict her recollections?

"Mall security," she said, stopping to inspect a glassed-in booth with uniformed men staring at a variety of screens, and Kay wondered if she was thinking that such men might have saved her, thirty years ago. "This is where Karmelkorn— No, no, *no*. I'm turned around. The new wing, with Hecht's, threw me off. It's not that the mall has gotten larger but that I was confused about the layout, transposed the two corridors."

She began moving so fast that Kay almost had to jog to keep up with her. "The movie theaters would have been down here," she said, skidding to a stop, then turning around, her pace picking right back up. "And if we go right here—yes, now it makes sense. The place where those escalators are, that wasn't Hoschild's but the J. C. Penney, which was still under construction that weekend. Here—this was the organ store, where Mr. Pincharelli worked on weekends."

"Here" was now something called Kid-Go-Round, a store that apparently catered to children who needed the equivalent of prom clothes, for weddings and the like. Next door was a store called Touch of the Past, which Kay found eerie until she realized that it sold Negro League memorabilia, expensive jerseys for teams such as the Homestead Grays and the Atlanta Black Crackers.

"Mr. Pincharelli?" Kay asked.

"The music teacher at Rock Glen Junior High. Sunny had the biggest crush on him for a while."

Heather stood transfixed, rocking slightly, humming again as she had in the car, hugging herself as if she were cold. "Look at those dresses," she said. "Flower girls, junior attendants. Did you have that kind of wedding?"

"Not quite," Kay said, smiling at the memory. "We married outdoors, in the backyard of a friend's house on the Severn River, and I wore flowers in my hair. It was the eighties," she added with a note of apology. "And I was all of twenty-three."

"I'm never going to marry, not for real." Heather's tone was not regretful or self-pitying, merely factual.

"Well, then at least you'll never have to get divorced," Kay said.

"My parents divorced, didn't they? I didn't get that at first. They split up. Do you think it's my fault?"

"Your fault?"

"Well, not my fault, obviously. But a consequence of what . . . happened. Do you think grief drove them apart?"

"I think," Kay said, picking her words with as much precision as possible, "that grief, tragedy, tends to magnify whatever is there, expose the fissures that are already there. Strong marriages get stronger. Weak ones suffer and, without help, may fall apart. In my experience."

"Are you saying my parents didn't have a good marriage before?" Her tone was fierce, straight from the schoolyard, the instinctive defense against even an implied insult against one's parents.

"I wouldn't know. I couldn't know. I was speaking in generalities, Heather."

Again the smile, the reward for using her name, for being the one who believed in her, perhaps even more than Gloria, whose dedication was billed hourly. "I thought everyone was dead. I just assumed everyone was dead. Except me."

Kay trained her eyes on the gossamer skirts in the windows, the heartbreaking kind of girly-girl dresses that her own Grace had never wanted to wear. *I just assumed everyone was dead.* If they were, it would be much easier to carry the lie. But would someone tell a lie like this just to get out of being charged in a traffic accident? If that were the case, now that she knew the little boy was going to be okay, couldn't she simply recant? She was so credible, yet the very fact that Kay was thinking along those lines might be the proof of how studied this all was.

Staring straight ahead, Kay could see Heather's reflection in the plate-glass window of where the organ store had once been. Tears were coursing down her face, and she was shaking so hard that her teeth, her perfect, no-cavity teeth, were chattering uncontrollably.

"It began here," she said. "In its own way, it began here."

CHAPTER 31

The business section of St. Simons—the "village," according to a local who helped Kevin find his way there—was lousy with charm. The main drag was lined with precious shops, the kind that specialized in selling useless things to people who shopped reflexively, as entertainment. It wasn't the high-end, name-brand type of shopping you saw in the Hamptons, where Kevin had worked landscaping jobs as a teenager, but it was a big step up from Brunswick. He understood now why Penelope Jackson had lived on the mainland, how out-of-reach the real estate must be for the people who scooped the ice cream, poured the beers, sold the pink-and-green dresses that seemed to dominate the window displays.

He had timed his visit to Mullet Bay for the late-afternoon rush, before the dinner hour started in earnest. The bar-restaurant was a typical resort establishment, another variation on the American dream, Jimmy Buffett version. Parrots, tropical drinks, no-worries-mon. It was hard to figure out how a going-on-forty woman had fit in here, a young person's joint where the waitstaff, male and female, wore shorts and polos. But the manager, a dark-eyed honey of a girl with glowing skin, cleared that up by explaining that Penelope was one of the line cooks.

"She was great," she said with a peppy enthusiasm that seemed to be her default setting, pronouncing it "graaaa-ate." The plastic bar pinned above her perfect left tit proclaimed her to be Heather, and the coincidence seemed a portent of . . . well, *something*. Then again, Heather was a pretty popular name. "Good worker, very reliable. Would fill in at the last minute, even bartended once or twice when the regular guy didn't show. The bosses would have dearly loved to keep her."

"Why'd she quit?"

"Well, she just needed a new start. After the fire and all." Even in expressing genuine sadness, this Heather retained a kind of indomitable enthusiasm, as if her beauty, her fine young limbs, supplied her with a constant, humming joy of self. Infante imagined arranging those limbs around him, absorbing a little of that sunny self-regard.

"What about this woman?" He pulled out the photo of his would-be Heather. "She look familiar? You ever see anyone like this with Penelope?"

"No. But then—I didn't really see anyone with her, not even her boyfriend. She spoke of him, and he came by once that I recall, but that was it." She wrinkled her nose. "Older fellow, kind of sleazy. He said some things to me, but I didn't tell Penelope. It was just beer talk."

"She say where she was going when she left?"

"No, not to me. She gave notice, and we even had a little party for her at the end of her last shift. A cake and all. But, you know, she was kind of private. I think—" She hesitated, touchingly sincere in her desire not to gossip, which made Infante like her all the more. So many folks he interviewed reveled in the opportunity to slander others in the name of their civic duty, volunteering all sorts of extraneous and derogatory information.

"Do you think she kept to herself because of her situation at home?"

An energetic, relieved nod. God, he wanted to fuck her. It would be like . . . like lying on a beach somewhere, only with the silkiest sand imaginable, warm and comforting, not the least bit gritty. There was nothing sour in this girl, no life taint. Her parents were probably still married, even still in love. She was breezing through school, popular with males and females alike. He could imagine birds alighting on her shoulders, as if she were some Disney cartoon princess.

"She came in once, with a bruise on her face? And all I did was look, just glance at her, and she got very upset. 'You don't know what's going on,' she said. And I told her, 'I didn't say anything, Penelope, but if there's something I can do,' and she was, like, 'No, no, no, Heather, you don't understand, it's not what you think, it was just an accident.' And then . . . then—" The girl swallowed, a little nervous, and Infante fought to keep his attention on her words even as he was trying to figure out how to persuade her to come out to his rental car and climb on top of him. "She said, 'Don't worry, it'll all be worth it. I'll come out on top.' That was around Thanksgiving."

"What did she mean by that?"

"I'm sure I don't know. We never spoke of it again. Was that . . . well, wrong of me? Should I have called someone, tried to make her get help? She was an adult, after all, older'n me. I didn't see how I could help her."

"You did just fine," Infante said, seizing the opportunity to pat her forearm. The moment stretched out, not at all awkward.

"Can I get you something? Food, a drink?" Her voice was a little lower, almost husky.

"I probably shouldn't. I have to drive back to the airport in an hour or so, catch a flight home to Baltimore."

He caught her stealing a glance at his left hand. "There are lots of flights out of Jacksonville. You could probably go first thing in the morning, and it wouldn't make much difference. Home at nine, either way, just A.M. or P.M. What's the diff?"

"I already checked out of my motel."

"Oh, well, accommodations could be made, most likely. People are real friendly here. And it's fun, St. Simons. You've hardly seen any of it, I bet."

He considered it. Of course he did. Here was a beautiful young woman, all but promising she would fuck him when her shift ended. He could sit at the bar, drink beer, let the anticipation build as he watched her twitch back and forth in those khaki shorts. She'd probably comp his bar bill, or at least sneak him a few under the table. And what was the difference—the *diff*—Saturday night versus Sunday morning? Nancy was doing the interview today, starting just about now, by his calculations. He had been cut out, through no fault of his own. Okay, through nobody's fault, but definitely through no fault of his own. Under the circumstances—and the circumstances were beginning to form in his mind, an accident on the causeway, nothing big, nothing that would make the news, but enough of a hassle to trap him on the island until after the last Baltimore-bound plane left Jacksonville, and who could prove it didn't happen?—no one would care if Infante came home tomorrow. It wasn't like you needed to be an exceptional detective to do an airport pickup. Let someone else baby-sit the mom when she arrived, shuttle her to the Sheraton and keep her company. Heck, Lenhardt would probably enjoy hearing about his southern-belle adventure. *Did you get a good meal on the department? No, but I got good pussy!*

He brushed her wrist with his fingertips, feeling all that warmth, the vitality of her youth, the strength that came from never having had anything really bad happen to you. Kevin had no use for actual virgins, but he liked this particular kind of innocence, born of the belief that some guarantee had been made, that life would always be a smooth, creamy ride. Maybe it would be for this Heather. Maybe everyone she loved would die in his or her sleep, at appropriate ages. Maybe she would never sit at a kitchen table with her husband, weeping over the bills they couldn't quite cover or arguing about the various disappointments he had banked. Maybe she would have children who brought her nothing but pride and joy. Maybe. Someone had to have a life like that, right? His line of work didn't specialize in them, but they had to exist.

He slid his hand from her wrist, shook her soft

little paw, and said good-bye, taking care to let her know, through his voice and expression, how much he regretted not staying.

"Oh," she said, surprised, clearly a girl who was used to getting her way.

"Maybe another time," he said, meaning, *Tomorrow, next week, I'll probably go home with another young woman I meet in a bar. But tonight I'm going to return my rental car and be a team player.*

On the way out of town, he stopped at a barbecue joint in Brunswick and bought Lenhardt a T-shirt, a muscle-bound pig modeling his biceps: NO ONE CAN BEAT OUR MEAT. Even with that pit stop for a pulled-pork sandwich, he got to the Jacksonville airport so early that he managed to get standby on a flight that would get him into BWI almost an hour earlier than his original flight, a nonstop that would take almost half the time of his original one.

CHAPTER 32

"You want a better chair?"

"No, no." Willoughby was embarrassed by the offer, by the sergeant's very solicitousness. He was neither old enough nor distinguished enough to warrant so much attention.

"Because I can get you something better than that."

"I'm okay."

"I mean, over a few hours you're going to feel that one."

"Sergeant," he said, intending to sound dignified and stoic, but achieving only cranky. "Sergeant, I'm fine."

The building was a different one from the one where he had worked the bulk of his career, and he found himself grateful for that. He had not come here to stroll down memory lane. He was the ref, the linesman, here to rule what was fair or foul. A manila envelope, slightly dusty, sat at his feet, waiting for its moment.

It was going on 4:30 P.M., an interesting time to begin a long interview. It was a drowsy time of day, when blood sugar dipped and people began thinking about dinner, maybe cocktails if they went that way. Earlier, Willoughby had watched the pretty detective eat an apple and several slices of cheese, washed down with a bottle of water.

"Protein," she explained when she realized he was observing her. "It doesn't give you a burst of energy, but it sustains you over the long haul."

He wished he had a daughter. A son would have been nice, too, but a daughter cares for her parents in old age, while sons tend to get sucked into their wives' families, or so he'd always heard. If he had a daughter, he would still have a daughter. And grandchildren. It wasn't that he was lonely. Until a few days ago, he'd been pretty happy with his life. He had his health, golf, his golf buddies, and if he wanted to keep company with a woman, there were several at Edenwald who'd be thrilled to volunteer. Twice a month he met some old friends, Gilman boys, at the Starbucks on York Road, the one where the old Citgo station had been, and they talked about politics and old times. They called themselves "ROMEO"—retired old men eating out—and the conversation was damn lively. The sad truth was, Evelyn had been so sick and so frail for so long that he couldn't really miss her. Or, more correctly, he'd been missing her for years, through the last decade of her life, and it was easier to miss her now that she was truly gone.

It was funny about Evelyn—she didn't like him to talk about the Bethany girls. Other cases, even ones that were far more gruesome in the details, didn't bother her so much. In fact, she liked how he played it both ways. His life as a cop had brought him real cachet in their social circles, even made him sexier, and Evelyn had reveled in the fact, all her friends jockeying around him, vying for his attention, plying him with questions about his work. But not the Bethany girls, never the Bethany girls. He'd assumed that the subject was too heartbreaking for her. Denied children, she could not bear to hear about another infertile couple who had gained them, almost magically, then saw them taken. Now, for the first time, he wondered if the real problem was that he never solved it. Had Evelyn been disappointed in him?

"You're late," Gloria snapped at Kay, taking Heather by the elbow.

"Heather told you what happened," Kay said, trying to convince herself that she wasn't lying, simply declining to contradict Heather's lie, another hair split in a growing series of split hairs, a whole headful of them. But when she tried to follow them into the elevator, Gloria stopped her.

"You can't come up, Kay. Well, you could come up, but you'll be left in some empty office or conference room."

"Oh—I knew that," she said, her second lie in less than a minute, but this one merely a cover for her embarrassment.

"It's going to be a while, Kay. Hours. I assumed that I would drive Heather home."

"But it's so far out of your way. You live up here, and I'm over on the southwest side."

"Kay . . ."

She should go home, Kay told herself. She was getting too close to Heather as it was, crossing all sorts of lines. The mere fact that Heather was in her home—well, technically not in her home, but on her property—could result in a reprimand, threats against her license. She was losing her way. But, having gone this far, she was not willing to go back.

"I have a book with me. *Jane Eyre.* I'll be utterly content."

"*Jane Eyre*, huh? I never could read her."

Kay realized that Gloria had confused Brontë's novel with the other Jane of nineteenth-century letters, Jane Austen. There probably wasn't room for much in Gloria's brain besides her clients, her work. Should Kay take her aside, tell her that they had visited the old mall? Would Heather volunteer this? Did it matter? Left alone, her eyes scanned blindly across the pages, following but not really absorbing Jane's flight from Thornfield, the stiff proposal from St. John, the adorable, adoring sisters who turned out to be Jane's cousins.

She wasn't happy to see a female detective in the room, although she tried to conceal her irritation and surprise.

"Are we waiting for Kevin?" she asked.

"Kevin?" the plump detective echoed. "Oh, Detective Infante." As if she didn't have the right to call him by his first name. *She doesn't like me. She resents me for being so much thinner, even though she's a lot younger.*

She's protective of Kevin. "Detective Infante had to go out of town. To *Georgia.*"

"Is that supposed to mean something to me?"

Gloria shot her a look, but she was beyond caring what Gloria thought. She knew what she was doing and what she had to do.

"I don't know. *Does* it mean something to you?"

"I've never lived there, if that's where you're going."

"Where have you lived, over the last thirty years?"

"She's going to take the Fifth on that," Gloria said quickly.

"I'm not sure the Fifth is relevant, and we keep telling you that we can get your client before a grand jury, grant her immunity on anything she did as far as identity theft goes, but—okay." Fake easygoing.

I know you, Detective. You're one of the good girls, the kind who gets to be class secretary, or maybe vice president. The one who always has a big jock boyfriend and fusses with his collar at lunchtime, already a little wife at age sixteen. I know you. But I know what it's like to be a real teenage bride, and you wouldn't like it. You wouldn't like it at all.

"As we've said repeatedly, this isn't about the legal side of things," Gloria said. "It's also the poking about, the prying. If Heather provides the details of her current identity, you'll start talking to her coworkers and neighbors, right?"

"Possibly. We'll definitely run it through all our databases."

Who the fuck cares?

But Gloria said: "You think she's a criminal?"

"No, no, not at all. We're just having a hard time understanding why she never came forward until she was involved in a car accident and facing hit-and-run charges."

She decided to challenge the detective head-on. "You don't like me."

"I just met you," she said. "I don't know you."

"When is Kevin coming back? Shouldn't he do the interview? Without him we'll have to go over a bunch of stuff I've already covered."

"You were the one who wanted to do this today. Well, here we are. Let's do it."

"Gary Gilmore's final words—1977. Were you even born?"

"That very year," Nancy Porter said. "And how old were you? Where were you that Gary Gilmore's death made such an impact on you?"

"I was thirteen in Heather years. I was a different age on the outside."

" 'Heather years'? You make it sound like dog years."

"Trust me, Detective—I *aspired* to the life of a dog."

CHAPTER 33

"Sunny told me that I could go to the mall with her, but I couldn't hang around her. And then, maybe just because she said that, I wouldn't leave her alone. I followed her to the movie *Escape to Witch Mountain*. When the previews began, she got up and went out. I thought she might have gone to the bathroom, but when the movie started and she still wasn't back, I went out to the lobby to check for her."

"Were you worried about her? Did you think something had happened?"

The subject—Willoughby was not ready to call her Heather yet, if only out of self-protection, wary of investing too much hope in this woman, this resolution—the subject thought carefully about the question. Willoughby could see that she was someone given to thinking before she spoke. Perhaps she was

317

simply a cautious person, but his suspicion was that she liked the drama created by her pauses and hesitation. She knew she was playing for a larger audience than Nancy and Gloria.

"It's interesting that you ask that. The thing is, I *did* worry about Sunny. I know that sounds backwards, me being the younger one. But she was—I don't know what the right word is. Naïve? I wouldn't have had any words for it at the time. I just know I felt protective of her, and it worried me when she didn't come back. It was unthinkable that she would buy a movie ticket and abandon the show."

"She could have gone outside and asked for a refund."

She furrowed her brow, as if considering this. "Yes. Yes. That never occurred to me. I was *eleven*. And besides, I found out right away why she left. She had sneaked into *Chinatown,* which was an R-rated movie. The way the lobby was set up—there were only two theaters—it wasn't so easy to do that, and they watched for it. But if you used the bathroom on the other side—if you said the other one was full, or dirty—you could distract an usher and sneak in. We had done that before, to get two movies for the price of one, but not to see an R movie. It never occurred to me to try to see an R movie. I was a bit of a goody-goody."

Sneaking into R-rated movies—did kids even have to do that anymore? And a movie such as *Chinatown,* what a disappointment that must have been if you were hoping for salacious kicks. Willoughby wondered if an eleven-year-old, back in 1975, could even grasp the big twist, the incest theme, much less follow the intricate land deal at the heart of the film.

"So I found her in the back row, watching *Chinatown,* and she got furious with me, told me to go away. Which attracted the usher's attention, and we both got thrown out. She was really angry. Angry enough to scare me. Then she said that she was done with me, that she wouldn't even buy me Karmelkorn as promised, and she didn't want to see me again until our father picked us up at five-thirty."

"So what did you do?"

"Walked around. Looked at things."

"Did you see anyone, speak to anyone?"

"I didn't speak to anyone, no."

Willoughby made a notation on the legal pad they had provided him. This was key. If Pincharelli remembered Heather, she should remember him. It was one of the few things the music teacher had been forthcoming about, eventually. He'd seen Heather in the audience, watching him play.

Nancy Porter, bless her, caught it, too.

"You didn't speak to anyone, okay. But did you see someone, anyone, that you knew?"

"Not that I remember."

"Didn't see anyone familiar. A neighbor, a friend of your parents'?"

"No."

"So you just wandered around the mall, by yourself for three hours. . . ."

"That's what little girls do at malls, from time immemorial. They go to malls and walk around. Didn't you, Detective?"

This earned a baleful look from Gloria, who was not enjoying her client's combative attitude. Detective Porter smiled—a sunny, sincere smile, the kind of smile her subject had probably never been able to deliver in her entire life—and said, "Yeah, but for me it would have been White Marsh, and I hung out in the food court, near Mamma Ilardo's pizza."

"Nice name."

"They made a good pizza."

Nancy bent over her legal pad, writing furiously. All for show, Willoughby knew. All for show.

6:20 P.M.

"Tell me again what happened at the end of the day, when it was time for you to meet."

"I told you."

"Tell me again." Nancy took a swig from a bottle of water. She had offered the woman repeated chances to have a soda, take a bathroom break, but she always said no. Too bad, because if they could get her prints on a glass, they could run it through the system in minutes, see if they got a hit. Did she know that?

"It was almost five, and I had wandered back to the center, beneath the big green skylight, where the food was. Karmelkorn, Baskin-Robbins. I was thinking that Sunny might change her mind and buy me a treat after all. I decided if she didn't buy me Karmelkorn, I'd tell our parents about the R-rated movie. One way or another, I would get what I wanted. Back then . . . back then I was very good at getting my way."

"Back then?"

"You'd be surprised how years of sexual servitude break your will."

Willoughby liked the way that the detective nodded, as if sympathetic, but didn't let this information throw her off her stride. *Yeah, yeah, years of sexual servitude, that old thing.*

"It's—what time is it, when you go to the Karmelkorn?"

"Almost five. I *told* you."

"How did you know the time?"

"I had a Snoopy watch." Recited in an oh-so-bored voice. "A yellow-faced watch on a wide leather band. It had belonged to Sunny, in fact, and she no longer wore it. I thought it was funny. But the way his arms moved, it was hard to ever know the exact time. So all I can say is, it was going on five."

"And where was the Karmelkorn?"

"I couldn't tell you in terms of north or south, if that's what you want. Security Square was shaped like a plus sign, only one end was much longer than the other. The Karmelkorn would have been on the short, stumpy end that faced where the J. C. Penney was going in, but hadn't opened yet. It was a great place to sit. Even if you weren't eating, the smell was so rich and buttery."

"So you were sitting?"

"Yes, on the edge of a fountain. It wasn't a wishing fountain, but people had thrown coins in. I remember wondering what would happen if I fished them out, if I would get in trouble."

"But you were a goody-goody, you said."

"Even goody-goodies think about such things. In fact, I would say that's what defines us. We're always *thinking* about the things we don't dare do, figuring out where the lines are drawn, so we can go right up to

321

the edge of things, then plead innocence on the ground of a technicality."

"Was Sunny a goody-goody?"

"No, she was something worse."

"What was that?"

"Someone who wanted to be bad and didn't know how."

7:10 P.M.

Jane Eyre finished—Reader, I married him, he was blind, what other choice did he have?—Kay realized she was without a book. She probably had one in the trunk of her car, but she wasn't sure they would buzz her back into the building if she left. She could ask someone, but she felt that strange adolescent self-consciousness that she had never quite lost. She studied the notices pinned to the bulletin board, the pamphlets. DARE—Drug Awareness Education. No, wait, that didn't add up: Drug Abuse Resistance Education. An infelicitous name, all to create an acronym that didn't work, in Kay's opinion. It was too close to Drug Abuse *Resists* Education.

The impromptu trip to the mall still bothered her. Should she tell someone? To whom did she owe her loyalty, if anyone? Should she leave? But all that waited for her was an empty house on a Saturday night.

7:35 P.M.

"You want a soda?"

322

"No."

"Because I do. I'll be right back, okay? I'm just going to get a soda. Gloria?"

"I'm fine."

Left alone, the lawyer said to her client, "They're listening to us, just so you know. If we want to speak privately, however, all you have to do is ask."

"I know. I'm fine."

7:55 P.M.

"So where were we?"

"*You* were getting a soda."

"No, I mean when I left. Where were you, in the story? Oh, yeah, on the edge of the fountain, thinking about the coins."

"A man tapped me on the shoulder—"

"Show me."

"Show you?"

Nancy perched on the table between them. "I'm you. Did he come up from behind you? Which side? Show me."

She approached Nancy from behind, flicking her left shoulder with a little more vehemence than a tap would require.

"So you turn and you see this guy—what did he look like?"

"He was just an old guy to me. Very short hair, gray and brown. Ordinary-looking. He was in his fifties, but I'd only find that out later. At the time the only thing I thought was, He's old."

"Did he say anything?"

323

"He asked if I was Heather Bethany. He knew my name."

"And did that seem strange to you?"

"No. I was a kid. Grown-ups were always knowing things about me that I didn't know how they knew them. Grown-ups were like gods. Back then."

"Did you know him?"

"No, but he showed me his badge, right away, told me he was a police officer."

"What did the badge look like?"

"I don't know. A badge. He wasn't wearing a uniform, but he had a badge, and it wouldn't have occurred to me to doubt anything he said."

"Which was?"

" 'Your sister's been hurt. Come with me.' So I went. I followed him down a corridor, where the restrooms were. There was an exit back there, marked 'For Emergencies Only,' but it was an emergency, so it made sense to me that we were going that way, rather than the usual entrances."

"Did an alarm sound?"

"An alarm?"

"You walk out doors marked Emergency Exit Only, an alarm usually sounds."

"I don't remember one. Maybe he disabled it. Maybe there wasn't one. I don't know."

"The corridor was . . . where?"

"Between the center atrium and Sears. It was where the restrooms were, and also where they did the surveys."

"Surveys?"

"Consumer stuff. Sunny told me about it. You could get, like, five dollars for answering questions. But you had to be at least fifteen, so I never got to do it."

Infante slipped into the room where Willoughby and Lenhardt were watching the interrogation.

"You're supposed to be at the airport, waiting for the mom," Lenhardt said to him, but not in a mean, ballbusting way, not to Willoughby's ears.

"I got in early, and she's going to be at least two hours late according to the monitors. I thought I had time to run up here, see how things were going."

"Nancy's doing good," Lenhardt said. "She's taking her time. She's had her going almost four hours now, and she keeps bringing her up to the edge of the actual kidnapping, then going back to the beginning. It's driving her crazy. She's bursting to tell us the bad shit, for some reason."

Infante glanced at his watch. "I'll have to leave for the airport by nine-thirty. You think I'll catch the main show?"

Lenhardt balled his fists and rotated his wrists, peering at his clenched fingers. "Magic Eight Ball says all signs look good."

"So you're outside, and . . . is it dark?"

"No, it's still light. It's March twenty-ninth. The days were getting longer. We got outside—"

"No alarm on the door?"

"No, no alarm on the door. And there was a van. He opened the door, and Sunny was inside. Before I could register anything—the fact that she was lying down, tied up, the fact that this wasn't a police car—he had caught me up and thrown me back there. I fought, if you could call it that, a little girl flailing her arms at a grown man. But it was completely ineffectual. I wonder—do you think he got Sunny the same way, with the same story? How did he *know* us? Have you figured *that* out, Detective? How did Stan Dunham know us? Why did he target us?"

"Stan Dunham's in a retirement community out in Sykesville." A pause. "Did you know that?"

"It's not as if we're *pen pals*." Said with dry disgust. Yet without worry, Willoughby noticed. Again, they had considered carefully what they would say about Dunham. They had no intention of telling her that he couldn't contradict his own name at this point. But the fact that he was still alive didn't seem to make as much of an impression as it should have. Even if she were telling the truth, shouldn't she be more taken aback by the revelation that her captor, the man who had ruined her life, was just thirty miles west of where she sat?

"Okay, okay—when he grabbed you, did you . . . lose anything? Leave anything behind?"

"What do you mean?"

"Just that. Did you leave anything behind?"

Her eyes widened. "The purse. Of course, I dropped my purse. How I mourned that purse. I know this will sound weird to you, but it was easier, in the back of that van, to worry about the purse than to think about . . ." She began to cry, and her lawyer handed her a tissue, although these were the kind of tears that no mere tissue could sop up, hard as rain.

"Can you describe the purse?"

"D-d-d-d-escribe it?" It was all Willoughby could

do not to reach out and grab the sergeant's hand. This was it, the moment that he and Nancy had planned this morning.

"Yes, could you describe it? Tell me what it looked like, what was in it?"

She appeared to be thinking, which didn't seem right to Willoughby. She knew or she didn't.

The lawyer spoke for the first time. "C'mon, Nancy. What does it matter if she can describe a purse she had when she was eleven?"

"She described her Snoopy watch in pretty definite detail."

"It was thirty years ago. People do forget things. I can't remember what I had for lunch yesterday—"

"Denim with red rickrack," she said firmly, her voice rising over her lawyer's. "Attached to a set of wooden handles by a set of white buttons. The purse had a muslin base, and you could attach various covers to change the look."

"And what was in it?"

"Why . . . money, of course. And a little comb."

"Not a key or a lipstick?"

"Sunny had the key, and I wasn't allowed to wear makeup yet, just Bonne Belle."

"That was the complete inventory of the purse?"

"What?"

"A little comb, Bonne Belle, and money. How much?"

"Hardly any. Maybe five dollars, less what I'd spent for the movie ticket. And I'm not sure I had a Bonne Belle. I just told you that's all I was allowed to have. I can't remember everything. God, do you even know what's in your purse right now?"

"Billfold," Nancy Porter said. "Tic Tacs. Diaper wipes. I have a six-month-old. Lipstick. Receipts—"

"Okay, you can. I can't. Hey, when they stopped me Tuesday night, I didn't even know why my billfold wasn't in my purse."

"We'll get to that."

9:10 P.M.

"So once in the van . . ."

"We drove. We drove and we drove. It seemed like a very long time, but maybe my sense of time was off. He stopped at some point and got out. We tried the door—"

"You weren't tied up, like your sister?"

"No, he was in a hurry. He just grabbed me and threw me in. I have no idea how he subdued Sunny."

"But you said, 'We tried the door'—"

"I untied her, of course. I didn't let her stay tied up. He stopped, we tried the door, it was locked from the outside. And there was mesh between the rear of the van and the passenger compartment, so we couldn't get out that way."

"Did you scream?"

She looked at Nancy blankly.

"While he was outside the van. Did you scream, try to draw attention to yourselves?"

"No. We didn't know where we were, if there was anyone out there to hear us. And he had threatened us, told us horrible things would happen—so no, we didn't scream."

Nancy glanced at the tape recorder but didn't speak.

That was good, Willoughby thought. She was using silence as a goad, waiting the woman out.

"We were in the country. There were . . . crickets."

"Crickets? In March?"

"Some strange sound. Strange to us. Perhaps it was the absence of sound." She turned to Gloria. "Do I have to talk about this part in detail? Is it really necessary?" Then, without waiting for an answer, she began the story that she claimed to be so loath to tell. "He took us into this house in the middle of nowhere. A farmhouse. He wanted to . . . do things. Sunny fought him, and he killed her. I don't think he meant to. He seemed surprised when it happened. Sad, even. Is that possible? That he could have been sad? Maybe he had always meant to kill us, kill both of us, but then it happened and he realized that killing wasn't something he was equipped for. He killed her, and then he told me that I could never leave him. That I would have to stay with him and his family, be a part of it. And if I didn't . . . well, if I didn't, then he would have no choice but to do to me what he'd done to Sunny. She's dead, he said. I can't bring her back. But I can give you a new life, if you let me."

Willoughby had a vision of a highway, the way it shimmered sometimes in the late summer, how the air seemed to get wavy at sunset. There was a similar quality in this story, although he couldn't quite put a finger on it. It began with the crickets, even though she had disavowed them. All he knew was that she was moving in and out of the truth, that parts were accurate but others had been . . . molded. Shaped. To whose expectations? To what purpose?

"His family? So there were other people involved in this?"

"They didn't know everything. I'm not sure what he told his wife and son—maybe that I was a runaway who he'd saved from the streets in Baltimore, a girl who couldn't go home for whatever reason. All I know is that he went to the library and read old newspapers until he found what he needed—a story about a fire in Ohio, several years before. An entire family had been killed. He took the name of the youngest child and applied for a Social Security number in that name. With that, he was able to enroll me at the parish school up in York."

"Without anything but a Social Security number?"

"It was a parish school, and he told them that it was all I had, that everything had been destroyed and it would be months before he could get a birth certificate. He'd been a police officer, well respected. People generally wanted to please him."

"So he enrolls you in school, sends you off every day, and you don't try to tell anyone who you are or what you've been up to?"

"This didn't happen right away. He waited until the next fall. For almost six months, I lived under his roof, with virtually no freedom. I was pretty broken down by the time I started going to school. I'd been told every day for six months that no one cared about me, that no one was looking for me, that I was dependent on him for everything. He was a grown-up—and a cop. I was a child. I believed him. Besides—I was being raped every night."

"And his wife put up with this?"

"She turned a blind eye to it, as families do. Or maybe she rationalized that I was at fault, that I was a baby prostitute who seduced her husband. I don't know. Over time you get numb to it. It was a chore, something I was expected to do. We lived between Glen Rock and Shrewsbury, which felt like a million miles away from Baltimore. Up there no one ever spoke about the Bethany girls. That was something that happened down in the city. And there were no Bethany girls anymore. Just a Bethany girl."

"Is that where you live now? Is that where you've been all this time?"

She smiled. "No, Detective. I left there a long time ago. When I was eighteen, he gave me money, put me on a bus, and told me I was on my own."

"And why didn't you take the bus back to Baltimore, find your folks, tell everyone where you'd been?"

"Because I didn't exist anymore. I had been Ruth Leibig, only survivor of a tragic fire in Columbus, Ohio. Normal teenager by day, consort by night. There was no Heather Bethany. There was nothing to go back to."

"So that's the name you've been using, then. Ruth Leibig?"

A broader smile. "You won't get it that easy, Detective. Stan Dunham taught me well. I learned how to search old newspapers, too, how to find unclaimed identities and make them mine. It's harder now, of course. People get Social Security cards earlier and earlier. But for someone my age there are still lots of little dead children's names to use. And you'd be surprised how easy it is to get birth certificates if you have some basic information and a few . . . skills."

"What kind of skills?"

"That's none of your business."

Gloria nodded. "Look, she's given you the story. Now you know."

"Here's the thing," Nancy said. "Everything she's given us so far leads to a dead end. The farm, where all this happened? Gone, subdivided years ago, and there's no record that any human remains were uncovered."

"Check the parish school, Sisters of the Little Flower. You'll find Ruth Leibig on the rolls."

"Stan Dunham is in a hospice, dying—"

"Good," she said.

"His wife has been dead for almost ten years. Oh, and the son? He died in an accidental fire just three months ago. In Georgia. Where he was living with Penelope Jackson."

"He's dead? Tony's *dead*?"

If Willoughby had been younger, he might have shot out of his chair. Infante and Lenhardt, already standing, stiffened in their posture, leaned toward the speaker-box that was bringing the words to them.

"Did you—" Lenhardt began, even as Infante said, "She wasn't surprised about the father, didn't give a shit about Penelope Jackson or Georgia, but the son has caught her off guard. And she knew his name, although Nancy didn't provide it."

On the other side: "Be still, Heather," Gloria said. "Now. Nancy, if you would give us a minute."

"Sure. Take all the time you want."

Nancy had walked out of the room, but she was practically prancing when she joined the circle of detectives. The girl was pleased with herself, as well she should be, Willoughby thought. She had done a good job. The thing about Pincharelli was a key omission.

And Miriam had always insisted that Heather had taken an unusually large amount of money that day to the mall, because her bank at home was empty.

But it wasn't good enough. He was the only one in the room who knew they had fallen short of proving she wasn't Heather Bethany. He'd stake his life on the fact that she was lying, but he couldn't prove it.

"Well?" she said to the three men.

"We waited for you," Lenhardt said.

Willoughby picked up the envelope at his feet and opened it, although he knew what he would find inside. A blue denim purse, with red rickrack. Even within the light-deprived confines of an envelope, it had faded a little over the years, yet it was just as it had been described, except for the contents. But that's only because there were no contents. The purse had been found next to a Dumpster, turned inside out, a tire mark on its side. The supposition had always been that Heather had dropped it during the abduction and that some opportunistic scum had stumbled on it, stripped it of whatever cash or items it contained, and tossed it aside.

Yet they couldn't contradict her memory of what it had contained, because they didn't know. Here was the purse, exactly as she'd described it. So if she was Heather Bethany, why didn't she remember seeing her sister's music teacher? Had Pincharelli been lying all those years ago? Had he broken down and told Willoughby what he wanted to hear because there was yet another secret he was hiding? He was dead, too. Everywhere they turned, people were dead or dying. That was the natural order of things, over thirty years. Dave was gone. Willoughby's Evelyn was gone. Stan

Dunham's wife and son were gone, and the man himself was as good as gone. Penelope Jackson, whoever she was, had disappeared, leaving behind nothing but a green Valiant. And the only thing they'd been able to establish with any certainty was that the woman in the interrogation room was not Penelope Jackson. Yet she had described the purse. Did that make her Heather Bethany? He thought back to the shimmer in the air, the moment he was sure that she was lying.

"Fuck me," Lenhardt said.

"Well, the mom will be here soon," Infante said. "It would have been nice if we didn't have to put her through that, if we could have told her when she landed what was what, but at least DNA's definitive. When we finally get it. Even with a rush, it will take a day or two."

"Yeah," Willoughby said. "About that . . ."

10:25 P.M.

The plane seemed to drone as sleepily as its passengers, most of whom were tired and disgruntled from being more than two hours past their scheduled arrival. In her first-class window seat, a luxury created by the necessity of buying a last-minute ticket, Miriam couldn't begin to sleep, and she stared at the floor of clouds below the jet. It took a long time to break through the cloud cover, but Baltimore was finally beneath her, for the first time in almost twenty years. It was vast in a way that did not match her memories, its lights spread across a far wider area, but she hadn't flown into Baltimore since 1968. The airport had still

334

been called Friendship then, and Miriam was returning from Canada by way of New York. In the summer after the riots, it had seemed a felicitous time to take her children to Ottawa, let them spend an extended vacation with their grandparents. Oh, how dressed up they had gotten for that return trip, the girls in matching dresses purchased by Miriam's mother at Holt Renfrew—striped shifts with scarves that attached to the collars with snaps. Sunny had been a mess twenty minutes into the journey, but Heather barely had a crease in her dress even upon landing. People could meet you at airport gates then. She remembered Dave, waiting for them inside the terminal, pale and round-shouldered, so beaten down by his job. A few years later, when he approached her with his dream of opening a store, that image came back to her, and she readily said yes. She had wanted him to be happy. Even when she was miserable, she had wanted nothing less for Dave than some sort of peace.

Suddenly there was a dead space beneath the plane, with almost no lights shining at all, an abyss. The plane had turned and was heading up the Chesapeake Bay. Although the final descent was quite smooth, Miriam's stomach twisted once again from that strange *turista*-like ailment she had never known in all her years in Mexico, and she fumbled in the seat pocket for an airsickness bag, but there wasn't one. Perhaps airlines didn't provide them anymore, perhaps people were supposed to be able to fly without getting ill, at least in first class. Or someone had taken it and the overworked flight attendants hadn't noticed. Miriam did the only thing possible, given the circumstances. She swallowed.

PART VIII
THINGS AS THEY ARE (1989)

CHAPTER 34

The last leg of Miriam's trip to language school was complicated by the fact that she didn't yet speak Spanish. *A true Catch-22,* she thought as she stood in the cavernous, chaotic bus station, where she had managed to purchase her first-class ticket to Cuernavaca with a minimum of misunderstanding. She had gotten through customs and finessed the Mexico City cab system to get there and was feeling very proud of herself up until the moment she left the ticket counter, her bus ticket for Cuernavaca clutched in her trembling hand.

But how to find the right bus among those lined up in the lanes outside, rumbling and belching black smoke? The announcements on the PA system were nothing more than bursts of static, incomprehensible in any language. There was no information booth that she could find, no one seemed to speak English, and the halting Spanish she had acquired in her introductory course back in Texas was of little use. People stared at her blankly when she stammered out her questions, then released a torrent of words, peppering her with sounds. They wanted to help. Their faces were kind, their gestures affectionate and warm. They simply did not understand anything she said.

She studied her ticket, noted that it was blue, then began looking at the tickets in others' hands. There was a woman whose ticket was also blue, a tired-looking woman with the kind of profile that one saw in Mayan art—the noble, hawklike nose, the flat forehead.

"Cuernavaca?" Miriam asked.

The woman considered Miriam's question cautiously, as if she had known a lifetime of simple questions that turned out to be sinister and dangerous.

"*Sí*," she said. "*Ya me voy.*" She turned away, as if she thought Miriam's question had been a subtle order to move along. When she glanced back over her shoulder and saw Miriam following her, she picked up her pace, which was difficult as she was traveling with two large shopping bags. But it was more difficult for Miriam, with her suitcase strapped to a set of rollers, and she began to fall behind. The woman glanced back again, saw Miriam struggling, then registered the ticket in her hand, that it was the same as hers.

"*Cuernavaca,*" she said, understanding. She waited for Miriam to catch up with her, then led her to the proper bus. "Cuernavaca," she repeated, smiling, as if Miriam were a child learning an essential word. "Cuernavaca," she said upon boarding, settling in a seat across the aisle. Then she dared a new bit of vocabulary, words that Miriam knew she should know, words that she had learned at some point, but were lost to her. The woman tried again, speaking more slowly. Miriam laughed and threw up her hands, mocking her own ignorance. The woman smiled and laughed, too, seemingly relieved that she would not have to try to make conversation with this gringa stranger for the hour's journey south. She settled back in her seat, rummaged through one of her bags, and pulled out something wrapped in waxed paper. She peeled the paper away, revealing a mango on a stick coated with a thick sprinkling of what appeared to be chili pepper. Now that she was safe on the bus, almost at her destination, Miriam was relaxed enough to find this wondrous. If she had seen it just five minutes earlier, when she was still lost, it would have struck her as disgusting.

¿De dónde es? That was what the woman had asked. *Where are you from?* It was too late to answer, and even if Miriam did—what would she say? She had boarded a plane in Austin this morning. Did that make her a Texan? Or should she say Canada, the place of her birth? Since her parents had died, she had no ties there. She still thought of Baltimore as home, but the fact was she had lived there a mere fifteen years, while Texas had been her home for the last thirteen. *Where was she from?* The only thing she was sure of was that she was getting out of Texas just in time, racing the recession as if it were an unruly wave sweeping up a beach.

She had been lucky, not smart. She had sold her own house eighteen months earlier, before the market began its precipitous slide. At the same time, she had divested herself of some longtime investments she had inherited from her parents. But it wasn't that she had predicted the stock market collapse in 1987 or Texas's real-estate woes on its heels. She had been toying with the idea of early retirement, so she had moved her money to CDs and other laughably conservative investments. And she hadn't bought a new house because she wasn't sure she wanted to stay in Texas. Her money would go so much further somewhere else. Lots of people didn't want to stay in Texas just now, and these people had cried in Miriam's office over the past few months, baffled by the concept of negative equity. "How can we *owe*?" one young woman had sobbed. "We bought the house, we made our payments, and now we're selling it. So why do we owe seven thousand dollars?" Bolder sellers tried to suggest that a Realtor should not be paid if the deal yielded no profit for them. It was an ugly time.

But even if things had been booming, Miriam would have made the same decisions. Her pathologically optimistic partners thought she was crazy, taking four weeks off just as the spring season was gearing up. "How can you leave now?" they asked. "Things are bound to pick up." They would think she was crazier still if they knew she didn't plan to return to work ever. She was going to study Spanish in a month-long immersion course, then find a place to live. In the United States, such a dream was at least a decade away. But here in Mexico, where a dollar currently bought you sixteen hundred pesos, it could be done. Not that she was sold on Mexico. Belize was a possibility, or Costa Rica.

In the blur of preparations for the first leg of her trip, she had not focused on the date right away. There had been so much to do, so many signatures, even more than a settlement required. Traveler's checks, the sublease agreement on her apartment, the sale of her car. (That alone should have alerted her coworkers she wasn't returning. Who could live in Texas without a car?) But three weeks ago, when she finally made the plane reservation, the date, March 16, had stared up at her from her Filofax. She decided it was a good omen, getting out of the country before another March 29.

The bus was winding through a mountain pass, and Miriam noticed the tiny white crosses along the roadside. Come to think of it, weren't buses always plunging down hills in Mexico? Such stories seemed a staple of the news. Bus accidents and mudslides and typhoons and earthquakes. On the cab ride from the airport to the bus station, she had seen abandoned buildings from the Mexico City earthquake of 1987, their fates still undecided. Most of the people she knew loved CNN, felt that it was an intellectual badge of honor to watch a cable channel with so much foreign news. Some called it the Crisis News Network, but Miriam felt that Ted Turner's ultimate subtext was, Be Glad You're Here. The rest of the world was shown as wild and unpredictable, prone to disaster and strife and civil war. Spend enough time with CNN and the United States seemed reassuringly stable.

At last the bus arrived in downtown Cuernavaca. Miriam had a hotel reservation and an address in her pocket, but she had one more linguistic hurdle before she could truly arrive. According to the note from the school, one must haggle for taxis, agreeing on a fare before the trip. How did one do that without being conversant in Spanish? When she got to the head of the taxi line, she offered the driver a thousand pesos, then fifteen hundred, then two thousand, but he kept refusing her. She was on the verge of getting flustered and angry when she realized that they were talking about a difference of a few cents.

The cab plunged into the congested streets, and Miriam's eyes felt drunk from what they were trying to take in—a castle, one of Cortez's, decorated with a Diego Rivera mural, the zócalo, thronged on a Sunday afternoon, with a group of men in some sort of indigenous dress. Eventually, her driver turned down a grimy, nondescript street. Miriam's heart sank. She had booked a room at Las Mañanitas, shockingly expensive by Mexican standards, the equivalent of an airport Marriott back in the States. It was to be her last splurge, her final extravagance. She had assumed the cost would guarantee quality and was dismayed when the driver stopped at a nondescript building. "Here?" she asked, then remembering. "*¿Aquí?*"

The driver grunted, all but threw her luggage on the sidewalk, and drove away. Suddenly a heavy wooden door was flung open and a trim blond man appeared, accompanied by two locals, who wordlessly took her bags. Ushered into an anteroom, she saw that the hotel was designed to be a glorious secret. It turned a blank face to the street, but it was situated on an expansive courtyard, with rooms ringing an emerald lawn where—of all things—white peacocks strolled. She felt like Dorothy in *The Wizard of Oz,* exchanging the black-and-white of Kansas for the Technicolor of Munchkinland.

Oz made her think of the girls, their annual ritual of watching the televised version of the movie beneath an old quilt, which they threw over their heads at certain scary moments—the bellicose trees, the flying monkeys. Not the witch, interestingly, never the witch, although her early incarnation as Elvira Gulch unnerved them a little. But Margaret Hamilton had squandered her ability to scare them by appearing in those coffee commercials.

Miriam's knees buckled, and she started to cry, just a little. How to explain, in any language, why she behaved this way? She had come to Mexico in hopes that she could stop explaining once and for all. She had come to Mexico to escape the phone calls, the ones where no one ever spoke. ("Dave?" she yelled into the empty air. "Who is this? Why are you calling me?" Once, just once, she had forgotten herself and said "Honey?" only to hear a sharp intake of breath.) She had come to Mexico to start over, and here she was, trapped in the same old life. Amazing, the levels of pain, the subtle variations, even after more than a decade. Miriam lived every day with a dull, chronic ache, like some permanent nerve damage she had learned to compensate for because there was no surgical fix. But no matter how careful she was, no matter how tenderly she protected these compromised joints and tendons, there were things that made the pain flare up, sudden and searing. Anything could trigger memories, even new experiences such as this, which she sought out hoping for a context in which the girls could not insert themselves. She looked at the white peacocks strutting across the lawn at a hotel in Cuernavaca, Mexico, and burst into tears for the children who would have been delighted by them.

But the beauty of a first-class hotel, the whole point

of paying seventy-five dollars a night when you could be just as comfortable for thirty, is that the staff is trained in unfaltering politeness. *The señora must be tired after her long day of travel,* the blond man told the hovering staff—in Spanish, yet Miriam could understand his Spanish, which was not as rapid, whose words did not run pell-mell into each other. She was escorted to a sparkling room, where a maid brought her fresh-squeezed orange juice. The maid then gave her a tour of the room's amenities. Nothing was too small, too trivial, to be explained. She indicated a rug on the floor. *For your little feet.* She showed her a bowl of fruit. *In case you have hunger.* And, at last, she placed a small pillow on the snowy white bed and urged her to lie down. *For your little head,* Miriam translated. *For your little head.*

Miriam pantomimed her desire for a glass of water, which would have to be distilled or purified, even in this shining place. She then tried to ask if it was necessary to dress for dinner, if she could wear pants, going so far as to unzip her suitcase and show the uncrushable silk trousers packed on the top. *Cómo no,* the maid responded. Not *why not* but *how not,* Miriam noted. Another idiom to master.

"*¿Tiene sueño?*" the maid then asked, and Miriam started. But she was only being asked if she was sleepy, not if she had dreams.

She surrendered to the bed and when she awoke, night had fallen and the hotel lawn was full of people having drinks and dinner. She sipped a kir royale, nibbled toasted pine nuts, and tried to shut out the language she already understood, allowing only Spanish into her head and heart. She was here to learn new words, a new way of speaking, a new way of being. She had already learned a few things today, and been reminded of others she already knew. She would now have hunger, not be it. Use the first-person pronoun only for emphasis. And, most important of all, she would swap why for how. *¿Cómo no?*

CHAPTER 35

"Barb, I lost my story!"

The cry, all too familiar at this time of the afternoon, came from the usual source, a messy desk in a corner of the newsroom, a desk piled so high with papers and reports that its occupant would have been virtually invisible if it weren't for her towering hairstyle. A tiny, formidably stylish woman, Mrs. Hennessey often lost her work on deadline, but seldom because of an actual computer crash or malfunction. Instead she had a habit of hiding her work in progress on the alternate screen or copying the entire story to a "save" key and then deleting it from the screen in front of her.

"Let me see, Mrs. Hennessey." Barb tried to swing the computer around on the pedestal that allowed it to be shared by two reporters, but Mrs. Hennessey had cunningly blocked the lazy Susan by piling reference books around it, so she seldom had to share. Barb tapped away, checking the usual traps, but Mrs.

Hennessey was right for once: She really had lost her work. When Barb found its ghostly twin in the backup system, it was just a blank template with a story header and the date it had been created, nothing more.

"Did you save as you wrote?" she asked, knowing the answer.

"Well, I tabbed at the end of every paragraph."

"The tab key doesn't *save*. You have to execute the save command, Mrs. Hennessey."

"I don't know what you mean." Mrs. Hennessey had been around since God was a boy, to use a localism. A thirty-five-year employee of the *Fairfax Gazette,* she had started in the women's section, as it was then known, and fought her way into the news section, where she had covered the education beat for the last two decades. Her seniority was unmatched, if only because the paper's most promising reporters seldom stayed for more than two years. She also was rumored to be a Holocaust survivor, but her thick gold bangles hid whatever tattoos she might have. She was, in short, tough as nails, but she reverted to a kittenish, helpless quality when her computer let her down. Or, more correctly, when she let the computer down, refusing to take the simplest steps to protect her work.

"If you hit 'Function 2' every 'graph or so, then the computer will store a copy of your file and continue to update it. You never saved this work. As far as the computer's concerned, it doesn't exist. It can't save what it can't see."

"What do you mean, it can't see it? It's right there," she said, gesturing at the screen with her be-ringed fingers. "It *was* right there," she amended, given that the screen was blank. "I could see it. These machines are useless."

Barb always felt defensive on the computer system's behalf, flawed as she knew it to be. The *Gazette,* part of a small chain, had the incompatible habits of being progressive in its thinking and tight with its coffers, a combination that had brought them this dinosaur of a system, one that wasn't intended for newspaper work. "It's a tool, like anything else. When you used typewriters, there was no copy unless you inserted carbon paper. It's a poor craftsman who blames his tools."

The saying, one of her father's, came out of nowhere. As usual, she felt wistful and sad and anxious all at once, as if this wisp of an echo could unravel her life.

"What did you say to me?" Mrs. Hennessey's voice abandoned kitten and moved on to lioness. "You impertinent . . ." Here, she uttered some oath in German or Yiddish, Barb couldn't be sure. "I will have you fired. I will—" She clambered out of her chair and over the piles of reports she had used to create a makeshift barrier around her desk, and raced to the editor's corner office on her tiny, perfect heels, quivering all over, as if Barb had threatened her with violence. Even her topknot—dyed into submission and touched up every two weeks so nary a root showed in the fierce chestnut red—shook as if in fear.

Barb might have been worried, if she hadn't witnessed the same performance at least twice a month since she'd started working in the newsroom last summer. Mrs. Hennessey raged up and down in the editor's office, shaking her tiny fists, demanding Barb's ouster. She huffed out of the room and, within seconds, Barb was summoned by electronic message.

"If you could just see your way to being a bit more tactful with her . . ." the editor, Mike Bagley, began.

"I'll try," Barb said. "I do try. Do you ask her to be more tactful with *me*? She treats me like her personal servant. Granted, the computer eats her work every now and then, but most of her problems stem from the fact that she refuses to do the most basic stuff correctly. I'm not her keeper."

"She's an"—he looked around as if fearful of being overheard—"an older woman. Set in her ways. We're not going to change her at this point."

"So that little tail wags the whole newsroom's dog?"

Bagley, a large man with thin gingery hair that had faded with age to the color of Tang, made a face. "That conjures up quite an image. Mrs. Hennessey's tail. My eyes! But look, Barb. Your career path has been unorthodox at best. Your people skills are less than . . ."

She waited, curious to hear what word he would put to it. Nonexistent? Crippled? But he didn't even try to finish the sentence.

"We are utterly dependent on you. When the system crashes and you bring it back up, your work saves us thousands of dollars. You know that and I know that. So let Mrs. Hennessey pretend that she's a person of consequence, as opposed to an age-discrimination suit waiting to happen. Just apologize to her."

"Apologize? It wasn't my fault."

"You called her a crappy writer."

"I . . . ?" She laughed. "I said that it was a poor craftsman who blames his tools. It's just an old saying. I didn't say shit about her writing. But she is, isn't she?" Barb mulled on this. It had not occurred to her before that she was entitled to have an opinion about the words that appeared on the screens she tended. She had been plucked out of the Classified department, a computer savant discovered in the newspaper's equivalent of Schwab's. She wasn't even conscious of reading the paper, but she had been, she realized, and Mrs. Hennessey *was* a crappy writer.

"Just say you're sorry, Barb. Sometimes the expedient way is the right way."

She looked at him through her lashes, eyes glowering. *Do you know what I could do to this system? Do you realize I could cripple this whole operation?* In her six-month evaluation, Bagley—who had no right to supervise her, given that he had no inkling what her job involved—had written that she needed to "work on her anger." Oh, she worked on it, all right. She banked it like a fire every night, recognizing it as her best source of energy.

"And who will apologize to me?"

He had no idea what she was talking about. "Look, I agree that Mrs. Hennessey is a handful. But she didn't say boo to you. And she *thinks* that you said she's a bad writer. It's just easier all around if you apologize."

"Easier for who?"

"For whom," he corrected. What an asshole. "Okay, it's easier for me. And I'm the boss, right? So just say you're sorry and let me get the hell out of this hen fight."

She found Mrs. Hennessey in the break room, a grimy alcove of vending machines and Formica-topped tables.

"I'm sorry," she said stiffly.

The older woman inclined her head with equal

stiffness, a queen staring down her nose at a peasant. That is, she would have been staring down at Barb if she hadn't been seated. "Thank you."

"It was just a saying." Barb didn't know why she felt compelled to keep speaking. She had done what she'd been told to do. "I wasn't implying anything about your writing."

"I've been a reporter for thirty-five years," Mrs. Hennessey said. She had a first name, Mary Rose. It appeared in her byline, but it was never used in conversation. She was always Mrs. Hennessey. "I've worked at this paper longer than you've been alive. Women like me, we made your career possible. I covered desegregation."

"Yeah? That was a big issue—" She stopped herself, just in time. She had been on the verge of saying "That was a big issue where I grew up." But she was Barbara Monroe, of Chicago, Illinois. She had attended a big-city high school, Mather. A big school in a big city was easier to fake than a small one, because anyone could be forgotten in a big school. But she wasn't sure if desegregation had been a big issue in Chicago. Probably, but why risk saying anything too specific? "That was a big issue in the seventies, wasn't it?"

"Yes, it was. And I covered it single-handedly."

"Great."

She had meant to sound sincerely impressed, but her voice betrayed her as it sometimes did, and the word came out a little sour, sarcastic.

"It *was* great. It was meaningful. More meaningful than tinkering with machines for a living. I'm writing the first draft of history. What are you but a mechanic?"

The would-be insult made Barb laugh. It was just so funny that this was Mrs. Hennessey's idea of a cutting remark. But her laughter provoked the old woman even more.

"Oh, you think you're so special, wiggling around the newsroom in your tight shirts and short skirts so the men all look at you. You think you *matter*."

The editor had told her that she did matter, that she was essential. "I don't see what my wardrobe has to do with this, Mrs. Hennessey. And I honestly think that your work was great—"

"Was? *Was?* Is. My work *is* great, you, you . . . guttersnipe!"

Again she wanted to laugh at the older woman's idea of an insult. Yet this one was more effective somehow, finding a soft spot. Sex, her own sexuality, was a touchy subject for her. She didn't flirt with the men in the newsroom, or anywhere else for that matter, and her skirts weren't short. If anything, they were long by the standard of the day, because her frame was petite, so skirts hung lower than they were supposed to, drooping on her hips. With her towering upsweep and high heels, Mrs. Hennessey was almost as tall as she.

Which could explain, perhaps, why she felt it was fair play to pick up the older woman's Diet Pepsi and pour it over her beautiful, quivering topknot.

They fired her. Of course. Actually, they gave her the option of attending counseling sessions or leaving with two weeks' severance. "No references," Bagley added. As if she would ask for one, as if it would have any application when Barbara Monroe

354

disappeared and another woman took her place. She took the severance.

She sneaked back in that night, using the newspaper's research tools, crude as they were. The newspaper's sole librarian was in her debt and had never dreamed why Barb wanted to know so much about the library, its capabilities. He'd been flattered, in fact, to show Barb all the things a well-trained librarian could do with a telephone and a list of reference desks in city libraries. Title searches, which kicked up property and court records, were also valuable, but they required time and money, neither of which she had right now, although she had sneaked a few through the newspaper's account over the past year. Dave Bethany was still on Algonquin Lane. Miriam Bethany remained missing, as she had been for some months now. Stan Dunham was at the same address—but then, she had never really lost contact with Stan Dunham.

Finally she picked out her new name and existence, just as Stan had taught her to do. Time to start over. Again. It was a burn, not being able to use this job on her résumé, but she had decided that she wasn't going to stay in newspapers. Once she got the formal training she needed, she would find a more lucrative home for her skills, in an industry used to paying for talent. She could do better than the *Fairfax Gazette,* even if they did have to push her out of the nest. Didn't it always work that way? Even in the worst situation, she had always needed someone else to force her out, encourage her to move on. How she had cried that day at the Greyhound station, while other people smiled and nodded, thinking she was nothing more than a scared teenager who couldn't bear to leave home.

Her research done, the last thing she did was write a little code, her going-away gift to the *Gazette*. The next day, when Mrs. Hennessey logged on, the whole thing crashed, taking with it every article in progress, even those that more responsible reporters had diligently backed up. By then she was already in a diner in Anacostia, waiting for Stan Dunham. He had tried to persuade her to drive farther north, but she told him that she wouldn't cross the district line into Maryland. And to this day, whatever she wanted from Stan Dunham, she got.

CHAPTER 36

"Because she was adopted, you know?"

Dave had been waiting in line for a cinnamon twist when this one sentence managed to break free of the general hum around him, flinging itself at him like a shoe or a small stone. The comment, however, was not addressed to him but was part of a conversation between two placid middle-aged women waiting behind him in line.

"What?" he asked, as if it had been their intent to involve him in their conversation. "Who was adopted?"

"Lisa Steinberg," said one.

"The little girl in New York who was beaten by her adoptive father? It's great that the bastard is going to jail. But they shoulda gotten the woman, too. No real mother would have sat idly by while that was going on. No way, no how."

They nodded, smug and content, the entire world known to them. They were doughy, pasty-faced

357

women, anti-advertisements for the baked goods sold at Bauhof's. Dave was reminded of a book that Heather and Sunny had loved, *Beastly Boys and Ghastly Girls,* with whimsical drawings by someone of note. Addams? Gorey? Something like that, very clever line drawings. One story was about a boy who ate nothing but sweets until he melted in the sun, just a puddle of gelatinous flesh with facial features.

"How can—" he began, but Miss Wanda, attuned to his moods after all these years as neighbors, diverted his attention the way a mother might have headed off a son's tantrum.

"Apple turnovers, today, Mr. Bethany. Still hot."

"I shouldn't . . ." he began. Dave was still at his college weight, but his own flesh was pretty doughy, too. Loose, with a slack to it that he couldn't seem to overcome. He had stopped running a few years earlier, no longer having time for it.

"C'mon, it's got apple in it. It's good for you. An apple a day, like the doctor said." And with the help of a turnover, Miss Wanda had him out of the store before he could lose his temper. A hot turnover, like a soft answer, turneth away wrath.

He had been out of sorts all morning, for the usual reasons and some news ones. His annual caller hadn't checked in. It had been years since the guy had actually said anything, now preferring the passive harassment of a hang-up call, but the call had continued to come every March 29. Strange to mind that of all things, but it gnawed at Dave. Was the guy dead? Or had he given up, too? Even the creeps were moving on with their lives. Then Dave had called Willoughby. The detective hadn't forgotten the date, far from it. He had offered the stoic understanding that Dave had come to expect, a wordless commiseration. No "Hey, Dave, what's up?" No pretense of progress. Just "Hello, Dave. I'm looking at the file right now." Willoughby looked at the file all the time, but he made a point of having it in front of him on this date.

Then Willoughby had dropped the bombshell on him.

"I'm retiring, Dave. End of this June."

"Retiring? You're so young. Younger than me."

"We can go at twenty with full pension, and I've racked up twenty-two. My wife— Evelyn's health has never been great. I'd like to spend some time with her before— They have these places, where you can live on your own, but then when you get sick, you stay on the premises, in your own apartment. We're not there yet, but in five years or so . . . I'd like to have—what do they call it?—quality time with her."

"Will you work at all? Freud believed work was essential to a man's well-being. A person's."

"Maybe volunteer somewhere. I don't need— Well, I have plenty of things to keep me busy."

Probably he had been on the verge of saying: *I don't need the money.* But even now, after knowing Dave for fourteen years, after speaking of things at once intimate and terrible, Willoughby had his pockets of reticence. Perhaps he was so used to being guarded about his trust-fund status around his colleagues that he couldn't break the habit with Dave. Once, only once, he had asked Dave to a Christmas party, a pity invite. Dave had expected a raucous cop blowout. Yearned for it, in fact, for such a party would be a novelty to him. But it was more of a family and neighborhood affair—and what a family, what a neighborhood. This was the kind of gentle, assured social ease that the Pikesville families of Dave's youth had been trying to achieve with all their noisy show and clamor, but it was impossible to imitate wealth at this level. Plaid pants, cheese puffs, gin martinis, thin-shanked women and red-faced men, all speaking quietly, no matter how much hard liquor they put away. It was the kind of event that he would have liked to describe to Miriam, if they still spoke. Miriam's phone had been disconnected. He knew this because he had tried to call her last night.

"What will . . . who will . . ." His voice had gotten thick and he felt almost overwhelmed with panic.

"The case has already been assigned," Willoughby said quickly. "A smart young detective. And I'll make a point of impressing upon him that you're to be kept in the loop. Nothing will change."

That's the problem, Dave thought bleakly. Nothing will change. Leads will pop up, only to evaporate like dew. Every now and then, a crazy person or a prisoner angling for special treatment will claim to have a tip, then be discredited. *Nothing will change. The only difference will be that the new detective, whatever he knows, whatever's in the case file, won't have been with me every step of the way.* It was, in some ways, more wrenching than the break with Miriam, and certainly more unexpected.

"Will we still . . . talk?"

"Of course. Anytime. Hell, I'll be keeping tabs, don't think that I won't."

"Okay," he said.

"I have to be politic, of course. Can't breathe down the new guy's neck too much. But this case will always belong to me. It's one of the two closest to my heart."

"One of two?" Dave couldn't help himself. He was shocked to hear that any other case had a claim on Willoughby's attention.

"The other one was solved," Willoughby said quickly. "Long ago. That one was about . . . good police work, in the face of difficult odds. It doesn't compare."

"Yes, I can see how a case that centered on good police work wouldn't compare to mine."

"*Dave.*"

"I'm sorry. It's just today. That today is today, that day. Fourteen years, and not even a bum lead, a wisp of a rumor, in the last two. I still don't know how to do this, Chet."

"This" being everything—not just his status as a perpetual victim of a crime that had never been delineated but his very existence. He had learned how to *go on,* because that phrase denoted a long, trudging trip to nowhere, pure inertia. Going on was easy. But he had long ago forgotten how to *be.* For the first time in years, he thought of his friends in the Fivefold Path, the ritual burning and meditation that he had abandoned because he could no longer pretend that he lived in any moment. In Alice's Wonderland, the rule was jam tomorrow and jam yesterday, but never jam today. In Dave's world, there was no today, only yesterday and tomorrow.

"No one's equipped for what you've been through, Dave. Not even a police. I probably shouldn't tell you this, but—the file's been in my house more often than not. Now, in light of my retirement . . . it has to go back, but it will always be in my head. You have my promise. I'll be here for you. Not just today, not just *this* day. Every day for the rest of my life. Even when

I *retire*-retire, it will be around here. I won't go to Florida or Arizona. I'll be here."

The detective's words had placated him, at least superficially. But Dave had been spoiling for a fight all the morning, and the mood didn't dissipate. The Steinberg case had made him crazy since it hit the headlines eighteen months earlier, and last week's sentencing had dredged up all those feelings again. Any story of child abuse or neglect by parents made Dave insane. Lisa Steinberg had been killed two weeks after the little girl in Texas, Jessica, had fallen into the well, and Dave had been angry about that, too. *Where were the parents?* His experience, strange to say, had made him less empathetic. He picked apart others as they had picked him apart. Adam Walsh, Etan Patz, the whole sad strange fraternity of bereavement—he wanted nothing to do with it.

Wind chimes sang as he entered the store, now known simply as TBG—or, as the low-key, lowercase sign had it, tbg. When he made the switch, he thought about trying to use the entire name—tmwtbg—but even he could see that it was a mouthful. The clothing section of the store now took up as much space as the folk art. It had become the very type of store that Miriam had nagged him into trying, much more accessible. It was a raging success. He hated it.

"Hey, boss," said Pepper, his current manager, a breezy young woman with thirteen hoops in her left earlobe and dark hair that had been razor-cut in the back yet kept long in the front, so long it fell into her eyes. She was Windexing the display cases. Pepper could not have been more proprietary about the store if it were her own, and Dave had yet to figure out what had made her so responsible at such a young age. She had a talent for deflection, a way of avoiding revelation. Dave had the same tendency, but he knew what had formed his temperament. Pepper might have known pain and heartache, but he could not imagine that this sunny, wholesome young woman—despite the hair, those thirteen hoops, she was a fresh-faced, all-American type—had anything truly tragic in her past. He'd thought about asking Willoughby to do a more thorough background check on her, claiming the pretext that he thought she might have sought employment with him because she knew someone or something connected to his girls' disappearance. But he had never misused his daughters that way, and he didn't want to start.

Pepper was beautiful, too, the kind of young woman noticed by the reluctant boyfriends and husbands dragged into the store. But Dave saw this only in the abstract. Whenever he met a woman, he estimated her age relative to what his daughters would be, and if she weren't at least fifteen years older, he wanted nothing to do with her. Sunny would have turned twenty-nine this year, he thought with a pang. Therefore, he wouldn't consider a woman of less than forty-five. Which should have been good news for the middle-aged women of Baltimore—a successful, available man who would never want a younger woman—except that Dave's relationships never worked. It had become common to speak of one's past as baggage, but Dave's past was so much larger, so much more burdensome, that it could never be understood as a single object that he dragged behind him. His past was like riding a monster with a lashing tail. He clung to it reluctantly, knowing that he would be crushed by its heedless feet if he ever relinquished his grip.

It was a quiet morning, so he went over the books with Pepper, taking her deeper into the workings of tbg than any previous employee had been allowed. He reminded her of the spring craft show, asked if she would like to be his representative there. She squealed, actually squealed, and bit a knuckle in delight.

"But you'd be with me, right? I'd be scared, making those choices all alone."

"I think you can do it. You have a great eye, Pepper. Just the way you display things, your attention to the store's look—I swear, even when I buy a dud, you find a way to make people want it."

"The kind of things we sell—they're dreams, you know? Visions of what people want to be. No one *needs* anything we stock, even the clothes. So you have to group them to tell a story. I don't know, I'm sure I sound crazy—"

"You make perfect sense. Before I hired you, I seldom took a day off. Now I'm capable of being away from the store for up to, oh, twenty minutes at a time."

Dave's workaholism was an old, familiar joke between them, and Pepper whooped with delight, a loud, raucous sound that made him wince. She did not know what day it was. She probably didn't know that Dave Bethany had ever had two daughters, much less what happened to them. True, their images lived in a silver frame in the back room, on his desk, but Pepper never asked questions. She was not incurious, he believed, merely careful about delving too far into

364

his past, lest he expect the same privilege in return. He really liked Pepper. He wished he could love her, or feel fatherly toward her, but that could never happen. Even if Pepper had been less reticent, he never would have allowed himself to feel paternal toward any young woman. In the past fourteen years, Dave had had lovers, women in his bed. But he never considered marrying again, and he had no desire to create daughters out of strangers. Pepper was his employee, nothing more.

Of course, people gossiped that she was more, later on. The next day, when emergency workers cut Dave down from an old elm tree behind his house, from the very branch where the tire swing had hung until the rope finally rotted away, they found a note directing them to a pile of papers on his desk, in the study where he had once chanted as the ghee burned at sunrise and sunset. *No one needs the things we sell,* Pepper had said, *so you have to group them to tell a story.* Dave hoped his groupings—his body, his papers, the balanced checkbook, the achingly neat house—would be understood. His letter might not be an official will, but its intentions were plain enough. He wanted Pepper to take over his business, while all his other assets, including those derived from the sale of the house, should be put in trust for the daughters that everyone else presumed dead, then released to certain charities in 2009.

"I feel awful," Willoughby confided over the crackle of the international line, having found Miriam through her former colleagues at the real-estate office. "It was just that day that I—"

365

"Don't feel bad, Chet. I don't. At least, I don't feel guilty about Dave."

"Yes, but . . ." The sentence, while unfinished, still managed to be quite cruel.

"I don't *forget* either," Miriam said. "I just don't remember in the same way. Which is to say, I don't wake up every morning and hit myself over the head with a frying pan and wonder why I have a headache, which was Dave's solution. The pain is there. It will always be there. It doesn't have to be stoked, or encouraged. Dave and I chose different ways to mourn, but we both mourned equally."

"I've never said otherwise, Miriam."

"I'm in language school here. Did you know that? I'm learning a new language at the age of fifty-two."

"I might do something like that," he offered, but she wasn't interested in what he was doing. *At least Dave pretended to care about me,* Willoughby thought.

"In Spanish there's a whole set of verbs where what would be the object in English becomes the subject. *Me falta un tenedor.* Literally, 'The fork is lacking to me,' not 'I need a fork.' *Se me cayó. Se me olvidó.* 'It fell from me.' 'It forgot itself to me.' In Spanish it's understood that things happen *to* you sometimes."

"Miriam, I've never second-guessed anything you or Dave did to cope."

"Bullshit, Chet. But you kept your opinion to yourself most of the time, and for that I love you."

He wished those words—so flippant, so unfelt—didn't hit him so hard. *For that I love you.*

"Stay in touch," he said. "With the department, I mean. If anything should come up—"

"It won't."

"Stay in touch," he repeated, pleaded, knowing all the time that she wouldn't, not forever.

A few weeks later, the day before his official retirement, he checked the Bethany case file out one more time. When the file was returned, any reference to the girls' biological parentage had been removed. Dave Bethany had always insisted that this part of the story was a cul-de-sac, a dead end, not unlike Algonquin Lane itself, which backed up to the more civilized edges of Leakin Park, an otherwise unruly bit of wilderness in the middle of the city. In the early days, just after the girls went missing, coarse, curious types drove slowly by the house, their rubbernecking intentions exposed when they had to turn around at the street's end. Others had come to the store, buying small items to assuage their guilt. How those people had pained Dave, how hurt he had been. "I'm a fucking freak show," he complained to Chet, more than once. "Take down the license plates," Chet advised him. "Make a note of the name if they pay by check or credit card. You never know who's driving by." And Dave, being Dave, had done just that. Taken down license plates, recorded every hang-up phone call, shook his family's life as if it were a snow globe, then set it back on the table and waited to see how the tableau might change. But no matter how many times he rearranged it over fourteen years, all the parts sifted back into place— with the exception of Miriam.

PART IX
SUNDAY

CHAPTER 37

"We can lie about the bones," Infante said.

"But we don't have any bones," Lenhardt said. "We can't find the bones."

"*Exactly.*"

Infante, Lenhardt, Nancy, and Willoughby were in the lobby of the Sheraton, waiting to take Miriam Toles to breakfast—a breakfast where they would admit they didn't have a clue as to the identity of the woman she hoped to meet today, the woman for whom she had traveled over two thousand miles. She could be Miriam's daughter. Or she could be a brilliant liar who had decided to fuck with everybody's head for a week or so. To what end? Money? Boredom? Out-and-out insanity? Or was she safeguarding her current identity because that name would pop out a criminal warrant for the person she now was? That was the only thing that made sense to Infante. He didn't believe for a minute that she was worried about her privacy. From his observation she grooved on attention, enjoyed their every encounter. No, she had something else to hide, and she was concealing it behind Heather Bethany's identity, using this infamous old murder to distract them.

"We've been obsessing over the bones because of all the things they could establish if we had them. The parents aren't biological, but the sisters are. Right?"

Willoughby nodded. Twentyfour hours ago, according to Nancy, she had to sweet-talk him into watching the interview. Now they couldn't pry him away and Lenhardt was humoring him, rather than risk hurting his feelings and seeing him on the nightly news. Infante still couldn't get over how he had screwed with the case file, then all but encouraged them to bring Miriam back to Baltimore before they knew what was what, who was who. What had the guy been thinking? How could he have removed crucial information? No possibility could be ruled out, as far as Infante was concerned. One thing that Nancy had told him about cold cases—the name was always in the files.

"We already told her we didn't find the bones," Lenhardt said.

"We told her that we didn't find them at the address she provided. But I've just come back from Georgia, right, where Tony Dunham lived? For all she knows, the son could have dug them up and taken them away before his father sold the property, to prevent their discovery."

"That would be impressive," Lenhardt said. "I can't even get my son to mow the lawn."

"Seriously—"

"No, I'm hearing you, just trying to think it through.

So we tell her we have her sister's bones. If she's lying, she capitulates—you *think*—because she knows she's going to have to submit to tests, and those will prove she's not related. But she's quick on her feet, this one. What if she says: 'Well, it could be some other body. Who knows how many times Stan Dunham did this, how many girls he killed?' "

"It's still worth a shot. I'd try anything right now to get an answer as quickly as possible out of her, to put the mother's mind to rest without making her go through the turmoil of meeting her, talking to her. If we could get her to confess . . ."

"Well, we're not going to figure out anything before breakfast," Lenhardt said, glancing at Willoughby. "We have to tell the mother how up in the air this is. She shouldn't have come, but I guess I should have known, as a parent, that nothing would hold her back once we called."

Infante usually hated it when Lenhardt invoked his standing as a parent, especially now that Nancy could nod solemnly, part of the club. But in this case Lenhardt seemed to be trying to mitigate Willoughby's guilt, so Infante didn't mind as much.

Nancy spoke up. "She would roll with anything we told her, somehow. That's my observation. You ever see that show, on cable, the one with the fat guy in glasses who does improvisations?"

The three men looked at her—Lenhardt and Willoughby completely lost, Infante clued into Nancy's vague pop-culture shorthand from their time as partners. "That piece of shit? You couldn't pay me to watch it. Although I did like it when the black guy, the super nice one, made fun of himself on that other

373

show. *Does Wayne Brady have to choke a bitch?* That was funny."

Nancy flushed. "Hey, you get up with a baby in the middle of the night and see what *you* watch. I only bring it up because she reminds me of that. She's quick, she thinks on her feet, and she gets what a lot of liars don't, that it's okay to make mistakes, because people do say the wrong stuff all the time. Like with the crickets? She didn't miss a beat when I pointed out it was March. She knows I caught her in a lie at that moment. But she kept going. Sergeant's right. You try that bones story on her, she won't blink."

The elevator opened, and Miriam Toles, after a quick look around the lobby, recognized Infante. Last night, when Infante met her at the airport, he had expected someone dressed more . . . well, Mexican. Not in a sombrero—he wasn't that ignorant. But perhaps one of those tiered skirts in bright colors, or an embroidered blouse. He also assumed that she would look older than her age, which records put at sixty-eight. But Miriam Toles had that sense of style that he'd seen in New York City women when he went into the city as a kid—silver hair in a severe, chin-level bob, large silver earrings, no other jewelry. He saw Nancy glance down at her own outfit, a pink shirt worn with a khaki skirt that was meant to hang a little looser than it did, and knew she was feeling dowdy and hickish. He bet that Miriam Toles often had that effect on other women. She wasn't truly pretty—she had probably never been pretty. But she was elegant and she had the remains of a killer figure.

Next to him he was conscious of Chet Willoughby straightening up a little, even sucking in his gut.

"Miriam," the old detective said, his manner a little stiff. "It's good to see you again. Although, obviously, not under these circumstances."

"Chet," she said, holding out a hand for a shake, and the old detective deflated. Had he been hoping for a kiss on the cheek, an embrace? It was weird, seeing this sixty-something guy all quivery with a crush. Didn't this ever end? Shouldn't it end? Lately, when every other commercial seemed to be about impotence—ED, as the ads called it, as if that were *better*—Infante had found himself thinking that it was silly to fight the body, that it must be almost a kind of relief to have your dick lie down on the job, done at last. *His* would never give up the ghost, of course, he knew that much about himself, and it would be a burn if you got impotence as a side effect of some medication. But he'd been counting on, even hoping for, the end of the emotional insanity, that giddy rush of caring what another person thought of you. Watching Willoughby, he realized that it ended as everything else did—with death.

Miriam stared down at the lackluster fruit she had plucked from the breakfast buffet, hard little pieces of things not quite in season. She didn't want to be one of those tiresome people who was forever championing her way of life, but she already missed Mexico, the things she had come to take for granted over the last sixteen years—the fruit, the strong coffee, the lovely pastries. She was embarrassed by this paltry brunch, much as the quartet of police officers seemed to find it a treat. Even the young woman was eating lustily, although Miriam noticed her plate was all protein.

"I would have come anyway," she told them. "Once I heard the detail about the purse. True, I wish your information were more . . . definitive at this point, that you knew one way or the other. But even if this isn't my daughter, she clearly knows something about the day my daughters disappeared. Perhaps everything. Where do we go from here?"

"We'd like to put together a comprehensive biography of your daughter, filled with details that only she could know. The layout of the house, family stories, in-jokes. Anything and everything you can remember."

"That would take hours, maybe even days." *And break my heart a thousand times over.* For thirty years Miriam had understood that she had to share her family's saddest secrets with investigators—her husband's failing business, her affair, the roundabout way that Sunny and Heather had come to be their daughters. But she was jealous of the happy memories, the mundane, quotidian details. Those belonged to her and Dave exclusively. "Why don't you tell me what she's told you so far, and see if any of that rings false with me? Why won't you let me see her?"

The female detective, Nancy—it was overwhelming for Miriam, meeting so many new people—flipped through her notes. "She's been consistent on birthdays, the schools they attended, your address. Thing is, most of that is on the Internet or in news accounts, if a person is inclined to dig deep enough, pony up for the archive searches. At one point, she said something about vacations to Florida and a person named Bop-Bop—"

376

"That's right. Dave's mother. She coined that hideous name for herself because she couldn't bear to be anything matronly. She hadn't enjoyed being a mother and being a grandmother really discomfited her."

"But that's not exactly proprietary, is it? Heather could have told that to kids at school, for example."

"Yet would it be remembered thirty years later?" Miriam asked, then answered her own question. "Certainly you wouldn't forget Bop-Bop if you ever met her. She was a piece of work."

Willoughby smiled.

"What, Chet?" Miriam asked, sharper than she intended. "What's so amusing to you?"

He shook his head, not wanting to say anything, but Miriam caught his gaze and held it. She shouldn't be the only person answering questions this morning.

"You're just so very much as I remembered. The . . . candor. That hasn't changed."

"Gotten worse, I would think, now that I'm an old woman and don't care what anyone thinks of me. Okay, so this person knows Bop-Bop, she knows what Heather's purse looks like. Why don't you believe her, then?"

"Well, there's the fact that she doesn't remember seeing the music teacher, when he was adamant that he saw her," Nancy said. "And in the original notes you told investigators that Heather had a little box in her room where she kept her birthday and Christmas money, but the money—somewhere between forty and sixty dollars, by your recollection—was missing. So Heather took her money to the mall that day, but when we asked for the contents of the purse—"

"The purse was empty when it was discovered."

"Right. *We* know that. However, Heather wouldn't, unless she emptied it herself and threw it down, and no one thinks that happened. This woman didn't mention it, however. She said there was a little cash, a brush, and a Bonne Belle lip moisturizer because she wasn't allowed to wear real lipstick then."

"We didn't have rules about makeup per se. I told her it looked silly on young girls, but it was her choice. Bonne Belle sounds right, however. Plausible, at any rate."

Nancy sighed. "Everything she says sounds *plausible*. At least when she describes the day, what happened. It's when she describes the abduction and . . ." Her voice faltered.

"Sunny's murder," Miriam prompted. "You have avoided speaking of that part to me."

"It's just so lurid," the young woman said. "Like something out of a movie. The details of the day—what they had for breakfast, how they took the Number Fifteen bus to the mall—again, something that's in the news accounts, as is the usher who remembered them getting kicked out of *Chinatown*—those things ring true. But being kidnapped by a cop who takes them to a deserted farmhouse and decides to keep Heather instead of killing her after she witnesses the murder of her sister? When she gets to that part, all the details fall away, and the story no longer rings true."

"Is it the cop part?" Miriam asked. "Is that what's so unbelievable?"

To their credit, the four detectives, current and former, did not protest too quickly or readily, did not swear to the heavens that they had found it easy to consider one of their own as a killer and sexual predator. Infante, the handsome one who had picked her up at the airport, spoke first.

"The cop part makes a lot of sense in some ways. That's how you would lure two girls away—show each one a badge, say you have her sister, that she's in trouble. Any kid would follow a cop."

"Maybe not Dave Bethany's children in 1975— Dave was given to calling police officers pigs, before we found ourselves in their debt, before Chet became a trusted friend." That was a conscious gift to Chet on her part, a way to make up for the sharpness in her voice earlier. "But okay, I see your point."

"It's just this particular cop, it doesn't really track," Infante continued. "He was in the theft division, a good guy, well liked. None of us knew him, but the guys who did are stunned by the idea that he could be involved in this. Plus, he's not even sentient, so he's an awfully convenient target."

"Dunham," Miriam said. "Dunham. Stan, you said?"

"Yes, and the son's name was Tony. Does the name mean anything to you?"

"Dunham rings a bell. We knew *someone* named Dunham."

"Not anyone you ever told me about," Chet began, his voice defensive. She put her hand on his forearm, wanting to comfort him, but also keen that he stop talking, so she could follow this train of thought.

"Dunham. Dunham. Dunned by Dunham." Miriam had a vision of herself at the old kitchen table in the house on Algonquin Lane. It was a rickety thing, a not-quite antique, passed down from Bop-Bop's apartment when she left Baltimore. *Foisted* on them, Miriam would have said, more stuff for the house with too much stuff. There had been days when she felt she couldn't walk across a room without bumping into a table or a footstool or some other object that Dave had dragged in. Dave had painted the table with taxicab-yellow lacquer and let the girls affix flower decals to it, which had looked good for all of two weeks, and then the decals had started to peel, leaving behind a sticky residue and pulling up bits of the paint. The green of the checkbook clashed horribly. Or maybe it just seemed that way because she was anxious when she paid their bills each month, watching them go a little further into the hole, playing the game of which creditor to appease this month, which one to let go a little longer. They had argued about expenses, but they could never agree on what was truly expendable. "Ghee costs nothing," Dave would say if Miriam suggested that the Fivefold Path was a practice the household could no longer afford. "Why can't you run her to and from school?" She would counter, "I have a job now, a job this family needs. I can't drop everything to chauffeur Sunny back and forth."

You could do the mornings. . . . But who would do the afternoons? . . . The guy is screwing us anyway, reversing the route in the afternoon. . . . We have to find some way to cut our budget.

It was an argument they had almost every month that year, and Miriam had prevailed every month, once again making out the check to Mercer Transportation, up in Glen Rock, Pennsylvania. She hadn't even known where Glen Rock was. But when the checks came back, they were endorsed by—

"Stan Dunham owned the private bus company,

Mercer, that we used to get Sunny to and from junior high every day."

"Mercer owned the property," the girl all but yelped. "It was an LLC, the previous owner before the development went in. I thought Dunham sold it to Mercer, but he must have simply transferred the deed to his own LLC. Shit, I can't believe I missed that."

"But we looked at the driver," Chet said. "It was one of the first people we checked out, and he had a solid alibi for the day the girls went missing. Stan wasn't the driver. *You never told me about Stan.*"

Miriam understood his frustration, for she felt it, too. No one had been sacred in their search for the girls, no one had been presumed innocent. They had turned their life upside down and inside out, looking for names and connections. Relatives, neighbors, teachers had been considered, whether they knew it or not. Employees at Security Square had been checked for minor sex charges, then brought in to talk to police, as if trafficking with a prostitute necessarily led to kidnapping two adolescent girls. Her coworkers, Dave's associates. They had even tracked down the man who drove the Number 15 bus route that day, the man Miriam always thought of as the one who had driven her daughters to their deaths, as sure as Charon ferried the dead across the river Styx. Suspicion was infinite, but energy and time proved finite. Dave's great, frantic fear, the anxiety that made life with him unbearable, was that they had not done everything they could, that there was always something else they should be doing, checking, examining.

And, sure enough, Dave had been right. *Dunned by Dunham,* he had sung. *Are we being dunned by*

Dunham again? He had been polite, but stern, and they had quickly learned not to put him in their monthly roulette of bills that may or may not be paid. They could not afford to offend him, lest he drop Sunny from the route. But Dunham was nothing more than a signature, very black and emphatic, on the back of a check that returned each month from a bank in Pennsylvania.

CHAPTER 38

Lenhardt was still trying to figure out the tip for brunch by the time Infante called the duty judge to alert him that they would need a search warrant for Stan Dunham's room in Sykesville. They met the judge outside the Cross Keys Inn, where *he* was having Sunday brunch, and in less than an hour Infante and Willoughby were on their way to the nursing home. Kevin had not wanted the old cop to come along, yet he couldn't help but indulge him. Something had been missed, a detail overlooked, all those years ago. No one's fault—once the driver was eliminated, why would anyone think of some faceless guy up in Pennsylvania, cashing checks? Still, he could tell that Willoughby was beating himself up.

"You know how we found the Penelope Jackson connection?" Infante asked. Willoughby was looking out the window, studying a golf course on the north side of the freeway.

383

"Some sort of computer search, I gather."

"Yeah, by Nancy. The first day I did the typical stuff—NCIC, all those databases. But I didn't think to check the fucking *newspapers,* on the off chance that Penelope Jackson had made news in a way that didn't generate a warrant. If Nancy hadn't done that, we wouldn't have made the connection between Tony and Stan Dunham. Even knowing what we did, we missed the timeline. Dunham's lawyer told me he sold the property a few years ago, but I didn't pin him down on the date. I assumed he was talking about the sale to Mercer, but he was talking about Mercer's sale to the developer."

"Thank you, Kevin," Willoughby said in a brittle voice, as if Infante had offered him an Altoid or something else utterly trivial. "But you're talking about an oversight you made in the first twenty-four hours of investigating a hit-and-run and a suspicious woman. I had fourteen years to work the Bethany case, and if the information about Dunham is correct, it means I never made a single significant discovery in the disappearance of the Bethany girls. Think about that. All that work, all that time, and I didn't actually learn *anything*. Pathetic."

"When Nancy started working cold cases, she told me the irony is that the name is always in the file, one way or another. But Stan Dunham's not in the file. You called the bus company, they gave you the name of the route's driver, you established it couldn't be him. Besides, we still don't know anything, other than the fact that there is some sort of connection between Stan Dunham and the Bethany family."

"A connection that a child wouldn't know about,

because no eleven-year-old knows who endorses a check." Willoughby's gaze returned to the passing scenery, although there wasn't much of note. "I can't decide if this makes me more inclined to trust our mystery woman or less. You know, she could be someone that Stan Dunham confided in, for whatever reason. Or Tony Dunham, more likely. A relative, a friend. Nancy told me that she was very insistent that you check the school records, that we'll find Ruth Leibig in the records at that Catholic school in York."

"But that won't prove she *is* Ruth Leibig, just that Ruth Leibig existed and went to that school. You know, they say you can't prove a negative, but it's turning out to be pretty damn hard to prove who this woman *is*. What if she just claims another identity, then another? Ruth Leibig is dead, after all. This woman is the goddamn Queen of the Dead."

They left the highway and headed north. The suburbs had crept farther and farther out in the decade since Infante first moved to Baltimore, but there were still some traces of country life here in Sykesville. Yet the facility itself was quite fancy, stark and modern, even more impressive than the one in which Willoughby lived. How did an old cop, one without a trust fund, afford a place like this? Then Infante remembered the sale of the property up in Pennsylvania, Dunham's interest in annuities when he was still relatively robust, according to the lawyer. The guy was a planner, no doubt about it. The only question was whether he had planned his crimes as carefully as he had mapped out the financial specs of his final years.

*

Willoughby shuddered a little when they were directed to the hospice wing where Stan Dunham was kept. That surprised Infante at first, but then he remembered: Willoughby's wife had died in such a place, had made the short, one-way trip from apartment to care ward when she was still in her fifties.

"Mr. Dunham has virtually no speech at this point," said the pretty young nursing aide who escorted them, Terrie. Nurses—he should date more nurses. They were a good fit for a police. He wished they still wore those white dresses, the ones that were tight at the waist, and those little caps with wings. This one had on mint-green pants, a flowery top, and some butt-ugly green clogs, but she was still striking. "He makes occasional sounds, some of which indicate what he's feeling, but he can't communicate more than his basic needs. He's late-stage."

"Is that why he's been moved to the hospice?" Willoughby asked, stumbling a little over the last word.

"We don't move people into hospice unless their life-span is expected to be less than six months. Mr. Dunham was diagnosed with stage-four lung cancer three months ago. Poor guy. He's really had nothing but bad breaks."

Yeah, Kevin thought. *Poor guy*. He asked, "He had a son, Tony. Did he ever visit?"

"I didn't know his son was alive. His lawyer is our only contact. Maybe they were estranged. That happens."

Maybe the son didn't want anything to do with the father. Maybe the son knew what went down, all these years ago, and he told his girlfriend, Penelope,

386

*and she told someone, someone who happened to be
driving her car.*

Kevin knew that someone with advanced Alzheimer's
couldn't provide any meaningful information, but he
was still disappointed when he saw Stan Dunham. This
was a husk of a man in plaid pajamas and bathrobe.
The only signs of life in him were the comb marks in
his hair, the fresh shave. Did the nurse do those things?
Dunham's eyes certainly brightened at the sight of her,
passed over Kevin and Willoughby with mild interest,
then returned to the nurse.

"Hi, Mr. Dunham." Terrie's voice was bright and
enthusiastic, but it wasn't overly loud or babyish.
"You have two visitors. Someone who used to work
with you."

Dunham continued to look at her.

"I didn't work with you," Infante said, trying for
Terrie's tone, only to come across like some hale and
hearty car salesman. "But Chet here did. He was in
homicide. You remember him? Probably best known
for catching the Bethany case. The Bethany case."

He repeated the last three words slowly and
carefully, but nothing registered. Of course. He knew
it wouldn't, but he couldn't help himself. Dunham
kept staring at pretty Terrie. His gaze was like a dog's,
affectionate and utterly dependent. If this man was the
Bethany girls' abductor, he was a monster. But even
monsters aged, became frail. Even monsters died.

Infante and Willoughby began systematically opening
drawers and closets, looking for anything. Looking for
everything.

"He doesn't have a lot of possessions," Terrie said. "There's not much point . . ." Her voice trailed off, as if the man sitting in the chair, the man who followed her face and voice with such determined attention, might be surprised at the news that he was dying. "But there is a photo album, which we look at together sometimes. Don't we, Mr. Dunham?"

She reached under the ottoman and unearthed a large, cloth-covered book, a satiny white that had faded to yellow. On the cover a blue-diapered baby crowed, "It's a boy!" When Infante opened the book, the handwriting was clearly a woman's, a fine up-and-down cursive hand that recorded the life of one Anthony Julius Dunham from his birth (six pounds, twelve ounces) to his christening to his high school graduation. His mother, unlike some, had never lost patience with the task of jotting down her son's every accomplishment. A certificate for completing a summer reading program, a Red Cross card noting that he had achieved "intermediate" status as a swimmer at Camp Apache. Report cards—not very impressive ones—were affixed to the pages with black triangles.

The photos made Infante wistful for his own dad. Not because there was a resemblance between Infante's dad and the younger, more robust Stan Dunham, but because the photos captured the generic moments of family life that everyone experienced. Goofiness around the house, landmarks on vacation, squinting into the sun at ceremonies. Each was carefully labeled in that same feminine handwriting. "Stan, Tony, and me, Ocean City, 1962." "Tony at school picnic, 1965." "Tony's high school graduation, 1970." In nine short years, the son had gone from a crew-cut towhead in striped T-shirt to a long-haired, would-be hippie. Hard on a cop, Infante thought, especially one of that era, but whatever Tony wore, the parents who bracketed him beamed with pride.

The last photo—Tony in what appeared to be a gas-station uniform—was labeled "Tony's new job, 1973." The book ended there, although there were still several pages left. Two years before the girls disappeared. Why had this woman stopped documenting every phase of her son's life? Did he move out in 1973? Was he there when his father brought home a girl in 1975? What had Stan Dunham told them, how had he explained the sudden appearance of a preadolescent girl?

"Kevin, check this out."

Willoughby had pushed aside pillows that may or may not have been arranged to hide a large cardboard carton on the upper shelf in a closet. Terrie interceded, staggering a little under the weight of the box, and Infante helped her, placing a steadying hand on her shoulder. She gave him an amused look as if she were used to such ploys, making him feel old and geezerish, another guy in her care trying to cop a feel.

The box was full of the kind of detritus that students collect. Report cards, programs, school newspapers. All from the Sisters of the Little Flower, Infante noted—and featuring the name of Ruth Leibig. No album for Ruth, whoever she was, although her grades were certainly better than Tony's. No photographs either, and nothing dated before the fall of 1975. There was a diploma, though, from 1979. Strangest of all, there was an old-fashioned tape recorder, a bright red box shaped like a purse. He pushed a button, but nothing happened, of course. The tape inside was Jethro Tull's

Aqualung. On the bottom of the player was an equally old-fashioned label, the kind made with one of those guns. "Ruth Leibig," it said.

Infante dug deeper in the box and found something stranger still: a marriage certificate, also dated 1979. Between Ruth Leibig and Tony Dunham, as witnessed by his parents, Irene and Stan Dunham.

Tony's dead? That, according to Nancy and Lenhardt, was the piece of information that had surprised the woman during their interview. Not saddened, however. Shocked and upset, even angered. But she hadn't been the least bit sad. At the same time, she had never mentioned Tony, not by name.

"What happened?" Infante asked Stan Dunham, who seemed startled by the tone of his voice, the loudness of it. "Who was Ruth Leibig? Did you kidnap a young girl, kill her sister, then screw the little one until she hit her teenage years, when you made a present of her to your son? What happened on that farm, you sick old fuck?"

The nurse was appalled. She wouldn't be kindly inclined toward him if he called her in a week or so. *Remember me? I'm the detective who cursed at the old man you think is such a sweetheart. Wanna go out sometime?*

"Sir, you must not speak that way—" Dunham didn't seem to notice that anything was happening.

Infante opened the photo album, pointed to the last picture of Tony. "He's dead, you know. Burned up in a fire. Maybe murdered. Did he know what you did? Did his girlfriend know?"

The old man shook his head, sighed, and looked out the window, as if Infante were the demented one, a raving lunatic to be ignored. Did he understand anything? Did he know anything? Were the facts locked in his brain or gone forever? Wherever they were, they were inaccessible to Infante. Stan Dunham returned to looking at his nurse, as if seeking her assurance that this disruption to his routine would end soon. *When's it going to be just you and me again?* he seemed to be asking her. She spoke to him in a soft, reassuring voice, stroking his hand.

"That's not actually allowed," she said with a worried glance at Infante. "Touching patients like that. But he's the nicest man, my favorite of all the ones in my care. You have no idea."

"No," Kevin said. "I don't." *God knows what he'd have done to you if he'd met you when you were a teenager.*

Chet Willoughby had continued to sift through the box of papers, returning to the diploma and the marriage certificate, which he studied through tortoiseshell reading glasses.

"Something's not right, Kevin. It's hard to be definitive, but it's highly unlikely, based on these, that Ruth Leibig is Heather Bethany."

CHAPTER 39

Kay's dining room had a set of French doors that separated it from the living room, and she had noticed over the years that her children seemed to feel invisible when the doors were closed. She often took advantage of this, situating her favorite reading chair so she could glance up and catch a glimpse of Grace or Seth at their least self-conscious, a state of being that was increasingly rare with each passing year. Adolescence was like a big scab, or scar tissue, a gradual covering of a soul too soft and open to be exposed to the elements. She liked the way Grace chewed on her hair while doing her math homework, a habit that Kay remembered from her own girlhood. Seth, at eleven, still spoke to himself, narrating his life in a quiet, unrushed monologue that reminded Kay of the commentary for golf tournaments. "Here's my snack," he would say, lining or stacking his cookies into precise patterns and structures. "Oreos, real

Oreos, because you can't fake Oreos. And here is the milk, low-fat, Giant brand, because milk is milk. Yesssssss!" The part about the milk was Kay's voice boomeranging back to her, from the early days after the divorce when she worried about money constantly and abandoned all brand names in favor of store labels, and even made the children submit to blind taste tests to show them that they could not possibly discern the difference among various brands of chips and cookies. Thing was, they could, so she had ended up compromising on that issue. Name brands for cookies, chips, and sodas, the store brand for milk, pasta, bread, and canned goods.

Sometimes her children caught her looking at them through the glass, but they didn't seem to mind too much. Perhaps they even enjoyed it, because Kay never laughed or teased them at such moments. Instead she shrugged guiltily and went back to her book as if *she* had been caught unawares.

Today it was Heather in the dining room, however, and she scowled when she saw Kay on the other side of the glass, even though Heather had been doing nothing more than reading the Sunday paper and Kay's only thought was how pretty Heather looked in the grayish light. Peering at the paper, which she held at arm's length as if slightly farsighted, she had no lines in her forehead and her jawline was still smooth and taut. Only a deep dent between her eyes betrayed her fierce concentration.

"When did the Sunday comics stop running Prince Valiant?" she asked when Kay carried her coffee mug into the room, trying to act as if it were her destination all along. Then, before Kay could answer—not that she had an answer—Heather decided for herself, "No, it wasn't the *Beacon* that ran Prince Valiant. It was the *Star*. We got the *Beacon* on weekday mornings, but on Sunday we got both papers. My dad was a news junkie."

"I haven't heard anyone speak of the *Beacon* for years. It merged with the *Light* back in the eighties, around the time the *Star* folded. But Baltimore being Baltimore, some people still talk about the *Beacon* as if it still existed. You sounded like a real old-time Baltimorean just then."

"I *am* a real old-time Baltimorean," Heather said. "Or was, at any rate. I guess I belong to another place now."

"Were you born here?"

"What, that didn't come up in any of your Google searches? Are you asking for yourself or for them?"

Kay blushed. "That's not fair, Heather. I haven't taken sides in this. I'm a neutral party."

"My father always said there was no neutrality, that even the act of being neutral involved taking a side." She was challenging Kay now, accusing her of something, but what?

"I didn't tell anyone that we stopped at the mall yesterday."

"Why would you?"

"Well, I wouldn't, but . . . you can see—it might have been of interest. I mean, if they knew . . ." Kay was grateful for the ringing telephone that interrupted her stammering, although she wasn't sure why she was the one who was flustered and embarrassed. From somewhere upstairs Grace's voice sounded with the usual frenzied excitement that the telephone provoked in her. "I'll get it!" Then, in a forlorn, flat tone that told the story of a million dashed expectations: "It's someone named Nancy Porter. She wants to talk to Heather."

Heather went into the kitchen and made a point of pulling the swinging door shut behind her. Even so, Kay could hear her short, brittle answers. *What? What's the rush? Can't it wait until tomorrow?*

"They want me to come back," Heather said, pushing through the door with such force that it stayed open. "Can you take me there, in about a half hour or so?"

"More questions?"

"I'm not sure. It's hard to believe there could be any more questions, after what they put me through yesterday. But my mother is here, and they want me to meet with her. Nice reunion, huh? In a police interrogation room, where our every word can be recorded, overheard. I bet they've spent the morning debriefing her, telling her that they think I'm a liar, begging her to prove that I'm not who I say I am."

"Your mother will know you," Kay said, but Heather didn't seem to hear the reassurance in her voice, the implicit promise that Kay *wasn't* neutral. Kay believed her. In fact, it occurred to Kay that Heather might be more credible when she wasn't trying to prove how credible she was. When she talked about Sunday comics and the things her father used to say, she was effortlessly herself.

"Look, I'm going to go back to my room, brush my teeth and hair, and then we can go, okay? I'll meet you back here in a bit." She crossed the small flagstone path that led through the backyard and to the garage, which was set far back on the property, bordering the alley. Stupid to say that thing about Google. What if they went into Kay's computer, traced her movements? Any competent technician could find her company's Web site and the e-mail she had sent her boss. Was Kay watching, did she have to go upstairs? After all, there was nothing there that she needed. The police had taken her key ring the night they stopped her. How grateful she'd been at the time that even her key ring couldn't betray her. It was just a lump of turquoise on a silver bar, something picked up in a thrift shop, an item of no significance. For obvious reasons, she had never been one to personalize her belongings, to embroider her monogram into things, although it had certainly been suggested that she do just that on various tea towels and aprons, back when she was in her teens and "engaged" to Tony Dunham. "Sure, Auntie. I'm just dying to have a fucking hope chest." She had been slapped for the "fucking," yet not for the fucking. What a household. What a goddamn messed-up, mixed-up place that had been, behind the gingham curtains and the ruffled petunias in the window boxes.

She wished she had some money or at least a credit card. Oh, if only her wallet hadn't been missing—stolen by Penelope, she was sure of that much now, the woman was clearly a schemer, incapable of gratitude—and she hadn't been so confused and disoriented that first night. She could have talked her way out of the traffic violation somehow, even with no license and a car registered to someone else. Although, knowing what she did of Penelope, she wouldn't be surprised to find out that the license plates had expired or that the car had multiple parking citations stacked up in some municipal computer somewhere.

She glanced back over her shoulder. Kay was still in the kitchen, drinking her coffee by the sink. Shit. She would have to go upstairs after all. Then what?

It was hard, opening the bathroom window with just one arm to press against the old, warped wood, harder still to squeeze through the tiny opening and drop a full story, but she managed. Adrenaline was a marvelous thing. Brushing the knees of her slacks— Grace's actually, and she felt bad about that, of all the things she'd done, she felt bad about taking a teenager's favorite slacks and getting the knees dirty— she got her bearings. The closest busy street was Edmondson, to her right. It led straight to the Beltway, but she couldn't hitchhike on the Beltway. She should try Route 40, but that ran east-west and she needed to go south. She'd figure it out. She always figured things out, eventually.

She began walking briskly, rubbing her arms. It would be cold when the sun went down, but perhaps she would get lucky, make it home by then. If she could get a lift to the airport and take the train— Did the locals run on Sundays? Amtrak did, and if they didn't catch her by New Carrollton, she could make it the whole way. Even on a local, she was willing to bet that she could stall a conductor for a few stops, persuade him that she'd lost her ticket, maybe even been mugged, although that was risky, for he would want her to report that to the police. *If only she'd gotten on the train Tuesday, the way she was supposed to.* She could tell the conductor that she had a fight with . . . her boyfriend, and he pushed her out of the car, that was it, and she was stranded and needed to get home. She could sell that story. Hell, she'd once seen a homeless woman ride free from Richmond to Washington, even as she chattered that she was going to meet with the president. It's not as if they put you off in the middle of the tracks, and if she could make Union Station, she had a shot. She'd call a coworker, or even her boss if necessary, maybe risk jumping the turnstiles on the Metro, anything to get home again. It was all she could do not to break into a trot toward the busy street, with cars rushing back and forth. She felt as if she were running toward the real world, a place of motion and confusion where she could once again safely disappear, that she would have to reach top speed to break through the wall between it and this make-believe kingdom where she'd lived the past five days.

But just as she came to the end of the alley, a patrol car surged forward and blocked her path, and that plump, smug detective stepped out.

"I called you on my cell," Nancy Porter said. "We weren't sure you would run, but we were curious to see what you would do when we said we wanted you to meet Miriam. Infante's at the other end of the alley. And, as you know, there was always a uniform out front."

"I'm just taking a walk," she said. "Is that against the law?"

"Infante went to see Stan Dunham this afternoon. He learned some interesting things."

398

"Stan Dunham's not capable of telling anyone anything, even if he were so inclined."

"See, it's really interesting that you know that, because you managed not to mention his incapacitation yesterday, and I made a point of not sharing it, because I wanted you to think he could contradict you. Yesterday you indicated that you hadn't had any contact with him for years."

"I haven't."

The detective opened the rear door. It was a proper police car, with a wire screen between the front and back seats. "I don't want to cuff you, because of your arm and because there's no charge on you—yet. But this is going to be your last chance to tell us what really happened to the Bethany girls, Ruth. Assuming you know."

"I haven't been Ruth for years," she said, getting into the car. "Of all my names, I hated Ruth the most. I hated being Ruth the most."

"Well, you're giving us your current name today, or you're spending the night in the Women's Detention Center. We've indulged you for five days, but time's up. You're going to tell us who you are, and you're going to tell us what you know about the Dunham family and the Bethany girls."

If she had to put a name to what she was feeling, it might have been relief, the knowledge that this was going to end once and for all. Then again, it might have been absolute dread.

CHAPTER 40

"We could show her to you, on the closed-circuit video," Infante offered Miriam. "Or walk her by you in the hall, let you get a look at her."

"There's no way she's Heather?"

"Not if she's Ruth Leibig, and she's all but admitted that was her name. Ruth Leibig graduated from high school in York, Pennsylvania, in 1979 and married the Dunhams' son the same year. Heather would have been sixteen then. The marriage would have been legal, especially with the Dunhams as witnesses. But how likely is it that Heather graduated high school two years early?"

"I was the one who picked up on that," Willoughby put in, but Infante didn't begrudge him that little bit of self-importance. Eventually Infante would have noticed it, too, the date discrepancy. But such facts as the Bethany girls' DOBs were burned into Willoughby's brain, much as the old man had tried to deny it.

"No, Heather was smart, but not so smart that she could skip two grades," Miriam admitted. "Not even in a parochial school in the Pennsylvania boondocks."

Infante had gone to Catholic school and thought it pretty rigorous, but he wasn't going to contradict Miriam on anything just now.

"So what did happen to my daughters?" Miriam asked. "Where are they? What does any of this have to do with Stan Dunham?"

"Our supposition is that he did abduct and kill your girls and that his son's wife, Ruth, somehow came to be privy to the details," Infante said. "We're not sure why she's safeguarding her current identity, but chances are she's wanted on a warrant for something else. Or she knows for sure that Penelope Jackson set the fire that killed Tony Dunham, and she's trying to protect her, although she keeps insisting she has no relationship with the Jackson woman. When we ask about the car, she takes the Fifth. When we ask her anything, she takes the Fifth."

Nancy leaned in, pushing a glass of water toward Miriam. "We've told her that if she'll give us Penelope Jackson on the murder of Tony Dunham in Georgia, we might be able to cut a deal with her on the hit-and-run here and whatever else she's running from, depending how serious it is. But other than admitting she was once Ruth Leibig, she's just not talking, not even to her own lawyer. Gloria's urged her to make a deal, to tell us everything she knows, but she seems almost catatonic."

Miriam shook her head. "That makes two of us. I'm numb. All along I kept telling myself that it was impossible, that she had to be an impostor. I thought

I had . . . insulated myself against hope. Now I realize I wanted it to be true, that I thought by coming here I could make it true."

"Of course you did," Lenhardt said. "Any parent would. Look, come tomorrow, Monday, we're going to be able to piece a lot more things together. We'll be able to check to see if Tony and Ruth ever divorced, what jurisdiction it was in, stuff like that. We'll track down people from the school, even if the parish is gone. For the first time, we have leads, solid ones."

"She's not Heather," Willoughby put in, "but she has the answers, Miriam. She knows what happened, if only secondhand. Maybe Dunham confided in his daughter-in-law after the diagnosis, maybe she was his confidante."

Miriam slumped in Lenhardt's chair. She looked every bit her age now, and then some, her good posture gone, her eyes sunken. Infante wanted to tell to her that she had accomplished much by coming here, that her trip had been worthwhile, but he wasn't sure it was true. They would have searched Dunham's room eventually, even without Miriam identifying the link between her household and his. Visiting the old man hadn't seemed urgent when his name first surfaced, because of the dementia, but they would have started poking around in his affairs soon enough. Hell, up until this afternoon Infante hadn't even been convinced that Dunham was connected to anyone but Tony Dunham and the ever-elusive Penelope Jackson. That was the one link they had established independently—mystery woman to Penelope Jackson to Tony Dunham to Stan Dunham.

Still, if he was being honest with himself, he had to

second-guess his own decision not to visit Dunham as soon as he had the name. Was it because Stan Dunham was a police? Had he hesitated, made a bum decision because he just couldn't believe that one of their own could be involved in such a sick crime? Should they have locked her up the first night and trusted the accommodations at the Women's Detention Center to provide all the encouragement she needed to talk? She had played them all, even Gloria, her own lawyer, stalling them, trying to figure out a way to keep from telling them who she was. But she wasn't gutsy enough, or depraved enough, to try to play the mother that way. Maybe that was the one shred of decency in her, the place where she drew the line. She had run because she didn't want to confront the mother.

Or maybe she had run because she believed that Miriam, with a glance, could do the one thing that they had failed to do this past week—eliminate with certitude the possibility that she was Heather Bethany.

"Walk her by me," Miriam said softly. "I don't want to talk to her—that is, I do, I want to scream at her, ask her a thousand questions, then scream some more—but I know I mustn't do any of those things. I just want to look at her."

Miriam waited in the lobby of the Public Safety Building. She thought of putting on dark glasses, then almost laughed out loud at her own heightened sense of drama. After all, this woman didn't know her. If she'd ever seen Miriam, it was in photographs from that time, and while Miriam knew she had aged exceptionally well, she would never be mistaken for her thirty-eight-year-old self. Fact is, her thirty-nine-year-old self had barely resembled the thirty-eight-year-old version. She remembered noticing how she had changed when the newspapers ran those photos on the first-year anniversary, that her face had shifted irrevocably. It wasn't age or grief, but something more profound, almost as if she'd been in an accident and the bones in her face had been put back together again, leaving it similar to what it had once been, but vaguely off.

The elevators were frustratingly slow, as she had learned on her own descent, and the wait in the lobby seemed interminable. But, at last, Infante and Nancy got off the elevator, flanking a slight, blond woman, holding her loosely by the elbows. Her head was tilted forward, so it was hard to see her face, but Miriam studied her—Ruth, was that it?—as best as she could, took in the narrow shoulders, the slim hips, the comically youthful trousers, so wrong for a woman verging on middle age. *If she were my daughter,* Miriam thought, *she'd have better taste than that.*

The woman looked up, and Miriam caught her eye. Miriam didn't mean to hold the gaze, but she found she couldn't turn away. Slowly she rose, blocking the path of the trio, clearly unnerving Infante and Nancy. This was not part of the plan. She was to sit and watch, nothing more. She had promised. They probably thought she was going to slap or push her, spit imprecations at the latest charlatan to appropriate Miriam's life story for her own amusement.

"Mi— Ma'am," Infante said, correcting himself, protecting her name. "We're escorting a prisoner. It's only because of her injury that she's not in handcuffs. Please stand back."

Miriam ignored him, taking the woman's left hand in hers, squeezing it as if to say, *This won't hurt a bit,* then pushing up the sleeve of the cardigan sweater she wore, careful not to disturb the bandaged forearm. On the upper arm, she found the mark she sought, the splayed and oh-so-faint scar of a vaccination that had been burst by the helpful application of a flyswatter, missing the fly but scattering pus and blood, creating a wound that had taken weeks to heal, a scab that had been picked continually despite all admonitions to leave it alone, that such picking would leave a permanent blemish. There it was, a ghostly mark, so faint that no one else would notice it. In fact, it was possible that it wasn't even there, but Miriam believed she saw it, so she did.

"Oh, Sunny," Miriam said, "what in the world is going on?"

405

CHAPTER 41

The wheels on the bus go round and round, round and round, round and round.

They wanted to know what she was thinking, what was running through her head, and that was it, exactly: The childhood song had come back to her that afternoon on the Number 15 bus, Heather sitting across the aisle from her, humming in that happily infuriating, infuriatingly happy way she had. Heather was still a little _girl_. Sunny was not. Sunny was about to become a woman. This bus, the Number 15, was taking other people to the mall, on ordinary errands, but it was taking her to meet her husband.

Buses were magic. Another bus had brought her to this place in her life, this moment where everything would change. She was running away, just as her mother had. Her _real_ mother, the one with blond hair and blue eyes like hers. Her real mother was someone who would have understood her, someone to whom she could have spoken of all the things locked up in her heart, secrets so explosive that she had never written them down anywhere, even in her diary. Sunny Bethany was fifteen, and she was in love with Tony Dunham, and every song she heard, every *sound* she heard, seemed to pulse with that information, even the thrumming wheels on the bus.

The wheels on the bus go round and round, round and round, round and round.

It had begun on another bus, the school bus, after the route was reversed at the other parents' insistence and Sunny ended up riding alone in the afternoons.

"Mind if I put the radio on?" the driver asked one day. He was a substitute, young and good-looking, not at all like Mr. Madison, who normally drove the route. "But you have to keep it a secret. We're not supposed to play the radio. My father, who owns the bus company, he's really strict."

"Sure," she said, embarrassed at the way her voice squeaked. "I won't tell."

Then—not the next time he drove, or the time after that, or even the time after that, but the fourth time, in November, when the weather was turning colder: "Why don't you move up here to the front seat and talk to me, keep me company? It gets awfully lonely, sitting up here by myself."

"Sure," she said, gathering her books to her chest, feeling stupid when the bus hit a pothole and she banged her hip hard against one of the seats. But Tony didn't laugh at her, or mock her. "My apologies," he said. "I'll try to keep the ride smooth from here on out, my lady."

Another time—the fifth time, or maybe the sixth.

Their encounters were frequent enough to blend together now, although she seldom saw him more than two or three times a month. "Do you like this song? It's called 'Lonely Girl.' It reminds me of you."

"Really?" She wasn't sure she did like the song, but she listened closely, especially to the final line, about the lonely boy. *Did that mean*—but she kept her eyes on her notebook, a blue binder. Other girls inked the names of their crushes on the cover, but she never had dared. A few weeks later, she tried doodling a tiny "TD" in the lower right-hand corner. "What does that stand for?" Heather had asked, nosy Heather, always spying Heather. "Touchdown," Sunny said. Later she transformed the initials into three-dimensional shapes she had learned to draw in geometry.

More and more, Tony talked about himself, over the music. He had tried to join the army, go to 'Nam, but they wouldn't take him, much to his mother's relief and his disappointment. Sunny didn't know there were people who *wanted* to fight in the war. Tony had a heart defect or something, mitral valve prolapse. She couldn't believe there was anything wrong with his heart. He had feathered hair, which he groomed frequently with a small brush he kept tucked in the pocket of his jeans, and he wore a gold chain. He smoked Pall Malls, but only after the other kids had gotten off the bus. "Don't rat me out," he said, winking at her in the rearview mirror. "You sure are pretty. Has anyone ever told you that? You should wear your hair like Susan Dey. But you're already a cutie."

The wheels on the bus went round and round.

"I really wish we could spend time together. Real time, not just these bus rides. Wouldn't that be nice, if we could be alone somewhere?" She thought it might be, but she didn't see how it could be arranged. She knew without asking that her parents, as open and freewheeling as they professed to be, wouldn't let her date a twenty-three-year-old bus driver. She wasn't sure, however, what would bother them more—the twenty-three part, the bus-driver part, or the wanted-to-go-to-'Nam part.

Eventually, Tony said he wanted to marry her, that if she met him at the mall some Saturday, they could drive up to Elkton, get married at the little chapel where people from New York got married, because there was no waiting period, no blood tests required. No, she said. He couldn't be serious. "I am, I will. You're so pretty, Sunny. Who wouldn't want to marry you?" She remembered that her mother, her real one, had run away at seventeen to marry her true love, Sunny's real father, and people grew up faster now. She heard her parents say that all the time. *Kids grow up so fast now.*

The next time she saw him, the week of March 23, she said yes, she would meet him, and now, a mere six days later, she was on another bus, heading to see him. She was going to go on her honeymoon tonight. She shivered a bit, thinking about that. They had never been able to do more than kiss, and only a little, but it had made her insides flip. Tony's father knew his schedule too well, questioned him closely if he returned home late, sniffed the interior of the bus and asked if he'd been smoking. It was funny, but being the son of the man who owned the bus company didn't get Tony any special privileges, just the opposite. The only reason Tony still lived at home, at age twenty-three, was that his mother would be heartbroken if he left.

"But we won't live with them, after we're married," he said. "She won't expect that. We'll get an apartment in town, or maybe over to York."

"Like the Peppermint Patty?"

"Like the Peppermint Patty."

The wheels on the bus went round and round.

And then Heather had to go and ruin everything, following Sunny not only to the mall but into *Chinatown,* where Sunny was supposed to rendezvous—his word—with Tony. Once they were thrown out, Sunny had fled, not sure what to do. How would she find Tony now? She went to Harmony Hut. Music was their common bond after all, the thing that had brought them together. Eventually he did find her, but he was angry and out of sorts, as if the ruined plan were all her fault. Then Heather had found *them,* spotted Sunny standing in Harmony Hut, right in front of the Who records, holding a man's hand. Heather began making a fuss, saying the same man had tried to talk to her by the organ store, that he was a creep. She said she was going to tell. They had to take her with them, right? If they left Heather alone, Sunny told Tony, she would tattle to their parents, and that would ruin everything. They promised Heather candy and money, said she could go home after they were married, that she could be the flower girl, the witness. The flower-girl part seemed to win her over. But out in the parking lot Heather decided she didn't want to go, and Tony grabbed her a little roughly and pushed her into the car. In the scuffle she dropped her purse, but Tony refused to go back for it, and she had cried and whined all the way up the highway about that stupid purse. "I lost my purse. With my Bonne Belle. And my comb, the souvenir one from Rehoboth Beach. I lost my purse."

Only there was no wedding when they got to Elkton. The courthouse was closed, so they couldn't get a marriage license. Tony pretended to be surprised, but he had made a reservation at a motel down in Aberdeen. *Why would you call ahead for a motel, but not check on whether the courthouse was open?* Sunny had a sick feeling in her stomach, not at all like the flips she'd felt while kissing. In the room with Tony and Heather—Tony glowering because he couldn't be alone with Sunny, Heather still whining about her lost purse—Sunny had felt trapped, confused. She wasn't sure if she was angry with Heather for interrupting her honeymoon or relieved. It was beginning to seem like a stupid idea. She wanted to go to high school and then college, travel through the world as her father had, with nothing more than a backpack. She volunteered to go across the street to a diner and buy them all dinner. She decided not to mention that she would be using the money she'd taken from Heather's bank.

The diner was called the New Ideal, and it was the old-fashioned kind her father loved best, where everything was made from scratch. Burgers like that took longer, but they were worth it. In fact, diners were the only place her father ever ate burgers. Even a health nut, he said, had to let loose every now and then. He had made them chocolate-chip pancakes that morning, and she hadn't finished hers. She wished she had. She wished she could go back to this morning, but that was impossible. Still, she could go home. She would go back to the room, ask Tony to take them home, come up with a lie and persuade Heather to back her up, bribing her with her own money.

She paid for the cheeseburgers, never guessing that her life had ended while she waited in the New Ideal Diner.

When Sunny returned to the room, Heather was lying on the floor, not moving. An accident, Tony said. *She was jumping on the bed making all this noise and I told her to stop, tried to grab her arm, and she fell.*

"We have to call a doctor or take her to a hospital. Maybe she's not really dead." Hopeless words, said over the body of a clearly dead Heather, the back of her head as collapsed as a pumpkin the day after Halloween, blood seeping into a towel beneath her once-blond hair. Why had he put a towel beneath her head? And how do you hit your head so hard falling off a bed? But those were questions Sunny would not even dare to consider for several years.

"No," Tony said. "She's dead. We should call my dad. He'll know what to do."

Stan Dunham was far kinder than the tyrant described by his son over those months of confessional talks on the bus. He did not yell, or scream, or say, as Sunny's mother often did, *What were you thinking, Sunny? Why didn't you use your head?* Sunny could see how he might be strict, but not scary, never scary. If you were in real trouble, you would want to talk to someone like Stan Dunham.

"This is the way I see it," he said, sitting on the motel double bed, his hands on his knees. "We have lost one life, and we can't get it back. If we call the authorities, my son will be arrested and charged. No one will believe it was an accident. And Sunny will have to live the rest of her life with parents who will blame her for the death of her sister."

"But I didn't . . ." she protested. "I wasn't—"

He held up a hand, and Sunny fell silent. "It will be hard for your parents to think otherwise. Can't you see that? Parents are human, too. They won't want to hate you, but they will. I know. I'm a parent."

She bowed her head, out of arguments.

"But here's how I see it, Sunny? I'm right, it's Sunny, isn't it? You and Tony made a plan. I'm not sure if Tony knew that a fifteen-year-old girl can't marry without her parents' consent in this state"—he shot his son a look—"but this was your plan, and we're going to see it through. That's honorable, doing what you said you were going to do. You'll come live with us, under a new name. At home you can be Tony's wife, just like you planned. You'll share a room, even. I'm okay with that. Outside the house, you'll have to go to school for a while, be someone else. And when you're old enough, you can have a proper wedding. I'll work it out. I'll make everything work. You have my word."

With that he lifted Heather as any father might pick up a sleeping child, cradling her broken head and arranging her over his shoulder, then carrying her out to his car, telling Sunny to follow him. To her

413

amazement she did—into the car, into another life, another world, where she would not have to be the girl who had caused her sister's death. Tony was to stay behind and clean the room, then spend the night there as planned, in order to keep people at the motel from becoming suspicious about events in room 249. *Tony never meant to marry me,* Sunny admitted to herself, sitting in Stan Dunham's car, her sister's body in his trunk. He was going to take her to this ugly motel off the highway, have sex with her, then return her home, counting on her shame and embarrassment to keep her from telling anyone.

It probably would have worked, too. She would have gone back to Algonquin Lane, concocted some story about what had happened, why she'd gone missing for several hours. But she couldn't go home now, not without Heather. Mr. Dunham was right. They would never forgive her. She would never forgive herself.

They called her Ruth, told people that she was a distant cousin, unknown to them before the fire that had killed her family. Outside the house that's all she was, a distant cousin who may or may not have been falling in love with her newfound boy-cousin, but she was Tony's wife from the day she crossed the threshold. She shared Tony's bed—and quickly discovered she didn't enjoy it. The sweetness, the compliments from their time on the bus—those were gone, replaced by an urgent, not-quite-brutal sex notable primarily for its brevity. When she felt wistful for home, when she dared to say that perhaps she should go back, that there must be a way, Stan Dunham told her that she had no

414

home. Her parents had broken up and drifted away. Her father was a failure, her mother an adulterer. Besides, she was an accessory now, someone who had helped to cover up a crime, and she would be charged if she came forward. "I used to be a police," he said. "I know what's happening with the investigation. You're better off with us."

It did not escape her that the Dunhams were the kind of family for which she had yearned in recent years. *Normal*, she would have called them, with a father who had a real job and a mother who stayed home and baked, tying bright aprons over her dresses. Irene Dunham seemed to have more aprons than dresses, in fact, and she baked every day of the week. Her piecrust was famous, she told Sunny, bragging on herself with a self-satisfied air that Irene found unacceptable in others. But her pie, for all the prizes it had won, was dust in Sunny's mouth, and she never finished a slice. Irene didn't seem to care for Sunny much, blaming her for everything that happened, standing by her son no matter what he did.

As Sunny got older, she sometimes tried to say no to Tony when he wanted sex, and he would hit her, blackening her eye on one occasion, dislocating her jaw another, punching her so hard in the stomach that she thought she might never breathe again. And one time, the last time, just about killing her. Admittedly, this was after she had struck him with the poker from the living-room fireplace, the same poker she had used to break the heads on Irene's beloved dolls.

This was their official wedding night.

It was almost midnight, and the elder Dunhams were asleep as usual, but for once they couldn't ignore the

415

noises coming from Tony's bedroom. Irene Dunham had gone straight to her son's side, although he had nothing more than a bright red line of blood across his cheek, the one blow that she had landed before he pulled the poker from her and began beating her, then kicking her. Stan Dunham had gone to her, however, and in the moment that he reached for her and their eyes met, Sunny saw that he *knew,* had always known. He understood that his son had killed Heather, that her death was not an accident. She hadn't fallen and hit her head. Tony had beaten her, or thrown her to the floor and pounded her head until it broke. Why? Who knows? He was a violent, frustrated man. Heather was a mouthy little girl who had ruined his plan. Perhaps that was reason enough. Perhaps there could never be reasons enough for what he'd done.

"You have to leave," Stan Dunham told her, and if his family heard his words as a punishment, an exile, she knew he was trying to save her. The next day, he found a new name for her, taught her the trick of disappearing into a little dead girl's unclaimed identity. "Someone born about the right time, who died before getting a Social Security card, that's what you want." He bought her a bus ticket and told her that he would always be there for her, and Stan Dunham was nothing if not true to his word. When she was twenty-five and decided she wanted to learn how to drive, he had come down to Virginia on weekends and patiently guided her through empty school parking lots. When she decided, back in 1989, that she wanted the training necessary to get hired on as a proper computer tech, he had underwritten it. When Irene died and Stan no longer had to worry about his wife's grudging oversight, he purchased an annuity for Sunny. It wasn't a lot of money, but it helped her make car payments and, lately, deposits to her savings account, which she hoped to use for a condo if the real-estate market ever cooled down.

It was only when Penelope Jackson showed up on her doorstep a week ago to the day that Sunny learned that Tony Dunham had an annuity, too. And that, when drunk, he had spoken of his crimes and his early marriage, telling Penelope that she would never get away from him because he had once killed a girl and covered it up, with the help of his father and the girl's very own sister.

"Here's where he grabbed out a square inch of my hair," Penelope said, showing a bald patch behind her ear. Then, tapping on a large, grayish front tooth, "This is a bond, and not a good one at that. Fucker pushed me down the front steps after I sassed him. When I found out that his father had paid for an annuity for some other woman, I thought I should come visit her, see what she went through that was worth getting money from the Dunhams. Because the only thing Tony's ever given me is a promise that he'll hunt me down and kill me if I ever leave him. He's after me now. You have to help me, or I'll go to the authorities, tell them what I know about you. You covered up a murder, and that's as good as being a murderer."

It had taken the better part of three days, but she used the methods that Stan Dunham had taught her long ago and found Penelope a new name, then obtained the documents she needed to create a new life. She also had taken five thousand dollars from her savings account and given it to Penelope, who then

417

booked a flight to Seattle out of Baltimore-Washington International. She had begged Penelope to pick another airline, one that flew out of Dulles or National, but Penelope was adamant about using Southwest. "You build up credits for free tickets with them really fast. Rapid Rewards, they call it."

So for the first time in almost twenty-five years, Sunny had crossed the Potomac and headed into Maryland, then up the Baltimore-Washington Parkway. "Keep the car if you want it," Penelope said, but Sunny couldn't imagine doing that. How could she explain some old junker with North Carolina tags? Her plan was to park it at the airport and take a train back into D.C., the Metro the rest of the way home. But, having come so close to home, she couldn't see the harm in going a few miles north, then doubling back. As she got closer to Route 70, she began to think about visiting Stan, something she had never dared, no matter how ill he became, because a visit would mean signing in, leaving tracks. But Penelope had said he was bad, demented and nearly dead. If they didn't ask for ID, she could give them a fake name. Or perhaps she could go drive past Algonquin Lane, see if it really was the cherished home of her dreams or merely a ramshackle farmhouse in a not-great corner of Baltimore.

And then the car had slipped away from her, her life had slipped away from her, and in her panic and confusion she'd begun to tell the truth, only to regret it instantly. "I'm one of the Bethany girls." If she told them everything else, they would bring back Tony and make her admit to the world that her sister's death was her fault. Besides, who knew what lies Tony would tell, what violence he might do to her? So she blamed everything on Stan, knowing he was safe in his own way, and said she was Heather Bethany. Heather, who had never done anything worse than snoop and spy on an older sister. Their resemblance had always been profound, and there was nothing about Heather's life that Sunny didn't know. It should have been easy, being Heather.

The moment she heard that Miriam was alive, she knew she would be exposed. Still, she tried to brazen it out, tried to give them plausible answers so she could slip away before Miriam arrived. Irene was dead and Stan was beyond the reach of any form of justice. If she had known all along that Tony was dead, she might not have hesitated to tell the whole story. But Penelope Jackson had said that Tony was alive, that she needed money because he was determined to hunt her down and make her miserable for leaving him. Penelope had all but said it was Sunny's fault that Tony remained in the world, still hurting women, and wasn't that true? *If she had called the police that night, in the motel. If she had just started screaming, bringing the other guests, the manager.* But she had been scared and silent, wanting to believe there was a way to avoid telling her parents that Heather was dead—and it was her fault. "Look after your sister," her father had said. "One day your mother and I will be gone, and you'll be all you have." It hadn't worked out that way.

"But—" Miriam began, then stopped, her voice faltering as if the task before her was impossible, as if there were so many questions still to be asked that she could never choose just one. Sunny thought of all the things that mothers ask, day in, day out. *Where have you been? What did you do? What happened in school today?* She remembered how she had begun to chafe at her mother's curiosity when ninth grade started and she met Tony, how she had learned to hide all her emotions and secrets behind the laconic wall of adolescence. *Nowhere. Nothing. Nothing.* Now she would gladly answer anything her mother asked, if only her mother could figure out what it was she wanted to know. Sunny decided to offer the simplest and most private information she had, the very thing that she had been so reluctant to give up, believing it to be the last thing, the only thing, that belonged to her.

"I'm an IT person for an insurance company in Reston, Virginia. I use the name Cameron Heinz, but everyone at work calls me Ketch."

"Catch?"

"Ketch, short for Ketchup. Heinz, get it? She was killed in Florida, back in the mid-sixties, in a fire. Fires are always good. I just want to be that person again. But I want to be Sunny, too, and spend time with you, now that I know you're alive. Is there any way I can do both? I've been the wrong person for so long, can't I be the right person again, without anyone knowing?"

Lenhardt said, "I think there is if you're capable of a little deceit."

"I think I've proved," Sunny said, "that I'm capable of far more than just a little deceit."

Two weeks later the Baltimore County Police Department released a statement that the bones of Heather Bethany had been discovered by cadaver dogs in Glen Rock, Pennsylvania. This was an out-and-out lie, and it amused Lenhardt no end how easily the reporters and the public swallowed it—cadaver dogs discovering thirty-year-old bones, which were identified quickly and automatically, as if there were no DNA backlogs, as if the theoretical possibilities of science could trump the day-to-day realities of overburdened bureaucracies and slashed state budgets. They said they had been able to identify the grave site with information developed from a confidential informant. This was technically true, if one considered Cameron Heinz a confidential informant, a person different and apart from Sunny Bethany. Police had determined that her killer was Tony Dunham and that his parents had entered into an active conspiracy to suppress his crime and hold hostage the surviving sister, Sunny. She had escaped from the family at an undisclosed time and was still alive, living under a different name. Through her lawyer, Gloria Bustamante, Sunny asked that reporters respect her privacy, grant her the anonymity that would be given to any sexual-assault victim. She had no desire to speak of what had happened. At any rate, said Gloria, who adored talking to reporters, her client was living in a foreign country, as was her only surviving relative, her mother.

"True enough," Lenhardt later said to Infante. "Reston, Virginia, is a fucking foreign country as far as I'm concerned. Ever seen that place, with all those office parks and high-rises? Anyone could disappear down there."

"Anyone could disappear anywhere," Infante said.

After all, Sunny Bethany had done just that, for more than thirty years—as a student in a parish school, as a Swiss Colony salesgirl, as a classified-ad clerk at a small newspaper, as an IT person in a large computer firm. Like a bird who moved into abandoned nests, she had inhabited the lives of long-dead girls, counting on no one to see her, and the world had been almost too eager to grant her that privilege. She was, by design, one of the anonymous women who streamed through streets and malls and office buildings every day—attractive enough, worth a second look, yet deflecting all attention. Would Infante, champion cataloger of women, have noticed her, in any of her guises? Probably not. Yet now that he bothered to look, really look, he realized that Sunny's face was remarkably close to the computer projection of how Sunny Bethany would have aged, although the forecast had erred a little on the wrinkly side, creating pronounced crow's-feet and deep grooves on either side of her mouth. She could have passed for five, ten years younger if she pushed it. But she had settled for a mere three.

Go figure, Infante thought, closing the computer window that contained the likenesses of the two sisters, *Sunny Bethany has no laugh lines.*

PART X
SWADHAYAYA

The fifth and final step of the Fivefold Path, swadhayaya, is liberation through self-knowledge: Who am I? Why am I here?

—Adapted from various
teachings on the Agnihotra

CHAPTER 42

The moment that Kevin Infante crossed the threshold at Nancy Porter's holiday party, he knew there was a potential fix-up in the offing. He could spot the unlucky lady a mile away—a brunette in a bright red dress, not quite watching the door. She was pretty enough. Actually, she was exceptionally pretty, although in the style that other women found attractive—slim figure, bright eyes, abundant hair. That was the tip-off. She was Nancy's choice, and he had to admit that Nancy had pretty good taste. Still, he hated even passive throw-them-together-and-see-what-happens matchmaking, which seemed to imply that he couldn't find women on his own, or that he was choosing poorly.

And so what if the latter was undeniably true? He was a big boy. Nancy should leave him to his own devices.

He scouted the room, looking for a conversation he could lose himself in, making him harder to approach.

No sense trying to chat up the hostess at one of these things. Nancy was bustling back and forth between the kitchen and dining room, replenishing plates, piling more food on the buffet table. Lenhardt hadn't posted yet, and Nancy's husband had never been that keen on Infante, but then, Andy Porter would have been inclined to dislike any man who spent hours alone with his wife, even in the most innocuous circumstances. Scanning, scanning, scanning, feeling the brunette getting closer, Infante's eyes fell on a familiar face, although he needed a second to place the woman—round-faced, pleasant. Kay what's-her-name, the social worker.

"Hello," she said, offering her hand. "Kay Sullivan. From St. Agnes?"

"Sure, the one who—"

"Right."

They stood awkwardly for a second. Kevin realized he would have to do better than this if he wanted even a temporary reprieve from Nancy's machinations.

"I didn't realize you and Nancy were pals."

"We became reacquainted, from the House of Ruth. She did a presentation for us on one of the county's oldest unsolved murders, the Powers case."

He remembered. He never forgot one of his own. A young woman, separated from her husband, a contentious custody battle. She had left work one afternoon. Neither she nor her car was ever seen again. "Oh, yeah, that one. How long has it been?"

"Almost ten years. Their daughter is in her teens now. Can you imagine? She has to know that her father was the number one suspect, even if nothing was ever proven. I didn't remember that he was a former cop, though, before he went into private security."

"Huh."

Another awkward pause, as Infante wondered why Kay Sullivan had brought up that one piece of information. Was she trying to say that Baltimore cops were, by nature, felonious? All Stan Dunham had done was cover up a murder.

"Do you ever . . . ?" Kay began.

"No."

"You don't even know what I was going to ask."

"I just assumed it was about Sunny Bethany." Kay's face flamed, as if embarrassed. "We're not in touch. I think old Willoughby checks in with her mother from time to time. Speaking of which—"

He swiveled his head, realizing that Willoughby should be among the party guests, too, and saw him in an argyle sweater, of all things—chatting up the brunette in the bright red dress. Willoughby had an eye for women, as Infante had learned since they started playing golf together. To his surprise—and, although he didn't want to admit it to himself, his gratification—Willoughby seemed to prefer his company to the stuffed-shirt crowd at Elkridge. He was more police than prep, after all. He also was one of those genteel letches, the kind who liked to bask in the glow that good-looking women threw off. He doted on Nancy, had lunch with her at least once a month. He was probably trying to work the brunette toward the mistletoe, angle for a little cheek kiss. "I should go say hi."

"Sure," Kay said. "I understand. But if you do hear from Sunny . . ."

"Yes?"

"Tell her that it was nice of her, to remember to

send Grace's pants back dry-cleaned and mended. I appreciated that."

She sounded forlorn but resigned, as if used to being abandoned in social situations. Infante speared a pierogi from the platter and dragged it through some sour cream—bless Nancy's Polack forebears, the girl knew how to put on a holiday spread. The events of last spring had been a job to him, but they must have been exciting to Kay Sullivan, a reprieve from a life spent . . . well, doing whatever hospital social workers do. Wrestling with Medicaid forms, he supposed.

"Grace?" he asked Kay. "Is that your daughter? How old is she? Is she your only kid?"

Kay brightened and began to tell him in great detail about both her daughter and son, while Infante listened and nodded, helping himself to more pierogies. What was the big deal? The brunette would keep.

"*¿Cómo se llama?*" asked the man outside the gallery, and Sunny had to make a conscious effort not to stare at the hole above his mouth. Her mother had warned her about Javier, said he was a little unsettling to look at when you first met him, and Sunny had automatically assumed his deformity would rob him of speech as well. Back in Virginia, immersed in planning for this trip, she had imagined him as a mute, a Quasimodo figure who communicated in grunts and sighs.

He persisted, unperturbed by how her eyes slid away from his face, probably used to that visual evasiveness, maybe even grateful for it. She would be. "*Es la hija de Señora Toe-lez, ¿verdad?*"

How do you call yourself? You are the daughter of Señora Toles, true? Although Sunny had been listening to Spanish-language tapes for weeks and was comfortable with the language in written form, she was finding that she needed to translate everything she heard, word by word, frame her answer in English, and then translate it back into Spanish, a less-than-efficient process. Her mother said it wouldn't always be that way, if she decided to stay.

"*Soy,*" she began, then corrected herself. Not "I am," but *Me llamo.* "I call myself." "*Me llamo* Sunny." What did Javier care about the other names and identities, what it said on her driver's license and whether that matched her passport or her high school diploma? "Cameron Heinz" was on her driver's license and her passport, and therefore on her itinerary as she made her way from airport to airport to taxi and, finally, to this street in San Miguel de Allende, in many ways re-creating her mother's journey sixteen years ago, although Sunny did not know that yet. She would learn that later, on their trip to Cuernavaca. Meanwhile, back in the States, Gloria Bustamante was waiting for CamKetchBarbSylRuthSunny to decide who she wanted to be. It was a complicated choice, made more so since Stan Dunham had died this summer, leaving behind a small estate that Gloria thought Sunny should contest, as Dunham's indirect victim and, briefly, daughter-in-law. Could she claim that inheritance? Should she? And if she reclaimed her real name along with the residue of Stan Dunham's savings, how long could she go without being discovered? As Sunny knew better than anyone, every computer keystroke left a trail.

429

Here, however, she could call herself whatever she wanted. For the next two weeks.

"*Me llamo* Sunny."

Javier laughed and pointed to the sky. "*¿Como el sol? Qué bonita.*"

She shrugged, at a loss. Small talk was hard enough in English. She pushed into the store, engaging a gentle wind chime. The Man with the Blue Guitar had a wind chime, too, she remembered, although its sound had been deeper, chunkier.

Her mother—her mother!—was with a customer, a short, squat woman with a grating voice, who pushed and poked at the earrings on the counter as if they had displeased her in some way. "This is my daughter, Sunny," Miriam said, but she was hemmed in by the counter and the customer's bulk, so she could not come forward and hug Sunny as she clearly wanted to do. *She does want to hug me, right?* The woman inspected Sunny briefly, then returned to torturing the jewelry. The pieces seemed to tarnish at her touch, to darken and bend in her stubby fingers. Sunny wondered if she would ever stop seeing strangers this way, if she would continue to focus on others' defects and try to figure out, as quickly as possible, whether they were inclined to help or hurt her. This one was clearly of no use.

"She must take after her father," the woman said, and Sunny recalled the joy of pouring a Diet Pepsi over Mrs. Hennessey's head in the *Journal*'s snack room. Regrets, she had a few, to put it mildly, but that wasn't one of them. In fact, it was one of her shining moments. She should tell her mother that story, on their trip. It was one of the few anecdotes she could share, come to think of it, one that wouldn't make either of them sad or anxious.

She was actually a little nervous about finding things to talk about with her mother, but it would turn out to be far easier than she anticipated. On the train into Mexico City the next day, they would begin by discussing Penelope Jackson, whereabouts still unknown, although she had stopped using Sunny's credit cards after the first forty-eight hours in Seattle, thank God. By the time they changed to the bus to Cuernavaca, Miriam would summon up the nerve to ask Sunny if she thought Penelope had actually killed Tony, and Sunny would say yes, but not for the money, that Penelope had thought about claiming the annuity only after Tony was dead and been surprised to discover it ended with Tony's death. "But she was definitely capable of killing a man. She had the meanest eyes . . . Mom. I was scared of her. From the moment I saw her, I knew I had to do whatever she wanted me to do."

They would discuss Detective Willoughby, who kept dropping elaborate e-mail hints about coming to Mexico to play golf, and wondering if there were any good courses near San Miguel de Allende. Miriam said she didn't want to encourage him, but Sunny thought she should, maybe just a little. What was the harm?

Eventually—not the next day, or even the day after, but several days later, sitting with drinks as the sun went down and the white peacocks strutted in the twilight at Las Mañanitas—Sunny would ask Miriam if she thought it was true, what Kay had said all those months ago, about how a tragedy only revealed the strengths or weaknesses in a person, in a family. *Fissures,* Kay had called them.

"You're asking," Miriam said, "if it's your fault that your father and I broke up. Sunny, it's never a child's fault. If anything, your disappearance might have delayed my leaving. I'd been miserable for years."

"But that's the thing," Sunny said. "When I looked back—during the years I was gone—I told myself we had a happy family, that I'd been silly to long for something different. Remember how we found all those doll dishes in the roots of the trees and under the bushes? Remember how Daddy bought two copies of *Where the Wild Things Are*, then broke the bindings and used them to create a border in Heather's room, so it told the full story of Max and his journey? I thought the house on Algonquin Lane was magical, but it was a prison to you. One of us has to be wrong."

"Not necessarily," Miriam would reply. "By the way, I created the border in Heather's room. But if I didn't tell you that, would the memory be wrong, would your father have loved you any less? I think not."

Finally, when it was dark, really and truly, when they could not quite see each other's faces and they were alone in the garden, or felt as if they were, they would get around to the subject of Stan Dunham. "Your father would have been tempted to do the same thing," Miriam said, "if you or Heather had done something wrong."

"I did—" Sunny began, but her mother wasn't having it.

"That's what parents *do*, Sunny, try to rectify their children's mistakes, protect them. Children can be happy when their parents are miserable. But a parent is never happier than her unhappiest child."

Sunny turned that phrase over in her mind. She would have to take her mother's word for it. If she knew anything about herself, it was that she wasn't equipped to be a mother. She didn't care much for children. In fact, she resented most of them, as if they had stolen her life from her, illogical as she knew that to be. She was the one who had been stealing lives, appropriating names and histories from girls who had never made it as far as first grade.

"Still, I like to think your father would never have caused anyone as much pain as Stan Dunham caused us," Miriam said. "You say he was kind to you, and I'm grateful for that. But I can't forgive what he did to us, even now that he's dead."

"Yet you forgive me." It was the bruise she couldn't stop fingering, the same way she'd been unable to stop picking the scab of her vaccination, which was what had made it so tender and vulnerable to helpful Heather and her flyswatter.

"Sunny, you were *fifteen*. There's nothing to forgive. Of course I don't hold you responsible. Neither would your father, if he were still alive. And no, *that's* not your fault either."

"Heather would. Hold me responsible."

Here her mother surprised her by laughing. "She just might. Heather could hold a grudge as tightly as she held a nickel. But I think even Heather has to acknowledge that you never wished her harm."

One of the peacocks shrieked, its voice chillingly human. Heather having her say? Sunny could never be as sure of her sister's benediction as her mother wanted her to be.

But all these conversations would come later, as time and travel and darkness made intimacy possible. Right now they were in the gallery, still a little strange and

433

unfamiliar to each other, and Miriam suddenly made a rude face above the oblivious head of her cranky customer, rolling her eyes and sticking out her tongue. *The kind of face I make,* Sunny realized, *when someone screws up the system by downloading something and I have to fix it as they dither.*

"Yes, she does take after her father," her mother said. "This is her first trip to Mexico, and we're going to Cuernavaca for Christmas, to stay at Las Mañanitas."

"You couldn't pay me to go to Cuernavaca," the woman said. "And Las Mañanitas is overpriced." She shoved away from the counter as if pushing back from a table after a heavy meal that had failed to please, and lumbered out of the store without so much as a good-bye or a thank-you.

"And to think," Miriam said, coming around the counter to embrace Sunny, "that was on the tip of my tongue. An invitation for that absolute charmer of a woman to join us on our trip. How was *your* trip, Sunny? Are you tired? Do you want to go to my *casita* and nap, or would you like to have a meal first? What time did you get up this morning? Did it take terribly long to get here?"

Just thirty years, Sunny wanted to say. Thirty years and an oil slick on a highway.

Instead she chose something simpler, something she knew her mother could understand, a need that her mother, any mother, could meet. Like Max in *Where the Wild Things Are,* she had tired of the wild rumpus, sailed home, and taken off her wolf suit. She wanted to be where someone loved her best, even if she believed she had long ago forfeited her right to that unconditional devotion.

434

"I *am* hungry," she said. "Planes don't serve real meals anymore, not in coach, but then, I haven't been on a plane since I went to Ottawa with you, when I was a little girl." A flash of Heather and her in their matching dresses, Sunny smeared from their shared package of M&M's, Heather impeccable and fastidious, the two of them forever the female versions of Goofus and Gallant. Hell, Heather had even known Tony was a creep, the first time she ever saw him. At eleven going on twelve, she was far wiser than her fifteen-year-old sister. "Can we go somewhere to eat?"

The two women linked arms and walked out into the bright, chaotic street, where Javier had to shout to be heard above a passing bus. Sunny couldn't begin to make sense of the words, but based on his elaborate gestures, Javier seemed to be insisting that they looked so much alike, that they were so beautiful, the mother and daughter, together at last. He locked his own fingers, pantomiming their connectedness, and Sunny was reminded of those straw tubes one found at carnivals, the way your fingers got caught if you fought the tube too hard.

She met his gaze, no longer scared of his face now that she knew where the hole was, what was missing there. If only she could so readily show the world what was missing in her. Who would avert their eyes from her face, who would be unable to look at her straight on?

"*Gracias,*" she said, then remembered the most important word that anyone can hear, what had meant so much to her, even when it was false and unearned, wholly wrong. In pretending to be Heather, Sunny had managed to bring Heather back to life, complete with all her maddening confidence, and that was one thing she could never regret. Of all the people she had ever been, or ever would be, Heather Bethany was her favorite. *"Gracias,* Javier."

AUTHOR'S NOTE

On Opening Day 2005, I was with a group of friends headed to the Washington Nationals game, forty-somethings who had all grown up in the Baltimore and Washington area. As we passed Wheaton Plaza, the boisterous conversation stopped abruptly and we turned to look at one another.

"Do you remember—" someone began. We all did. We had been teenagers when two sisters, Shelia and Katherine Lyon, disappeared from the area around Wheaton Plaza on March 25, 1975. The mystery of their disappearance has never been solved. They left behind their parents and two brothers, a family that bears no resemblance to the Bethany family. So why did I choose a date four days later for this wholly fictional story about two missing sisters?

It wasn't my initial intent. Although I needed to set the action of this story on an Easter weekend, I thought I could use any year in the mid-1970s as the backdrop.

437

But after reading newspapers from that era, it turned out that 1975 best suited the story I wanted to tell. I would be remiss if I did not make it clear that this novel has nothing to do with the Lyon family's tragedy. But I would be disingenuous if I didn't acknowledge the similarity in the dates.

It should be implicit that a writer's publishing house is always key to these enterprises, but my editor, Carrie Feron, and her assistant, Tessa Woodward, really went above and beyond on this book, with the full support of everyone at Morrow and Avon—including Lisa Gallagher, Lynn Grady, Liate Stehlik, and Sharyn Rosenblum. A special shout-out to the men and women at the HarperCollins distribution center in Scranton, Pennsylvania, for the cake and the company, both exquisite.

Technical advice/hand-holding was provided by Vicky Bijur, David Simon, Jan Burke, Theo Lippman Jr., Madeline Lippman, Susan Seegar, Alison Gaylin, Donald Worden, Joan Jacobson, Linda Perlstein, Marcie Lovell, Bill Toohey, Duane Swierczynski, Sarah Weinman, Joe Wallace, James R. Winter, and many of the contributors to the Memory Project, who were generous with their recollections of 1975. I'm also grateful to the Enoch Pratt Free Library for its very accessible microfiche files of local newspapers—and to Kristine Zornig of the Maryland Room. A word to the nitpickers out there: Please remember that movies were often rereleased into theaters, especially after winning Academy Awards, so, yes, *Chinatown* was at Security Square Cinema in 1975 and the *The Sound of Music* was playing at a downtown theater when the blizzard of 1966 hit. As for Southern readers, another plea: I have nothing but affection for Brunswick, Georgia. It is, after all, my father's birthplace. The less-than-complimentary descriptions of Brunswick come from Kevin Infante, a Yankee detective having a very bad day. Myself, I'm quite partial to the area, which I visit every spring.

The book is dedicated to two women who have provided support and friendship from my earliest days as a novelist. Fittingly, Fellows is a teacher and Norris is a librarian. But they are, first and foremost, passionate readers. In singling them out, I am really dedicating this book to all readers.

If you enjoyed *What the Dead Know*

DON'T MISS

ANOTHER THING TO FALL

by Laura Lippman

Out now in Orion Paperback

ISBN 978-0-7528-8415-8

FIRST SHOT
MARCH

There she was.

Smaller than he expected. Younger, too. But the primary shock was that she was human, a person just like him. Well, not just like him – there was the thirty-plus age difference to start – but flesh and blood, standing on a street in Baltimore, occupying the same latitude and longitude, breathing the same air. Look at her, sipping one of those enormous coffee drinks that all the young people seemed to carry now, as if the entire generation had been weaned too early and never recovered from the shock of it. He imagined a world of twenty-somethings, their mouths puckering around nothingness, lost without something to suck. Figuratively, not literally. Unlike most people, even allegedly educated ones, he used those words with absolute precision and prided himself on the fact, as he prided himself on all his usage, even in the sentences he formed in his head, the endless sentences, the commentary that never stopped, the running voiceover of his life. Which was funny, as he disdained voiceover in film, where it almost never worked.

Yet even as the vision of a suckling nation took shape in his head, he knew it wasn't his exclusively, that it had been influenced by something he had seen. Who? What? A small part of his brain wouldn't rest until he pinned this fleeting memory down. He was as punctilious about the origins of his ideas as he was about the correctness of his speech.

He liked young people, usually, thrived in their company, and they seemed to like him, too. *Crabbed age and youth cannot live together* – the bard couldn't have been more wrong on that one. The young people he invited into his home, his life, had given him sustenance, enough so that he didn't mind tolerating the inevitable rumors. *Baltimore bachelor . . . lives by himself in that old house near the park . . . up to strange things with all that camera equipment. People swear he's on the up-and-up, but who knows?* But those things were said by the neighbors who didn't know him. When he selected the children, he got to know their parents first, went around to the houses, showed them what he did, explained his methods, provided personal references. It got so parents were calling him up, begging him to take on little Johnny or Jill. Gently, tactfully, he would explain that it wasn't just another after-school program, open to any child. It was up to him, and him alone, who would be admitted.

Now that he had this one in his viewfinder – would he have chosen her, seen something in her when she was eight or nine? Possibly, maybe. It was hard to know. Faces coarsened so much after adolescence. Personalities more so. This one – she was probably sweet, once upon a time. Affection-starved, the kind who crawled into your lap and cupped your cheeks with her baby-fat palms. Patted your cheeks and stroked your hair and stared straight into your eyes with no sense of boundaries, much less the concept of personal space. He loved children when they were unself-conscious, but that phase was so swift, so fleeting, and he was left with the paradox of trying to teach them to be as they once were, to return to a time when they didn't understand the concept of embarrassment, much less worry about what others thought. But it was the eternal struggle – once you realize you're in Eden, you have to leave. He watched the teenage years approach with more anguish than any parent, knowing that it marked the end.

The lens was a powerful one, purchased years ago. He was no Luddite – there was much new technology on which he doted, and even more for which he yearned – but he could not sacrifice his old Pentax for a digital camera. Besides, the kind of SLR system he would need was out of reach. The Canon he had priced online was $2,500 at discount, and that was for the body alone. No, he would stick with his battered Pentax for now. Come to think of it – how old was this camera? It must be twenty-five, thirty years ago that he had taken the plunge at Cooper's Camera Mart. A memory tickled his nose – what was that wonderful aroma that camera stores once had? Film, it must have been film, or the developing products, all outmoded now. Consider it – in his lifetime, just a little over a half-century, he had gone from shooting photos with a Kodak automatic, the kind with a detachable wand of flash bulbs, to shooting movies that he could watch instantly at home, and if anyone thought that was inferior to trying to load an eel-slippery roll of film onto a reel then they had his sympathies. No, he had no complaints about what technology had wrought. Technology was wonderful. If he had had more technology at his disposal, even fifteen years ago, then things might be very different now.

Look up, look up, look up, he urged the image he had captured and, just like that, as if his wish were her command, she lifted her eyes from the paper in front of her, stopped sipping her drink, and stared into the distance. Such an open, innocent face, so guileless and genuine. So everything she wasn't.

Her mouth, free from the straw, puckered in lonely dismay and he knew in that instance the image that had been tantalizing him – *The Simpsons*, the episode that had managed to parody *The Great Escape* and *The Birds* with just a few deft strokes. He had watched it with his young friends, pointing out the Hitchcock cameo, then screening the real movies for them so they could understand the larger context. (It was the only reason he agreed to watch the cartoon with them, in order to explain all its cinematic allusions.) They had loved both movies, although the explicit horror of killer birds had seemed to affect them far more than the true story behind the men who had escaped from Stalag Luft III, only to be executed upon their capture. He was ten years old when the movie came out – he saw it at the Hippodrome – and World War II, an experience shared by his father and uncles, loomed large in his imagination. Now he found himself surrounded by young people who thought Vietnam was ancient history. They had reeled when they learned he was old enough to be in the draft. This one – she, too, considered him old, and therefore a person she was free to ignore. She probably didn't even remember the Persian Gulf War. She might not know there was a war going on even now, given how insular she was. Insular and insolent.

He watched the rosebud of her mouth return to the straw and decided that the image that had been teasing him, literally and figuratively, was Lolita. The movie version, of course. No heart-shaped sunglasses, but she didn't need them, did she? *You'll be the death of me*, he lamented, clicking the shutter. *You'll be the death of me*.

Literally and figuratively.

PART ONE:
KISS KISS BANG BANG

Fall came early to Mount Vernon this October – much to the neighborhood's disgust. According to Mandy Stewart, vice president of the Mount Vernon Neighborhood Association, workers for *Mann of Steel* stripped leaves from the trees in order to create the late autumn atmosphere required for the miniseries, which is being produced by Philip "Flip" Tumulty Jr.

"They just came through in late September and ripped the leaves from the trees, then put up a few fake brown ones in their place," Stewart told the *Beacon-Light*. "They stole our fall out from under us! And they've made parking a nightmare."

Steelworkers are equally peeved with *Mann of Steel*, which they say has shown a marked indifference to portraying the industry with accuracy. "These guys couldn't find Sparrows Point on a map," said Peter Bellamy of Local 9477. "They're just using us for cheap laughs."

He said retired steelworkers are considering

informational pickets at the series' various locations around the city, but disavowed any connection to the series of mishaps that have befallen the production.

The Maryland Film Commission and the city's film liaison both said they had received no complaints, insisting the production had been an exemplary, polite presence in the city. Tumulty refused repeated requests for comment, made via his assistant.

Tumulty is the son of the Baltimore filmmaker Philip Tumulty Sr., who first attracted attention with lovingly detailed movies about Baltimore's Highlandtown neighborhood in the 1960s and early '70s, such as *Pit Beef* and *The Last Pagoda*. But he turned his attention to more conventional – and far more lucrative – Hollywood blockbusters, including *The Beast, Piano Man* and *Gunsmoke*, the last a reworking of the long-running television show. The younger Tumulty, after a much-heralded independent film, written with childhood friend Ben Marcus, has worked exclusively in television.

His latest project, *Mann of Steel*, has extended the city's long run with Hollywood, which has been an almost constant presence in Baltimore over the last fifteen years. Yet, although this series centers on Bethlehem Steel and Baltimore belle Betsy Patterson, Maryland almost lost the production to Philadelphia, which has more architecture dating from the early 19th century. Special tax incentives helped to lure the production to Maryland.

Unlike previous productions, *Mann of Steel* has had a rocky relationship with the city from the start. Complaints from neighbors and steelworkers are only part of the problems they have faced. There have been a series of small fires set near some of the locations and rumors of bad behavior by up-

and-coming actress Selene Waites, 20, who keeps popping up in local bars.

"We are grateful to Baltimore and Maryland for all they've done to make this film possible," said co-executive producer Charlotte MacKenzie when asked for comment. "We just wish others were grateful for the $25 million we're spending, half of which will go directly into the local economy."

Community activist Stewart is not about to be mollified: "The economic benefits of film production are wildly exaggerated, based on the stars' salaries, which may or may not be taxed by local authorities," she said. "The bottom line is that *Mann of Steel* is a pain in the butt.

The *Beacon-Light*, Oct. 15th

MONDAY
CHAPTER ONE

The headphones were a mistake. She realized this only in hindsight, but then, what other vision is available to a person heading backwards into the world?

True, they were good old-fashioned headphones, which didn't seal tightly to the ear, not earbuds, which she loathed on principle, the principle being that she was thirty-two going on seventy. Furthermore, she had dialed down the volume on her Sony Walkman – yes, a Sony Walkman, sturdy and battered and taxicab yellow, not a sleek little iPod in a more modern or electric shade. Still, for all her precautions, she could hear very little. And even Tess Monaghan would admit that it's important to be attuned to the world when one is charging into it backwards, gliding along the middle branch of the Patapsco in a scull and passing through channels that are seldom without traffic, even in the pre-dawn hours.

But Tess had painstakingly rationalized her way into

trouble, which, she decided later, is pretty much how everyone gets into trouble, one small rationalization at a time. She wanted to row yet she felt obligated to listen to her boyfriend on a local radio show promoting the Oktoberfest lineup at her father's bar. Besides, he planned to play some songs by Brave Combo, a nuclear polka band that Tess quite liked. She would row a path that was familiar to her, and trust the coxswains for the fours and eights to watch her back, literally, a courtesy offered to all scullers.

It did not occur to Tess to row a little later, or skip the workout altogether. The rowing season traditionally ended after Thanksgiving, a mere month away. She had to take advantage of every waning day, especially now that Baltimore was in its full autumnal glory. If aliens had landed in Baltimore on this particular October morning, they would have concluded that it was the most perfect city on the globe they were about to conquer, truly the Charm City it claimed to be. The trees were tinged with gold and scarlet, the breeze was light, the sky was slowly deepening into the kind of brilliant blue that reminded people they once knew the word "cerulean," if only because it had been on the vocabulary lists for the SATs.

Tess set out for Fort McHenry at the distant tip of Locust Point, rationalizing every stroke of the way: She knew the route so well, it was so early, the sun not even up. She had beaten the other rowers to the water, arriving in darkness and pushing off from the dock at first light. She wouldn't wear the headphones on the way back. She just needed to hear Crow on WTMD, listen to him play a few snippets of Brave Combo, then she would turn off the Walkman and—

That's when the police boat, bullhorn blaring,

crossed into her line of vision and came charging toward her. By the time she registered everything that was happening – the approaching boat, the screams and shouts coming from all directions, the fact that someone was very keen that she stop or change course – the motor boat had stopped, setting up an enormous, choppy wake that was going to hit her sideways. Tess, trying frantically to slow and steady her scull, had a bona fide moment of prescience. Granted, her vision extended only two or three seconds into the future, but it was uncannily exact: She was going to go ass over teakettle into the Patapsco, a body of water that even conquering aliens from a water-deprived planet would find less than desirable. She closed her eyes and shut her mouth as tightly as possible, grateful that she had no cuts or scratches into which microbes could swim.

At least the water held some leftover summer warmth. She broke the surface quickly, orienting herself by locating the star-shaped fort just to the north, then the wide channel into the bay to the east of the fort, toward which her vessel was now drifting. "Get my shell," she spluttered to the police boat, whose occupants stared back at her, blank-faced. "My shell! My scull! MY GODDAMN BOAT." Comprehension dawning, the cops reached out and steadied her orphaned scull alongside the starboard side of their boat. Tess began to swim toward them, but a second motorboat cut her off.

A man sat in the stern of this one, his face obscured by a baseball cap, his arms crossed over a fleece vest emblazoned with a curious logo, *Mann of Steel*. He continued to hug his arms close to his chest, a modern-day Washington crossing the Delaware, even as two young people put down their clipboards and reached out to Tess, boosting her into the boat.

"Congratulations," said the male of the pair. "You just ruined a shot that we've been trying to get for three days."

Tess glanced around, taking in everything her back had failed to see. This usually quiet strip around Fort McHenry was ringed with boats. There was an outer periphery of police boats, set up to protect an inner circle, which included this boat and another nearby, with what appeared to be a mounted camera and another fleece-jacketed man. There were people on shore, too, and some part of Tess's mind registered that this was odd, given that Fort McHenry didn't open its gates to the public until 9 a.m. Farther up the fort's grassy slopes she could see large white trailers and vans, some of them with blue writing that she could just make out: *Haddad's Catering Service*. She squeezed her ponytail and tried to wring some water from her T-shirt, but the standing man frowned, as if it were bad form to introduce water into a boat.

"The sun's up now," said the young woman who had helped Tess into the boat, her tone dire, as if this daily fact of life, the sun rising, was the most horrible thing imaginable. "We lost all the rose tones you wanted."

The stern man threw his Natty Boh baseball cap down in the boat, revealing a headful of brown curls, at which he literally tore. He was younger than Tess had realized, not much older than she, no more than thirty-four or thirty-five. "Three days," he said. "Three days of trying to get this shot and some stupid rower has to come along at the exact wrong moment— "

"Tess Monaghan," she said, offering a damp, sticky hand. He didn't take it. "And I'm sorry about the accident, but *you* almost killed *me*."

"No offense," said the younger man, the one who had helped to boost her into the boat, "but that might have been cheaper for us in the long run."